No Coincidence

Copyright © 2020 by TMP Publishing LLC/Tiffany Patterson

All rights reserved.

This is a work of fiction. Names, characters, businesses, places, events and incidents are either the products of the author's imagination or used in a fictitious manner. Any resemblance to actual persons, living or dead, or actual events is purely coincidental.

A special thank you to Melissa at There For You Editing (thereforyou.melissa@gmail.com) for editing.

Chapter One

Resha

"Oh my damn," I whispered in shock. With ballooned eyes, I stare up and up into the hazel eyes of the man I met not too long ago. "Is that ..." I swallowed, feeling shy as hell all of a sudden, "what I think it is?"

A rumbling chuckle, that started at the deepest part of his belly, rippled up his large, muscled chest and spilled out of the sexiest mouth I'd ever seen.

"You've never seen a cock piercing, doll?"

My heart rate quickened and I blinked, shaking my head, not believing the position I found myself in. "Of course, I have," I retorted, because ... what? Was I supposed to tell the truth?

"Don't worry, it doesn't hurt."

Gulp.

I swallowed, not out of fear, but to keep myself from asking, "What if I wanted it to hurt?"

Shit. It's been way too long, girl. Get yourself together!

My womanly parts bellowed for me to not mess this up.

"Give me your hand," he insisted, but instead of waiting for me to actually give him my hand, he took it into his much larger one, pulling me closer to him. The heat emanating from his body elicited an immediate response from mine. My nipples perked up and I felt the insides of my thighs being lubricated with the essence of my own arousal.

"Oh," I gasped when he guided my hand to his very large member, allowing me to feel the length and girth of him, along with the curved, metal bar that possessed two small balls at either end. The bar that had been pushed through the flesh of the tip of his cock. I tightened my hand around his shaft, but found that my fingers couldn't touch. Smoothing my hand down his shaft, I ran my thumb along the tip.

I flinched when he hissed, his body tightening at the move.

"Careful there, doll. You don't want this to end before it begins."

Feeling froggy, I lifted my gaze to meet his and raised an eyebrow. "If that's the case, maybe I wound up in the wrong room." I added a little purr to my enunciation.

His eyes narrowed and a small wrinkle appeared between his dark blond eyebrows. He didn't say a word, but the warning alarm that went off in my stomach told me that I just poked a bear. My second indication was the gasp that escaped my lips when, without warning, he lifted me from the ground as if I weighed only a few pounds.

"You like talking shit," he murmured, close to my ear at the same time he forced my legs around his waist, carrying both of our nude bodies over to the bed. In the blink of an eye, I found myself on my back, him hovering over me, eyes scanning my face as our breathing patterns synced up with one another's.

"That could get you into trouble where I'm from," he warned before leaning in and letting his lips cover mine.

Sighing into his mouth, I extended my hand to entangle in his long, strawberry-blond hair. He took control of the kiss, or rather, I surrendered control the moment his lips touched mine. But when his large hands began massaging my very full breasts, pinching the nipples, I had to break free from his mouth to let out a wild moan. It'd been a long time since a man had touched me there, and an even longer period of time since a man had touched me there in the *correct* way. His pinches weren't too hard. But they weren't delicate either. He applied just the right amount of pressure to cause a small amount of pain, which turned into an immense amount of pleasure.

"Oohh," I sighed.

"You like having your tits sucked?" he questioned.

I didn't hesitate to nod. The next thing I knew, his head was dipping lower and that moist, hot tongue of his was capturing my left nipple.

"Oh shit!" I blurted, my back arching.

With his hands still on my breasts, he began to slide his body down mine and I held my breath.

I moved to play with the loose strands of hair that had spilled out of his man-bun, but then I blinked because suddenly it got brighter inside of the hotel room. Startled, I glanced around the room, which appeared to be getting lighter by the second.

"What's—"

Beep! Beep! Beep!

"Shit!" I yell, sitting up in my bed, pushing the sleep mask from my eyes, and blinking as I look around the room.

My bedroom.

I was at home.

Not in a hotel room, in a different city, with a very delicious man hovering over my body.

I let out a deep sigh. "You need to let that go," I groaned to myself as I started to lay back down once I hit the snooze button on my sunrise alarm clock. Unfortunately, my head wasn't even given a chance to hit the pillow before my phone started ringing. The same phone I intentionally left in my living room before heading to bed the previous night.

Blinking, I looked at the clock on my glass nightstand. It read 8:02. Only two people in the world would call me this damn early. I had half a mind to ignore the ringing phone, but then I thought it could possibly be my Aunt Donna. And given her health condition, I would feel horrible if she called because she needed me and I wasn't there for her.

"Ouch! Dammit!" I barked after stubbing my toe on my coffee table as I lunged for the phone, fearful the caller would hang up before I had a chance to answer. I didn't even get the opportunity to see who the caller was.

"Hello?"

"You sound breathless. Did you finally get laid? Am I interrupting a morning quickie before you kick him out?"

Frowning, I pulled the phone from my ear and put it on speaker. "Only your nasty behind would be calling me this early with these types of questions," I retorted to my cousin, Destiny.

"Nasty? Ha! I'm a married woman."

"Yeah, and I'm surprised Tyler let you come up for air this long."

Destiny giggled into the phone. "That's only because he's in the nursery changing Tristan and Travis while I snuggle with Miss Annalise. She was up most of the night with the sniffles and a little cough."

"Aww, my poor baby. How's she doing this morning?"

"Better. She's sleeping comfortably now. I've got the humidifier on in here."

I nodded even though Destiny couldn't see me.

"So, back to the nature of my call. Did you finally get some? Is that why your ass was huffing and puffing as you answered the phone?"

"You get on my damn nerves, you know that, right? My sex life, or lack thereof, is none of your business. And I was huffing and puffing because the only running I do is to get to the phone as it rings early as hell in the morning, while I'm trying to sleep."

"Whatever. You should be up by now anyways. It's after eight o'clock."

"Just barely," I mumbled. "And besides, I had that launch party last night across town so I didn't get to bed until almost three in the morning."

"Oh yeah, I forgot about that."

I rolled my eyes. Of course she'd forgotten. Destiny was busy with her husband, three kids, and running a successful business.

"You're still coming to the shelter today, right? To work with the women. They really need your help."

"I'll be there, it's on my schedule."

Oh, and on top of being a wife, mother, and entrepreneur, Destiny also opened and ran a women's shelter here in Williamsport, along with her mother-in-law and three sisters-in-law.

I ignored the pang of sadness that rose in my chest just thinking about everything she had going on in her life.

"You remember it's at eleven, right?"

"I got it. I'll be there. I've already got what I'm bringing packed and ready to go. I'm going to sit down, write out a couple of new posts, respond to some emails, and get ready to go. I'll be there," I promised.

"Good. I think I'll bring Annalise 'cause she's a bit clingy when she's not feeling well. See you there, sis."

"See you there."

I hung up the phone, forgetting to respond with the usual *love you* that I typically give when getting off the phone with my sister, slash cousin, slash best friend. Technically, Destiny and I were cousins. But ever since her parents, my Aunt Donna and Uncle Daniel, took me in at the age of twelve, we've been more like sisters. That has led to a great friendship and partnership as we hosted a very successful podcast together as well.

Sighing as I disconnected the call, I allowed my gaze to travel around my two-bedroom, spacious condo that I utilized for both living and work. I loved my living room with its large, floating white entertainment center, complete with my sixty-inch flatscreen, surrounded by my many plants. Wandering down the hall, I headed to my spare bedroom, turned home office. However, as soon as my bare foot made contact with the plush white carpet, I paused.

"Coffee," I commented, snapping my fingers with one hand and rubbing my eyes with the other. I definitely needed some coffee. It hadn't been a fib that I told Destiny the previous night was a late one for me, due to working an event.

I made a beeline for the kitchen, straight for the Keurig, one of the more luxury items I've chosen to purchase for my home for comfort. It took less than five minutes for me to fill up the

Keurig with water and prepare a steaming cup of my favorite vanilla-flavored, caffeinated beverage in my hands. Taking the first sip of my drink, I let my eyelids close and inhaled deeply. And just when I started to savor the taste of the coffee, images of the previous night's dream float to mind.

"Seriously?" I hissed out loud to the empty room. I pushed out a frustrated breath even as chills ran down my spine at the remembrance of the dream. The damn problem was that it wasn't just a dream. It was a memory. I could still feel his strong hands on my body. And at the point at which goosebumps began popping up on my arms, I suppressed the memory with a shake of my head.

"I've got shit to do," I bemoaned, taking my coffee and carrying myself to my office to sit down at my desk.

The first task of the day was tackling the long list of emails that I needed to respond to before I began writing. They mainly consisted of the typical inquiries from brands, notices of payments, which always made my day, and requests from other bloggers to guest post or show up to their events. A few of my emails were from Shauna, the virtual assistant I hired eighteen months ago. Shauna had been a huge blessing, helping me in getting organized, staying on top of payments, and ensuring that I was making the appointments I'd agreed to.

It took just about thirty minutes to get through all of the work emails when I came to the final message, but as soon as I read the subject line, a chill ran down my spine. My fingers stopped abruptly, hovering over the keyboard as I read the short tagline of the email.

Hey there.

That's all it said, but I wasn't unfamiliar with those two words. Clicking on my mouse, I moved the pointer over to the email, opening it.

You looked beautiful in that picture you posted yesterday. I would love to see you in that outfit up close.

"Shit!" I cursed as the shaking of my hand on the mouse accidentally caused me to delete the damn thing. I started to go into the trash to retrieve it but stopped myself. I didn't need to read those words again. I'd memorized them in just the few seconds I spent with the email.

I shuddered to think about meeting whoever was behind that strange message. This had been happening off and on for the past few months. I would post something on my Instagram page or on my blog, and then this person would send me an email or DM saying they wished my picture was for their eyes only. I tried not to think too much of it once I blocked them. I believed it was just some lonely ass man with nothing better to do. However, it was starting to make me very uncomfortable.

Before I could get too lost in my thoughts, a window popped up on my desktop, ringing.

"Good morning," Shauna chimed, smiling as I answered her video call.

"Hey."

Shauna's full lips turned downward as she frowned. "Is something wrong?"

I shook my head even though I had completely forgotten our usual Monday morning check-in call.

"No, everything's fine. Just tired. I didn't sleep well, and woke up a little earlier than usual when Destiny called."

Shauna's eyes drifted from the screen to the open planner in front of her. I was familiar with it. She always kept it close by during our calls.

"You have that appointment this morning at the shelter, right?"

I nodded. "Yup. She called to make sure I was still coming for some reason. I think the whole mom thing is going to her head. She double checks on everything now," I laughed.

Shauna giggled as well. "I get it. It's what us moms do."

I shrugged. "I wouldn't know." It was supposed to have come out as a mere response but even I heard the distress in my voice. And if I hadn't, the weight that settled in my chest at the reminder of my single and childless status would've alerted me.

"Anyway, I'll be there until early afternoon, I think, and then I'm headed to the business meeting at Nordstrom to speak with a couple of their execs about the campaign they want me to do. Later, I have that video call with that other brand to be added as one of their plus size models."

"Have you decided to move ahead with that?"

I pushed out my lips and sat back in my chair, folding my arms over my chest. "I don't know. The money they were offering last time seemed nice, but I spoke with a few other bloggers they approached and they were offered more." I frowned at just thinking about being lowballed by a brand.

"What're you thinking of doing?"

I pondered for a few heartbeats. "We could hold out for a little more. Destiny taught me the value of getting paid what I'm worth," I commented, remembering how early on she encouraged me not to accept just anything just to get paid.

"It's a good thing you have her."

"True. Five years ago I would've taken one look at that offer and signed my life away." Pushing out a breath, I looked to my right, at the large window, at the beautiful skyline view my tenth floor apartment view afforded me. Turning back to the screen, I faced Shauna. "Today, I know the value I offer to any company and am less willing to settle."

She nodded her approval. "Amen to that. And you haven't talked to Destiny about the other brand deal yet, have you?"

Shaking my head, I said, "Not yet. I'll get to it, eventually." I found myself keeping more and more from my cousin lately.

We talked for another fifteen minutes about what was on the agenda for the following week, how she was doing in uploading the posts to my social media feeds, and what type of responses I was getting back from the posts. We both agreed that I needed to use my Instagram stories more often to engage followers.

"They *loved* the stories you posted last night while out at the Sip and See," Shauna commented.

"I noticed. I was up for an additional hour and a half responding to inquiries once I got back last night. Most of them were asking who the guy I was dancing with was." I rolled my eyes because I was *always* getting asked by my followers who I was dating, how do I maintain a relationship, and more.

"He looked cute from behind," Shauna quipped.

"Yeah, too bad he's married to the owner of the store. We weren't really even dancing and he kept himself at a respectful distance. But followers see me within five feet of a guy, and they have questions." I didn't mind it, however. I enjoyed sharing parts of myself with my blog followers and podcast listeners. I just wasn't divulging anything too personal, which I had made very clear. And, to top it off, there was absolutely nothing to report in that area of my life.

"All right, seems like we've got the week planned. I need to go get ready to leave."

"Okay, catch you next Monday. I'll email if anything comes up."

"Thanks, Shauna."

Even though I said I was going to get ready to head out, I remained at my desk working for the next forty-five minutes, writing up two posts for the blog and uploading the corresponding images to go up the following day and the following week. Once that was completed, and realizing I was about a half an hour behind schedule, I hustled getting dressed, opting for a light-brown, pleated skirt, cream-colored, scoop neck top that I tucked in at the waist, and a three-quarter length blazer-style jacket. And even though it was fall and somewhat chilly out, I chose to pair the outfit with some strappy, leopard-print heels and my brown leather handbag. I took one final look in the mirror and nodded in approval. The look was both appropriate to show the women at the shelter how to pair a stylish, fun, and professional outfit, while being a little flirty, and also, it was perfect to wear to my business meeting after the shelter.

I fluffed the long, silky, dark brown tresses that I'd just had installed a week earlier. The tips of the hair were a golden blonde which I loved and felt right given the impending colder weather. I'd become so occupied with my outfit and making sure I gathered all the perfect clothing items, makeup, and other accessories that I lost track of time.

"Damn!" I cursed, glancing at the clock on my wall. "I gotta go," I said to no one as I looked around for my keys, which I somehow always seemed to forget to place on the key rack that was mounted right next to the front door.

"Oh!" I gasped, spotting my keys on the kitchen counter. Grabbing them up, I hooked the briefcase I would need throughout the day over my left shoulder and grasped the handle of the suitcase where I'd packed everything with my left hand and headed out the door.

Pressing the down button on the elevator, I mentally went over everything I had to ensure I hadn't forgotten anything.

"Oh, excuse me!" I blurted out when I walked right into the chest of my next door neighbor as he attempted to exit the open doors of the elevator.

My head rose and the way his lips spread into a familiar smile made my insides groan.

"Not a problem at all, little lady."

I bit the inside of my cheek hard to keep from rolling my eyes.

"Excuse me, Jarvis," I muttered, not wanting to get entangled in any drawn out conversation.

"In a rush? It seems like I've barely seen you in the last few weeks." His smile was meant to be charming, I assumed, but all

I saw was the chipped front tooth of his and the fact that he obviously wasn't a regular when it came to exfoliating.

"No, I guess you haven't." Stepping around him, onto the elevator, I punched the button to the garage level of our building.

Spinning around, I looked one final time at Jarvis. "Been working. You know how it is." I plastered a fake smile on my face just as the doors closed on him saying something that I couldn't and didn't want to discern.

I shook my head. Jarvis was nice and all, but since the day he moved in two years ago he gave me creepy vibes. I could never quite put my finger on it, but I always felt the desire to get as far away from him as possible. Unfortunately for me, Jarvis seemed to want the opposite, always making it a point to stop and talk to me whenever we encountered one another in the hallway or elevator.

Brushing thoughts of my weird neighbor aside, I stepped free of the elevator and headed toward my pride and joy. My wine-colored Lexus RX 350. She was a 2018 and I paid for her in cold, hard cash, at the insistence of my cousin, Destiny, of course. She was a stickler when it came to finances in general, and avoiding debt, specifically. If she'd had things her way, I would've gotten an older model to save even more money, but I wasn't about that life. I worked hard and had the money. I got what I wanted.

But this day, instead of feeling the usual pride I felt as I strolled closer to my car, a warning feeling began in the pit of my stomach. I paused a foot away from my car, swinging my head from left to right to see who, if anyone, was around. There was no one. Regardless, my spine tingled, the hair on my arms standing as the feeling that I was being watched filled my body. Without another thought, I raced to my car, yanking the door open, and practically threw myself inside, slamming the door shut door and locking it behind me. I moved so fast I was breathing heavy by the time I fully settled inside. The breathing hard may've also had something to do with the fear combined with adrenaline coursing through me as well. All I could think of was the email from that morning. There was another message in my Instagram DMs. A sickening feeling overcame me, as my knees started feeling weak.

Wrapping both of my hands around the steering wheel and trying to steady my breathing, I worked hard to not freak the hell out.

"It's nothing, Resh. Don't make a big deal out a few messages," I told myself. It was just some messages from a stranger on the internet. They could be halfway across the country, or hell, living in an entirely different country while I was imagining they were hiding out in my building's garage, secretly watching me.

"That's it. No big deal," I whispered repeatedly as I pulled out of my parking spot and started the drive to the community center.

****

"You're late."

My eyes rolled without any direct communication from my brain to do so. It was an automatic response.

"Don't act like you don't know me by now," I retorted to my cousin even as I widened my arms to pull her into a hug. "Ouch! Damn you!" I grunted from her pinching my arm as we pulled apart.

Destiny placed her hands on her small hips—that had gotten slightly bigger since birthing triplets, but she was still naturally tiny.

"I do know your ass, which is why I had that pinch waiting on your always late behind all morning."

I shook my head. "No faith in me."

"Oh, I have faith. Faith that you're going to be *at least* fifteen minutes late."

"Ha!" I gasped and pointed at the clock high on the wall of the lobby behind Destiny. "According to the clock, I'm only twelve minutes late."

"Whatever." Destiny waved her hand. "So what was it that kept you this time? Please say it was a man you were trying to get rid of this morning."

My mind immediately went back to messages from that morning. A fluttering of fear rose in my stomach. I shook my head. "There was an accident on the highway, reducing it to one lane for like three exits."

Destiny sighed. "I hope everyone's okay."

I nodded, thankful she hadn't picked up on the lie. There was an accident, but if I'd left at the time I intended I would've made it on time. It was all the other happenings of the morning that had me running behind schedule. However, I wasn't up for sharing that right then.

"Well, you made it. That's what matters," a voice stated from behind Destiny.

I look over my cousin's shoulder to see Patience, one of her sisters-in-law, headed toward us.

"Patience, good to see you." I pulled her into a hug, which she warmly received before pulling back, smiling as she cupped my arms in her hands.

"We're glad you made it. This place isn't the same when you're not around."

My insides warmed because she was genuine when she said that. It was as if when Destiny became a part of this family,

I did as well. Instead of responding directly, I looked back at Destiny and stuck my tongue out at her.

"See, at least *someone* is happy to see me."

Patience giggled.

"We're all happy to see you," came another voice. That was Kayla, another sister-in-law of Destiny's.

Soon enough, Kayla, Patience, Destiny, as well as their mother-in-law, Deborah Townsend, were greeting me and showing me into one of the large conference turned dressing rooms.

"Resha, I ordered breakfast since the likelihood that all of us have eaten before getting out of the door this morning was slim to none." All the women, including myself, laughed because she was right. "Please help, yourself."

All the other women had at least one child, but Patience had five and Destiny had three. I was certain their mornings were crazy and getting time to eat before making it into the office was a near impossibility.

"And, Resha, just doesn't eat breakfast," Destiny added.

I frowned, playfully, because she was right. Typically, I wasn't a breakfast eater but seeing as how it was nearing eleven thirty, my stomach started to growl. Picking up a chocolate chip scones, I placed it on one of the porcelain plates along with some sliced strawberries and green grapes.

I took a bite of the scone. "Oh, this is good," I moaned, looking at Deborah.

She smiled. "It's from this new little bakery down the street. They have all kinds of things. One of our girls actually works there."

Kayla nodded. "Yeah, Suzette. She's been there for what? Three months now?" she asked, her head turning to ask the other women.

Patience nodded. "I think so. About a month after it opened."

"Suzette," I repeated. "The one with the two-year-old little boy, right?"

"That's her," Destiny answered.

"I remember giving her some makeup tips. How's she doing?"

"Really well," Deborah responded. "She started taking classes at the community college for culinary arts. She loves baking."

"Good for her." I remembered Suzette as being incredibly withdrawn and reticent upon first meeting her. There was a heaviness in her eyes that was so familiar it almost pained me just to see. Honestly, most of the women, who came through the doors of this center, had that look. That forlornness was something I recognized in just about all of them.

"So," I began, clapping my hands, ready to think of something else, "I brought more clothes and makeup, and some accessories I think will work with some of the other clothes that have been donated. It should only take me a few minutes to get set up, and then I can start working with the ladies."

"Great," Kayla replied. "As you can see, we've rearranged the conference room since you were here last to make this the changing room. It offers so much more space than the last room."

I nodded in agreement, looking around at the racks of clothes that were neatly lined on one side of the room, and the partitions that had been set up on the other side, allowing privacy for dressing.

"And you even have a few vanities. Perfect."

"Naturally. We want the ladies who come here to be equipped with the basics to help them go out and conquer the world. That starts from the inside, of course, but helping them look good on the outside doesn't hurt, either," Deborah chimed in.

"I couldn't agree more."

There was little conversation after that as I busied myself with setting up all the items I'd brought and making sure there was an assortment of outfits for the women to choose from. The purpose of this fashion session was to get the women who have never been in the working world, or who'd had an extended period away, to feel comfortable dressing up for interviews and their first days at a new job.

"Welcome!" I gushed as a timid looking woman entered. "What's your name?"

"Emily."

"Nice to meet you, Emily. Please, come in." I noted the blonde tresses that would look much better after a trim. And my mind immediately went to the perfect foundation for her skin tone.

I greeted three more women as they entered with Kayla.

"This is Charlotte, Mary, and Tammy," Kayla introduced.

I shook hands with all of the women and began asking some basic questions on what it was they were looking for. Two of the women had job interviews later that week, one would be starting a new temp position the following week, and Emily was just starting out in pursuit of a career, and had no idea what style of clothing worked for her.

After giving the women a quick introduction of myself, I taught them some basics of dressing for success before taking them over to the racks of clothes to begin searching for items they liked and that looked good on them.

"Also, remember, if you see something you like, but it might not fit quite right, consider tailoring."

"Tailoring?" Emily appeared befuddled.

"Yes. It just means having your clothes cut or sewn to fit *your* body. Most clothes are made according to whatever standard the manufacturer deems right. There isn't even a standard of sizing across the board. It's why you can walk into one retail store and fit perfectly into a size twelve jeans, but then go in another and be able to fit a size ten, or even go up to a fourteen in another retailer's clothing. It's a mess. Just remember, it's *not* a reflection of your body. And *please* don't get me started on why so many retailers refuse to put actual pockets in women's jeans."

"Right?" Tammy gasped. "I thought it was only me who noticed that."

I shook my head along with Kayla.

"You are certainly *not* alone. My favorite pair of jeans that hugs me in all the right places is perfect, except …"

"They don't have any damn pockets," I finished.

"That! They have the little sewn part that *looks* like a pocket but it's just a design."

"And who the heck needs a designer pocket? Give me a real pocket."

"Please!" Tammy added, causing all of us to giggle at the shared frustration.

That little tangent broke any of the remaining ice, and all of the women opened up more and more, feeling comfortable sharing their struggles in dressing for their body types. I got lost in the conversation, answering questions and applauding when each woman found the perfect outfit for them. I visibly saw how each woman's confidence became more pronounced as they began to shake off the assumptions that their bodies were wrong or improperly built for the clothes.

"You were so great with them," Kayla noted after the women left and I started packing up my belongings to head over to my afternoon meeting.

I smiled wide as I placed a few items in my briefcase. "I love doing this. I learned from Aunt Donna that clothes are meant to adorn what we already have. They don't make us."

"I love that. Wish most girls grew up learning that. Oh, speaking of raising daughters, you're coming to Victoria's birthday party this Saturday, right?"

I stopped short in the hallway, having forgotten all about the one-year-old girl's birthday party I RSVP'd to. Why the hell a one year old needed an RSVP to her birthday party was beyond me.

"Yeah, I'll be there."

"Good. Remember, it starts at three. Don't feel obligated to bring anything either. That little girl has everything she could ever want." She playfully rolled her eyes.

"I wouldn't think of showing up to anyone's home without a gift. Aunt Donna raised me better than that."

Kayla chuckled. "If you insist. See you there. I have to go help Patience with something before leaving. Thanks again for coming." She gave me another hug and turned, heading in the opposite direction just as Destiny rounded the corner.

She frowned. "Were you trying to sneak out without saying good-bye?"

I wrinkled my forehead. "Of course not," I lied because that's exactly what I was planning on doing.

"Better not had. Where are you headed to now?"

"Have a meeting with a major retailer. To possibly be one of the new faces of their new plus size line."

"That's awesome, Resh! Who is it?"

I shook my head. "I'm not saying yet just in case this doesn't go through."

Destiny paused as we came to the entrance of the center, turning to me and frowning. "Since when do we keep things from each other?"

I lifted an eyebrow. "You mean like getting married?"

Raising her hands and face heavenward, Destiny sighed. "I can't believe you're still bringing that up. I told you, Tyler and I—"

"Didn't tell anyone ... yeah, yeah, yeah. You've said it all before," I chided. Truth was, I wasn't as pissed about Destiny and Tyler's elopement anymore. I just used it to throw in her face for some petty reason.

"Resha, you know—" Destiny started, taking my hand in hers.

"D, I'm just playing. Relax. I'm not keeping anything from you. I just don't want to jinx it, or get too excited about this opportunity, so I'm playing it close to the chest. I promise if it goes through you will be the first to know about it."

She paused, looking me in the eye.

I held firm in my conviction, not allowing myself to be swayed by the spark of sadness I caught in her brown eyes.

"Okay, I understand. Hey, you'll be at the party on Saturday, right? Mama's coming, too."

I nodded. "I just confirmed with Kayla."

"Good. Maybe you'll bring a date. Oh," Destiny snapped. "Better yet, maybe I can hook you up with one of the guys who'll be there."

"Don't!" I warned. "First of all, I'm pretty damn sure all of the men there are married with children of their own. Shit, at one pathetic time in my life I may have been down to be some man's mistress, but at thirty-seven I am not about that life—"

"Resha, you know damn well I would never hook you up with someone like that—"

Holding up my hand, I cut her off. "And second of all, I can find my own date."

"Good then bring someone."

"I'm celibate for a reason."

"Which is?"

"I'm finding myself."

I laughed at the *bitch stop playing* look on my cousin's face.

"Yeah, just make sure you find your ass to Kayla and Josh's this Saturday at three for Victoria's birthday party. No, better yet, how about you pick up Mama early and come over my house at noon to have lunch together before the party. The kids have been dying to see you."

I didn't bother telling my cousin that her barely one year old children probably didn't even remember me from one day to the next, although we FaceTimed often when I was away.

"Okay, I'll come over early," I conceded. "I gotta go." I didn't wait for Destiny's response. I gave her a hug and moved passed her to the door, toward the elevator.

Sadly, on my way out, I reflected on how distant I felt from my closest friend in the world. Destiny's life had changed so much in the past couple of years, as it should've. The free time she used to have was now eaten up by family obligation, which I understood. But it left me having to figure out where I stood sometimes. Not to mention, seeing her so happy and full, at times, reminded me of what my life was still lacking.

And now, nearing forty, I wondered if my happily ever after would happen.

Chapter Two

Resha

"Hey, Auntie Donna," I gushed as soon as she opened the door to her apartment. Bending low, I let her wrap her arms around me for a hug. I sighed a little as my face nuzzled against her shoulder before taking a step back.

"I don't understand why you don't just use your key, girl," she chided.

I laughed, shutting the door behind me as I fully stepped inside. "You know I don't want to interrupt what you may have going on up in here, Auntie."

"Girl, you know I'll still put you over my knee. Talking fresh like that. Don't think I don't know what you meant."

I laughed again because the idea of my sixty-nine-year-old aunt with Parkinson's disease putting me over her knee was laughable, even though I knew she'd try if she could.

"I was just kidding. You look cute," I told her, staring down at the cobalt blue dress she wore. "Did the aide help you put that on?"

"She sure did. Left about five minutes before you got here."

I nodded, knowing full well the schedule of the aides who worked with my auntie. "She could've stayed until I arrived," I stated, not liking the idea of my aunt being left alone, if only for a short period of time.

"Girl, if you wasn't running late, you would've made it to see her here."

I pursed my lips but didn't respond because she was right. I was running late, per usual, but only by about five minutes or so. Anyway, I was glad that my aunt finally relented and made the decision to move in with Destiny and Tyler, after all three of us had been begging her for months. She hadn't wanted to get in Destiny and Tyler's way, but we all had grown uneasy with her living by herself even though she did live in a very reputable retirement community, with nurse's aides who helped her much of the day. However, they weren't family.

"Let me help you put your coat on. Which one do you want to wear? The pastel pink one or the black peacoat?"

Aunt Donna frowned. "You don't think it's too hot for those? Isn't it supposed to get up to the low sixties today?"

Pulling out my phone, I rechecked the weather. "You're right, but it may dip down to the mid-forties tonight and we don't know how long we'll be out."

My aunt waved a shaking hand at me. "I'll be fine in that fancy Lexus of yours. I'll just wear my long sweater."

I grabbed the fall cashmere sweater out of the closet, admiring the sandy color and softness. "This goes well with your dress."

Aunt Donna nodded proudly as if she had it all figured out already.

I helped my aunt with her walker, not bothering to ask if she wanted to bring her wheelchair since she already kept one at Destiny and Tyler's home. To be honest, she could leave her apartment now and comfortably move into their home since they already had an in-law suite added to their home as it was built. Aunt Donna didn't need to add anything aside from her clothes and herself.

"So, I see there's no man in here," Aunt Donna stated, looking around the inside of my car, once we'd gotten in.

"Here you go," I muttered as I started the vehicle.

"I'm just sayin'. Destiny told me you're still on this celibacy thing or whatever."

"Why are y'all talking about my private business?"

"Because your business is *our* business, miss thang."

"Oh my God," I groaned as we turned out of the parking lot of her building. I truly wanted to turn on the radio, a podcast, *something* to prevent the conversation from heading down the road in which I knew it was going but that would've been rude. Aunt Donna might curse me out if I did that, so I just listened.

"You want to tell me what that's all about?"

I shook my head. "Not really."

"Girl, if you don't open your mouth and tell—"

"There's nothing to explain. I'm just abstaining from men for a little while. My career has been busy, taking off lately, and I'm traveling a lot, and—"

"And hush up with all that mess. Destiny was busy owning her own business and she still made time to date and find Tyler."

I bit my bottom lip to prevent myself from reminding my aunt that while Destiny was single, my aunt had very much been up her butt about finding a man and settling down. She'd been on my case as well, but while D was single, Aunt Donna had to split her chiding between the two of us. Now that Destiny was wifed up, I was getting a double dose of this mess from my aunt.

I pushed out a breath as I listened to her tell me for the millionth time that she wanted to see me happy. Happy the same way she was with my uncle for so many years.

"I wanna leave this Earth knowing that both of my girls are happy and well taken care of."

My gaze moved over to her in the passenger seat. "Leave this Earth? What are you talking about, Aunt Donna?"

"Don't go getting all scared, girl. I didn't mean anything by that. I mean I'm getting up there in age and whatnot, is all. It would do my aging heart some good to have some grandkids."

"You have three grandkids already."

"Yes, and more are in order. Destiny has done her part. Now it's your turn, chile."

I bit the inside of my cheek at the same time my heart pushed against the walls of my chest. If my aunt only knew how much I wanted the same thing. I wouldn't lie this time by going off on a tangent about how women could be happy and fulfilled with a great career, loving friends, and extended family. Not all of us needed a husband and children to complete us.

I said those words repeatedly to my aunt at one time or another, on my podcast, to Destiny and other friends. It was the truth.

It just wasn't necessarily *my* truth.

"Oh, look, we're here." I pushed out a relieved breath when we pulled up in front of Destiny's house some twenty minutes later.

I honked the horn to let them know we'd arrived, and within minutes, Tyler was pulling my passenger door open to help my aunt out of the car. I looked at him and sighed, knowing my cousin had done a hell of a job when she married him.

"Hey, Resha," he said, with his gaze still on Aunt Donna as we helped her with her walker.

"Hey, Ty. Where's—" I didn't fully get my question out before Destiny pushed through the front door with two babies on her hip, one of which was crying.

I giggled. "Looks like we made it just in time."

Tyler chuckled. "It's party central up in here."

I followed Tyler and my aunt to the front door and then leaned in, pressing a kiss to D's cheek before plucking Annalise out of her arms.

"What's all that crying about?" I cooed. "Huh? You're too pretty to be making such ugly noises," I teased and rubbed my nine-month-old niece's belly, before tickling it, making her laugh. "That's better."

"It's their nap time and no one wants to go to sleep. Well, Travis went right out. But these two weren't having it," Destiny explained as we entered the house. "Hey, Mama."

I watched as Aunt Donna and Destiny greeted one another, and I stepped in to also take Tristan from Destiny's arms. As I knew he would, he came right to me, calmly laying his head against my shoulder.

"You're a natural," Tyler remarked, smiling down on me. "I don't know how you do it every time."

I glanced down to where his gaze was planted to realize that Annalise had also laid her head against my shoulder. And although her eyes were still open, they were drooping and she was fighting to keep them open.

"I know where these two go," I whispered, and without another word I moved around the three of them and headed upstairs to the children's nursery.

Pressing the door open, I heard the white noise machine Destiny and Tyler used to play while the babies were sleep. I tiptoed across the room and checked in on Travis who was sound asleep. He was the best sleeper out of the three of them. For a brief second I wondered how I was going to maneuver with two babies in my arms, to lay them down in their cribs.

That was when I felt someone standing over me.

"Let me help with that," Tyler stated in a low but deep voice as he pulled a now-sleeping Annalise from my arms.

I placed Tristan in his own crib, covering him with his blanket and lightly running my hand over his soft, curly mane before stepping back. Tyler moved next to me as I stared down at Tristan.

"I got a job for you if you ever want to change careers."

I covered my mouth to prevent the giggle from escaping. He turned and held the door open for me as I stepped through.

"Seriously though, they love you. You're great with kids. Maybe you should reconsider that whole celibacy thing and have a few of your own."

"Oh my God!" I shrieked while also punching Tyler in the arm. "I'm going to kill Destiny for telling you my business."

"You also mentioned it on your podcast."

I groaned. "So I did. Whatever. I just spent the last twenty-five minutes in my own car getting told by my damn near seventy-year-old aunt that I needed to *get some* as she put it."

Tyler cocked his head back and let out a hearty laugh. I couldn't hold back my smirk. Somewhere along the way Tyler and I had developed an almost brother and sister relationship. It didn't feel awkward having these types of lighthearted discussions with him, not in the least.

"Maybe you should listen to her."

"And maybe *you* should stay out of grown folks' business," I retorted as we entered the kitchen.

"Hey, my husband's a grown ass man."

"Thanks, precious," Tyler responded to Destiny before lowering a kiss to her lips.

"You're welcome, baby."

"Whatever, you both need to stay out of grown folks' business ... in particular, *my* business."

"See," Destiny pointed at me with the wooden spoon she held in her hand, "all that animosity is pent-up sexual frustration. You need to work that out."

I glowered at my cousin. "No, this animosity is from hunger. What are you feeding me? And it better not be your cooking either."

Tyler let out a laugh. "You know that's one thing neither of us do in this house."

Destiny nodded.

"Who cooked?"

"We ordered from that Mexican place you like."

"Good. What'd you get me?"

"Your fave chicken nachos but I did cut up some veggies and made a salad."

I narrowed my eyes at the wooden bowl that Destiny brought from the kitchen counter.

"Don't give me that look. Come on, food's getting cold."

I followed Destiny and Tyler into the dining area where Aunt Donna was already sitting. The smell of the food hit my nose, reminding me that all I had that day so far was a cup of coffee. Sometimes I wondered how I still thoroughly filled out my size fourteen clothing, while forgetting to eat half of the time. As I looked over the food, I remembered it was because the other half of the time I did eat, I went all out. Mexican was one of my favorite cuisines to order out with all the cheese, sour cream, and guacamole I could get. I also loved cooking and baking for others and for myself, and I indulged whenever I got the chance.

"It's just us for lunch?" I questioned, looking around the table once the plates had been filled.

"Yep. I'll be heading over to Josh's after lunch to help him finish setting up the barn for the party."

I wrinkled my brows after swallowing my first bite of my nachos. "Barn? You're setting up a barn for a birthday party?"

Tyler scoffed. "Hell yeah. Get this, it was my father who insisted on the damn thing …" He paused. "Sorry, Ma," he stated contritely, glancing at my aunt.

"I know Deborah taught you better than that," Aunt Donna retorted.

I laughed behind my napkin. If it wasn't his own mother, it was my Aunt Donna getting on Tyler about his mouth.

"Yeah. Anyway, Father wanted his little princesses to be able to ride ponies and whatnot for their birthday. That man doesn't play about his duties as a grandfather."

"He's already started talking about the triplets' party," Destiny added.

"Oh yes, Robert, Deborah, and I had a conversation last week about it."

I blinked as I glanced in my aunt's direction.

"Oh Lord," Destiny grumbled.

I cracked up laughing at how my aunt started going on about the different themes for the party they discussed and how many presents per child they should get and whatnot. Destiny and Tyler remained respectful while my aunt was looking, but every time she lowered her gaze they gave one another the *this is insane* look. I, for one, was just happy the attention had been taken off of my love life, or lack thereof. I cheerfully ate my nachos in peace.

"The babies should be up by the time we have to head over to the party," Destiny stated about forty-five minutes later once the food, dining area, and kitchen were cleaned up. "Mama, do you want to lay down for a little bit?"

"Yeah, baby. I'ma head to my room to rest." Aunt Donna then turned down the hallway toward the in-law suite that was designated just for her.

I watched until she entered the room, shutting the door behind her. I knew she'd be okay in the room by herself as Destiny and Tyler had purchased furniture especially to accommodate her disability.

"Let me show you the outfits I picked out for them," Destiny insisted, grabbing my hand to follow her.

Over the next thirty minutes we killed time by looking at the children's outfits, and Destiny allowed me to help pick out an outfit for her to wear to the party. The children woke up one by one, and Destiny and I changed, fed, and then redressed the kiddos before I went down to get my Aunt Donna to head over to the party.

We arrived in perfect timing, which of course we did since Tyler and Destiny lived on the same block as Joshua and Kayla, just a few houses down. My heart squeezed at how close all the family members were. I wondered what it would've been like to have grown up in a large family surrounded by cousins, aunts, uncles, and loving parents on all sides.

"Resha, you made it," Kayla chimed, sounding surprised when I entered the door behind Destiny and my aunt.

I blinked. "I told you I was coming."

"I know, but Destiny said sometimes you have to cancel for work stuff. Anyway, I'm glad you made it." She pulled me into a hug, causing her not to see the glare I threw Destiny's way over her shoulder.

"I'm glad to be here, and here's a little something for the princess." I handed Kayla the gift-wrapped toy I'd purchased for Victoria.

"Thank you but you didn't have to bring a gift," Joshua stated as he came up behind his wife.

I opened my mouth to respond but Kayla cut me off.

"I already explained that to her, babe, but Resha wouldn't hear of it."

Smiling, I shrugged. "My auntie taught me better than that. You'll have to take it up with her if there's a problem." I jutted my head in my aunt's direction as she stood by Destiny cooing at Annalise.

Josh chuckled with his arm wrapped around his wife's shoulders.

"Where's the birthday girl?"

Josh rolled his eyes. "With her grandfathers. Neither one of them will let her out of their sight. They're out back on the patio."

I nodded, knowing that Kayla and Josh had recently installed a covered patio to the back of their home, allowing for semi-outdoor parties year round. It was something Kayla enjoyed having, according to Destiny.

"Oh shit, I bet Buddy twenty bucks you weren't going to show up," Josh suddenly barked out, laughing, looking over my head toward the entranceway.

Stepping aside to let Josh greet whoever he was speaking to, I went to pivot to turn in that direction when Kayla moved beside me.

"Excuse my husband. As much as he gripes about mine and his father spoiling Victoria, he's even worse. This man invited *everyone* he knows to the party."

I giggled, but the deep baritone I heard behind me suddenly stole all the air from my lungs.

"Twenty bucks? What's the problem, Townsend? Family going bankrupt? My showing up is worth *at least* a Benjamin."

"Or two," Kayla added over my shoulder to the man.

"Now that's what I'm talking about. Your wife knows what's up."

I swallowed, trying to dislodge the lump that had formed in my throat but it was useless. Frozen in place, I wondered if anyone would notice if the ground opened up and swallowed me whole. I knew things like that don't happen but I wished for it to occur, harder than I ever had in my life …. well, almost any other moment.

"Resha, this is Joshua's good friend, Connor."

I blinked, wishing I could knee Kayla as she grasped my arm to spin me around to face *him.*

I didn't need an introduction. As soon as I turned and my eyes met his hazel orbs, that same jolt I felt rush through my body the first time I met him occurred. The man was magnetic, literally. I felt myself being pulled to him before I was consciously aware of taking a step forward.

"N-Nice to meet you, Connor," I managed to get out in a relatively normal voice, if I do say so myself.

His eyes narrowed at the same time his larger hand slipped around mine. And I'd be damned if my entire body didn't shudder. He didn't speak at first as we shook hands, but his eyes did the talking for him.

They told me how much of a liar and coward I was.

Lowering my gaze, I dropped my hand from his without responding to his unuttered condemnation.

"You too. Tasha was it?"

My lips pursed and I lifted my head, shooting him a lethal glare because he knew damn well what my name was.

"*Resha*," I corrected.

He grunted and nodded.

"Well, where's the little angel at? I didn't come to look at your ugly mug," he said to Josh.

Both Josh and Kayla chuckled, and Josh went to show Connor to the patio where the party was starting to ramp up.

"Are you okay?" Kayla paused, giving me a worried expression.

"Who me? Yeah, sure. Um, do you have anything to drink? I am a little thirsty."

"Yes, of course. We've got everything ... soda, juice, tea, water."

"Diet Coke?"

"Yup, Destiny said that was your drink of choice." Kayla plucked a can out of the fridge and handed it to me. "Let me get you a glass."

"No, that's fine. I'll just grab a straw. Thank you." I took one of the colorful straws that'd been placed on a plate by the food, next to the cups, and opened my soda to take a drink. The first sip didn't do anything to alleviate the lump in my throat, not that I thought it would at that point.

Stepping out onto the patio, I was taken by surprise at how big it was. And although it was covered, the sliding doors were open to let in a breeze from the outside. I was thankful that it wasn't too cold out but I still glanced over at my aunt to make sure she had her sweater on. I wasn't surprised to see her sitting next to Joshua's mother, Deborah, the pair involved in a lively conversation.

I smiled, happy that Destiny's in-laws had taken my aunt in as much as they had when she became a part of the family.

"Hey, what're you thinking about?"

"I'm thinking about how someone should've taught you not to walk up on people, surprising them like that," I retorted as I spun around to face Destiny.

She giggled. "Girl, what're you so jumpy about? You're surrounded by family."

My mind went back to the creepy emails and messages I'd been sent earlier in the week. The last few messages were scarier because the person writing them had references specific locations I'd been at, or what I was wearing on a day of the week when I hadn't posted on social media. I looked around, avoiding my cousin's gaze.

And as my eyes moved to the other side of the patio, they instantly locked with Connor's. Another reason I was feeling uneasy. Even my damn dreams, as vivid as they'd been, hadn't compared to the real life version.

"How did your meeting go?"

Destiny's question pulled me back to her. "What meeting?"

"The one you refused to tell me about."

I blinked. "Oh. That one." I shrugged. "It went well, I think. Still waiting to hear back from them. If they send over a contract that meets what we discussed, I'll send it to my lawyer before agreeing to anything."

"And your financial advisor to make sure they're paying you what you're worth."

I grinned. "Of course. If it gets to that stage, I'll definitely be pulling you in to help negotiate the final numbers."

"I know you will. I saw your latest post on fall sweaters. Loved it."

Smiling, I adjusted the leopard print sweater I was wearing, emphasizing that it'd been one of the sweaters I featured on my blog that week.

"It looks good on you, but then again, there's not much that doesn't."

"Thanks, sis."

"Girl bye, you know you look good. I'm loving this fall weave you've chosen."

I did a hair flip. "She cute, right?"

We laughed just as Patience with one of her youngest twins on her hip joined us.

"Let me guess. This is Thiers," I stated, leaning down and smiling at the baby. If I remembered correctly, he was close to eighteen months.

"Yup. I would ask how you know, but he's the clingiest of all of my children," Patience laughed. "He's *always* on my hip. Even the baby isn't as clingy."

I grinned and shook my head, because Patience and Aaron also had a daughter they named Anastasia. She was the youngest of all the children and was probably somewhere with her father while Thiers stuck close to his mother's side.

And just like clockwork, as if we were taking too much of his mother's attention, Thiers squirming.

"He's hungry. Excuse me," Patience uttered before rushing off.

"Resha, loved this week's post," Michele commented. She was another one of Destiny's sisters-in-law.

"Thank you." I smiled across at her. "I love those braids," I commented on the long, chestnut braids she'd had installed since I last saw her.

"Thanks, I needed a change. I can't remember the last time I got my hair braided."

"They look great on her, don't they?" a deep male voice interrupted.

No one was surprised to see Carter pop up behind Michelle, staring down at her lovingly, with a twinkle in his cerulean eyes just before he pressed a kiss to his wife's cheek.

"Then again, my lady would look good with no hair on her head whatsoever. I'm a lucky man," he complimented while wiggling his blond eyebrows.

Michele stared at her husband, a light rose color making its way on her caramel cheeks as she ate up his compliments. I stared down into the can of Diet Coke I still held, something tightening in my chest.

"All right, you two, that's enough of the love fest, break it up," Destiny admonished.

Carter chuckled and pressed another kiss to Michelle's cheek before heading in the direction of the birthday girl, who was still being indulged by her grandfathers.

Those men love hard.

"They sure do," Michele and Destiny stated wistfully, at the same time.

I blinked, not even realizing that I'd stated my thoughts out loud. Thankfully, neither woman had noticed the longing I heard in my own voice. They were too busy eyeing their spouses across the room. That was also when another tall, blond male just so happened to look up and turn my way, catching my gaze.

His glare was hard, penetrating, as if he could see right through me. I loathed that feeling above all else, and, I averted my eyes once again, looking down at the Diet Coke.

"That was a great topic on this week's podcast. I love that you ladies are doing a whole divorced series for women on how to bounce back with their finances," Michelle stated, bringing my attention back to her.

I nodded. "Yeah, we get so many emails from women going through a divorce or separation who've let their spouses handle the finances for years and just don't know where to start."

"It's surprising that in this day and age how many women are so willing to turn over financial responsibility to their husbands that easily."

Destiny shrugged. "It makes sense if you think about it. In most households, women are still shouldering the role of being the primary caretaker, homemaker, and holding down a full-time or part-time job. With all of that burden, it just seems easier to let their husbands take over managing the money."

"Burden?" I questioned with a raised eyebrow.

Destiny rolled her eyes. "I didn't mean it like that."

Michelle giggled. "I know you didn't. And I get it. Carter is totally the hands-on type of father, loves cooking, and truth be told, he's even a little cleaner than I am. I think it's a result of his time in the military. He still folds all the clothes very nearly the way he was taught in the army. Anyway, what I'm saying is we share the duties in the house, but I could see if raising our kids were left mainly to me along with keeping the house clean and managed ... well, I'd feel utterly overwhelmed with managing the finances on top of that."

"Right, and that's exactly where many of the women who message us are coming from. Not all, of course, and things are changing. More marriages seem to be evolving to a true partnership but there's still a ways to go."

"And is that why you've yet to take the plunge?"

I tossed my head backwards. "Oh, here we go," I groaned at Destiny's question.

"I'm just saying."

I made a long, suffering sigh.

"Resha, are you dating anyone?" Michelle decided to chime in.

"Ah man, y'all are as bad as Aunt Donna."

They both laughed but that didn't end the procession of questions.

"I'm just saying, marriage can be a beautiful thing. Maybe it's time for you to rethink this whole celibacy thing."

I parted my lips to respond to my cousin, but a deep chuckle behind me had me pivoting on my heels, staring directly up into the hazel eyes that I'd been trying to avoid since he arrived.

That damn look. He wasn't shy about the fact that he overheard our conversation and knew my secret.

Clearing my throat, I turned back to my cousin.

"Connor, hey, I didn't know you were stopping by," Destiny spoke up.

I blinked as a pit began to form in my stomach. How the hell did these two know each other?

"No other place I'd rather be than a one-year-old's birthday party," he responded, sarcasm filling every syllable.

Michelle and Destiny giggled.

"This lame made it a point to stop by because I would kick his ass if he didn't," Joshua added from out of the blue as he approached Connor's side.

Connor's head angled down at Joshua, who at a few inches over six-foot was tall in his own right, but Connor had to be at least six-foot-six, ensuring he towered over just about anyone standing next to him.

I love tall men.

Why the hell my subconscious thought it was appropriate to remind me of that damn fact remained a mystery.

"Have you met my cousin?"

I bit back the groan that wanted to escape my mouth as Destiny eased beside Connor, looking in my direction. I could see in her eyes what she was doing.

"We've made our acquaintance."

His eyes never left my face, and all of a sudden I could feel my body temperature begin to rise in spite of the cool breeze coming from outside.

I cleared my throat and looked over at my cousin, avoiding Connor. "I need to go to the bathroom."

"Oh, we were just about to cut the cake and open presents," Kayla stated breathlessly as she joined our circle with Victoria in her hands.

I gave her a pasted-on smile. "I'll be quick." I didn't pause for a reaction or a response, and I turned and made my way back inside and down the hall toward the first floor bathroom.

****

Connor

Well this is an interesting turn of events, I thought as I watched her ass sway from one side to the other in the dark denim jeans she was wearing. I didn't even bother hiding my ogling of her backside. I'd barely spoken a full sentence to her since I arrived, but it was time to change that.

"Save a slice of cake for me, will ya?" I told Josh without even looking before moving in the same direction as that ass.

"Don't tell me …" he mumbled.

"Then I won't," I retorted prior to exiting his presence.

I'd been to Josh's house before so I didn't need any directions on how to find the bathroom—assuming, of course, that's where Resha went. I was right on the money when after only walking halfway down the long hall, I saw none other than Resha exiting the bathroom door.

"Imagine running into you here, *Pilar*," my words somehow came out on a growl.

Stunned, those dark, coffee-colored eyes of hers widened, and the full, heart-shaped lips pinched before she spoke.

"Or it is Resha?" I questioned while folding my arms over my wide chest. I couldn't stop myself from looking her over. Her skin held the deep cinnamon color that I remembered from our night together; however, her oval face was bracketed by dark brown curls that were blonde at the tips. That night, her hair had been styled in a short, jet black bob that hadn't even touched her shoulders. Naturally, I let my eyes dip lower to the leopard print sweater that silhouetted her ample breasts and stopped at the small waist. The jeans looked as if they were clinging for dear life as they hugged those bountiful thighs of hers.

"It's both actually," she finally answered with her chin lifted as if she'd one upped me somehow.

I approached, stepping closer, lifting an eyebrow and daring her to elaborate.

"My middle name is Pilar. My first name is Resha."

Dropping my arms, I nodded in understanding. She hadn't lied that night, not completely, when she told me her name was Pilar.

"And what are you doing here, Resha?" Nope, I didn't miss the way the vein in her neck doubled in speed at my mentioning her name for the first time.

She took a step backwards, only to be met by the closed door she just exited.

"Destiny is my cousin, *not* that it's any of your business."

"If it wasn't my business you wouldn't have answered me."

Her eyes narrowed and I instantly recalled it was the same look she gave me that night after I told her I was going to fuck her to sleep. Defiance. And I felt my body react to it the same way in which I was reacting that moment. Sheer determination.

"And what are *you* doing here, Connor?" She folded her arms over her breasts.

My eyes dipped before returning to meet her gaze again. "A good friend of mine invited me to his kid's birthday party." I added a one-sided shoulder shrug.

"You don't seem like the type to make it a habit of attending kid's parties. Or have many friends."

I stepped even closer, crowding her space. "I'm pretty certain that was supposed to be some sort of insult on your part, but I don't insult easily. How long you been celibate?"

She gasped and it pulled a chuckle from my lips. I had to keep going.

"Was that vow of celibacy taken before or after I fucked you to sleep in my hotel room?"

Another gasp. Her eyes were so large they looked as if they were ready to pop out of her head.

"What the—" She stopped and didn't say anything further before using one hand to push at my shoulder, as she made her way around me and charged down the hallway.

Again, I watched the sway of her ass in those jeans. And try as she might to come across as genuinely offended, I spotted the quickening of her pulse and the way her bottom lip quivered ever so slightly.

"Resha Pilar ..." I murmured, wondering what her last name was. Of course, I had my ways of finding out. I made a mental note to do just that as soon as I had the time.

Chapter Three

Resha

Was that before of after I fucked you to sleep in my hotel room?

"Who says something like that?" I blurted out into the night air. It was a few hours after the birthday party and I was back home. Aunt Donna had chosen to stay the night over Destiny and Tyler's, and we all had dinner together after the party.

Now, after having made myself a tall cup of my favorite pumpkin latte, complete with whipped cream on top, I was taking time to utilize my favorite part of my condo—the balcony. Unfortunately, as I prepared to sit down on the white wicker loveseat, memories of my encounter with Connor flooded my mind.

An instant chill ran through my body. I tightened the blanket I brought out with me over my body, although I knew that wasn't the real reason for my body's distress. Thinking the latte would help warm me from the inside out, I took a sip, and although it was good, I still felt as if I was missing something.

... I fucked you to sleep ...

He truly had. On more than one occasion that night. I vividly recalled him waking me up after round one to go at it again.

I sighed.

For months I'd endured dreams of being in that man's arms after only one night together. I'd had no intention of ever seeing him again. But just my luck, out of nowhere, in the midst of my cousin, my aunt, and even Destiny's sister-in-laws questioning me on my decision to remain celibate, there he appeared.

I had tried to forget that night with him. On busy days, I could do so easily. I filled my days with work, meetings, writing, social media postings, photoshoots, recording, and whatever else I needed to do. Or told myself I needed to do. But nighttime always got me. Even on the nights when I practically crawled into my bed with exhaustion, swearing this would be the night where my brain was just too tired to even think about dreaming of him. But I was the fool, because tired as I might have been, my memories of that one evening in New York with Connor always seemed to make their way to the forefront of my mind.

I sat back in the loveseat and lifted my legs to place them on the low-sitting glass patio table, careful not to disturb the lavender candle that sat, burning at the center. My balcony space truly was my little oasis. As much as I loved my entire condo, working from home sometimes made it difficult to discern where work ended and my private space began. Though I had a space for my desk and office, I often worked in my bedroom, kitchen table, and living room. But the balcony was my getaway.

I'd had it adorned with a cream-colored, fluffy throw rug, comfortable patio furniture—including the loveseat, table, and chair—my plants, of course, and I'd strung up an array of lights around the wall so it was perfect for reading at night. But now, my little sanctuary was being impeded with thoughts of a man I swore I would only have one encounter with. One unforgettable night, across the country. I'd been in New York during fashion week for a couple of appearances by some companies I was working with. I wasn't new to working at fashion week, but after a late night meeting, I opted to stop in a random bar for a quick drink by myself. About fifteen minutes after I sat down at the bar, someone took the stool next to me, asking the bartender for a beer. His voice had me hooked before I even saw his face.

When I did, I knew it was time to go. From that angle, I could only make out his profile—which was, for lack of a better word, perfect. His long, strawberry-blond hair hung low, past his shoulders, but when one massive hand came up, swiping his hair out of his face, my gasp caused him to look my way. *Lord, why did he do that?*

Those penetrating eyes of his were what I saw next, and the intensity matched the hard lines and planes of his face. Even in the darkened bar I could make out the five o'clock shadow that peppered his lower jaw and top lip. It gave a rugged look to his already handsome face. But he wasn't handsome in the J. Crew model sort of way. The crooked line of his nose spoke to it having been broken at least once in his life, and the danger that emanated from his eyes backed up my assumption that this man was well versed in handling himself.

He didn't say anything for a long while, he just stared at me. And, had it been anyone else, I'm sure I would've found it creepy and awkward as hell. But there was no underlying macabre vibes involved in that first stare.

"Thanks," he said as he stared straight into my eyes.

Wrinkling my brows, I parted my lips to ask what he was thanking me for, but out of the corner of my eye, I saw movement. I realized he was thanking the bartender for bringing him his drink, while still holding my gaze. I lowered my line of sight to see him toss the bartender a few bills, more than enough for his beer.

"That's for her drink as well."

I didn't say anything, too caught up in trying to figure out what it was he was angling for.

"What are you drinking?"

I took another sip before answering.

"An apple martini."

He grunted and chuckled at the same time. It was the sexiest thing I'd heard in a long time. So much so, that my thighs instantly clenched.

"Figures."

I didn't like that tone, however. "What figures?"

"You'd be drinking a prissy ass drink like that."

Slightly offended, my head pushed back and I stared down at his drink. "What, instead of a *real* drink like beer?"

Smiling, he nodded before taking a long sip of the dark beer he ordered.

In spite of myself, I watched his Adam's apple bob up and down as he swallowed. Again, it was damn near erotic to watch.

He sat the now half-empty glass down and leaned in closer, placing one hand on the side of the stool I sat on, while the other rested against the bar. His face was mere inches from mine.

"Damn straight," he responded. The breath he let out skirted across the skin of my neck and goosebumps rose along my collarbone. His eyes dipped and then narrowed, and I knew he had noticed my body's reaction to his closeness.

Slowly those irises of his lifted to meet mine again.

"You're here alone, aren't you?"

I nodded. Why? I had no fucking clue. I'm generally a cautious woman. I don't go around telling men I just met that I was out alone. But for some odd reason I *wanted* him to know I wasn't there with anyone else.

"I'm Connor," he finally introduced.

"R— Pilar," I blurted out, giving him the name I used when I didn't want someone to know my real name or get too close. It wasn't a total fabrication since that was my middle name. I cleared my throat. "Pilar." I stuck out my hand.

He reached for it.

Big hands.

My eyes dropped to the ground.

Big feet.

I was a fully grown woman. Had been sexually active for a number of years prior to my decision to remain celibate. I'd been tricked more than once by the big hands and big feet belief. Not every man with large hands and feet had the size to match in his pants, if you know what I mean. However, I just knew that wasn't the case with Connor.

He had … what were the younger millennials calling it these days?

Big. Dick. Energy.

It wasn't just confidence, or even cockiness, which, trust me, he had in spades. It was in his damn aura. His shando! He could handle his own in *any* situation.

"My hotel is right across the street."

Those seven little words had my nipples pebbling against the designer bra I wore. I'd been celibate for two years, three months, and thirteen days up until that point. And to be completely honest, the desire to be with a man hadn't truly bothered me. I began my celibacy journey because I wanted more than sex from a man, but somehow all the ones I'd come across seem to just want that one thing. Sure, nights were lonely, but I had a toy that I kept in the nightstand next to my bed that always helped get me through the rough spots. And unlike most men I'd encountered in my life, my toy never let me down. All he required was that I kept his batteries fresh. It was little to ask for so much pleasure in return.

Yet, as I sat across from Connor, watching him finish off that beer while his free hand still rested against my bar stool, I knew that even my trusty toy that I traveled with wouldn't be enough to satisfy the urges he was stirring inside of me. Still, I couldn't make it easy on him either.

"What makes you think I give a damn where your hotel room is, Connor?"

A smile that rose all the way to his eyes again had my insides tingling. My inner voice was already beginning to tell me to shut the hell up before I talked myself out of some amazing orgasms that night.

"For one, the way you keep biting that lower lip of yours is a pretty decent indication." He punctuated his commented by raising his hand and tugging as my chin, causing my lower lip to pop out from between my teeth, proving his point. "Secondly, your flared nostrils and that beating vein in your neck practically scream, *'Come fuck me, Connor.'*"

My eyes bulged. I couldn't believe his vulgarity … or maybe I could but just couldn't believe how much more it turned me on.

"Don't worry, a stór, I'll fuck you to sleep. I can tell by the look in your eyes, it's been a long time since you've had a man do that for you."

My jaw clamped shut because I wanted to refute his statement but couldn't. It had been a long time since anyone has fucked me good enough to put me to sleep. And I'm talking about long before I decided to close up shop down there for a while.

"You … you're …" I struggled to find the word that identified exactly what my thoughts of him were.

"Incorrigible? Sexy? Dangerous? A little crazy?"

"All of the above," I responded.

He chuckled, and that truly sealed the deal. But again, I couldn't make it that damn easy.

"How do I even know you'll be worth my time?"

A grin formed on his lips. The type the Grinch makes when he knows he's just succeeded in his plans to foil Christmas.

An instant later those same lips were barreling down on mine, connecting us physically for the first time since this encounter began. He hadn't asked, hadn't tried to move in slow or even romance me into this kiss. I asked a question and he responded.

And oh boy what a response!

I'd forgotten that kissing was an art form. Very few men, at least in my experience, were versed in how to do it the right way. Connor wasn't one of those men. Though this kiss had begun rather abruptly, it was patient and rushed all at the same time. His lips were soft yet unyielding. His tongue was just the right mix of prying and exploring. He ran his tongue against the corner of my lips, causing me to shiver. Then his tongue moved to lick the top of the inside of my mouth. My panties became the recipient of a waterfall. And that was when I felt Connor's hand on my ass. Somehow we'd both moved from our positions on the stools, to standing.

By some miracle, I realized that we were standing there making out right in front of the bar for the bartender, customers, and God to see. I pulled back.

It took me a moment to steady my breathing, and for words to actually form in my brain.

"I-I think we should go. *Now,*" I managed to get out.

For a man of his size, Connor moved fast as hell. Tossing the bartender's tip on the bar, he then grabbed the small, black clutch I'd had sitting on the bar and placed it in my hands. Then wrapping a long arm around the small of my back as we exited the bar.

He was right, his hotel was directly across the street. And I had spent that night yelling his name at the top of my lungs before an orgasm-induced exhaustion forced me to sleep.

****

Connor

Resha Pilar McDonald.

I'd found out her last name. All it took was a simple Google search. I opted for that instead of going directly to Josh to ask him. I didn't need his shit. And it turned out, she ran a successful plus size fashion blog, had thousands of followers across her social media pages, and hosted a podcast with her cousin, Destiny. I easily found all of that out with one simple Google search. And yup, she lived right here in Williamsport.

The woman who'd interrupted my sleep many nights from our one encounter had the damn audacity to be living in my city the whole time.

"Nice work!"

I grunted as I heard my brother's voice echoed on the walls around us. I ignored him, continuing with my double unders to finish out this round of jump roping. Out of the corner of my eye, I saw Mark wheel around one of the concrete pillars of the basement of this building to move in front of me.

"Working out pretty intense, bro."

Again, I said nothing as the timer of the workout app I was using on my phone went off, signaling the end of that round. Instantly, I dropped the jump rope, and picked up the gloves by my feet, placing them on and moving to stand in front of the hanging punching bag. Once the timer bell chimed again, I began a series of right and left jabs against the bag, pivoting on my toes, to circle the bag in its entirety.

"Planning on getting in a fight tonight? It's been a while."

My focus was acutely on the punching bag, though I clearly heard Mark.

"Oh, for fuck's sake, how long are you going to keep this shit up, Connor?"

Hearing the distress in his voice, I paused and briefly looked at him. "You still fighting?"

He nodded. "Yes."

I grunted and continued punching the bag without another word. The timer sounded again, and I tossed the gloves on the floor and moved to my jump rope again, lifting it to begin another round until the timer went off.

"You know you can't keep ignoring me."

I grunted.

"I'm your little brother. Your *only* brother."

Nothing.

"You're here early before the fights begin. Are you doing two a days now?" Mark inquired, not seeming to get the picture that I wasn't in the mood to talk.

"What the hell, Connor?" he finally uttered again, sounding frustrated.

"Ah, don't fret over his grumpy ass. He's having woman troubles."

Ah fuck! I cursed in my head as Buddy emerged from behind the door of the changing room. There was an entrance into the building that only a few people were aware of or had access to. Buddy, the guy who trained most of the guys who came to our Underground fighting group, was one of the few. He also was a pain in my ass when he wanted to be, having been my own trainer throughout my professional career as a professional mixed-martial arts fighter.

"Woman troubles?" Mark inquired, wearing a smirk on his face. It reminded me of myself whenever I had the one up on somebody.

"Both of you need to mind your fucking business," I growled, tossing the jump rope to the ground and turning the workout app off, since my workout was completed. Grabbing the water bottle I'd brought, I squirted water into my mouth as I fought to catch my breath. The sweat running down my back, arms, chest, and face spoke of the ninety minute session I just endured. And to answer Mark's question from earlier, yes, this had been my second workout of the day.

And unfortunately, Buddy was accurate when he attributed my extra workout session to *woman troubles.* But it would be a cold day in hell before I admitted any of that to these fuckers.

"What's her name?" Mark asked as he wheeled himself next to me.

I wanted to put him in a headlock to get rid of that stupid grin he wore on his face.

"I wouldn't try it if I were you, O'Brien. This kid may be a cripple but you've been out of the ring a while and he's faster than he looks," Buddy teased with as little tact as possible.

Even Mark laughed. Everyone knew Buddy didn't mince words, nor did he seem to care about sparing anyone's feelings. Truth be told, him calling Mark a cripple was a term of endearment in Buddy-speak. Anyone else and I would've put them on their ass.

"Who you got me going against tonight?" Mark asked.

"I was thinking Brick."

"Fuck no!" I yelled, glaring at Buddy.

Buddy barely reacted to my outburst while Mark let out a deep sigh.

"We can't keep going through this shit, Connor. I'm fighting and that's that. If Buddy puts me in the ring with Brick, so be it. The bigger they are, the harder they f—"

"Fuck that, Brick is twice his size even with a pair of functioning legs. He's faster than he looks and he's mean when he wants to be."

"Exactly, the kid's ready for him."

"I'm not a damned kid," Mark squealed, reminding me of when he was ten years old and used to beg me to take him to my workout sessions just so he could be around other fighters. When I told him that he was too young, he would respond with that exact phrasing.

"He'll be fine, O'Brien. Don't get your panties in a twist. Right, kid?"

"Fuck you, Buddy. I ain't a damn kid."

Shaking my head, I grabbed my gloves, water bottle, phone, and jump rope to head for the changing room to shower. I wouldn't be staying around for tonight's fight if Mark was getting in the ring. I was liable to jump in the ring and beat any bastard black and blue who dared to even graze the top of my kid brother's hair.

"Hey, wait up, I need to speak with you."

I sighed but slowed down and turned to face Mark, lifting an eyebrow.

"I really came here early to talk to you about your underperforming social media pages."

"Not this shit again."

"Yes, this shit again. As your social media manager—because you absolutely *refuse* to hire a real one—I have to keep you updated on what's happening. Look, you know I believe in your product and what you're selling, but between my own full-time job, fighting, and having a social life of my own, I think it's necessary to tell you, that you really need to hire someone for this. Your products aren't getting the attention they deserve because your social media presence is lacking."

"What are you talking about? My protein shakes alone brought in just over one million in revenue last year. The supplements brought in another five hundred thousand."

"Yeah, and you could've doubled or even tripled that amount had you had the right marketing in place."

Frustrated, I pushed a hand through my long hair, noting how sweaty it was. I owned and operated a number of businesses. However, my focus, as of late, had been on my dietary supplements and protein shake company, TKO Supplements. Our most popular product line was our TKO protein powders and shakes. We'd been growing steadily over the past three years.

"It's time you became the face of TKO."

"Hell no." I shook my head adamantly at Mark's ridiculous suggestion. This wasn't the first time he brought it up.

"Come on, Connor. People know you. They'll trust TKO even more with your face at the forefront because they know your reputation for fighting, and more importantly, for *winning.* All the pictures on TKO's social media pages right now are just images of the protein powders, the labels, and whatnot. Put your face in it, or take pictures of you drinking the stuff after a tough workout session and I bet you orders will pick up instantly."

"I'm not doing it."

"Fucking stubborn ass," he grunted.

"Watch your mouth."

"And what the hell are you going to do about it?"

I narrowed my eyes at my brother as he sat there boldly staring up at me from his wheelchair, daring me to make a move.

"Little shit."

His laughter hit my back as I turned and stormed into the changing room to shower and head home for the night. Usually, I stayed for the Underground fights, but not if Mark was getting in the ring. I didn't need to watch that shit. And Buddy and every man involved in this fighting club knew that if my kid brother got hurt, there was nowhere on this Earth the person who did it could hide to escape my wrath.

****

Instead of heading straight home, I chose to head to a twenty-four hour grocer to pick up something to eat. All I had at my place was bottle of protein shakes and I knew that wouldn't be enough to satisfy me for the night. Not the way my stomach was growling after such an intense workout.

Inclining my head, I acknowledged the older Asian woman who ran the store along with her husband. She gave me a curt nod as she always did when I entered.

Making my way to the back of the store where they kept their daily prepared meals, I grabbed a chicken salad sandwich, bag of chips, an apple, and a bottle of water. Once I got to the register, I added one of the banana muffins that were wrapped in Saran wrapped to my order and waited for the woman to put all my items in a plastic bag and hand me my change before exiting. I only lived a few blocks from the store, but since I'd driven from the building where the Underground fought, across town, I started in the direction of where I parked my Kawasaki which was about a half a block down the city street.

"Ahh! Help!" a feminine voice shrieked as I walked past an alley close to where my bike was parked.

The hairs on the back of my neck stood up as I recognized that voice.

"Leave me alone!" she yelled again.

That was when I turned my head, and thanks to the streetlight I could make out a larger figure standing over a woman, raise his hand and punch her across the face. My bag was thrown to the ground and I sprinted down the alley to reach the pair.

"Get the fuck off of her!" I growled at the same time I reached for the man by the back of his neck and practically threw him into the brick wall of the building behind me. Yet, hearing his shriek of pain wasn't enough satisfaction. I grabbed the bastard by his shoulder, spinning him around and quickly landing my own fist against the side of his face. The familiar sound of bone crunching echoed in that dark alley. I would've kept going but the dumbfuck had a jaw made of glass and was instantly knocked out cold after one hit.

I turned to the woman, who was still standing there, breathing heavily. The lighting gave me a clear view of one dark brown eye that was filled with fear. The other was covered with her hand.

"Resha," I breathed out, going to her. "What the hell happened? Are you okay?" My hands went to her waist to hold her steady because she appeared as if she was on the verge of passing out.

"What's going on down there?" someone yelled.

I looked down the alley to see two people standing there. "Call 911. She's just been attacked!" I ordered, and the man quickly pulled out a phone and began calling. I vaguely heard his telling the operator our location and the situation.

Staring down at Resha, I saw she appeared terrified. "You're okay," I consoled, pulling her close to me. Her lush body fell against mine as if she desperately needed the comfort.

"H-He tried to rob me," Resha was explaining ten minutes later to the police officers.

"Is questioning her again necessary? She's already explained this to the female officer who arrived first and she needs to be taken to the hospital." My level of patience was running out, especially as I watched how swollen Resha's face had gotten in the last ten minutes.

"Okay, we'll let you get some medical attention and we'll be in touch if there are any follow-up questions."

I didn't bother thanking the officers, as I placed my arm around Resha and walked her to the paramedics.

"What are you doing? They already checked me out."

"I know, but you need to be taken to the hospital, and I've only got my bike with me tonight. I don't think it's safe to have you ride on the back of my motorcycle. Not until we know for certain you don't have a concussion. So, I'm going to follow the medics to Memorial."

"I don't think—"

"Ma'am, we do think it's best that you go to the hospital with us."

Resha sighed, but when I thought she was going to give more protest she didn't, nodding her head instead and allowing the paramedics to escort her into the back of the ambulance.

Good thing, too, because I was damn sure ready to strap her over my shoulder and ride one-handed on my Kawasaki if need be.

The entire time as I rode behind that ambulance all I could think about was her shrieks for help followed by the sound of the punch that fucker had given her. It had me tightening my hands on the handles of my bike, fighting the urge to speed up and get to the hospital first in search of the would-be thief. He'd remained passed out as the cops cuffed him and the paramedics loaded him into the ambulance.

Dumbfuck.

I parked as soon as we pulled into the parking lot of the hospital and ran to meet the ambulance just as they were opening the doors to let Resha out of the back. I could see she was able to move about relatively fine but that didn't seem to stave off the worry that continued to course through my veins.

"Thank you," she mumbled to the paramedics as they loaded her stretcher off the ambulance and rolled her through the doors of the emergency room. I practically pushed the smaller male medic out of the damn way once they placed her in one of the exam rooms.

I listened intently as the medics conveyed the necessary information to the in-take staff of the ER. Once that 'medics transferred Resha to one of the hospital's beds, we were shown to a private room, at my insistence, and told a doctor would be in to see us shortly.

"We didn't need a private room. I could've waited out in the lobby," Resha argued as I helped her sit down on the examination table.

"You could've but why the hell should you? I've got an in with a few of the people on the board of this hospital." I was also a stake-owner in the hospital as well but that didn't need to be said out loud.

"Thanks," she simply stated before clearing her throat.

"And why the hell were you out so late at night, by yourself, in a dark alley anyway?" I charged, uncaring of my tone.

Resha's forehead wrinkled and she gave me a sharp look with her unswollen eye.

It pissed me off just to see her other eye.

"I didn't know it was a crime for a woman to be outside at night alone."

"Not a crime but pretty fucking stupid."

Her mouth fell open. I guessed she expected me to mince words. *Tough shit.*

"You've got the mouth of a sailor."

"You'd know better than most."

Her lips pinched.

"If you must know, I was going out to that twenty-four hour grocery store to get some ic— dinner. Some dinner. The alley is a straight shot from my building two blocks over to the grocery store. I always take that shortcut."

"And do you always do so at ten o'clock at night?"

"I didn't realize it was that late. I lost track of time working."

"And why the hell didn't you just give that asswipe your bag?"

Frowning, she tightened her arm against the large, black and brown, leather shoulder bag she had with her. The same one the guy had tried to separate her from. When she chose not to give it up so easily was when he hit her. That's when I came along.

"It's my favorite bag! This is real leather," she defended.

I rolled my eyes and started to tell her how stupid that sounded when a knock on the door sounded and a doctor entered.

"Ms. McDonald, I'm Dr. Wilkes. I'll be checking out your injuries just to make sure there's no concussion," he explained all this while extending his hand for her to shake.

"And this must be your husband." He reached for my hand.

"He's not—"

"Connor."

"Pleasure to meet you. Well, of course, we wish it was under different circumstances."

I grunted. "Are you a resident?" I looked up and down his green scrubs, noting the absence of a white coat.

"I'm a first year fellow, actually."

Another once over and I felt my lips forming a frown. "We need a *real* doctor. Where's Dr. Hollstein at?"

"Connor," Resha admonished, "I'm sure Dr. Wilkes is just fine."

He nodded, which made me dislike him even more. "I assure you, I've gone through as much training as Dr. Hollstein and got into Memorial's very rigorous fellows program."

"I'm sure you're fine, Dr. Wilkes. Please don't pay any attention to him."

The doctor looked from me to Resha and back to me again.

"You better be."

He pushed out the breath he was holding and pulled the small, laser flashlight thingy from the pocket of his shirt.

I watched dutifully as he told Resha to follow the light with her eyes. She was able to do so with her right eye but her left was nearly swollen shut. Dr. Wilkes put in a request for her to get some additional tests just to make sure nothing was broken.

"Well, thankfully, nothing appears to be broken," he informed us about thirty minutes later as he held up Resha's X-ray.

"Are you sure?" I was on the verge of requesting a second opinion. The only thing that stopped me was glancing over and seeing Resha's unharmed eye drooping. Adrenaline from the attack was starting to wear off and she was getting tired.

"I'm certain. She'll need overnight observation, or for at least the next twelve hours just to ensure there's no concussion or more serious brain injuries."

"That won't be necessary. Besides, I don't even have—"

"I've got it covered, Doc. Anything else?"

"If you're in any pain, I can write you a prescription for some extra strength Tylenol. I wouldn't recommend anything stronger than that."

Resha immediately shook her head. "I don't want any medication."

Her adamant refusal sparked my interest but I left the question unspoken. I could circle back on that once we were alone.

"Thank you, Dr. Wilkes."

I moved from the far side of the room, taking Resha by the arm and waist to help her down from the observation table to the bathroom so she could change back into her clothes from the hospital gown she'd worn for x-rays. After some final directives and a writing out of the prescription he'd mentioned, just in case she changed her mind, Dr. Wilkes left us.

"You sure you don't want that?" I asked as Resha crumbled up the prescription.

"Positive." She tossed the script in the trash as if it were burning a hole in her hand.

"Which one of your parents was on drugs?"

A tiny gasp escaped her lips as she spun around with her good eye wide and forehead wrinkled.

I shrugged. "Not too difficult to figure out. Most people who react the way you do to a simple drug prescription typically have some experience with drug addiction. Either themselves or close a relative. I took an educated guess."

"That's none of your damn business," she sassed.

I shrugged again as if I didn't give a shit whether she told me. "Suit yourself. Let's go."

"I need to get a cab or an Uber."

"No shit. And I'm not letting you catch one alone. I'll have to leave my bike here overnight, I guess. No big deal, the parking lot's got cameras." Pulling out my phone, I brought up one of the car service apps I had and ordered a car to … "Hey, what's your address?" I questioned Resha as we stood out in the lobby of the emergency department.

Only when I didn't get an answer did I peer up from my phone.

"God dammit," I growled as I watched her sauntering off in the direction of the entranceway as if she was about to go it alone. "Hell no. Where the hell do you think you're going?"

She halted abruptly due to my hand encircling her arm, spinning her around to face me. "I'm going *home*."

"That's where I was just trying to get you to until you walked off."

"I'm going home *alone*."

"Bullshit you are. You did hear what the doc said, right?"

She waved a hand in the air dismissively, and even with her left eye swollen shut I could see the defiance written all over her face. *Stubborn ass woman.*

"He was just being cautious because he doesn't want to be sued if something goes wrong. I'm fine. A little pain but nothing I can't sleep off. At home. By myself."

"He was being cautious because this could be a big deal. You could have a concussion, and sometimes concussions don't show up immediately. Trust me, I've had one or two myself. They're not called traumatic brain injuries because the shit sounds pretty. The last thing you want is to be at home alone and start experiencing the dizziness, loss of consciousness, headache, vomiting, and a multitude of other symptoms that come with a concussion."

Her forehead wrinkled. "You go to med school or something?"

I chuckled. "Nah, why?"

"You seem to have a certain familiarity with some of the hospital staff and you rattle off the symptoms of a concussion like you studied it."

"I'm just a former pro fighter who's had more than one visit to the ER for getting knocked on my ass."

"So you weren't a very good fighter?" she retorted with arms folded over her breasts.

"I was one of the best, sweetheart." I moved closer. "But to become the best, one of the first things you learn is how to get knocked down and keep going."

She tilted her head to the side, her good eye glancing over me as if deciding something. I didn't have time for her to make a decision. Instead of waiting, I pulled up the app on my phone yet again and then handed it to her.

"Put your address in. I'm taking you home and watching you overnight."

Either she recognized the severity of the issue at hand or she was just really tired, because she gave no resistance. Less than five minutes later, our Uber was pulling up to the entranceway of the ER and I held the door open for Resha to get in before slipping inside behind her.

The very woman who'd kept me restless in my sleep for months now, was the same one who was going to keep me up the rest of the night.

Chapter Four

Resha

"I should've known," he said with a cockiness that made my body ripple in interest, in spite of the pain I was feeling.

Try as I might to have been Miss Independent at the hospital, the events of that night were starting to weigh heavily on me. My head was throbbing, and although I'd only been hit in the face, it felt as if the rest of my body had been attacked as well. Every step felt like a chore.

"Known what?" I questioned groggily as I stepped aside, allowing him to fully enter my condo. At this point, I was too far gone to even recognize the absurdity of letting him in my home in the first place.

"That your place would be decorated like this," he answered with arms wide.

"Like *this*?"

"All feminine. Pinks and greys, candles and plants."

"Don't come for my plants. They give this space life."

He chuckled. "Trust me, a stór, I'm not *coming* for your plants."

I silently watched as he removed the leather jacket he wore and causally hung it on the wooden coat rack I had next to my door.

"You're probably one of those women who likes people to remove their shoes whenever they enter their place, huh?"

"Shoes track in dirt and germs."

"Pssh," was all he commented before kicking off the sneakers he wore and placing them next to the coat rack.

"You got any ice?"

I blinked and watched as he began sauntering toward my kitchen in his socks and jeans.

"What?"

He tossed me a look over his shoulder. His eyes narrowed and he paused as if he was observing me. Before I could fully blink, he stood directly in front of me, staring down into my face, not in a sensual way but caring, as if he was inspecting every centimeter of my face, my reaction for what, I didn't know. But when his hand came up to cup my cheek, I found myself nuzzling my face against it.

"Are you feeling dizzy?"

"Umhm."

"You are?"

I blinked, not realizing my eyes had actually closed. "What?"

His lips frowned. "Dizzy? Are you feeling dizzy or nauseous?"

I shook my head.

He nodded but his hands grasped my shoulders and led me to the grey sectional and helped me sit down. I let out a sigh because I couldn't remember the last time I'd been treated with such gentleness. Wait, I could remember.

It was the last time I'd been in this man's arms. Rough around the edges he might be, but Connor also had a softness about him that one wouldn't assume upon first seeing him.

"I'm going to get you an ice pack for that eye."

I leaned against the couch, pulling the plush, rose pink throw blanket I kept on the back of the couch, around my body to warm me up. The pounding in my head was beginning to increase and I felt my entire body growing heavier and heavier. Sleep was inevitable. Hopefully, by the time I woke up, the pain would be gone and I wouldn't be regretting my decision to toss out that prescription the doctor had given me.

Just when I thought exhaustion had won out, I felt a shadow move over me.

"You shouldn't be sleeping," Connor stated as he kneeled down to the floor in front of the couch. "Here, put this against your face." He didn't wait for me to move, instead taking my hand and placing the cool ice pack in my palm before pushing both to my face, covering my injured eye.

The ice pack was cold but not painfully so because he'd wrapped it in one of the dishtowels I kept in the drawer by the sink.

"Good thing I spotted the ice packs in the back of the freezer. I thought I was going to have to use that bag of frozen vegetables."

I gave him a small smile. "Better that than the steak."

"That would've been my next option."

Just as he finished that declaration the beeping sound of my microwave went off.

"Oh." He jumped up quicker than anyone would suspect a man of his size being capable of and padded his way into the kitchen.

I didn't bother asking him what he was preparing in there because the ice pack was feeling too good on my face. It was helping to alleviate much of the pain in my face and even my headache.

"You need to eat. Sit up."

To say I was surprised to see Connor standing over me with one of my silver serving plates complete with a bowl of homemade chicken and dumpling soup from my freezer would've been an understatement. There were two bowls, actually, and after taking the tray, Connor sat next to me, plucking one of the bowls and spoons and began eating. I followed suit once I placed the ice pack on the coffee table.

"This is good. Why the hell would you go out for dinner when you had this right in your freezer?"

I grinned, remembering that this whole encounter had started because, stupidly, I'd wanted to pick up something for dinner and decided to take a walk to the grocer a few blocks over to get there.

"I made this last week and stuck the leftovers in the freezer, and forgot they were there, honestly." Truthfully, I was on my way to the grocer mostly for ice cream but didn't want to tell him that I was planning on having ice cream for dinner.

"Made this yourself? No shit." He sounded impressed.

"You like it?"

"Yeah."

My insides warmed. I loved when people enjoyed my food. Maybe that was why I hadn't wanted to eat the leftovers. I got joy out of cooking for other people instead of just myself.

I took a spoonful of the soup and let it warm me from the inside out, which Connor had already started the process on. Somehow I found myself leaning closer and closer to him. His body warmth was magnetic.

"I can't believe you were out in just a T-shirt and jacket. It's close to forty degrees out tonight," I commented, noting the dark cotton V-neck he had on under his leather jacket.

He grinned down at me and I noticed, not for the first time, the perfectly straight, pearly white teeth of his. I loved a man with great teeth.

"Irish blood, sweetheart. We're used to shitty weather."

"Are you from Ireland?"

"Parents are. Second generation Irish here. Born and raised in the good ol' US of A."

I took another spoonful of soup and then another, realizing how hungry I actually was.

"Oh no you don't," he warned at the same time I yawned.

"What?"

"Falling asleep. You need to keep those eyes open for at least another few hours."

I gave him a deadpan expression. "In case you haven't noticed, only *one* of my eyes is actually open." And just in case he didn't get my drift, I pointed to my swollen eye.

He visibly flinched and his lips pinched as he scowled while looking at my swollen eye. However, in a flash the expression was gone and he steeled his face. "I noticed." His voice sounded heavier, angrier.

"You got a deck of cards?" he asked. "And put that ice pack back on."

Again he didn't wait for me to respond to his order, instead stuffing the cool pack back in my hand and pressing it to my face. The movement was quick but it was gentle.

"How am I supposed to get you the deck of cards with this on my face?"

"Easy. Tell me where they are and *I'll* get them."

I rolled my good eye because that solution was all too easy. "Whatever. In the hallway closet, second shelf, next to the rest of the games."

Connor followed the direction I just gave him, and I was surprised at how lithe and limber he truly was. It wasn't the first I've noticed it, obviously, but he truly was light on his feet for such a big man. He hardly made a sound as he strode down the hallway.

"Of course." He rounded the corner sounding disgusted.

"What?"

"Pink playing cards? Who the hell has hot pink playing cards?"

"They were for breast cancer awareness month," I retorted, snatching the cards from his large hands. "And they're cute."

"If you say so." He chuckled, again taking the cards from me and removing them from their box to shuffle them on the table. I watched the muscles in his arms bunch and bulge as he shuffled the cards like a professional. There was something about the way he handled everything he did as if it was no big deal; required only minimal effort on his part to do a task perfectly. And I did mean *everything.* Starting with the way he'd easily handled my body the first night we met, to taking care of my attacker with such confidence, to the hospital staff.

"How long were you a professional boxer?" I questioned, desiring to know more about this man who was taking up so much space in my home, and my thoughts as of late.

He inched back from the coffee table and placed his elbow on the couch, turning to face me.

"Not a boxer, a fighter. And little over ten years."

"Why'd you retire?"

He peered over the cards he ceremoniously dealt out. "I'd had enough. Take your cards." He jutted his head toward the small pile of seven cards he'd placed in front of me. "What made you go into fashion?"

"How'd you know I work in fashion?"

"I looked it up. Give me your kings."

He jumped from one topic to the next.

Blinking, I looked down at my cards and realized what we were playing. I began giggling. "I can't believe we're playing *Go Fish*."

He shrugged with a grin on his face. "There's only two of us, not enough for spades. I'd offer a round of strip poker, but you're not up for that this evening. This is what I pulled out of my ass to keep you awake and let me know if you're able to follow instructions. Now give me your kings."

I plucked the king of hearts that I had in my hand and handed it to him.

"No way," I charged when he made his first book, obviously having the three other kings in his hand. "How did you have three kings already out of a seven card hand?"

His broad shoulder rose and fell. "Lucky, I guess."

"Or, you cheated when you dealt out those cards."

"Not a day in my life, sweetheart." Those pearly whites were on full display and I noticed that at some point he'd removed the hair tie he'd been wearing. Now, his blond locks fell in waves around his shoulders and it took all my strength not to reach out and run my fingers through it.

"It was my mother," I finally blurted out a few minutes later.

He lifted a curious brow.

"She was the drug addict."

It took all of two full seconds for him to put two and two together, recalling his question at the hospital.

"I don't take drugs if I can help it."

"It was only some acetaminophen."

I shook my head. "Not if I can help it. The pain isn't unbearable."

His face turned somber as he peered down at his cards. "I get it. My ma' liked booze a little too much. She was a good ma when she wanted to be but she liked alcohol more."

"But you drink. Give me your nines."

"Go fish."

I plucked a card from the deck, happy that I'd pulled a nine of spades. One card closer to making another book.

"Not often. Guess it was just dumb luck running into you at the bar that night. I rarely go into bars."

I'd heard many lies in my life. A ton came from my mother when she would tell me that she was done with the drugs. Most of the others came from various men throughout my life. They'd lie about wanting to be in a relationship only to tell me it wasn't that deep, or lies about not sleeping with someone else when it was obvious they were cheating, the *I love you* lies, and on and on. I'd become adept at discerning lies. Or just not believing much of what came out of a man's mouth.

So when I stared into Connor's eyes, and instantly believed what he'd just told me, this was a new experience.

"You're not lying," I whispered.

"The hell do I have to lie about?"

I shrugged and peered down at the cards in my hand. "Most men lie in one way or another."

"Like the lie about you being celibate?" he scoffed.

I raised my sharp gaze, lowering my hands. "I *am* celibate ... or was."

"Hate to break it you, sweetie, but what we did in New York sure as shit doesn't qualify as celibacy by *anybody's* definition of the word."

And if I had been a few shades lighter, I'm certain my cheeks would be noticeably burning red.

"I was celibate for two years and a few months before our ... encounter."

He grunted but kept his eyes on his cards. *"Encounter,"* he mocked.

"I'm serious. I—" I went to say that I hadn't been with anyone since him either but why the hell did he need to know that? I clamped my mouth shut.

"You haven't been with anyone since, either."

It wasn't a question. A statement of fact. He knew, but again, I couldn't just let him get away with that without any pushback.

"That's none of your business."

He inched closer, his lips hovering just above mine. "You sure it ain't my business?"

My lips parted to respond but nothing came out.

"Thought so."

And when I thought he was about to seal his declaration with a kiss, he pulled back. "This ice pack's done for the night. I'm going to grab the bag of vegetables for that eye of yours. Another twenty minutes with it on and then you can get some shut eye for a little while."

We played Go Fish for another twenty minutes as he said and then I laid down on the couch, covered myself with the throw, placed one of my pillows under my head, and fell fast asleep. Unfortunately, my rest didn't last too long because some thirty minutes later, Connor was shaking me awake.

"Wh-What's happening?"

"Just checking. What's today's date?"

"I don't know," I grumbled, swatting his big hand away.

Connor remained unperturbed. "What year are we in?"

"2019."

"What's my name?"

"Connor."

He smirked. "Of course, even with a concussion you still can't forget my name."

"I don't have a concussion," I challenged.

He chuckled. "That has yet to be determined, but you look like you're in the all clear. Go back to sleep." He pulled the throw up to my shoulders, and I took comfort in his warmth next to me as he sat at the edge of the sectional, down by my feet.

"You can turn on the TV if you want," I mumbled. "I can sleep with it on."

He shook his head. "Nothing good on at this time of night. Go to sleep."

I wondered if he'd gotten any sleep that night, thinking it must be something like two o'clock in the morning. But I didn't express that as I fell back to sleep. And on the rest of the night went in the same manner.

****

Connor

"You need to call someone."

Resha frowned as she stood up from the kitchen table, after eating the ramen soup I'd ordered for the both of us. I let her sleep in late since I'd had to keep waking her up throughout the night to check to make sure she wasn't experiencing symptoms of a concussion. She woke around eleven, and while she showered and changed clothes, I ordered from a restaurant that wasn't too far from here.

"Call who?"

I shrugged with my forearms on the white, circular dining table. "Someone who'll sit with and observe you over the next twenty-four hours just to make sure you don't have a concussion. Sometimes symptoms are delayed."

She pushed out a gush of air, and I carefully watched as the oversized T-shirt she wore clung to the shape of her body just enough to silhouette her hourglass figure. All of her clothes seemed to do that by design. As if they'd been created with her specific body in mind. The black leggings she wore aided in giving the perfect outline of her legs and hips.

"Last night wasn't enough?"

Hell no, my mind instantly responded. When I rose my gaze to meet hers as she placed both of our bowls in the sink, I realized she was talking about something else entirely.

Pushing away from the table and out of the comfortable upholstered chair, that was, of course, a pink color, I moved behind her at the sink.

Surprised, she turned to face me, but didn't try to move away from me or push me away. I knew she wouldn't.

"You should be watched for at least twenty-four hours to make sure you're in the clear. I'd do it but I have to leave on a business trip in a few hours."

"That won't be necessary, you've done more than enough. I can't thank—" She was about to thank me and I didn't want to hear it.

So, to silence her I bent low and placed a kiss to her lips. I had every intention on making it short and sweet.

I got the sweet part right, just not the short part. The same feeling I'd had in New York when we shared our first kiss overcame me standing there in her kitchen. She felt it, too. The moan she let out, followed by a sigh told me as much. I let my tongue caress her lips and make its acquaintance with her mouth.

Before I could get too involved and start thinking with my cock instead of my head, I took a step back.

"Where's your phone?" I questioned against her lips.

"Living room."

I pulled back, hating that I had to do so, and headed in the direction of the living room, spotting her cell phone resting on the coffee table. Grabbing it, I took it to her.

"Call someone. Destiny, your aunt, someone."

She frowned and I stood there, arms folded, daring her not to follow my direction.

"Don't think I won't cancel my business trip."

Her eyes narrowed.

"Fine," she huffed.

I watched as she pressed the buttons on her phone and made the call.

"Hey, D, it's me. … Yeah. Anyway, I got into a little, uh, scuffle last night. Nothing major, but um, I need to be observed just to make sure I don't have a concussion. Could you spare some time to come over?" She paused and I narrowed my eyes, angling my head to the side. "Great! See ya in a few." She pulled the phone from her ear, ending the call. "She'll be here in about thirty minutes. Tyler's home and is going to watch the kids so she doesn't have to bring them."

I nodded and glanced at the watch on my wrist. "My flight leaves in three hours. Otherwise I'd wait with you—"

"Oh, that won't be necessary." She waved her hand. "I'll be fine. You've really done enough. Honestly. I don't know what I would've done if you hadn't shown up last night."

Moving in, I took her chin in my hand. I brushed my free hand over the left side of her forehead and down to her cheek, still hating to see how swollen her eye was. The ice packs had helped but time was the true healer of all things, including black eyes.

I pressed a kiss to her forehead, nose, and finally her lips. Resha didn't protest, and I stepped back wondering what the hell had gotten into me. Without another word, I turned on my heels and headed to where my sneakers rested by the door. Stepping into them, I then lifted my jacket from the coat rack, pulling it on, wondering how the hell I was going to get my bike from the hospital, make it home to shower, grab my suitcase, and make my flight on time.

"Thanks again."

I nodded and gave Resha one final look before opening the door. I didn't bother making any promises to see her again or to even follow up with her. Typically, I was a man of very few words. Actions spoke louder than words. So when the door shut behind me and I heard the lock sound on the other side, I pulled out my cell phone and called Joshua.

"What's up, Connor?"

"I need your brother's phone number."

"Which one?"

"The youngest, Tyler."

"For what?"

"I need to speak to his wife because I'm sure her cousin just tried to bullshit me."

Chapter Five

Resha

An hour after Connor left, I found myself sitting at my desk, staring at my computer. I was supposed to be writing. I'd had three blog posts I wanted to get through, and thank goodness I'd already taken the pictures for them the previous week. But all I could think about was the night before.

I hadn't been as scared as I was the previous night in a long time. Years. And I kept mentally kicking myself for walking down a dark alley alone, even though I'd taken that same route many times before. I'd lived in my condo for the past three years and never felt unsafe in my neighborhood. But that goes to show, crime can happen anywhere. The police had told me that the guy was likely some junkie who saw an easy target. I shuddered at that word. It brought back many memories I would rather keep at bay.

Just when I placed my fingers over the keyboard to begin typing, a loud pounding at my front door had me jumping out of my desk chair.

"The hell?"

"Resha, open this door before I have to use my damn key!" Destiny shouted through the door, still pounding.

I rushed from my seat at my desk, out of my office, and down the hardwood floors of my hallway and living room to yank open my door.

"What's going on?"

"Oh my God!" Destiny recoiled in response.

I flinched, almost forgetting the sight that was my face. Yeah, the swelling was still very apparent even though some of the pain had subsided.

"Who did this to you?" Destiny demanded as she pushed her way through the door. It was only then that I noticed an angry looking Tyler standing behind her. He shut the door after they entered.

"What are you doing here?" I questioned, feeling exposed and confused at the same damn time. Two emotions I hated.

"What am I doing here? The only one asking questions should be *me*. Like, for example, why the hell didn't you call me as soon as this happened?"

"Ah hell," I grumbled as Destiny planted her hands on her hips, looking pissed off. And even though my cousin was only about five-foot-three and petite she was a damn powerhouse. I'd seen her cut down more than one grown man verbally and physically.

"Ah hell is right. Why the hell did I have to find out that my cousin was *attacked* last night and needs to be under observation for a possible concussion from Connor O'Brien?"

I closed my one good eye, spinning around and moving to my couch to sit down. "I'm going to murder that man." Somehow he must've figured out that I'd made a bogus call to Destiny while he was here and managed to reach out to her on his own.

"Oh, you don't have to worry about him, because you still have to deal with *me*. Wait 'til I tell Mama about this."

I sighed. "Tyler, can you control your wife, please?"

Tyler responded by shaking his head, still looking pissed off. "Normally I would, but Destiny's right, Resha. What the hell? You were out at night alone and didn't think to call your family while you were at the hospital?"

Did I say my headache had gone away? Because it was starting to come back with each word they spoke.

"I'm fine."

"You're not fine. Thank God Connor was there and was willing to stay with you throughout the night for observation. But according to him, keeping an eye on a possible concussion for *at least* twenty-four to forty-eight hours is best."

"It is. You don't make it to the NFL without seeing a concussion or two. Which doctor did you see at the hospital? Did they do X-rays and a CT scan or MRI? And who is this fucker that attacked you?" Tyler growled, rattling off questions with the same intensity and hostility that my cousin spoke.

"Ty, babe, can you grab an ice pack out of the freezer?" Destiny asked.

"Yeah."

I watched Tyler enter the kitchen before turning back to Destiny who was sitting next to me on the couch, grilling me.

"Where're the babies?"

"Don't you dare play that with me. Why the hell didn't you call me, Resh?"

I flinched at the hurt and anger I heard in her voice. "D, I didn't want to disturb you. It was my own dumbass fault for walking through a dark alley at night because I had a hankering for some chocolate chip cookie dough ice cream."

"Resha, don't give me that. And I know damn well you're not sitting up here blaming yourself for what happened."

"I'm just saying it could've been avoided. Don't get all up in arms and on your feminist rant about how women should be able to go anywhere at anytime without thought or concern for our safety."

"We should, and last I checked, I'm not the only one prone to that same feminist rant."

I giggled and sat back against my couch, realizing that the throw was hanging next to my head. Unconsciously, I turned my face into the throw and inhaled, smelling Connor. My entire body electrified at the smell as I remembered placing the throw over his body a few hours earlier as I'd gone into the bathroom to take a shower. It was a smell that one could never forget. Manly, strong, and unyielding, like him.

"Put this on," Destiny insisted as she took the ice pack from Tyler.

"I used these last night," I grumbled while still putting the ice pack over my eye.

"Good, and you're using them again today. Now, who was this fucker that attacked you?" Tyler insisted.

I pushed out a breath because these two were almost as bad as Connor.

"I don't know. Police think he was an addict out looking to rob someone for their money to get more drugs."

"Yeah, well, he's gonna get more than he bargained for," Tyler growled. "I've already spoken with the captain of the station he was taken to."

"Tyler, that wasn't necessary. Besides, he already got more than he bargained for when Connor knocked him out cold. I'm pretty sure he's hurting much more than I am today."

"Serves his ass right. You're coming home with us."

"What?" I shrieked, looking at my cousin as if she'd lost her mind.

"You heard me. You need to be observed for a few more hours, including overnight, so it's best you come back with us."

I shook my head adamantly. "That is not needed. Do not overreact to this, D. I'm fine. Yeah, my eye has seen better days, but in a day or so the swelling will have gone down and I'll be back to my normal self."

"Yeah, in a day or so. And at that time, you can come back to your home. But for now, you need to be around family. We need to be close by to make sure you're all right."

"D, I'm fine," I reiterated again, tossing myself against the sofa and pouting. I truly didn't have the energy to go up against Destiny and Tyler but I really didn't want to leave my home. "How about this," I proposed. "I'll call you every hour on the hour so you know I'm fine? That way I can stay here and get some work done, and you two can go and tend to your day as you had planned."

I looked up at both Tyler and Destiny, hopeful.

Destiny's frown and Tyler's look of displeasure spoke before their mouths moved.

"Or, you could just stop being so damned stubborn and bring your ass over to our house like I just said."

My head fell to the back of the couch. "D, look, I'm fine. See?" I held my arms out wide and then touched the tip of my nose with each pointer finger one at a time, similar to that roadside test police use for suspected drunk drivers.

"My full name is Resha Pilar McDonald. I live at 3340 Palmetto Drive, on the tenth floor, apartment letter C. My phone number is 512–"

"Fine, and what's the name of your favorite tailor?"

"Mr. Kim, works right on the corner a few buildings down."

"And how long have you been going to him?"

"For almost ten years. He's how I found this great building before the condos were even on the market." I smirked at my cousin cockily.

"And when's the last time you been to the gym?"

"Ha! Trick question. I don't go to the damn gym. Last time I went was in support of you a few months after you had the triplets. Damn near died in that damn Zumba class," I scoffed, shaking my head.

"Yeah, she's her normal self, I suppose."

"Like I told you."

"Fine, we'll just hire a nurse to come watch over you for the next twenty-four hours," Tyler decided to add.

"A nurse?" I shrieked, sitting up way too fast. Grimacing, I placed my hand to my head.

"See," Destiny yelped, moving to sit next to me, pressing her hand to mine. "You're obviously feeling uncomfortable."

"It couldn't possibly have anything to do with you two bullies standing over me, pressuring me to do as you say."

Destiny frowned. "We're your family. And you're coming home with us."

I sighed. "I know, D. I just don't need the extra bruhaha made over nothing. I wanna forget last night ever happened." A twitch in my chest told me I was lying because as soon as the words were free from my mouth an image of Connor staring back at me with his arms folded over his massive chest came to mind.

No, I didn't want to forget everything about the night before.

The attack? Sure.

Connor's overbearing presence in my home and the way he cared for me from the moment he spotted me in that alley until he left my place a few hours earlier? Not so much.

"Besides," I continued, pushing thoughts of six-foot-six, blond, second generation Irishmen out of my mind, "you all have three kids. No offense, because I love my niece and nephews, but your house isn't exactly, uh, quiet and conducive to someone potentially recovering from a brain injury."

Destiny turned to Tyler, and they exchanged a glance between them, as if considering my point of view.

Tyler was the first to speak. "You're right. The triplets are anything but quiet. So, then it's settled …"

I sighed, but my relief was too soon.

"I'll call the private nursing company my family uses. They'll send someone over within the hour and we'll sit with you until she arrives."

Destiny nodded, agreeing as if I didn't need a say in who was to be coming and going in my own home.

And like I said, I was starting to feel too tired to actually argue with either one of them. If allowing a nurse to come in and sit with me over the next twenty-four hours was what would get them off my back so be it.

I kept quiet while Tyler and Destiny made the arrangements with whatever company they used for house calls. I was too busy plotting on exactly how I was going to get Connor back for going behind my back and ratting me out to my cousin.

****

Connor

Maybe I should've stayed with Resha. To make sure she was okay. I'd been having that same persistent thought all night and well into the next morning, as I prepared for a very important business meeting.

Even after I'd called Tyler again and gotten reassurances from him that he and his wife had checked on her with their own eyes and that she was doing fine. He'd explained that

Resha had refused to come home with them, so they'd opted to hire a private nurse to watch over her for the next day or so, in her home, just to double check that she was doing fine.

Those assurances didn't stop the persistent thought that it should've been me staying with her. A nurse was fine, sure, but I'd had experience with *actually* having a concussion. And Resha being as stubborn as she is, was less than likely to immediately speak up if she was feeling off or out of sorts. I reminded Tyler of that, and again, he'd assured me that Destiny knew her cousin well and would be keeping a diligent eye over her.

"You ready for this?" Wilt, my attorney, questioned as I stepped off the elevator and into the hotel lobby.

"I'm here, aren't I?"

He chuckled and shook his head, used to my attitude at these sorts of things. I hated business meetings, even lucrative ones. Hell, they all were lucrative, lest I wouldn't be showing up to them, but I hated the hobnobbing that went along with it all.

"You are definitely here. In your standard leather, jeans, and T-shirt."

"They can have me in my leather or not at all."

We passed through the glass doors of the hotel to be met by the chauffeur of our car.

"Mr. O'Brien," he greeted, holding the door open. He was the same driver we had the night before from the airport, which was how he immediately recognized me.

"Thanks," I grunted as he shut the door.

"Did you have any last minute questions you wanted to go over before we step into this meeting?" Wilt inquired. It was something he always did when we were on our way to a business meeting.

"You read the contract, right?"

He nodded. "Read it over again last night in my room."

"And?"

"I hold firm that it's a solid contract. A few kinks to iron out, which I wrote out last night. But signing with Jersey's will place TKO protein and supplements in thousands of stores across the country, ensuring exponential market growth."

"In other words, sign the damn contract."

Wilt chuckled. "Once all the details are taken care of. I would if I was you."

"And because you get ten percent for brokering the deal."

He adjusted his suit jacket. "Small price to pay."

I didn't say anything because he was right. Wilt's been my attorney since my early days as a fighter. Buddy had introduced me to him. They knew each other from their neighborhood coming up. Wilt was scrappy, like Buddy, but he wasn't a fighter. Not in the ring, anyway. He was a damn pit bull of an attorney, however. After I retired from fighting, I kept him on my team for the various other businesses I had, and he's long since proven his worth.

Ten percent of this current deal would easily garner him a seven figure payout, but that still paled in comparison to what my company would earn in potential profits.

"Then let's see what they have to say," I finally responded.

We arrived to the headquarters of one of the nation's largest retailers and were escorted up to the third floor by one of the men Wilt and I had been corresponding with over the past few months. Without even thinking about it, while on the elevator, I pulled out my phone to see if I had any missed calls.

Nothing.

Not from Joshua or Tyler. Not that I expected either one of them to keep me informed if something did go wrong with Resha.

And that was when I also remembered that I hadn't given her my number to call me if she needed. Not that I'd thought she use it but I mentally kicked myself for not at least getting her number. I was going to have to bite the bullet and either get it from Destiny or wait until I got back to Williamsport to get it my damn self.

"Are you paying attention?" Wilt questioned, interrupting my thoughts.

I peered down at him, pissed off because no I hadn't been paying attention and he had the goddamn audacity to impede on my thoughts about a woman who was increasingly taking up more and more of my headspace.

"What?"

"Martin Chapman, the head of new operations for the retailer, will be joining this meeting. I've been trying to get him to make it in to meet us for weeks."

"Get off his cock, Wilt. He's just another man," I gritted through my teeth as we entered a huge conference room on the fifteenth floor of the building. There were at least five other men there, all in dark business suits with professional smiles on their faces as we entered. Like I said, I couldn't stand these types of meetings. I much preferred having these things over conference calls, or hell, even via email. That way I could be at home or in my office, lounging in sweatpants while talking shop with these types, instead of in a stuffy ass office.

"Just let me do most of the talking," was the final thing Wilt whispered under his breath to me as we were greeted by the first of the group.

I shrugged and gave no response because that was my typical response whenever Wilt made that comment, which was often.

"Mr. O'Brien, what a pleasure it is to meet you in person," a grinning jackal with over gelled dark hair greeted. "I'm Connor

Walsh. We have the same first name. Irish blood." He chuckled as if he expected me to join in on the not-so-funny joke.

I gave him a deadpan expression and he quickly sobered up. "Call me Connor," I stated. I really hated formalities.

Wilt and I were introduced to the rest of the team and shown our seats round the conference table.

"I'll sit here," I said after being shown to the seats where my back would be facing the door.

"Mr. O'Brien doesn't like having his back to the door. Once a fighter always a fighter," Wilt explained, causing the men to chuckle and give me knowing nods.

I gave them a cool look because I wasn't about to explain myself to anyone. But Wilt and I had been working together for so long, he knew my style well enough that he could smooth out any feathers I happened to ruffle.

"And here comes Martin," the man we'd met in the lobby announced, peering back into the room. The rest of the men in the room immediately tensed up and straightened their suit jackets, putting on their business expressions.

"Mr. Chapman," the man greeted.

In walked a tall, lanky figure, about the same age as Wilt. He had an air of superiority but I didn't find it off-putting as I did with most others. Unlike the underlings in the room, this guy looked me straight in the eye.

"Gentlemen, sorry I'm late. An early morning meeting ran behind. Let's not take up anymore time, shall we? You must be Connor O'Brien," he stated, extending his hand for me to shake.

"I must be." I shook his hand and then turned to Wilt. "This is my lawyer, Wilt Mendoza," I introduced.

"The name is certainly familiar. Nice to finally meet in person as opposed to the many emails we've exchanged."

"Pleasure." Wilt nodded while shaking his hand.

"Okay, let's jump right into it. Mr. O'Brien, our store, Jersey's, has extended the offer of exclusively offering your product on our shelves. As you know this is an extremely lucrative deal for any small business owner such as yourself."

"I'm well aware, but there are some questions we need to clear up before moving forward." I tilted my head toward Wilt, signaling that it was his turn to bring up our concerns with the contract.

Wilt adeptly went over the problems with the contract, the parts where we thought Jersey's would be getting too high of a percentage of the profits, issues with the chain of command, and whatnot. Once all those areas had been adequately addressed, I gave Wilt a look informing him that I was okay to sign. His eyes narrowed in the way they do when he's silently telling me that he agreed with my decision.

"There's just one thing we need to discuss, Mr. O'Brien." That statement was made by a guy who sat directly across the table from me. He'd been mainly silent up until this point.

"And you are?" I questioned, lifting an eyebrow.

His eyes seemed to widen at my tone. "Larry … Larry Bivens from the marketing department."

I stared at him, waiting for him to continue.

"Well, the deal looks great, and certainly, Jersey Retailers believes in your product, lest this offer wouldn't be on the table. The only problem is your marketing."

"My what?"

"M-More specifically your social media marketing presence, or rather, lack thereof."

"Lack? I've got all the requisite social media pages." My voice had deepened with annoyance. I was ready to get the hell out of this meeting. Most of the hard negotiating was over and now this douche was holding me up over some goddamn social media issues.

"Yes, you do, Mr. O'Brien. That's how we initially came across your products. But to say there are some areas in which your social media presence could be, uh, heightened, would be an understatement."

First Mark now this guy who's name I'd forgotten as soon as he spoke it. I turned Wilt and grunted.

"Trust me, Mr. Bivens, I've been talking to Connor about increasing his social media marketing and influence. I think he understands the importance of improving his marketing and advertising on his pages."

I turned back to the guy. "You have anything in mind?"

"Yes, our team came up with a few ideas on how to grow your online presence and still keep in line with your company's mission. If we could—"

"Great, email it to me," I insisted, rising from my seat. I was done. We'd been in this meeting that was only supposed to be thirty to forty-five minutes or so, for over two hours. "I'll read it over and get back to you. Anything else?" I questioned, looking around the table.

Chapman, of course, was the first to speak up. "I think that's all, Mr. O'Brien. We thank you for taking the time to come all the way out to the East Coast from Williamsport and we hope this is the beginning of a very long and advantageous union."

"That went very well," Wilt said, sounding proud of himself as we pulled off in the same chauffeured vehicle that'd dropped us off. We weren't done for the day by any means, needing to make some appearances later on at some promotional events at the local sports arena.

I grunted in response to Wilt's comment. "Hey, Wilt?" I spoke while scrolling through my phone, seeing I had a few text messages and emails to respond to.

"Yeah?"

"Don't ever fucking talk about me like I'm not in the room again." I rolled my eyes away from my phone screen and up to Wilt so he could see the look in my eyes.

He nodded contritely. "Sorry, Connor. You know I get excited and ahead of myself from time to time."

"I do. Don't let it happen again." My gaze moved back to my phone.

There was nothing left to be said. Wilt was a hell of a lawyer and someone I respected but he knew better than to try that condescending shit with me. I may've been on the verge of a lucrative deal, spearheaded in part by Wilt's above-average negotiating skills, but I'd burn everything to the ground if he or anyone else thought they could talk over or condescend to me.

Chapter Six

Resha

"Coming!" I yelled at the chiming computer as if it could hear me or acknowledge me in some way. I made it to my desk chair in a huff, slamming my body down against the seat and pressing the button to answer Shauna's call.

"Hey!" I blurted into the pop-up video screen of my smiling virtual assistant.

"Hey, you out of breath?"

I rolled my eyes. "Yeah, was in the living room. Got a late start to the morning and damn near forgot our call."

"No worries if you need to reschedule and take more time off."

I swallowed the sip of my vanilla bean latte that I'd just taken, shaking my head as I placed my mug on the marble coaster I kept desk to my desktop.

"No, please. After four days off with nothing to do, that is the last thing I need." I'd ended up taking a few extra days off after the attack last weekend. The nurse Tyler and Destiny hired ended up staying with me for a full forty-eight hours at their insistence. She'd noted that my blood pressure was a little high, and after noticing just how much swelling my face had done, she recommended taking time off. The tiredness and grogginess I continued to feel forced me to concede and do as she suggested.

Thankfully, however, I was feeling better, the swelling had greatly improved and was barely noticeable, and the nurse was gone. I only needed to apply a somewhat thin layer of concealer to hide the bruising that was still evident on my face. I'd posted a picture on social media just that morning of my outfit of the day, and out of the hundreds of comments that post had gotten so far, not one person noticed anything abnormal about my face.

"Let's go over what's in store for us this week."

"Glad you're feeling better."

I smiled at the screen, feeling guilty for telling Shauna that I'd needed time off because I'd come down with the stomach flu.

"Thanks." I took another sip of my latte just to avoid her sympathetic look. "So, you were able to reschedule with that sustainable clothing brand for the photoshoot, right?"

"Yup, they were actually relieved because as it turned out, all of their merchandise hadn't arrived."

"And that's rescheduled for next Tuesday?"

"Ten a.m."

"Perfect. Oh, one sec, Shauna," I blurted, surprised by the knock I heard at my front door.

Moving from my office down the hall to the door, I yelled, "Who is it?"

"FedEx! Delivery for Resha McDonald."

I peered through the peephole and was satisfied when I saw the usual delivery guy at my door.

"Oh wow," I exclaimed as I pulled open the door and saw a beautiful bouquet of pink and white lilies in a glass vase.

"Just need you to sign here."

Grinning, I took the pen from John, my delivery guy, as my heart rate quickened. "I wonder who these are from," I questioned out loud, picturing a certain six-foot-six, blond-haired, second generation Irishman, in spite of myself.

"Thanks, John," I stated after giving him a tip.

He nodded his head and tossed me a friendly smile before heading in the direction of the elevator.

I closed my door with my foot and held the vase in one arm as I locked the door. Holding the vase out in front of me so I could admire the beautiful petals of the flowers, I headed back down the hall to my office.

"Look at those. And lilies are your favorite," Shauna gushed.

"I know."

"Who're they from?"

"I dunno, let me check." I sat the vase down, turning it a little to find the card. Spotting it, I plucked it from the middle of the bouquet and opened the cream-colored envelope.

I'm sorry about that awful encounter you had last week. I hope these lilies bring you some comfort.

-S

A cold chill ran down my spine, extending out to all four of my limbs.

"Shit!" I yelped when the feeling in my arms caused them to give out, nearly dropping the vase to the ground. Luckily, I stood close enough to the desk that the vase fell on it instead of the floor where it surely would've broken.

"Well, who's it from?" Shauna questioned happily.

"What? Um, oh, uh, from that makeup brand I did a campaign with last month."

"That was so sweet of them. For a second, I thought you had a secret admirer," Shauna giggled.

"No, not that," I mumbled, moving the vase as far away from me as possible. I'd throw them out as soon as I was off the call with Shauna.

"What else is on our agenda?" I questioned to speed this call along so I could be rid of the bouquet I'd thought was so beautiful just a few moments earlier.

"Let's see, payment from that shoe brand you worked with months ago finally came in."

I nodded, only half paying attention to Shauna. While I was able to maintain my end of the conversation, my mind still wondered who the hell was behind sending me those damn flowers.

"That's it for the week. Talk next Monday?" Shauna finally said about thirty minutes later.

Nodding, I told Shauna good-bye before disconnecting the call. The next thing I knew, I was in the kitchen, tossing out the bouquet, but that didn't feel complete enough. I didn't want these flowers in my home, at all. So, I tied up the garbage bag I'd discarded the flowers and vase in, slipped my feet into my slippers, and headed out my front door, and down the hall to the trash shoot. Opening the door, I tossed the garbage bag down the shoot and heard it make a plopping sound as it landed in the huge trash holder at the bottom.

"Resha."

I groaned inwardly as I spun around to see Jarvis, my neighbor, grinning in my direction. He looked as if he'd made a special diversion from unlocking his front door to move in my direction as soon as he saw me.

"Hey, Jarvis. How's it going?" I mumbled, not wanting to come across rude.

"Better now that I've seen your beautiful face."

My eyes widened in horror at his obvious yet oblivious attempt at flirtation. "Uh, okay. Well, hope you have a great day." I tried to scurry past Jarvis but apparently that was a no-go because he stepped directly in front of me, blocking my pathway.

"Resha, I was wondering if you would like to go out to dinner sometime? Nothing too fancy, heck, maybe even at my place?" His dark brown eyes narrowed and he seemed to leer at me, awaiting my answer.

I began shaking my head almost instantly. "I'm sorry, Jarvis, but that wouldn't be possible."

"Why not?" He frowned.

Why the hell can't he just take no for an answer? I glanced back over my shoulder, looking at the closed door of the trash room, and remembered the flowers.

"Jarvis, do you, uh, do you know what my favorite flowers are?"

He seemed stunned by my question. "Flowers, uh, roses, right? Every woman likes roses."

I shook my head, almost feeling relieved. "Yeah, sure. Look, Jarvis, I've gotta go. Thanks for the invite but I won't be taking you up on it." *Ever.* "Enjoy your day."

Stepping around Jarvis, I made a beeline for my door, thankful that I'd left it unlocked to easily move inside without having to insert my key. Relief flooded me once I was back inside of my own home, but not for long. Being around Jarvis always seemed to creep me out, but add to that whomever had been sending me strange emails and DMs now sent me something directly to my front door. They knew where I lived. And how did he know about the attack the previous week?

I hadn't told anyone except for Destiny ... hell, I hadn't even told her. Connor had. My Aunt Donna wasn't even aware, since I'd begged Destiny not to tell her.

I paced my living room floor, feeling super uneasy in my own home. The worst feeling one could imagine. I'd lived uneasy in the place I called home as a young child and it was something I never wanted to go back to.

Making a decision, I called down to the front desk of my building.

"Yes, Ms. McDonald," the receptionist answered. Every resident had their name and number programmed to come up when we called downstairs.

"Yes, could you please have all deliverymen removed from my 'allow' list. I'd like a call from the front desk to come down if I have anymore deliveries."

"Sure thing. Anything else I can do for you today?"

"No, that's it. Thank you."

Hanging up the phone, I felt a little easier. My building was secure and had cameras just about everywhere, except the garage, which was the building's worst kept secret. Management insisted they were working to fix that problem as soon as possible.

I re-entered my office and sat down to do some work but what I ended up doing was picking up the phone and dialing Kayla's phone number. I knew she was working at the women's shelter that morning.

"Hey, Resha? Everything okay? How are you feeling?"

I pulled the phone from my ear, looking at it because of the concern I heard in Kayla's voice. "Feeling?"

"Yeah, we heard what happened the other night. I chose not to call because Destiny said you were taking some time off to rest and get better."

I gritted my teeth at my cousin, but to Kayla I said, "I'm feeling much better. Just a little bruising. Nothing to get worked up about. Listen, I wanted to ask you if you knew the address, for uh, Connor's company, TKO Supplements." I squeezed my eyes shut, proud of myself for getting the words out.

"Uh, yeah, I think I have it in my phone. Hang on a sec."

I paused and waited a few heartbeats.

"Here it is. You have a pen?"

"In my hand."

"The address is ..." she rattled off the address and phone number of the office where Connor ran his company out of.

I was surprised to be familiar with the street the building was on. It was only a few blocks over from my home.

"Thank you."

"Not a problem. Why didn't you ask Destiny? I'm sure she knew this information as well."

I stopped short, my mouth hanging open as I searched my brain for an explanation. "You know, I didn't even think to ask her. I know Connor and Joshua are such good friends so I figured you would know the information off-hand."

"You do?"

"Do what?"

"Know how close Joshua and Connor are?"

Again, I was caught off-guard by the question. "Uh, yeah, well, I mean, he was at your daughter's birthday party. So, I figured ... Destiny told me that Joshua doesn't particularly like having anyone he doesn't consider family over to his home. And aside from his brothers, parents, and your family, the only non-relatives there were Connor and his other friend, Damon, and his wife, Sandra, and their daughter, Monique. But um ... thanks for the info."

I clasped my hand over my mouth to keep me from talking so damn much. I was starting to sound guilty to my own ears. And I hadn't even done anything wrong. Sure, the truth was, I knew Destiny likely had the information for Connor that I sought out, especially since he'd obviously been in communication with her to tell her of my attack, but I just didn't want to ask her.

"You're welcome. Hey, we'll see you again soon down here at the shelter, right?"

"Yes, I think I'm scheduled to be there in another two weeks. I wish I could give more time, but—"

"No, please, don't apologize. We appreciate every minute of your time that you're able to give us. The ladies all agree on that."

"Thanks, Kayla. I'll see you soon. Bye."

I hung up the phone and moved to my bedroom to change into a pair of my favorite skinny jeans, my suede, cognac-colored thigh-high boots, and an off-the-shoulder black sweater. Thankfully, I'd already done my makeup earlier that morning to take a few headshots of myself. I quickly curled the weave I still wore, making a mental note of the next time I would need to go back to my beautician to get it redone, grabbed my bag, peacoat, and the paper I'd written the information Kayla had given me. I was out the door less than twenty minutes after getting off the phone with her.

I needed something to take my mind off of the events of that morning and heading over to see Connor seemed like the next logical move. Why? I had no idea but I wasn't going to question it.

****

Connor

"Mr. O'Brien, there's a Resha McDonald here to see you."

My head immediately perked up from my desk. "Thanks, Layla. I'll be right out." I disconnected the call and frowned, wondering what Resha was doing here at my office, and pissed off that she made her way to me, before I was able to make my way to see her. Ever since getting back in town, it'd been one thing after another. I was getting two and three calls a day from the people over at Jersey's to discuss operations for my products, dates when my supplements would be available, calls from their lawyers needing me to sign waivers, and all types of shit. That just for my TKO Products. It didn't include the business I still had to carry out for the gyms, laundromats, and gas stations I owned or partially owned around the city. All before taking care of the Underground fights in and outside of Williamsport.

I was busy, but I still kept myself informed on what was happening with Resha. I didn't even care that Joshua would call and give me shit whenever I spoke with Tyler to ask him what was happening with Resha. I'd all but insisted he make that nurse he hired stay for an additional twenty-four hours, offering to pay for it myself. He turned that offer down, obviously, but also made sure the nurse stayed until Resha was given the all clear.

I watched her coming down the hallway before she was able to see me. Her cinnamon skin glowed, in spite of the fact that the left side of her face was still swollen. Though, her makeup covered much of the remaining bruising without looking too caked on.

"You look better than the last time I saw ya," I grunted as I entered the lobby of my office. Leaning my elbow against Layla's front desk, I let my eyes travel over Resha's body as she rose from the chair. I especially appreciated the skintight jeans she wore along with the thigh-high boots she wore over them. Suddenly, I wanted to ask if she had more than one pair of these sort of boots but I'd have to save that question until we had some privacy.

"I'm going to take that as a compliment," she returned.

Dipping my head, I lifted my brows on a smirk. "Take it however you want. Layla, hold my calls." I jutted my head for Resha to follow me down the hall to my office, shutting the door behind us as she entered.

I watched her from behind as she glanced around at fighting plaques and pictures of me with Buddy and a number of other prominent people in the fighting world.

She stopped short at one of the pictures on my oakwood desk, raising it. "I know him," she remarked, facing me with a wrinkle in her brow.

Moving closer, I took the picture from her hand. I didn't miss the tingle that occurred in my hand when my fingers brushed over hers. And I know I saw Resha's breath hitch ever so slightly, informing me that she felt the same thing.

"Mark."

"He works for Aaron Townsend, right? I think I've seen him at the women's shelter a time or two."

I nodded. "He's my kid brother."

"No way." Taking the picture from my hand, she studied it for a moment. "I see he got all the looks in the family."

I chuckled and moved in closer behind her, trapping her body between mine and the desk. Turning, she lifted her face. That vein in her neck was already beating rapidly. I let my gaze linger there before brushing my fingers across the skin that covered the vein. A tiny gasp escaped her lips.

"Your words say one thing but your body says something entirely different, a stór."

"What does that mean?"

"What?"

"A stór."

I blinked, not even realizing I'd used the Irish term of endearment.

"You used it in New York, too."

I was sure I had. The word seemed to fall from my lips easily when speaking with her. Never had that happened before.

"It's an Irish term. What're you doing here?" Stepping back, I placed the picture frame in its original place on my desk.

"You need help."

My head popped up and my gaze moved to Resha. "Care to elaborate?"

Her lips spread into a knowing smile, and I swear to fucking God I had to fight my own mind to shake loose the image of sliding my cock in between those lips.

"Yes. You need help *bad*," she emphasized. "I was looking over your social media pages and it doesn't look good."

I groaned. "Not you too."

"Oh, so I'm not the first one who's mentioned how crappy your social media marketing is?"

"First one today. And no one has said *crappy*."

"But I'm guessing you've been told that your social media marketing could use some help, am I correct?"

I frowned.

"Thought so. Anyway, that's where I come in. I'm a social media pro. Literally."

"I've seen your blog."

A perfectly arched eyebrow raised and those coffee-colored eyes widened in interest. "Never would've mistaken you for having an interest in a plus size fashion blog."

"Haha," I intoned with a deadpan expression.

She giggled, which did some funny shit to the inside of my chest.

"Don't think I'll forget about you checking out my blog. Anyway … as I said, I was perusing through your posts and I see where you need some major improvement. And I'm willing to help you out. As a thank you."

I furrowed my brows. "Thank you?"

She nodded. "Yeah, for helping me out and all."

My scowl deepened. "I already told you, I don't need a thank you for that shit."

"Yeah, *you* don't need but what if I need it?"

Again, my expression was one of confusion.

She pushed out a heavy breath and bit her bottom lip, appearing as if she didn't want to reveal what she was about to say. "Look, I just don't like owing anyone anything. It's not how I like to live my life. And what you did for me the other week, though it may not have been a big deal to you, was a big deal to me. Even though you went behind my back and ratted me out to my cousin." She pointed a finger at my chest, trying to seem angry.

"And I'd do it again, too."

She rolled those big eyes of hers, and I happened to remember a very similar expression on her face as she rode my cock in New York.

"I'm sure you would. Anyway, it would mean a lot to me if you'd let me help you out."

"You don't owe me shit." I moved in even closer, leaving hardly enough room between our bodies for air to pass through. "But maybe there is something you can do for me," I growled by her ear, not knowing where my comment had even come from.

A small moan pushed past her lips. My hands dropped to her waist and my fingers crawled underneath the sweater she wore, feeling the soft flesh of her belly. Lowering my head, I nuzzled the space between her neck and shoulder.

"I-I'm celibate."

I let out a laugh against her skin. "A stór, you haven't been celibate since the moment you took all nine and a half inches of my cock in New York," I growled in her ear.

The goosebumps that rose along her skin were a direct response to my words and my hands still prodding her abdomen.

Her resistance was apparent so I made a decision.

"Fine. I'll take you up on your offer." I pushed back to stare down at her but kept my hands locked around her waist.

"You will?"

Nodding, I responded, "You seem to know more about this social media shit than I do. My brother and this new company I'm working with have been up my ass about paying more attention to my analytics and whatnot. You think you could help me with that?"

"Of course. I already came up with some ideas on where to start on my way over here. I was also thinking …" By the way she trailed off, I already knew I wasn't going to like the next words that came out of her mouth. "We'll need to do a photoshoot."

That didn't seem too bad. Maybe I'd begun overreacting.

But that was when she dropped the rest of her thoughts.

"With you … preferably shirtless."

"No." I shook my head adamantly. "Hell no."

Her shoulders slumped as she sighed. "I knew you were going to react this way."

"Then why did you even bother to bring it up?"

"Because it's what's best for your products and it won't be as bad as you're thinking."

"How the hell do you know what I'm thinking?"

"Because of your reaction. Look, it'll just be a few lights, some cameras, a little studio set up, your products offered. Probably wouldn't take more than half a day."

"But I'd be shirtless, correct? And greased up in baby oil and shit, right?"

"Nobody uses baby oil anymore. Not with coconut oil and shea butter around," she mumbled.

"Resha," I growled.

Giggling, she held out her arms. "Okay, okay. Look, TKO is your product?"

"Yes, but *I'm* not the product."

"You are, though. Listen, in today's day and age consumers want to feel as if they know their product and who makes them. They don't want impersonal advertisements and social media posts. *You* are your product. Why did you start TKO Supplements?"

I folded my arms across my chest and cracked my neck, angling my head from side to side. I could already feel my argument waning just by staring at those large, dark brown eyes of hers.

"I wanted a product that wasn't full of chemicals and bullshit."

"Well, we'll have to find a better way to explain that in your captions but keep going."

Grinning, I shook my head. "What else do you want to know?"

"What made you turn to creating your own products and supplements? What makes your product so special above everyone else's?"

"I was tired of drinking the same chalky protein shakes that were full of sugar and shit I couldn't even pronounce. I knew there had to be some healthier alternative to help with my recovery after workouts." I shrugged and took a step back from Resha, letting my gaze fall over her body once again before moving to my desk chair. "Spent some time researching and hooked up with some nutritionists and chemists and TKO was born."

I blinked when I noticed that Resha had actually pulled out her phone and was typing something as if taking notes.

"That's good. Couple that with your extensive fighting record and you've got gold. No wonder Jersey Retailers wants to partner with you."

My lips pulled downward into a frown. "How'd you know Jersey wants to work with me?"

Giving me a *get real* expression, she spun around, placing her hands on my desk and leaning in.

My gaze dipped to where her sweater dropped ever so slightly, exposing more of her soft, supple brown skin. I ran my tongue along my bottom lip.

"Nothing's a secret on the internet. Besides, I know some people at Jersey, and while they never came out and said as much they did hint at some new protein powders and supplements coming out soon. So, how about we book the photoshoot for this weekend?"

"No." My tone was clipped as I stood from my chair.

Resha sighed heavily, her shoulders falling. "Come on? How are you still saying no? I'm a professional at this kind of thing. I do this for a living, and sure, I'd need to conduct a little research on your target market and whatnot since your product is out of my realm of expertise, but I know I can help with your online presence to give your company a little boost. All you need to do is cooperate and agree to take a few pictures. That's it. Totally painless."

I gritted my teeth and started to shake my head again but then an idea popped into my head which had me grinning.

"Why am I getting a bad feeling about that look?"

Moving around my desk closer to Resha, I stopped about a foot away from her. "You take pictures for a living and post them online?"

"Well, sort of. The way you just said it made me sound like some sort of cam girl or something. But, more or less, yeah, that's what I do."

"So you're comfortable using a camera, right?"

"Of course. Took a course on photography years ago at the community college prior to starting my blog. I take one every few years to keep my skills updated. I don't want to brag but I know a thing or two." She lifted her hand and used it to brush imaginary dust off her shoulder.

I nodded. "Then you'll take the pictures."

"Yeah, I'll take the— Wait, what?"

"You heard me. You know how to wield a camera. No need to involve another photographer or a whole damn set. You can take the pics."

"But what about …"

"About?" I questioned when she trailed off.

"I know a number of photographers right here in the Williamsport area that would love to do this photoshoot for you. I can give them a ca—"

"It's you or no one. Final offer."

Her mouth snapped shut in defiance and she narrowed those impossibly long eyelashes are she peered at me. I smirked because in spite of the rebellion I spotted in her expression, I could feel her already agreeing.

She didn't want to but she would. I knew it and she did, too.

"This Saturday then," I stated with finality.

"I never agreed to doing the shoot."

"You didn't *not* agree either."

Silence was her reaction to that but she folded her arms across her chest.

Stepping forward, I pulled her to me by the waist. "You came here wanting to thank me for saving your ass, this is how you're going to do it."

She scrunched up her face. "I thought you said I don't owe you a thank you."

A smirk crossed my lips. "I changed my mind."

"That's not—"

I didn't know what she'd been about to say because by then I couldn't hold out any longer. It was as if my hand on her body was the spark my instincts needed to finally take over. Dipping my head, I captured her lips with mine. Her moan and sigh were instantaneous. I tasted and explored her mouth until I felt all of her resistance melt away.

I would do the photoshoot with her behind the camera. Not because she owed me jackshit, but because it gave me yet another opportunity to be in this woman's presence. Another chance to feel those thick lips of hers.

I pulled back with my hand at the nape of her head and our foreheads touching. "Saturday."

Resha silently nodded, but when I thought she was going to move out of my hold, she reached up with both of her hands and loosened the tie I had holding my hair back in a bun. My hair fell in waves around my shoulders.

"Wear your hair down."

I pressed another kiss to her lips before releasing her. "For you, I will."

She dipped her head almost as if feeling shy or bashful at my comment.

"Saturday morning. I'll pick you up," I finalized.

She looked surprised but didn't protest. "I'll be ready."

"Make sure you are."

Chapter Seven

Resha

"I can't believe I agreed to this," I murmured as I watered my newly acquired fern plant that I chose to hang above the toilet in my bathroom. I sighed as a tingle moved through my body at the remembrance of Connor's lips capturing mine in his office. All of a sudden, I recalled exactly why I agreed to do this photoshoot.

My original idea had been to hire an up-and-coming photographer I knew to take a few pictures. I would sort through them, create some great images to go on Instagram and FaceBook with some appropriate captions, and that would be that. Naturally, things couldn't be that easy because my hormones decided they wanted to act the hell up and get all smitten.

I moved from the bathroom with my watering can to nourish my spider plant and the others plants I had around the living room and a few that were out on the balcony. Satisfied once that task was completed, I looked over the bag I'd packed to take with me to Connor's photoshoot—the shoot in which I still didn't know exactly where the location was. He wanted to take the pictures on his own terms, in a location he specified, of course. The man just seemed to want to make things difficult.

I happened to raise my gaze and caught my smiling reflection in the mirror. Thinking about how adamant he was when I first proposed his taking pictures made me grin. He was obviously uncomfortable with being the face of his own products but too bad for him. The man was fine as hell and in just the way that would spark the interest of those wanting his product. The men would take one look at his pictures and want to be him, thereby buying the shake and supplements, or the women would want to be *with* him, thus buying the product to feel closer. Or better yet, buy the product for their man, subconsciously hoping it'd somehow turn their significant other into the image they saw.

I had it all figured out. What I couldn't figure out was why thinking of other women seeing images of Connor and their wanting him caused a pang of jealously to rumble through my chest.

"He's not my man," I reminded myself out loud.

So what ... he kissed like his lips had been waiting their whole life just to feel mine. It was no big deal that whenever I was in the same room as him the electricity was damn near palpable. Really, it didn't bother me that he fucked like a stallion.

Oh God.

Thinking about that night in New York had my entire body getting warmed up. And since the night of my attack, the dreams of our time together in New York had only increased, growing more vivid.

"Shit, Resh. Pull your shit together!" I bullied myself and just in time because my phone rang as soon as I slipped my feet into the athletic sneakers I chose to wear for the photoshoot, figuring I'd been on my feet much of the day.

"Hello?"

"Ms. McDonald, there's a Connor O'Brien at the front desk for you," the building's security-slash-receptionist explained.

"I'll be right down." After hanging up the phone, I quickly gathered all of my equipment and the oversized bag I placed everything, including a couple of props, and headed out my door, making sure to double check the lock, as I usually did.

As soon as I rounded the corner from the elevators, I easily spotted Connor's imposing figure while he stood over Tom who was our building's security and receptionist during the day on Saturdays. I giggled to myself as Tom peered up at Connor from his desk, thinking about how useless he would be if Connor were actually trying to break into the building or something.

"Hi, you ready for this?" I greeted.

"As long as you're still taking the pics, I'm ready for anything you throw at me, sweetheart."

My eyes bulged because I wasn't expecting that response. Or, more like I hadn't been expecting the candor in his voice when he said what he said. His tone had every hair on my body standing on end with just his words and that deep stare of his. I was sure if the real hair on my head wasn't braided down, underneath my weave, it would be standing as well.

And to make matters worse, instead of saying anything in return, Connor moved his hand around my waist and kissed me with all the earnestness he could seem to muster. Right when I got into the kiss, he pulled back, but not before nipping my bottom lip. My nipples instantly became hard.

"What was that for?" I groaned.

"That was for making me do this dumb ass shoot."

I folded my arms over my chest ... more so to hide my nipples just in case the sports bra I wore wasn't doing enough. "Ha! Like I could *make* you do anything."

He leaned down and had the nerve to nip my bottom lip again, pulling a gasp of air from my mouth.

"You could make me do a lot of things, a stór," he growled close to my ear.

I was preparing to respond when a movement out of the corner of my eye forced me to remember that we weren't in the privacy of my own home. Looking from Connor to my right, I caught sight of my neighbor, Jarvis, as he passed us, his face scowling and lips turned downward.

I didn't spare him a second look.

"All of that to take some pictures?" Connor questioned, regaining my attention.

I glanced down at the bag over my shoulder with everything I'd placed in it. "Yes, I needed to stock up on baby oil."

I giggled at the face me made.

"Ouch!" I yelped after he slapped my ass.

"Keep talking shit."

I was so tempted, but Tom clearing his throat again reminded me of the fact that we weren't alone.

"My car's parked in the garage. I guess I'll follow you wherever we're headed," I suggested.

Connor shook his head before turning to the desk, and that was when I first saw two motorcycle helmets sitting there. He picked up the pink and black one and handed it to me.

"Or you'll ride with me."

My eyes widened. "Uh, I've never been on a motorcycle before."

"First time for everything. Don't worry, I'll take it easy on the curves. I figured you'd like a pink helmet."

I started to protest, telling Connor that I'd never been on a motorcycle and that I didn't have any intentions on making that day my first ride either, but he was too busy taking my free hand in his and ushering us both out the front door of my building. As soon as we exited, it was unmistakable which vehicle was his. Almost directly in front of the building sat a midnight blue and black motorcycle that looked as if it'd been spit shined to perfection. In large white letters it read Kawasaki across the body. As soon as I saw it, I knew I had to get at least a few images of Connor on his bike for him to post.

"This is gorgeous," I stated, in awe. I'd never been one to care too much about motorcycles before, but this one had captivated my attention. Probably because the sleek yet powerful look of the bike reminded me so much of its owner.

"Custom made to my specifications."

I whistled low. "I'm impressed."

"You should be, I don't let just anybody sit on this beauty."

I looked him in the eye, wanting to ask if that meant that he hadn't taken any other women out on this bike, but I bit my tongue. His past was none of my business.

Connor took the helmet from my hands. "Let's make sure this fits correctly." He gently lowered the helmet until it fit snug around my head. He then secured the chin guard thingy and tightened is just enough that the helmet wouldn't move or go flying off.

"How's that?"

"Feels heavy."

He nodded. "It's supposed to. You'll get used to it." Pulling me closer to the bike, he gave me some instructions on how to properly get on and off the bike, how to hold him while riding, and how to lean into the curves when making a turn.

"I could know all of this already? I could own my own motorcycle."

Connor frowned. "You just said you've never been on a motorcycle before."

"Oh yeah." I rolled my eyes at my own silly pettiness.

"Do I need to go over any of this again?"

I started to shake my head but the helmet made it uncomfortable to do so. "No, I got it all."

"Cool, let's ride." He straddled the seat, and I groaned inwardly. My eyes immediately went to his muscular thighs that were, unfortunately, confined by the dark jeans he wore.

I moved closer and held firmly onto his shoulders as I got on the bike, placing my feet exactly where he'd instructed me to. I secured the bag I had with me in my lap and then lowered my arms to wrap around his waist.

"Tighter," he ordered over his shoulder.

I had no idea what he meant until his hands moved to my arms, pulling them in tighter and fully pressing my chest against his broad back. Inhaling, I let his manly scent invade my nasal passages. Again, that feeling of safety and security rose all around me and any fear I might've had about taking this ride with him evaporated.

"You good?"

I nodded because words didn't seem to want to form in my brain.

He turned his head forward, nodding, and started the bike. A small gush of air rushed from my lips as we took off. Instinctively, my arms tightened around Connor's body and I inched forward just a little to get closer to him, wanting to feel more secure.

I had no idea where we were going nor how long it would take to get there but I decided not to ask questions. For a little while, I could go with the flow.

Resting the right side of my head to Connor's back, I watched the streets pass us by, one by one. Fewer and fewer people were on the streets as we moved closer to the main highway that led out of Williamsport. A tiny fission of nervous energy began to grow in the pit of my stomach thinking of going on the highway on a motorcycle, but at the intersection before the highway turnoff, Connor made a right instead of a left. A sigh of relief fell from my mouth. Connor angled his head back, briefly looking over his shoulder at me before turning his attention back to the road. It was short-lived but his gesture conveyed that he'd felt my fear and that he was taking care of me.

I had to fight my growing emotions to calm down. I'd made it a habit in my younger years to get caught up and became too trusting way too soon with men I barely knew. Men who didn't deserve or earn half of the trust I put in them. And I got burned each and every single time. I hoped to God I wasn't starting back on old patterns with Connor.

It took about another fifteen minutes until Connor said over his shoulder, "Just around this corner up ahead."

I nodded but my heart sank a little. Oddly, I was already missing the end of this ride and having to separate myself from Connor's warm body.

Get your shit together, Resha! I scolded, reminding myself this man wasn't mine. Nor should he be. Connor wasn't my type at all. I was just out here to do him a favor. That's it and that's *all.*

"We're here."

I blinked, staring at the sight before me, having been totally caught up in my own thoughts. I squinted and looked around after I pulled the helmet from my head.

"The hell? Are you trying to kidnap me?" I shrieked, feeling on high alert as I stared at the deserted building.

****

Connor

I started to chuckle at Resha's ridiculous question, but once I pulled my head free of my helmet, and really looked into her enlarged eyes, my laughter ceased. There was real, genuine fear there. Those coffee-colored eyes closely examined one part of the building to the other, scanning the entrance for what I wasn't sure.

Stepping back, I glanced over my shoulder just to see what had her so damn spooked but there was nothing and no one there. No one besides the two of us. I turned back to face Resha to see her bottom lip tucked in between her teeth. She still remained on the bike, as if seriously considering whether or not she could drive it all on her own to hightail it out of there.

Moving closer, I held out my hand, taking hers into mine. "If I wanted to kidnap you, there are a hundred other better looking places I could bring you to, a stór."

Her eyes dropped to meet mine and she visibly swallowed. Her fingers tightened around mine.

"I don't like abandoned buildings."

My eyes narrowed. Her words were laden with memories of the past. I could tell. "What's got you to so spooked?"

Her lips parted, but that was where whatever she'd been about to say died, in one breath. She shook her head slightly. "I guess it's the attack. I must still be on edge from that night." She blinked and gave me a bullshit smile as if that would explain her reaction adequately.

It didn't.

Stepping closer, I took her chin in my hand and looking down deep into her eyes, searching for the truth.

"The police reach out to you?" I questioned when I didn't quite find what I was looking for.

She nodded. "He confessed to trying to steal my bag and for hitting me. He's being charged with assault and attempted robbery, I think."

I knew all of that already, having spoken directly with the police captain.

Resha's body shuddered. "I was just being uptight. I know you're not trying to kidnap me. What is this place?"

Her eyes skirted away from mine to look over my shoulder. I released her chin and stepped to the side so she could have a clearer view of the entranceway.

"I own this building. It's where I host my Williamsport Underground fights," I stated candidly. I didn't make it a habit of revealing my Underground fighting club to just anyone, especially women. Yet, I'd brought Resha here because if I was going to take pictures for my TKO products, this was the only place I'd do it at. And she was the only woman I'd allow in this facility to take said pictures.

"Underground? What's that?"

"Let me show you." Taking the large bag she carried from her, I hoisted it over my shoulder and took her hand in mine to help her off the bike.

"You're just gonna leave it parked out here like this?" she questioned, looking worried.

That time I did chuckle. "No one's touching my shit. Trust me." I squeezed her hand reassuringly.

"If you say so, cocky. But I better not end up walking back home."

"I'd carry you on my back before I'd let that happen."

She didn't respond verbally, but I felt a shudder in her body followed by her lowering her gaze, avoiding mine. She was so damn sexy when she did shit like that. I wondered if she knew it.

Nah, she doesn't.

Pulling my key free from the pocket of my jeans, I unlocked the heavy metal door that led inside, sliding it over before stepping aside to allow Resha to pass through. She gave me a hesitant look before something shifted in her gaze and she stepped over the threshold. I slid the door closed and locked it behind us and then did something I rarely do, which was to reach over and turn on the light switch, illuminating the entire first floor of the building.

"Is that a boxing ring?"

"Fighting ring," I corrected, glancing across the spacious room to where Resha was pointing.

I watched as her eyes and head circled the bottom floor of this abandoned-looking building. On the far side, a large, square fighting ring stood, surrounded by neatly arranged metal folding chairs for the audience to observe as fighters dueled it out. To the far right of the ring, almost toward the corner of the room, hung a punching bag, the middle of which had been repeatedly wrapped with duct tape. I'd been hitting that bag since I first went pro. Buddy had been begging me to buy a new one and I had, but for the other fighters to train with. I stood by old faithful.

"What do those doors lead to?" Resha pointed ahead to the doors beyond the ring.

"Changing rooms for the fighters."

She turned to me and placed her hands on her hips. Her fear had turned to curiosity.

My eyes dropped to her hips, appreciating the leggings she wore that cupped those hips the way my hands itched to. I moved closer, as if being pulled by an invisible string. I stared as she sucked in her bottom lip, but fear wasn't the motive this time around.

"Is this like a secret fighting ring or something?"

I snorted. "Not *or something.* That's exactly what we do in here, doll."

Her nose wrinkled at the pet name. I swear I didn't even realize I knew so many damn pet names until that moment. And hell, if I'd ever used any of them before.

"You run a secret fighting ring?" She sounded mystified.

I didn't answer, but again I took her chin into my hand. "I thought you were here to take my picture not ask questions."

A small smile arose on her lips and my chest expanded. "I can do both, can't I?"

My eyes dipped to her lips. "You can do whatever the hell you want," I growled before lowering my mouth to hers. Any thoughts of fighting immediately transformed to images of fucking. Resha's thick thighs wrapping around my back as I pushed inside of her. The little mewling sounds that began pouring from her mouth, the same damn ones she made our night in New York, grabbed the attention of my cock. My entire body sizzled with need as my hands slipped in between the opened peacoat she wore and underneath the Nike sweatshirt she had on.

Her arms reached up, her fingers intertwining in my hair, causing a few strands to break free of the band that held the bun in place. But before the kiss could turn into something else, I pulled back. Even though the chances of our being interrupted were slim since no one would be showing up here for a few more hours, I didn't want to risk it. Not yet, anyway. Resha had been way too jumpy the moment we arrived. The last thing I needed was to be interrupted while stripping her naked and having my way with her and have her think it was some sort of set up.

"Let's get this shit over with before I change my mind," I stated, peering down into her eyes, noticing the deepness of my voice.

"We could if you keep your lips to yourself."

Reaching around, I slapped her ass. "Fat chance of that happening."

Regrettably, I moved back from Resha and started toward the ring, removing my leather jacket. "So how do you want to do this?" I asked once I tossed the jacket on one of the chairs in the front row and folded my arms over my chest.

I grinned when I watched Resha's nostrils flare as her eyes grazed over the muscles of my arms and chest.

"Uh ..." She cleared her throat and blinked a few times. "Do this ... the photos, right. Okay, I bought a few of your products and supplements." She began removing the familiar black and blue bottles of my TKO protein powder and supplements from the bag she'd brought with her that I set in the chair next to my jacket.

"You purchased those?"

She paused and looked up at me. "Yeah."

"Why? I brought plenty and have some in the back."

She shrugged. "I needed to see what the product was about for myself so I could come up with a concept for the shoot."

"You tried any of it?"

She nodded. "The vanilla protein powder is my favorite. Do these supplements really work?" she questioned as she looked over the multi-vitamin bottle she held in her hand.

"Of course. I wouldn't put my name on shit that doesn't get results." I took the bottle from her hands, holding it up. "But these are meant to be used in conjunction with a whole foods diet and exercise to get the best results. Most people who take supplements think just taking a vitamin of some sort will do all the work they don't do."

"Maybe some people are just *busy*," Resha retorted, snatching the vitamin bottle from my hand.

I raised an eyebrow. "Touchy?"

With one hand on her hip she said, "Not at all. I'm just telling you that not all people who take vitamins think they're gonna do all the work. Maybe they have the right intentions and try to eat right or whatever but you know, life gets in the way." Her nose wrinkled in irritation and her lips pursed as if she were defending her very way of life.

I couldn't help the chuckle that escaped.

"What's so funny?"

"You, a stór." I laughed some more. "You don't have to defend shit to me. I'm not judging anyone or anything. I'm just telling you how the product is made to work."

Her shoulders slumped. "That obvious, huh?"

"Just a little."

She pushed out a breathe. "I get a little defensive about lifestyle choices at times."

I moved closer. "What for?"

She shrugged.

"Bullshit. You know why."

Her eyes narrowed, not liking being called out in her lie. *Too bad.* I held firm, awaiting her answer to the original question.

Finally, she rolled her eyes heavenward. "My job has me somewhat in the public eye. I'm not a celebrity by any means but I am sort of social media famous and I'm not exactly a size two. And while the majority of the feedback I've gotten from readers of my blog and social media postings has been extremely positive, there are still that small percentage who scrutinize my weight. Most of the time, it's random men sending those messages. They ask about what I eat or just flat out tell me I should be eating less and I need to get a gym membership instead of deals with major fashion brands."

By the time she'd stopped talking I was livid. My hands had tightened into clenched fists at my sides, and I could feel my heart rate increasing the blood flow circulating through my body. I wanted to take somebody's goddamn head off.

"Who are they?"

Resha blinked at the nearly lethal tone of my voice. She shook her head and waved her hand dismissively. "No one important.

Typically, they're just losers on the internet with nothing better to do than make others feel bad about themselves. Seriously, most of the time it doesn't bother me. Not so much anymore. It's just old stuff from growing up a fat kid, too. Really, it's not a big deal."

I peered at her through narrowed lenses to discern whether or not she was telling the truth or just trying to calm me down. It was a combination of both. But the same look in her eye that lured me in as I watched her in that bar in New York pulled me to her then.

Cupping the right side of her face with one hand, I let the other slip around her waist, bringing our bodies flush against one another. "You know you're beautiful, right?" She had to know that.

Her lips formed a thin line. "Sure."

She didn't sound convinced.

"Any motherfucker who deliberately goes out of their way to make a woman, let alone a stranger, feel bad about themselves is a shitstain who is miserable in their own life. Their real problem is they want you but deep down know they're not good enough to have you."

Her eyes widened as if she'd never heard those words before. As if the very truth of what I'd just told her had never even occurred to her. Damn, who the hell had this woman been with before? In that moment, it became my mission to get her to recognize the truth of who she was. To wipe away that longing look that resided deep in those coffee-colored orbs of hers. Not ever had a woman I wasn't related to awakened my need to protect, serve, and encourage, more than she had in this moment.

I released her, with that silent vow, taking a step back and allowing her to direct me to get this photoshoot over with. I had plans for the both of us once the work was out of the way.

Chapter Eight

Resha

"Perfect. Now reach up and grab for the top of the bag with your right hand. Let's see how that looks."

He's a natural, I thought to myself, and I smiled while looking through the lens of my camera, snapping picture after picture. We were a couple of hours into the shoot and I swear with each passing second, Connor looked better and better. It didn't hurt that he'd removed his T-shirt, spent a few rounds jumping rope to get all sweated up, and changed into a pair of grey jogging pants. All of that was the mere icing on the cake.

Connor's body was a masterpiece. Sketched out by years of training and fighting. And once we started taking pictures, I saw why he'd chosen this place for the shoot. This was his home. Not where he lived, obviously, but where he felt most comfortable. This dark, grungy abandoned building with seemingly nothing inside but a fighting ring, some training equipment, and folding chairs. All of it surrounded by huge concrete pillars that held the building up, was where he felt free and relaxed enough to allow me to turn the camera on him.

"Okay, here," I stated, lowering my camera and picking up both the vanilla and chocolate protein powder canisters, taking them to him. "Hold these in your hands like this."

He held a bottle in each hand, up around his chest with a stern face.

I bit my lip as I looked at him through the camera lens. His blond hair fell around his shoulders as the sweat rolled down his face and chest. Each droplet of sweat clung to muscles rippling over his tight abdomen, and for one second I wished I could be that droplet of salt, water, and whatever the hell else sweat was made out of.

My finger moved, snapping picture after picture of Connor and enjoying every second of it. He peered directly at me with each picture, silently conveying messages with his eyes that were unmistakable. I tried hard as hell to convince myself that this was just returning a favor to a man who did something nice for me, but I knew it was bullshit, and the gleam in Connor's eyes dared me to continue lying to myself.

That look was not to be misinterpreted. It said everything his lips didn't—and they had said plenty from the moment he kissed me once we first entered the building. My body hummed with excitement and anticipation that I couldn't ignore or downplay. But my mind, she was much more reticent.

Every failed relationship I ever had, which had been plenty, played over and over. My mind and memories reminding me that I was terrible when it came to choosing men. I couldn't trust myself, and hadn't been able to for a very long time.

"Stop thinking so much, Resha, and take the damn pictures so we can get out of here."

Connor's growl pulled me from those stressful thoughts of the past.

"We're almost done," I retorted. "I just want to get a final few shots with all of your products and supplements arranged in the middle of the fighting ring."

"I'm not laying down in that ring, half naked like some sort of fucking Fabio look-alike with TKO products spread all around me," Connor grunted, wearing an expression of disgust.

I nearly doubled over laughing at the image he painted. "Are you sure? Because I was thinking—"

"Resha," he warned in that guttural tone that caused ripples of awareness to roll through my body.

"F-Fine. I was kidding anyway. No, this shot will just be TKO products and supplements. I think I got all the shots of you that I need. You're very photogenic."

He grunted as he stuck his arms through the dark T-shirt he had stowed away in the back changing room. He helped arrange the products the way I wanted, and then I spent the final thirty minutes of our shoot taking shots from every angle, trying to get the products on display with the grittiness of our surroundings.

"These look good," I said excitedly when I finally stopped to look through the hundreds of images on the memory card with the camera's playback feature.

He didn't say anything but I could feel Connor behind me, standing over me. Suddenly, his hands covered mine, pulling the camera free. I let him as he held the camera out in front of us with his body pressed against my back, essentially trapping me from all sides. Yet, I didn't feel trapped. I felt as if this was exactly where I'd belonged my whole life.

His warm breath caressed the side of my neck as his chin lowered to my shoulder. His fingers pressed the arrow buttons of the camera, moving from one image to the next. My core temperature rose as his arms continued to bracket my body, and I stared at picture after picture of Connor in his element. That feeling of wanting to know everything I could about the man in the pictures, the man holding me, breathing down my neck, intensified. Suddenly, staring at the pictures wasn't enough. I needed to see the real thing.

Spinning around in Connor's arms, I reached up on my tiptoes, and wrapped my arms around his shoulders. He wasn't put off or surprised by my moves. No, he was expecting it. The heat that had built up between us throughout the morning and early afternoon, he wasn't immune to it anymore than I was.

So when his lips captured mine, we both were ready for the fireworks that ignited. His low, guttural groan, caused an almost painful need to course through my body. My nipples pebbled and I moaned the second his tongue met mine, somewhere in the middle of our kiss.

"Oh shit! I didn't mean to interrupt."

Startled, I jumped and clutched onto Connor's arms, almost digging into them with my fingernails. But Connor wasn't frightened at all as he peered over his shoulder. He did look pissed off and irritated.

"The hell are you doing here so early?" he questioned the older looking man who moved closer, wearing a grin on his face.

"Meeting a new recruit to the Underground early prior the first fight. He wants to train before getting into the ring. I left a message on your voicemail. You must've been busy." The man's smiling, brown eyes slid over to me, and the wrinkles increased as the smirk on his lips grew to a full on smile. "Ma'am, nice to meet you. I'm Buddy," he greeted.

I released the breath I'd been holding, realizing this guy wasn't a threat. In fact, the playful devilishness I saw in his eyes and the way Connor glared at him actually made me like him almost immediately.

"I'm Resha."

"Well that's a pretty name."

I grinned. "Thank you, Buddy."

I didn't get the chance to say anything else since Connor moved in front of me, blocking both Buddy and my line of sight to one another.

"Cut the shit and stop flirting with my woman," Connor growled.

I stiffened, sure that I heard him wrong. But when I peeked around Connor's broad body over at Buddy, the surprised expression on his face told me two things. One, that I wasn't wrong in hearing the way Connor had referred to me. And two, that wasn't a statement he made flippantly or frequently.

"We were just leaving," Connor finally said.

"I bet you were."

"What's all of this, anyway?"

"We did a photoshoot," I responded, beating Connor to the punch as I stepped around him. Out of the corner of my eye, I saw his eyes narrow on me but I didn't pay him any mind. "Your friend here's a natural in front of the camera."

Buddy laughed. "I've been saying that for years, but he just tells me to shove it up my ass."

I giggled. "That sounds like our guy all right." I turned to Connor, whose eyes were burning with warning. Daring me to keep trying him.

Oh, how I wanted to take him up on that offer but I was too much of a chicken. I had my limits.

"I'll clean this stuff up and get out of your way, Buddy."

"No, leave it. You two probably have important shit to do. I'll take care of it," Buddy insisted, when I started to gather the TKO products that still sat in the center of the ring. "Mark and I have been trying to convince Connor to take some more pictures for social media of his products for months now." Buddy paused. "If I knew you had this planned, I wouldn't have been pestering you so much."

"Maybe next time you'll leave me the hell alone when I say I know what the fuck I'm doing."

Buddy chuckled as if to say *fat chance of that happening.*

I grabbed my equipment that I brought for the shoot, save for the TKO products, and stuffed everything into my bag again.

"Let me help with that," Connor insisted as I moved to put on my peacoat. I smiled over my shoulder as he assisted, feeling womanly and cared for when he even helped to pull my hair from underneath my coat so it didn't get stuck.

"You hungry?"

"Yup," I responded, staring up into those eyes, not even knowing what the hell he'd just asked.

"You have a taste for anything in particular?"

I blinked, shaking my head, realizing he was talking about food. I shrugged. "I could go for a slice of pizza ... or two." I had to be honest. I was never a one slice of pizza kind of girl. Two or more. Always.

Connor grinned. "Perfect."

It was one short word, but the gleam in his eyes when he said it told me he wasn't referring to my response. I dipped my head and turned to see Buddy giving me a wink and grin as he went about whistling and picking up the TKO products from the ring floor.

I didn't know what the hell I'd just agreed to but I opted not to question it or myself.

****

Hours later, I found myself grinning and smiling as Connor and I passed through the front doors of my building. We'd gone to get pizza at a little hole-in-the-wall shop that wasn't far from the building we did the shoot at. The pizza was delicious but paled in comparison to the company. After eating, Connor dared me to allow him to take me on a tour of the outskirts of the city on his motorcycle. Not being one to easily turn down a dare, I said yes and got to enjoy watching the city of Williamsport pass us as we sped by on the motorcycle, sometimes going up to sixty miles an hour. I had a feeling Connor had no problem or fear going even faster but restrained himself for my sake.

"What're you thinking about?" he questioned in my ear as soon as the elevator doors closed behind us.

I found myself with my back pressed against the mirrored wall and Connor hovering over me.

"How great your pictures are going to come out," I lied, causing him to frown.

"Bullshit."

I giggled. "You have such a potty mouth."

The mischievous gleam in his eyes was his only response just before he dipped his head, bringing his lips closer to my ear. "That's not all I got, a stór." And just like that, his lips were on mine again.

I'd questioned throughout our day together how our evening would end. I wondered if I would have the guts to actually go through with letting him inside of my place again, but this time, allowing him into my bed. Sure, we'd slept together in New York, and I'd be a lying fool if I said I didn't want to do it again. However, that was different. We'd been strangers then. He was just a man who was out in a bar, in a city, far from the one I lived in. A city I was leaving the next morning. I could go back home and pretend it hadn't happened at all. But now? He was so much more than that.

Connor pulled away from the kiss, his hand moving to the nape of my neck, cupping it. His callused thumb ran along the side of my lower jaw, caressing. "This won't be New York."

Confused, I wrinkled my forehead, giving him a quizzical look.

"This isn't a one and done type of thing anymore."

His voice was so tender yet firm in resolution—his thumb continuing to trace a line down my jaw—and the gleam in his eye all caught me off-guard. But before I could ask just what he meant by it all the elevator dinged as it stopped at my floor.

Connor glanced over his shoulder just as my neighbor, Jarvis, prepared to step onto the elevator.

"Oh," Jarvis startled, his eyes widening when they moved from Connor to me and then back to Connor again. His lips thinned and his expression completely closed off. "Resha." He nodded curtly before stepping aside.

"Jarvis," I returned just as short as I moved off the elevator, Connor not far behind me. I glanced over my shoulder to see Connor standing over Jarvis as he moved passed, glaring down at him. It wasn't until I took another step that I realized he firmly clutched my hand in his, assuring that I wouldn't get too far from him, not that I was trying to.

He glared at Jarvis for another heartbeat before moving past him and following me down the hallway to my door.

I didn't even have a chance to get my key from my bag when Connor reached over my shoulder, pulling it free from my hand

and inserting it into the lock for me. Turning the knob, he pressed the door open. I made a move to step inside but that was when Connor spun me around to face him, intent on finishing the kiss that we'd shared in the elevator.

I sighed into his mouth, my body obviously wanting whatever it was he was willing to give. All my thoughts became fuzzy and were drowned out by the rising heat that threatened to scorch the both of us.

"W-We should take this behind closed doors," I was just barely able to say as I pulled back from the kiss.

"He an ex or something?"

I blinked and shook my head. "What? Who?"

Connor's hard set eyes moved to the elevator and then back to me.

"Jarvis?"

He scowled. "Whatever the hell his name is."

"No. Hell no. He gives me the creeps, actually. What makes you think he was an ex?"

"The way he looked at you. Just now and earlier today in the lobby."

I was stunned, not even realizing that Connor had spotted the extra hard look Jarvis had given us that morning.

"I see everything," he stated as if answering my unasked statement.

"He's not an ex."

"But he wants you."

It wasn't a question. It was a man making an observation about another man.

Folding my arms over my chest, I raised an eyebrow. "Jealous?"

He grinned. "Why the hell would I be jealous? I'm the one who has what he wants."

I parted my lips to ask him how he knew he *had* me but Connor pushed the door open and moved forward, causing me to step backwards into my condo. My entire body began to fill with excitement of what was to come once the door closed. However, as soon as I flicked on the lights and before I was even fully inside of my place, Connor's entire body stiffened.

He instantly became on high alert, pulling me closer to him with one long arm around my waist.

"What?" I questioned, turning around and gasping at the sight before me. My home had been ransacked. It was a mess. "What the—" My shriek was cut off when Connor, pulled me from my apartment, slamming the door behind us.

"What are you doing?" I demanded, turning to re-enter my home to see the damage that had been done.

Connor already had his cell phone in his hand before answering my question. "Whoever did that could still be in there. We need to go wait in the lobby for the police."

He began throwing out orders like it was his job when the 911 operator answered the call. The hand free of his cell phone tightened around mine, pulling me in the direction of the staircase. I followed, feeling so damn confused and out of place, in the building I lived in for years. I heard Connor barking orders and directions into the phone, telling the person on the other end the name of my street and my address, while informing them that the person who did this may still be inside. I shuddered thinking that might be true. Whoever had ransacked my home might still be there. They could've been inside lying in wait for me. Just when the fear began to overwhelm me and felt like too much to handle, Connor's strong arms bracketed me, pulling me into the secure warmth of his body. It was as if my body melted against his, needing his strength.

Somehow, with me still clinging to his side, he made it to the front desk of my building, loudly informing the on-duty security guard-slash-receptionist that my condo had been broken into.

"I'll call the police," the guard I knew as Randy stated.

"Already done. They're on their way. You'll need to cough up any video footage you have of her floor over the past few hours."

"Um, s-sure but I'll have to check with my management fi—"

"That wasn't a request, dipshit," Connor growled, leaning over the desk.

I glanced over at Randy who appeared terrified. He had to be nearly a full foot shorter than Connor's six-six frame, and was much scrawnier.

"Connor, calm down," I whispered.

Connor's lips pinched as he looked down at me.

I stood taller, straightening from underneath his arm and raised my chin, trying to appear more confident than I felt. "We need to remain calm. The police are on their way. They'll help sort all of this out."

God I hoped so.

It only took about five minutes for the police to arrive, thankfully. And as soon as they did, Connor was there, directing them up to my condo and telling him what we saw.

"And this is your apartment, ma'am?" one of the officers questioned.

"Yes.

"Okay, stay down here while we go take a look."

I nodded in agreement, and watched as they headed toward the door to take the stairs to my tenth floor condo.

"Who would do this?" I questioned, looking up at Connor.

He shook his head. "We're sure as fuck going to find out." His eyes moved over my head to peer down at Randy again.

The police took about ten minutes to call down to the front desk and have Randy inform us that we were in the all clear and that it was okay for me to come up. Knowing whoever had been in my place wasn't still there should've offered some relief but it didn't.

When we made it to my floor, a cold chill ran down my spine as I came to the entrance of my home. The officers stood just inside the door, awaiting Connor and I. He entered behind me, keeping close, which I believe he somehow knew I needed. I was relying on his strength because I was still in utter disbelief. Looking around my apartment, I flinched at the sight of my broken glass coffee table, my ripped pillows, and torn throw blanket.

"We need to know if anything was taken, ma'am," one of the officers informed me.

I nodded and took a few tentative steps inside of the place that had felt like one of the safest places on Earth to me, just that morning. I moved to check on the entertainment center in my living room where I sighed in relief seeing that my television and entertainment equipment hadn't been touched. A number of the drawers had been opened and my heart rate quickened until I looked and saw that the box I kept my spare cash was still there. Pulling the wooden box out of the drawer, my mouth dropped when I opened it and saw that the money hadn't been touched.

Confused, I looked up at Connor who stood over me with a deep scowl on his face. He stared at the money and then back to me.

I turned to the officers. "Whoever this was, didn't take the money I leave here."

One of the officers shrugged. "Maybe they missed it. Did you count it all to make sure it's there?"

I tucked the box under my arm and counted. Three hundred and eighteen dollars. The same amount I'd counted the last time I checked this box weeks ago.

"It's all here."

"They probably just missed it."

I stared up at Connor whose scowl deepened as he glared at the officers. "Or maybe whoever did this didn't give a shit about the money. Is Detective Brookes on the way?" he questioned impatiently.

The officer nodded. "He'll be here shortly. We just got a call over the radio with his ETA."

"Tell him to move his ass." Connor turned back to me. "Anything else missing?"

I looked around the living room, my heart sinking at the way my plants had been ripped from their planters and tossed around the floor. I shook my head and moved silently down the hall. The bathroom had been untouched but the same couldn't be said for my office. I gasped as soon as I pushed the door of my office open. The damage that had been done in my living room didn't compare to the state of my office.

My beautiful glass desk, the one I'd searched for six months for, had been cracked in three different pieces, sending everything that sat on it to the ground. My desktop computer had been smashed with something. My first thought was a baseball bat since that was the only thing I could think of that would do that type of damage. The screen was gone due to it being bashed in. The back of the screen was all dented up and almost complete broken in half. The metal cabinet that I kept all of my important documents in had been dented on all sides, but the drawers remained sealed shut.

"Whoever did this must've been pissed," one of the officers said.

"Is that your professional opinion, asshole?" Connor angrily questioned.

"Look, buddy—"

"Don't fucking call me—"

"Connor, please," I implored, not wanting to have to deal with him getting into a fight with the police on top of all of this.

"Where's Detective Brookes?" he asked.

"Just arrived," another unfamiliar male voice interrupted.

I glanced up to find a plain clothes detective standing at the doorway of my office. I knew he was a detective because of the badge he prominently displayed on his belt buckle at his waist. His serious, dark, almost charcoal eyes took in the room before they landed on me.

"You must be Ms. McDonald."

I nodded.

"I'm Detective Brookes. Sorry we had to meet like this." He looked over at Connor and nodded. "O'Brien."

"Brookes."

It was a short welcome but it made it obvious that these two knew each other.

"Did you get pictures?" Brookes questioned over his shoulder at one of the uniformed officers.

He shook his head and Brookes rolled his eyes, grumbling, "Of course not. Fucking idiots. Go stand out front with your partner," he ordered, and the uniformed officer left, looking forlorn.

I watched as Brookes pulled out his phone and began taking pictures of my office with it.

"Nothing's missing so far," Connor informed the detective.

I didn't pay attention to his reply, needing to remove myself from my office. The place where I spent so much of my day during my working hours was destroyed. I moved across the hall to my bedroom, expecting to find a disaster there, but I stopped short at the door due to the almost pristine nature of my bedroom. If I recalled correctly, my bedroom appeared to be cleaner than when I'd left.

"This isn't right," I mentioned out loud.

"What?"

"It's too clean," I told Connor, glancing up at him over my shoulder. "I know I had a pile of clothes on my bed this morning from the laundry I did last night. I left it out with intentions of folding it once I got home today and—" I stopped talking as I looked around. "The lines in my rug … I haven't vacuumed in over a week." I moved from the doorway, going to my bedroom closet, but as soon as I reached for the handle, both men behind me called out, stopping me.

"We don't want you to touch anything," Detective Brookes warned. "That handle could have valuable fingerprints on it."

Connor wrapped his hand around my arm, pulling me back and out of the way for Brookes to use the handkerchief in his hand to pull the door of my closet open.

There stood my vacuum cleaner. I didn't touch it but I moved closer, looking it over, and then turned back to Connor.

"It's been used today." I pointed at the clear plastic component that was the receptor for all the dust and debris that I knew had been empty that morning. "There's dust in there. Whoever did this destroyed my living room and office, but vacuumed my bedroom, folded my laundry, and put it away? This doesn't make any sense." I began rubbing my temples with my fingers.

"No, it doesn't," Brookes stated.

I watched as he moved from the closet to my bed. With the hand that held the handkerchief, he lifted the white comforter that rested there, pulling it all the way back to reveal the lavender sheets underneath.

I gasped at what I saw in the middle of the sheets. "Is that ..."

"Semen," Detective Brookes finished. "Most likely."

"Son of a bitch," Connor cursed behind me.

Feeling nauseous, I turned away from the bed. I needed to get out of that room. Fleeing, I rushed past Connor, back into the hallway, my breathing increasing. I moved down the hallway, past the damage of my living room and out onto the balcony, needing some fresh air.

Connor wasn't far behind me. I could feel the fear start to cloud the working parts of my brain, taking over all of my senses. That was when his arms surrounded me from behind.

"Wh-Who would do this?" I turned and asked him.

His large hand cupped my face. "Someone who's going to regret the day they were born," he growled.

"Ms. McDonald?"

Connor moved to my side, his arm moving around my waist, to allow me to see Detective Brookes standing at my patio door.

"I'm going to need to ask you some questions. I've got forensics on the way. Although much of the scene has been compromised already, we might be able to find some prints and DNA from the bedsheets." He frowned as he wrote something in the small notepad in his hand. "I wouldn't recommend staying here tonight."

"She's won't be," Connor quickly responded. "She'll be staying with me."

My eyes widened and I stared up at him.

"Okay, sounds good. Let me check on a couple things. A few more guys should be here soon to dust for fingerprints. I'll have some more questions and I'll need to get your contact information, Ms. McDonald, and then you can be on your way," Detective Brookes stated before writing something else in his notebook and departing.

I turned again to Connor. "Staying with you?"

"That's what I said," he responded without hesitation. "If Brookes allows it, you can pack a few things from here to bring. Otherwise, we'll make a trip to the store to pick up whatever you need."

He was so assured and his voice so calming and full of sternness that I didn't even think to go against what he was saying. The truth was I didn't want to.

About thirty minutes later, after answering more of Detective Brookes' questions—like what time I'd left that morning, if I had any idea who could've done this, etc—I was able to go to my bedroom and pick out a few items to pack up and take with me. Walking back into my bedroom again felt eerie. I stared at the bed that, even though I hadn't been here at the time whoever was in my home had been, caused me to feel violated just knowing what they'd done there.

"That thing is getting burned to the ground."

"I'll light the matches," Connor firmly stated behind me, stroking my arms up and down as chills ran through my body. I leaned into his strength for comfort.

Sighing, I moved to my closet, pulling out a suitcase to pack my clothes in. Most of the clothing in my closet hadn't been touched, and I felt okay taking them with me. I'd been assured by Detective Brookes that his team had taken photographs and done whatever they needed to do to get the necessary DNA samples and fingerprints. Next, I moved to my off-white, old-fashioned style dresser that I'd loved when I first purchased. Pulling the top drawer open, I removed a few of my leggings, T-shirts, and comfortable pajama sets for lounging and sleeping in.

"Oh my God!" I gasped when I opened the second drawer, where I kept my intimate apparel.

"What?" Connor questioned, immediately standing behind me, peering down.

"He stole my underwear." I looked up at Connor, completely mortified.

"Brookes!" Connor yelled.

"No! Don't tell him," I begged, feeling more embarrassed than I ever had.

"What do you mean don't tell him?"

"Yeah?"

"The fucker stole her underwear. Probably jerked off in there, too. Did your guys even check out her dressers?" Connor's voice was filled with anger I'd never heard anyone express on my behalf before. His anger must've transferred to Brookes as well because his dark eyes seemed to glow with indignation.

"Larry!" he yelled.

A few minutes later, one of the uniformed officers arrived at my bedroom door.

As Brookes explained the issue, I silently begged for the ground to open up and swallow me whole. Here I was standing in a room with four other men, listening to them talk about how some *perp* had broken into my home, destroyed much of my belongings, ejaculated in my bed, and then stolen my underwear.

This night just needed to end.

"I'm taking her home." I heard Connor's voice above everyone else's, and soon I felt his hands on my body, guiding me to the door. My feet moved without specified directions from my brain to do so. We were following Connor's direction as if he was the primary heat source I was seeking.

And he was.

I had no idea what lay ahead of me, but for now, I was just fine with following wherever Connor led.

Chapter Nine

Connor

She'd been so quiet ever since we walked into her apartment and saw the mess that was made. Save for answering the questions from Brookes and the other officers, she'd been quiet and her face was a mask of confusion and fear. Nothing tugged at me more than seeing those emotions swirling around in those dark brown eyes.

As I slid the large elevator door open, revealing my loft-style home, I moved to the side to allow Resha to enter first. She hesitated, peering up at me before turning and stepping off the elevator. My chest tightened at the look of fear that still danced in her eyes, despite her trying to hide it. It'd taken everything in me to allow her to even drive herself in her own car, to follow me on my bike to my place. I was only comfortable with her driving her own car after Brookes and another officer had thoroughly checked it out to make sure the perp hadn't left anything on her vehicle or it hadn't otherwise been tampered with.

"I'll take that," I stated, pulling the large bag she was clutching to her side from her, along with the suitcase I'd carried from her car. "Make yourself comfortable. I'll put these upstairs and then order us some food."

She nodded over her shoulder before moving across the hardwood floor toward the living room to the black leather couch. I watched for another heartbeat and then fully closed the elevator, taking her bags upstairs to the open space I'd designated as my bedroom. Being that it was loft there were no doors, everything was open, save for the first floor bedroom that I rarely used, but since I lived alone, I liked it that way. However, as I stared down at Resha who sat on the couch, looking through her phone, I briefly wondered if she liked this style. If she would be comfortable here.

"Okay," I began as I made my way down the stairs, "there's a good Chinese takeout not too far from here. There are two Italian places but they're just okay. A Thai place and a vegan spot. Any preference?" I questioned as I rounded the couch and took a seat next to her.

She shook her head. "I'm not that hungry."

I frowned. "It's been hours since we ate lunch. You need to eat. What's your preference?"

She sighed and peered over at me, giving me a side-eye look.

I smirked because I enjoyed the feisty side of her. Hell, I was quickly becoming a fan of *every* side of her.

"Fine. Chinese. You have a menu?"

I grinned and sat up, my arm reaching for the hidden drawer of the black, low-sitting coffee table at the center of my living room. Opening it, I ruffled through a couple of motorcycle and fighting magazines before pulling out the menu to the Chinese spot, and handed it to her.

She looked over the menu and told me what she wanted.

"Cool. I'm gonna order. You should call Destiny."

Her forehead knitted. "Why?"

I blinked and gaped at her as if she were crazy. "She's your best friend and sister pretty much, right? You don't think she'd want to know what happened today?"

Shaking her head, Resha waved a dismissive hand. "It's late."

I pressed the button on my phone to display the time. "It's barely a quarter after eight."

She rolled her eyes. "That's late for her these days. The kids' bedtime is eight o'clock and I don't want to call her in case the ringing of the phone will wake the children. I'll just talk to her in the morning."

I stared at Resha. "You seriously think she'd be upset if one of the kids woke up because you called to tell her your home had been broken into?"

Rising, she shook her head and ran her hands over her arms as if trying to keep herself warm. "It's no big deal. I'll call her in the morning. Don't you have a call to make? I'm starting to get hungry."

I and gritting my teeth so much so I could feel the flexing of the muscles in my jaw. She was scared shitless. I could see it, but she tried to downplay it, to hide it as if that would make it go away. And for some reason she didn't want to contact the person I knew she was closest to. I didn't say anything.

I gave her a curt nod and dialed the number to order our food.

"They'll be here in about twenty minutes," I told her after disconnecting the call. "Do you want to take a shower or change or anything?"

"A hot shower sounds great right now."

I directed her to the bathroom before handing her a towel, washcloth, and an extra bar of soap. Moving down the stairs, as Resha shut the door to begin her shower, I headed straight to my phone.

Picking it up, I sent a text to Joshua.

I need to meet with you and Brutus. Important.

I paced the floor, waiting for his response. It came about three minutes later.

What's up?

Tell you tomorrow. What time can you meet?

10:30. My office or at the Underground?

Office.

I tossed my phone back on the couch once that was over. Turning the television on, I flipped to the sports channel to get the latest updates on football games I'd missed that day ... at least that was what I told myself. I really just needed a distraction while Resha was in the shower. I had the biggest urge to barge into the bathroom and wrap my arms around her and let her know that there was nothing and no one that I'd let get to her but I held back. There was so much I was still piecing together in my own mind.

Earlier that day, her reaction to the building where we took pictures had me wondering. The same fear I'd picked up in her eyes later at her condo, I'd seen as she stared at what she thought had been a completely abandoned building. And that had been way before she was even aware of what'd taken place at her home. Also, I watched her as she answered Brookes' questions. He'd asked her if there was anyone she could think of who would've done this. Her immediate answer was *no*, but I'd seen awareness pop up in her eyes as if there was something she'd put together but didn't want to say out loud. Resha held a lot of secrets. And that wasn't even including the fact that she was so hesitant in telling Destiny, her cousin, adopted sister, best friend, and part-time business partner.

Before my thoughts could delve too deeply into what was truly going on inside of Resha's head, the buzzer from downstairs sounded. Moving to the door, I pressed the button, allowing me to see an image of the Chinese takeout delivery guy. I buzzed him up and paid for our food.

By the time Resha was out of the shower and dressed in a matching pumpkin pajama set, I had the food plated and set out on the coffee table.

"I've got Diet Coke, regular Coke, apple juice, and sparkling water."

"Diet Coke," she responded.

I grabbed a glass and a can of diet soda along with a bottle of water for myself.

"Feeling better?" I questioned as I placed her drink in front of her plate, opening the can and pouring it into the glass for her.

"Much," she sighed and smiled at me.

I pressed my palm against my chest because that tightening feeling started happening again. Unconsciously, I moved closer to her, using my hand to rub her back. She leaned into me, sighing.

"Thanks for letting me stay here. I'll have to do another photoshoot for you as payback."

I growled. "You don't owe me shit for this. We're going to get whoever this fucker is that broke into your home."

She looked up at me, pausing the bite of the chicken and broccoli she ordered. "How do you know?"

"Because I do. And I don't ever say shit I don't mean."

A small, pondering smile crossed those full lips, and I leaned down to kiss them.

"Have you always been like this?" she questioned once her eyes opened.

"Like what?" I took a forkful of the vegetable fried rice I ordered.

"A straight shooter. So assured and ... I don't know ... caring?"

I stopped chewing to look over at her, staring for a moment. I analyzed the words she just used to describe me. Shrugging, I responded, "I'm just me."

"Add modest to the list, too," she laughed.

We finished eating, and after placing the dishes in the dishwasher, I moved to the couch, pulling her in my arms, which she came willingly. She nestled her head against my chest, sighing contentedly as I wrapped my arms fully around her.

"You want to talk about why you're so hesitant to call Destiny?" I finally asked into the silence.

Her arm tightened around mine and she dipped her head, burying it farther inside of my chest.

"I'll take that as a no. How about whatever it was that you were holding back from Brookes?"

Her head rose and she gave me a questioning look. "How do you know I was holding something back?"

"I could read it on your face, a stór. Do you know who broke into your home?"

She shook her head. "I don't know who it was, but ..."

"You have an idea."

"Not quite. I just ... I've been getting strange emails for a few months now."

I lifted her chin higher to meet my glare. "What kinds of emails? From who?"

"Creepy emails. I get a lot of emails, DMs, and comments on my blog from readers and followers. Mostly its women interested in fashion or who listen to the podcast. Fans. But this one person has been sending strange emails, saying that they liked the outfit I wore that day. I remember the first one was like six months ago, maybe, and it felt odd because I hadn't even posted anything online that day of what I wore."

"That was the first but not the last email."

"Not at all. I didn't get them that frequently, so I didn't think much of it, honestly. Between traveling, attending work events, the podcast, helping at the shelter from time to time, I just pushed it to the back of my mind. The messages would come only a few times a month or so. Then they increased to a couple of times per week over the last few of months. He always signed the messages off with 'S'. And then there was the feeling that I was being watched ..."

"What?" I barked.

"I would feel it sometimes when I went out to my car in the garage of my building. I wouldn't see anyone around, at least not anyone out of the ordinary, but the hairs on the back of my neck would stand."

"S ..." Connor ruminated, thinking. "Do you know anyone whose name starts with the letter S?"

She shook her head. "I mean, I meet a lot of people for work events and whatnot. I'm sure I've met a ton of Stevens, Samuels, or last name Smiths, or whatever, but no one is ringing a bell. No one stands out as overly interested, or as making me uncomfortable."

"And what about your neighbor?"

Her brows knitted. "Jarvis?"

My jaw clenched at the sound of his name. "Him. You said earlier that he gives you creepy vibes and that he's far more interested in you than you are in him, right?"

She looked off, trying to wrap her mind around the suspicion that her next door neighbor could be responsible for all of this.

"But his name doesn't start with an S."

"Could be a nickname or just something he used to throw you off. He knows where you live, he has access to the parking garage where your car is parked regularly. He saw us out this morning. That could've sparked his anger and jealousy to push him to break into your home while we were out."

"You really think so?"

"It's a thought." A thought that I'd be looking into as soon as my eyes opened tomorrow. I didn't like that motherfucker from the moment I spotted him that morning. Considering this new information Resha just told me, he was the first person who came to mind.

"How do we even know whoever sent those emails, and had the flowers delivered are the same person?"

"Flowers? What flowers?"

Her eyes widened. "Oh yeah, about a week or so ago, there was a vase of white and pink lilies delivered to my door. I thought it was a brand I'd worked with at first but then I opened the letter. It was signed 'S' just like the emails and the note on my car."

"Do you still have it?"

Resha shook her head. "I threw it out because I couldn't stand seeing it. Just looking at that vase and those flowers made my skin crawl." She shuddered and tucked her face deeper into my chest.

I reached around, tightening my hold around her body. And before I thought better of it, I shifted until she was lying underneath me on the couch. Lowering my head, I pressed a kiss to her lips, which she eagerly received. I pulled back from the kiss and hovered over her, gazing into her eyes. I moved my hand underneath the cotton material of her pajama bottoms, feeling the softness of her skin, moving up to cup her breast.

A tiny moan pushed passed her lips.

"I can make you forget everything that's happened tonight. Or, I can make you forget your own name. Or, even better, I can have you screaming my name at the top of your lungs. Which one do you want me to do, a stór?" My voice was deep, laced with determination.

Resha sat up on her elbows, rising until her face was only a few centimeters from mine, and licked my lips before responding, "All of the above."

****

Resha

I think I just woke a sleeping giant.

Connor's nostrils flared, and as soon as the words departed my mouth, his lips covered mine, pulling a moan of need and want from me. His large hand tightened around my breast almost painfully, but the feeling prompted a flooding in my panties. His calloused thumb rubbed across my nipple and my brain stopped functioning for at least a heartbeat or two.

"We'll have to take this upstairs. There's not nearly enough room on this couch to do all that I want to do to you."

That statement fell around my ears and it was as if someone had turned the temperature up in the apartment by at least ten degrees. Connor helped me up the stairs while effortlessly stripping me of every ounce of clothing, one by one. He'd barely even touched me and all the fear, questions about who had broken into my home, and especially the loneliness that had felt like a blanket following me everywhere I'd gone for the last few years now dissipated.

He flicked on the light in the bedroom, allowing himself to see me fully in the nude. I didn't feel the need or want to hide from him. And the way those hazel eyes of his ate me up from head to toe had me standing proudly in front of him. As he moved closer, my hands unashamedly went for the belt buckle of the jeans he wore, undoing the belt along with the clasp holding his pants together.

Connor's lips fell to mine as his hands continued to make their acquaintance with my breasts. I moaned into his mouth and felt the moisture in between my legs increasing. Just when my legs began to shake with the anticipation of the moment, Connor stooped low, bending to pick me up and move to the bed. He used his broad body to separate my thighs, inching in closer between them to hover over me.

"I feel safe with you," I confessed in a whisper.

A genuine smile crossed his lips and he kissed me again before pulling back. "That's my purpose in your life." He pressed a kiss to one corner of my mouth before moving over and kissing the opposite corner. Lowering his head, he moved his lips closer to my ear. "To wipe away the loneliness that lingers in your eyes, to keep you safe, and …" He kissed my cheek and earlobe before pulling back.

"And what?" I questioned.

But he didn't answer. Not verbally. Instead, he kissed the life out of me before spreading my knees apart with his hands. Lowering himself down the length of my body, he brought his face to the most intimate part of my body.

I gasped because just the feel of his warm breath caressing the sensitive flesh that resided down there almost felt like too much. But that was nothing compared to the sensations that flowed through me when he opened his mouth.

"Holy shit!" I cursed when he began licking the folds of my labia. My hips bucked instinctively, and Connor used his hands to hold my body in place, exactly where he wanted me. I had thought my memory of our time together in New York was sharp and clear. The many dreams I'd had over the past three months, of that one night, were a constant reminder of what we'd shared there. And still, still, I wasn't ready for Connor's mouth on my body again.

My toes dug into the soft bed and I reached down with one hand, letting my fingers entangle in the silky strands of his hair while my hips attempted to raise, to get closer to his mouth. When his tongue repeatedly moved over my clitoris, I let out a howl that I didn't even know was there. My breathing quickened and my first orgasm of the night felt just in reach.

"C-C-Connor!" I bellowed when he clamped around my sensitive button, giving it his full attention. My body shook, my hand tightened in his hair, and my back arched into the feeling of pure bliss. My orgasm washed over me, taking with it any remaining thoughts of what happened earlier in the day, fear of possible stalkers, and images of creepy neighbors. All I felt was wrapped up in Connor's warmth. And as I opened my eyes, all I saw was his face, looking down on mine, observing me, searching my gaze for something only he knew.

Cupping his face, I brought his lips to mine. I tasted myself on him. How that made me hotter, I had no idea. I'd never enjoyed tasting my essence on another man's lips. But truthfully, no other man had actually gotten me off with his mouth either.

Connor's hands were everywhere on my body, squeezing and caressing my breasts, then rubbing my stomach, moving over my hips and firmly gripping my thighs. I was completely surrounded and caught up in a haze of him, and I was certain of one thing: I didn't ever want to come out.

My hands moved under his shirt, feeling the hard muscles that resided there. Pushing it up, he assisted by raising his arms, allowing me to pull the shirt over his head, completely exposing the top half of his body. And even though I'd seen it just that morning while taking pictures of him, his bare chest didn't fail to turn me on in ways that I didn't realize were even possible. Moving in closer, I locked eyes with him before reaching my tongue out and licking one of his nipples.

I watched as the veins in his neck bulged and his jaw went rigid. His hand went to the back of my neck, holding me in place. He liked my mouth on him. In that moment, I felt freer to explore his body with my mouth and hands. Other men I'd been with hadn't liked their nipples licked or touched for fear it made them look less manly or whatever. Connor reveled in it.

Pushing the tops of his undone jeans down past his hips, I watched as his thick rod sprang out from its confinement.

I gasped and pulled back at the sight of the tip of his aroused cock. How could I have forgotten about the Prince Albert piercing? I licked my bottom lip, swallowing at the sight of the rounded metal bar with two rings on either end, remembering how this little instrument had enhanced our coming together in New York.

I peered up at Connor—the expression on his face was serious yet tender.

"Let me make you forget your own name, a stór," he implored while intertwining his hand in my hair and pushing me back down against the pillows. With his hand still in my hair, he tugged, causing my back to arch slightly. He lowered his lips to my neck, allowing his teeth to trace the sensitive skin that resided there. With his free hand, he managed to maneuver the rest of the way out of his pants, kicking them to the floor before using his knees to separate my legs even farther apart.

   I felt stretched as soon as he began to enter me. This was a feeling I very much remembered from our night in New York. At the time, I told myself it was just because I hadn't been with anyone in a very long time. Now, I knew the truth was that Connor's just big all over.

"Breathe, Resha," he instructed.

I pushed out the breath I'd been holding on a shudder.

Connor continued to push inside of me and my breathing hitched again.

"Resha, breathe."

Who the hell is Resha? My mind swirled with questions but no answers came because all there was was this feeling of being fed and filled by the man holding me in his arms.

When he pushed all the way inside, I let out a shaky breath and moved my hands to his already receding hips.

"Oooh," I bellowed as the metal bar attached to his shaft grazed against my G-spot. It felt as if an entire bolt of lightning filled with spine tingling pleasure zapped through my body. With each stroke he made, that feeling overcame me over and over again.

When he lifted my leg by the knee, moving it damn near my armpit, allowing himself to penetrate even deeper, my entire body began to shake uncontrollably. I could hear words or sounds coming from my mouth, but for the life of me, I couldn't discern whether or not they made any damn sense.

This man was actually making me lose my damn mind.

My second orgasm was inevitable and it rippled through me like a tidal wave rips through the beach, barreling through any and everything standing in its way. The constant pressure from Connor's ring pressing against my G-spot, the added tension of his thumb rubbing against my clit, and the massaging of my inside walls from the pulse of his shaft all sent me spiraling into oblivion.

It had to be the longest and most intense orgasm I'd ever experienced. Heightened by the fact that I wasn't alone. Peering up at Connor, I recognized the straining muscles in his neck, the protruding veins in his forehead, and the darkening color of his eyes. He was also coming. He lowered and buried his head into the crook of my neck, grunting as we both came together.

I don't even remember what happened after that. All I remember is falling into pure euphoria, enveloped by the warmth I'd only felt with this man.

Chapter Ten

Connor

Peeling my eyes open, one by one, I glanced down to find my arm wrapped around Resha's shoulders as her head laid across my chest. Small snores escaped her open mouth as she slept. And while I knew she'd be pissed about it, I reached for my phone, and snapped a picture of her in this position. I wanted to remember her like this, all mine, first thing in the morning, her hair wild after a night of being fucked thoroughly.

Sex shouldn't be that damn good.

That was my final thought of the night. After my third orgasm because I somehow couldn't keep my hands off this woman. Even once I'd given her a number of orgasms, and had finished myself, my body had turned into the fucking Energizer bunny. As if she had flicked on a switch I hadn't even known existed. And once it was turned on the shit couldn't be extinguished. I probably kept her up until two in the morning with some part of my body—hands, mouth, cock—in or on her, pulling from her orgasm, screams, and shouts of pleasure.

But now it was nearly eight in the morning, which was sleeping in for me. And while I never lingered in bed upon first waking up, I wanted nothing more than to stay there, beneath those sheets, preferably with Resha writhing beneath me for the next few hours.

"Mmm," she moaned, pulling me from my ruminations. "Morning," she murmured against my chest.

"How'd you know I was awake?" I questioned, because I hadn't move too much as to not disturb her sleeping.

"Your breathing pattern changed." She sat up and covered her mouth with her hand to let out a yawn.

Reaching out, I allowed my fingers to trace the side of her face, pushing a few stray hairs out of the way.

Resha frowned as she touched her hair, and rolled her eyes. "I can't believe I let you pull my weave last night. Now it's all messed up."

I chuckled. "That's not all you let me pull, darlin'."

I laughed harder when she swatted her hand at me.

"At least I had an appointment for today anyway."

It was my turn to frown. "What time?"

Her brows pinched together in thought. "Umm, ten-thirty. What time is it now?"

"Almost eight."

She nodded. "Good. I still have enough time to make it to the shop."

"*We* have enough time."

Her forehead wrinkled and she cocked her head to the side. "What do you mean *we*?"

I reached up and kissed her forehead before fully sitting up and moving the sheets from over me.

"Just what I said. You're not going anywhere alone." Rising, I stretched my arms over my head and lengthened my neck, working the kinks out from sleep. I didn't miss the way Resha's eyes traced over my body. I usually slept naked, and of course, I hadn't seen a need to change that routine last night.

"Uh, um, what?"

I grinned. "I'll get started on a pot of coffee."

Grabbing a pair of boxers out of my dresser, I put them on before heading downstairs.

"Hair ... that's what we were talking about." She snapped her fingers as if coming out of a stupor. "I'm still going to my hair appointment!" she called down.

"Never said you weren't," I responded from the kitchen. "You just won't be going alone," I firmly added.

She might not like it but Resha wouldn't be going anywhere by herself until we found out whoever it was that was stalking her.

"Shit," I grunted when I realized the time and that I was going to be late to my meeting with Joshua and Brutus that morning. As Resha made her way to the bathroom to shower and get dressed, I headed back upstairs to grab my phone and tell Josh we needed to push back our meeting by about thirty minutes. Luckily, he was free to do so. Smirking at the phone, I grabbed a fresh set of clothing and headed to the bathroom to accompany Resha in the shower, since killing two birds with one stone seemed to make the most sense, and I wanted to hear her scream my name again that morning before we had to leave.

****

Resha

"Why are we at Townsend Industries on a Sunday morning?" I questioned as I looked across at Connor from the passenger seat of his car. As it turned out, the motorcycle wasn't Connor's only method of transportation. I only discovered this when I told him that I was not about to ride around on a motorcycle all day after getting my hair done, as it would completely defeat the purpose. That was when he informed me that the champagne-colored Infiniti QX80 I'd parked my car next to the night before in his building's garage actually belonged to him. I still tried to tell him that I could drive myself to my appointment, but he wasn't having it. And he reminded me that whoever was stalking me, obviously knew what my car looked like and could somehow be following me. After that, I decided it was best to allow Connor to chauffeur me around, at least for the time being.

"We're here to talk with Josh and his head of security."

"About what?" I frowned, not understanding what they could have to do with me.

Connor gave me a curious expression. "What do you mean about what?" He didn't allow me time to answer his question as he turned the car off and got out, shutting the driver's side door behind him.

I watched as he circled the front of the car, coming to the passenger side and pulling the door open for me. I hated the way I inwardly swooned as he took my hand in his and helped me down from the car. I wasn't used to chivalry.

"Thank you."

He nodded and placed a hand at the small of my back as we moved closer to the elevator.

"This isn't the main entrance, is it?" I questioned. I'd been to the building once before to meet Destiny for lunch, but I'd entered through the front entrance where just about everyone who came in the building entered ... or so I thought.

"Private entrance. Only family and security use it."

"And close friends, obviously," I added, while adjusting the baseball cap I wore over my hair. I'd insisted on wearing one of Connor's hats since he'd sprung on me that we would be making a stop before heading to my hair appointment. I wish I'd known it would be at Townsend Industries, I would've tried to look a little more presentable. Something about being in this building made me feel like I needed to pull it together and look my best.

"You look fine," Connor told me low in my ear, his hand moving to my waist, pulling me closer.

I glanced up at him through narrowed eyes. "Easy for you to say. You look great in a T-shirt, jeans, and leather jacket. Like you just stepped off the pages of a magazine shoot. Me? Not so much."

The scowl that appeared on his face was instant, but the door of the elevator popped open at the same time. However, Connor's expression kept my gaze locked on his.

He lowered, getting right in my face. "The next time you say some dumb shit like that, I don't give a damn where we are, I will strip your ass naked, put you over my damn knee, and redden your ass until you beg me to stop. Understood?" he growled.

Oh God!

"Do. You. Understand?"

I pulled my trembling bottom lip in between my teeth and nodded. And that was when I heard someone clearing their throat.

Peeling my gaze away from Connor's, I gasped at the sight of another burly man standing in front of us. This wasn't Joshua

Townsend, I realized as I peered up and up at this man. He was about the same height as Connor, but broader.

"Brutus." Connor nodded.

"O'Brien, good to see you again." His words were friendly but the heavy scowl on his face belied his words.

This was the family's head of security, Brutus. I'd seen him before, plenty of times, over Destiny and Tyler's house, or out with the family. As we stepped onto the elevator, I hoped to God he hadn't heard what Connor had just said to me.

"Ms. McDonald," Brutus greeted, dipping his head.

"Brutus ..." I cleared my throat. "H-How are you?"

He didn't answer with words—another nod of his head before punching in a code on the elevator, allowing the doors to shut and take us to the top floor of the building. As soon as the doors opened, we were greeted by a smiling Joshua.

I was almost stunned as I watched Joshua pull Connor into a bear hug, to which Connor shoved him back, causing Joshua to burst out in laughter. The mutual respect and friendship was easily seen between these two.

"What's up, O'Brien?" Joshua eventually questioned before turning to me. His eyes widened slightly. "Resha? How're you?"

I grinned. "Hey, Joshua. I'm doing well. How about yourself?"

"I'd be better if I knew why my old friend dragged me out of bed so early on a Sunday morning." His green eyes moved back over to Connor as Brutus moved past me.

"It's not early," Connor quipped.

"To you it's not, but for me, anything before eleven in the morning on a Sunday is early a fuck."

"Watch your language around my lady," Connor challenged.

I blinked and looked between Connor and Joshua, who was now grinning as if he'd discovered some secret between the two of us. I would've had a mind to choke Connor for what he'd just said, but admittedly, I didn't mind being called his lady, his woman, his *whatever.*

I could mentally kick myself for being so damned sprung.

"Excuse me, Resha. Didn't know the big guy's ears were so sensitive," Joshua joked.

I cleared my throat and again adjusted the baseball cap on my head. "No worries. This one curses like a sailor anyway, so I don't know why he's fronting now."

Connor glared down at me with a raised eyebrow. *Damn, he looks so handsome when he does that.*

"Anyway, had I known w-we were coming up here, I would've dressed a little d-differently," I stammered, turning my attention to Joshua. "Excuse the hat. I, uh, had a hair situation this morning." In spite of myself, my eyes guiltily shot over to Connor before moving back to Joshua.

My stomach dropped when I saw the grin on his face grow. "Yeah. Kay often has one of those *hair situations* you're talking about," he snickered.

My face flamed in embarrassment.

Connor growled but Joshua didn't pay him any attention as he strolled down the hall in the same direction Brutus had disappeared. For a man of his size, I was surprised at how swiftly and quietly he could move.

"We've got a situation," Connor started as soon as we entered what I presumed was Joshua's spacious office. For a minute, I was taken aback by the nearly three hundred and sixty degree view the office offered of the city of Williamsport. But Josh and Connor both seemed to take it all in stride as we moved to the couch that sat opposite his large, wooden desk.

"What's up?"

Connor placed his hand on my knee, making direct contact with my skin, and my body instantly warmed since I was wearing a pair of jeans that had a rip at the knees. The movement wasn't lost on Joshua either, as his attention dipped to Connor's hand before rising up to look at his friend again.

"Someone broke into Resha's home yesterday."

Joshua's face immediately changed from playful to serious. The change was so swift I had to blink just to make sure I wasn't seeing things.

"You contacted the police?"

Connor nodded. "Personally called Brookes to get his ass over there."

I looked to Connor, confused. I didn't know he'd made a private call to Detective Brookes. I'd just assumed he was the detective the police station sent out to handle this type of thing.

"He had them take prints and forensics is running the DNA on the mess that fucker left in her bed …" He paused, glancing at me when I began squirming.

I still didn't want to think about a stranger in my home, getting in my bed and jerking off. It pissed me off, scared me, and disgusted me all at the same damn time. I didn't know what telling Joshua all of this was going to do.

"He made sure they were thorough, but he's still a cop and cops have—"

"Procedures and rules," Joshua finished.

"Right. Which slows them down. I want to find this fucker now. We think we know who it is."

"That's where I come in, right?" Brutus interjected, emerging from the opposite corner of Joshua's office.

I'd forgotten he was even there.

"Yup," Connor responded.

"You know whatever you need is at your disposal," Joshua added. "Besides …" he looked over at me, "Resha is family. I'm surprised Destiny isn't here with Tyler."

I inhaled deeply, having almost forgotten how close this all was to Destiny. "She doesn't know. And please don't tell her," I blurted out.

Three pairs of confused eyes settled on me, demanding answers.

Shit.

Just one of these men's intense glares would be too much to handle, but all three had me wanting to bolt for the door.

The only thing holding me in place was Connor's hand still firmly planted on my knee.

"Destiny's busy, and if she finds out, she's going to tell Aunt Donna who's already sick and she doesn't need to be worried about me. I'll tell them after all of this blows over."

"Resha—" Connor started.

I shook my head. "No. Destiny can't know. I don't want her to know," I implored, staring Connor directly in the eye.

The edges of his eyes wrinkled as he scowled at me, appearing confused and angered by my reluctance to include my cousin in on what was going on in my life. Turning from Connor, I looked to Joshua.

"I'm sorry, but I'm asking you not to tell Destiny, either. And that means keeping this from your wife and your brother. Please, I just don't want …" I broke off, not wanting to explain my reasoning to the men in this room because I truly didn't understand it myself. All I knew was that this was something I was certain was going to blow over anyhow, so why get my family involved?

Connor's hand squeezed my knee, and I looked back to him. He didn't say anything but his eyes spoke for him.

"We'll discuss this later," they said, and I pushed out a heavy breath, half thankful that he wouldn't press this issue right then, but still worried that eventually he would push for more. For me to open up.

"I won't tell Kay or Tyler ... for now."

I swallowed and dipped my head at Joshua. "Thank you."

"Tell me what you know," Brutus interjected, moving behind Joshua with his massive arms folded over his chest.

I shrugged. "I don't know much." I glanced over to my left before speaking again.

"Start with what you do know."

"I started receiving some strange emails about six months ago ..." I went on to tell them the same story I'd told Connor the night before.

"And you kept this information from Brookes?"

"I didn't even put it together until I was talking to Connor last night." I turned to him for comfort, and he wrapped his arm around my shoulders.

"We think we might know who it is."

"Who?" Joshua asked.

"Her neighbor. First name's Jarvis …"

Within minutes, Brutus and the four of us were sitting around Joshua's office table staring at my neighbor's personal information on the screen of Brutus' laptop. I had no clue how he was able to pull up Jarvis' information so quickly but he was able to not only get his full name, address and occupation, but also medical, dental, and school records.

"His first name isn't Jarvis," I exclaimed, surprised that the man I'd been calling Jarvis for the past two years was actually named Sebastian. "Sebastian Jarvis Caldwell."

"S," Connor stated grimly.

Our eyes caught and my stomach dropped.

The rest of that meeting was a bit of a blur for me. I heard Connor mention something about making a visit, but I just assumed he meant going to the police or Detective Brookes about what we found out. If this was true, hopefully the police could put two and two together and this would all be over. Regardless, to think the neighbor I'd been living down the hall from, had ridden in the same elevator with, the one who I thought of as a little creepy but pretty much harmless, was the person stalking me, scared the hell out of me.

Yet, it did make sense. His first name matching up with the way my stalker signed off on all his emails. Jarvis, or Sebastian rather, had access to my building as a resident there and the garage where I parked my car. He could've been following me in the parking lot garage of our building and just hiding from plain sight.

"We need to head out," Connor informed the room.

Glancing over at the clock, I saw we only had about twenty minutes before my scheduled hair appointment. We said our good-byes and returned to the garage.

"How long do you think your appointment will take?" he questioned, climbing into the driver's seat of his SUV, as I buckled myself in.

"No more than two hours. Missy's pretty good about getting clients in and out, and it's Sunday. She only takes two clients on Sundays."

Connor nodded while he pulled up the car's navigation system. "Plug in the address. I'll drop you off. I have to run an errand, and then I can swing back to pick you up."

"I can just grab an Uber back, it won—" I firmed my lips shut at the thunderous look he gave me.

"I'll drop you off at the salon and then pick you up once I'm done. My errand won't be too long. And you won't be getting into any fucking Uber, Lyft, or other car sharing service until we know the bastard who broke into your home is taken care of."

I shivered at the words *taken care of*. He didn't say, "*until he's behind bars,*" or, "*until the police arrest him.*"

No.

Taken care of were his words, and it was on the top of my tongue to ask him what he specifically meant by that, but I held back.

"Fine," I finally agreed with my arms folded over my chest.

Connor snorted as we pulled out of the Townsend Industries' parking garage.

Chapter Eleven

Connor

It'd been quite a while since I waited in the backseat of someone's car for them to come out. And as I laid there, prone, in the backseat of Sebastian Jarvis Caldwell's F-150 truck, I had to control the anger coursing through my body. Just after taking Resha to her hair appointment, I called Brutus back for him to give me the information he was able to pull up on Caldwell. Turns out, he had a spotty past.

Caldwell came from a well-to-do family, but he himself was a slacker. He'd been a middle school teacher for a few years right out of undergrad, but when it was found out that he'd actually been having an affair with one of the eighth grade students, he was abruptly fired, and rightfully so. However, his family's money kept him out of jail and off the sex offender registry list. But that didn't slow Sebastian down. A few years later, in Sebastian's old neighborhood there were reports of a Peeping Tom in the area. The police never caught the guy but there were two neighbors who swore they saw Sebastian running from the scene where the peeping took place. Unfortunately, he'd had an alibi that his mother just so happened to back up. And surprise, surprise, the Peeping Tom seemed to go away once Sebastian moved out of that neighborhood. That move brought him to Resha's building, where he began going by his middle name, Jarvis.

The more I found out about this guy, the more the pieces seemed to fall into place. Just when my patience was starting to wane, a shadow befell the backseat of the car, moving to the front. I ceased breathing, remaining completely still as Jarvis or Sebastian, whatever the fuck his name was, pulled open the driver side door and climbed in behind the wheel.

Before he could insert the key into the ignition, I sprang up from behind him and circled his neck with my right arm, pulling him hard against the headrest of his seat. My left arm came up to hook onto my right shoulder, completing the circle and leaving his windpipe completely vulnerable to whatever I wanted to do with it.

"Wh-Wha—" he struggled to talk.

"Don't speak unless spoken to. That's the one hope you have of saving your own life right now, understood?"

He tried to nod, and I took that as a yes. Reaching forward with my left hand, I lowered the sun visor and pushed the mirror component open to allow me to see Sebastian's face, but due to my position he couldn't see mine.

"I'm going to ask you a series of questions. They'll be yes or no questions. You're going to blink once for no and twice for yes. Do you understand?"

He went to nod his head, and I tightened the hold I had around his neck.

"You don't seem to fucking understand English. Is that the case, Sebastian? Do I need to speak another fucking language for you to understand what I'm saying? Blink once for no and twice for yes."

Staring in the mirror, I watched his eyelids close and open twice.

"Good. Now, understand this. This hold that I have around your neck currently isn't life threatening. I can tighten it and eventually the pressure against your windpipe will cut off oxygen flow to your brain, causing you to pass out. If I were to let you go, you'd still live after that and be fine. But, if I continue to hold for say … one minute … two minutes … five minutes … ten minutes, you would die. And trust me when I say it would be the worst minutes of your life before you passed out. But, Sebastian, *you* are the one who is going to determine whether you live or die today. Understood?"

I paused and glared into his eyes in the mirror. He blinked twice.

"Great. Let's get started. Did you break into Resha's home yesterday?"

His entire body stiffened and his eyes widened in horror—not that they weren't already filled with immense fear, but this was a renewed, stunned type of horror. He blinked once.

"Do you know who did?"

Another solitary blink. I'd expected him to answer no to those questions anyway, but I wanted to look him in the eye as he answered.

"Have you been sending her emails?"

One single blink.

"What about a bouquet of flowers? Did you send her a bouquet of flowers, Sebastian?"

One blink.

"Do you find Resha attractive?"

A double blink. And even though I found his answer to be truthful, my arms tightened around his neck.

"Put your fucking hands down!" I demanded when his hands moved to my arms as if he was going to try to push me off of him. If he knew anything about fighting he would've known that that move was no use anyway. I had him exactly where I wanted him and could do anything to him, including take his very life.

And when I began to seriously consider doing just that, a knock on the passenger's side door window stopped me. I let out an annoyed breath before reaching over and pressing the button to unlock the door.

Sebastian, aka Jarvis, began squirming in his seat, trying to look over at the man who was now getting into the passenger seat beside him, shutting the door.

"I see you got started without me," Brutus said over his shoulder.

I shrugged. "Couldn't resist."

"You get anything?"

Frowning, I looked back to the mirror. "Not much," I admitted, my heart sinking as if filled with the realization that this guy likely wasn't Resha's stalker, in spite of the feeling I had earlier.

"Where were you yesterday, Sebastian?" Brutus questioned.

I loosened the hold I had around his neck, until my arms dropped to my sides, but when he didn't respond quick enough I slapped the back of his head. "Answer him!"

"I-I-I—"

"Use your fucking words!" I demanded, slapping him again, so hard his forehead banged against the steering wheel.

"I w-was out all day."

"Out where?" Brutus followed up.

"W-With some friends."

"You don't have any friends."

Sebastian's eyes went to the mirror as he peered up at me, now able to see me in the mirror. His eyebrows raised with recognition. I didn't give a shit about being recognized. If he was in any way smart, he'd realize the fact that I hadn't disguised my face wasn't a good look for him. But again, this guy wasn't the cream of the crop when it came to intelligence.

"Phone records indicate you made a call to a Ms. Wendy Mansion. A well-known Madame. So you spent the day with an escort?"

Sebastian sputtered, his eyes bulged, and he shook his head.

"What did I tell you about lying, Sebastian?" I warned.

He immediately ceased his denial and pointed his gaze at the floor of his truck.

"He was out most of the day. And I'm betting his phone records verify it. I'll get in contact with Ms. Mansion herself. Better yet, how about we take a trip to go see her?" Brutus proposed even though it really wasn't a question.

Sebastian, the fool he was, however, didn't realize this. "I-I can't," he stammered. "I'm supposed to be going to my momma's today."

"See your *momma* some other time," I demanded. "Sebastian, you're about to take a trip with my friend, here. And he's going to call me and tell me how that trip went. What he finds out will determine whether you live or die."

"He—" He started to scream for help and tried to open the door but he was much too slow.

I again wrapped one arm around his neck, pulling the door closed and locking it with the other hand.

"That was just fucking stupid." I squeezed his neck, cutting off the oxygen to his brain by blocking his windpipe but not crushing it like I wanted to. Only once he passed out did I let go.

"Go ahead, I'll handle this and call you later when I have more information."

I sighed and dipped my head in Brutus' direction, getting out of Sebastian's backseat. Slamming the door behind me, I felt defeated. I'd been all but certain this son of a bitch was the bastard behind whoever was stalking Resha, but my suspicions weren't quite panning out. Besides the fact that Sebastian seemed to have an alibi for the day before, something in his eyes told me he wasn't the stalker. He appeared too surprised when I mentioned the emails and flower arrangements sent to Resha. He may have a spotty history with women, and Resha was probably right when she said he gave her creeper vibes, but that didn't make him her stalker.

****

Resha

"I love it." I grinned in the mirror as I swung my head from side to side, admiring the new weave I just had installed. My stylist had done a long, curly style. The long, curly locks fell a few inches past my shoulders and there was a pop of color with the honey brown highlights around my face while the rest of the hair was a dark, deep brown.

I sighed, feeling a little more like myself than when I'd first walked into Missy's shop.

"You look good, girl," Missy purred while fluffing the sides of my hair. "Not that you don't always look good, but, chile, that mess you came in with this morning." She clucked her tongue and sucked her teeth, shaking her head. "Looking like who did it and ran. If I didn't know any better I'd say you was up late doing something you had no business doing."

I rolled my eyes because I knew Missy was fishing for information. Connor hadn't been shy about escorting me into the shop before dropping me off. Nor had he been shy about giving me a departing kiss on the lips before reminding me not to try to order an Uber, and that he'd be here within the next two hours to pick me up.

"But I know someone's still on her celibacy kick … at least that's the last I heard," Missy continued to pry.

"Hey, Missy, can you take some pictures of me and my hair so I can post on Instagram?" I questioned, ignoring her previous comments.

"Sure thing." Missy took my phone and snapped at least a half a dozen images of me from different angles, allowing me enough poses and angles that I could go through and decide which images looked best for me to post.

"Ooh, I like that one," Missy exclaimed as she looked over my shoulder while I scrolled through the images.

"I think so, too. I'll post this one. Hey, come on in here with me so I can post you on my IG stories."

Missy, never one to turn down an opportunity to get the word out about her shop, was eager to join me in my Instagram stories.

"Hey, y'all, how's everyone's Sunday going so far?" I cheerily questioned into my phone screen. "I just got finished getting my hair styled by my girl, Missy." I wrapped my arm around her shoulder to bring her in closer. "Tell them about your shop, Missy."

"Hey, IG! I'm Missy, owner of Hair by Missy down on Kensington Street. If you're in the Williamsport area, come and check me out."

"Missy is the one who keeps my hair looking right at all times," I gushed, and spun my head around so the viewers could see my hair. "She also keeps my natural hair under this weave strong and healthy as well. I've posted all of her contact information in my bio. Check her out. Bye!" I waved to the camera before letting go of the button and posting the video to my stories. When I peered up from my phone, my breath caught as my gaze locked with Connor's angry hazel eyes.

I frowned, wondering what had him looking so upset.

Missy must've picked up on the tension as well because even she, queen of running her mouth, piped down.

"Thanks, Missy," I stated to break up the silence. "I'll call you later this week to make another appointment in a few weeks or so." I waved and headed out, leaving Missy's tip on the receptionist desk.

"Bye, girl." She waved.

Connor looked from me to Missy, nodding at her before pushing the glass door open for me to pass through. He didn't say anything as he walked me to the passenger side door of his car and held it open, his hand taking my arm to assist me into his vehicle.

"You want to explain what the hell that was in there?" he demanded as soon as he got into the vehicle himself.

"What?" I questioned, wrinkling my nose with a frown.

"That. Inside of the shop with posting your location and who you're with."

My head jerked backwards at the same time he pulled off from the parking spot that was directly in front of Missy's shop and started off in the direction of his place.

"I always do that. Missy gives me a huge discount for posting her on my IG because it gets her a lot of customers."

"And how often do you do that?"

"What? Post at Missy's?"

"Post your exact location."

"I know where you're going with this. Not often, okay?" I started to get pissed off. "Why the hell do I have to change my life and what I do for this jackass that I didn't invite into my world? What? Am I not supposed to go out anymore? Post about what I'm doing? That's like fifty percent of my job description."

Sighing, Connor looked over at me as we came to a red light. His hand moved to my shoulder, massaging it, and the strain that had threatened to consume my body began to recede just from his touch. "Look, we're going to get this son of a bitch, but in the meantime you're going to have to change some of your lifestyle."

I sucked my teeth and started to turn my head to look out the window, but Connor's hand caught me by the chin, pulling my attention back to him.

"We'll figure this out, and I swear on my life, this motherfucker won't ever touch you. I'll die before I let that happen. Unfortunately, you need to be a little more guarded for the time being, okay?"

My eyelids grew heavy as I peered into his gaze. His unflinching stare held my own eyes captive and I couldn't look away even if I'd wanted to … which I didn't. Simply staring at him made me feel safer, cared for, and most of all, wanted. Within a heartbeat, Connor's face was mere centimeters from my own and his lips were covering mine. He solidified his promise with a kiss, and I opened up to receive it.

My body flamed with need, my nipples hardened with desire, and I suddenly wanted nothing more than to feel him inside of me. Stalker be damned.

Connor, however, pulled back before we could get too carried away in the middle of traffic.

"A stór, I have zero qualms fucking you right here in the middle of this street, but the way your stomach is growling tells me I better get some food for us before you pass out."

I shrunk back, lowering my head and giggling at the sounds my stomach was making. I was hungry, seeing as how I hadn't had anything besides a cup of coffee that morning.

"There's a Jamaican place not too far from here."

"The Jerk Shack. Oh my God, they have the *best* jerk chicken and oxtails," I damn near moaned, my hunger growing by the second at the mere mention of the restaurant.

"Guess I know where we're ordering lunch," Connor quipped, making a sudden right turn onto the street where the Jerk Shack was.

"And we definitely need to go grocery shopping later on today," I commented.

I laughed at the confused look Connor gave me. "Why grocery shop when you can eat out?"

I shook my head. "Such a guy thing. We need to go shopping because I'm in the mood to cook. Eating out gets expensive anyway."

"Whatever, I'll order groceries once we get back home."

I shook my head. "No, this weekend is the last weekend of the farmer's market before it closes up for the winter. They have the best produce, and I wanted to get some of their canned fruit spreads to last me for the next few months."

Connor sighed but a small smile played at his lips and I knew I didn't need to do anymore asking.

"Thank you," I stated happily as we pulled into the parking lot of the Jamaican restaurant.

****

"How am I going to work tomorrow?" I suddenly paused from scraping the crumbs from Connor's plate into the disposal, and stared across the spacious kitchen to the circular dining table where he still sat.

"Can't you take a few days off?"

I shook my head adamantly. "Absolutely not. I have my usual weekly call with my virtual assistant, Shauna, every Monday morning. And then I have like three posts from brand endorsements I need to put up this week, and a photoshoot with a new sustainable apparel brand I'm working with. Plus, the podcast is supposed to resume this week so Destiny and I will have to meet up at the studio."

My shoulders slumped thinking about all that I had to do this week and the fact that the main computer I used to get my work done still laid in fragments on my office floor. I got angry all over again picturing the damage done to my apartment, mainly my office that was in disarray and the things I'd worked so hard for just broken and thrown about because some asshole thought ... I don't know what the hell he thought.

"Hey, hey, hey!" Connor exclaimed, coming over to me and wrapping his arms around my body, his hands taking the fork and porcelain dish out of my hands. "We're gonna put this in the dishwasher because I don't want you breaking all of my shit," he grunted.

I watched as he placed the dishes in the washer and closed it. Then he came to stand over me as I leaned back against the sink. His hands moved to either side of my body.

"Tell me what you need to make it happen."

I raised an eyebrow. "Just like that?"

He nodded. "Exactly like that. Tell me."

"I need a laptop at least. All of my files are saved on the cloud, and I can access them through my phone or my tablet but it's easier for me to see everything on a bigger screen."

"That's it?"

I blinked. "What do you mean *that's it?* That's important."

"I get that. What else do you need?"

"Oh ..." I mumbled, feeling silly for my outburst. "Um, space to work, obviously."

"Obviously. We've got plenty of space in my office. Only myself and my receptionist are there full-time. My other employees come and go as needed. You can use one of the offices we have available."

"Really?"

He pressed a kiss to my lips, and I tasted the red wine I paired with the meatloaf, parmesan and chive mashed potatoes, and roasted Brussel sprouts I'd made for dinner. Connor only had a sip of the wine from my glass.

"Yes, really," he responded, his voice heavy with emotion as his arms moved to my waist and he pressed forward, firming our bodies together.

My body responded without hesitation.

"Anything you need," he added before kissing me again.

My arms raised and my fingers intertwined in his hair, and suddenly all of the worries I seemed to have only a few moments ago were erased. The feeling of his kiss, and his hands slipping underneath the T-shirt I wore, replaced the worry.

A yelp escaped my lips when Connor's sudden move had me with my legs hoisted up around his waist. I gripped his shoulders tightly, concerned he'd drop me, as he moved from the kitchen, through the living room, and up the stairs to his bedroom. The ease of his movement astounded me. I wasn't a small girl, and while, for the most part, I'd come to terms with my size, intimate moments like this still had me on edge a little.

"Relax, a stór. I'd cut my own hair off before even thinking of dropping you," he growled and nipped my bottom lip with his teeth, causing me to giggle.

"Why do I feel so safe with you?" I questioned and then bit my tongue, not having meant to blurt that question out loud.

Connor's eyes darkened as he lowered our bodies to his bed. For a long while he just hovered over me. Then he leaned in and kissed my forehead, and I swear it was one of the most intimate things I'd ever experienced. The moment his lips touched my skin it was as if an electric current shot down from the top of my head to the tips of my toes, causing them to curl.

"Because you are," he finally declared.

I stared up at him and so many questions swirled around in my head. Like, how the hell was this even happening? How did I happen to walk into a random bar in a city halfway across the country after not wanting to go back to my hotel room solo, and end up in this man's arms and feeling so cherished all these months later?

I didn't have answers to those questions, nor did I truly want to hash out those answers while laying underneath

Connor's body. So instead of contemplating anymore, I reached up, cupping his face and raising my head to meet his lips. He controlled the kiss, but he did it with such enthusiasm and fervor that I didn't mind letting him have control.

I let my fingers dance in the softness of his hair, pulling the strands free of the band he always kept them tied up in. His hair fell around us, as if cocooning us in our own little world. I allowed my hands to travel down his chest and abdomen, and then up and underneath his shirt to feel the ripples of muscles that laid there beneath smooth skin.

A moan pushed through my lips when his hands did the same, only his hands were full of intent as they quickly undid the front clasp of my bra, allowing my breasts to spill out of their confinement. A gush of air made its way out of my lungs at the feeling of freedom that came with the undoing of the bra. Connor pushed the shirt I was wearing up and over my head, tossing it to the floor. The shirt was soon followed by the bra. And he lowered his mouth, covering one nipple with his hot mouth.

"Don't stop!" I pleaded, arching my back to receive more of what he was giving. My mouth grew dry due to the gasps and moans that continually escaped my lips from the pleasure he was feeding my body. He pinched and twisted my other nipple with his calloused hands to the point of pain. Somehow the pain merged with the pleasure of his mouth and I'd be damned if I didn't find my legs trembling and an orgasm ripping through my body.

Calling out the only name who'd ever given me an orgasm from playing with my breasts, my voice went hoarse. Yet, we were just getting started.

I barely had time to come down from my first orgasm when Connor's insistent hands were pulling at the skinny jeans I'd worn that day, removing them from my body. My lace panties were soon to follow.

I gasped at the tearing sound. "Connor!" I yelped. "Those are one of the only pair I have left," I reminded him seeing as how a certain stalker had left me with only a few of my own underwear."

"Too bad."

I would've called him on it not sounding apologetic in the least. I would have if he wasn't so damned fast in flipping our bodies over so that I straddled his. Not only that, but he hoisted me up, pushing himself down farther on the bed, somehow making it so that his face was directly beneath my aching core as I sat up on my knees.

Stunned by our new position, I leaned forward, placing my hands against the wooden headboard as I stared down, opened mouth at Connor. The mischievous sparkle in his eyes had my pussy dripping wet and he hadn't even touched my womanly folds as of yet.

But oh my God! Once he did, my head fell back and the yell that emanated from my throat was enough to disturb his neighbors. I was sure of it, and yet, I didn't care either. Connor ate me out like a man on a mission, and no one was about to get in his way.

"Fuuuuck!" I croaked out when his tongue whirled around my clitoris for what felt like the hundredth time. His hands held firmly to either side of my asscheeks, keeping me in place. If I had any fears about potentially crushing his airway in this position, they were laid to rest when Connor pushed my hips down, pressing my knees further into the bed and trapping me in place.

He was so good at what he was doing that my vision began to blur with tears. The man was actually bringing me to tears. I felt them streaming down my face as I repeatedly yelled out his name, begging him to stop, and yet, pleading with him to keep going. My hips began pumping wildly as the shaking in my thighs kicked up. My body needed its release like a plant needs water and sunlight to grow. I was on the verge of dying. I was sure of it. And when I opened my mouth to tell Connor this, a silent scream escaped my lips instead.

I rocked against Connor's incessant mouth as he tried to suck my very soul through my clitoris. It was all his for the taking when that second orgasm hit me like wildfire. My entire body shook and convulsed almost to the point of pain. My fingers ached from gripping the headboard so harshly and my feet strained against the curling of my toes.

"Holyyy fuck!" I cursed, beating my fist into the wall behind the headboard. I swear if I had the energy to beat Connor black and blue when his ass had the nerve, the *gall* to laugh at my reaction, I would have. But I was just about done.

Oh, but he wasn't.

Of course, he wasn't.

"Connor, what—" My question was cut short when I soon found myself positioned on all fours, Connor behind me. "Ooh," I hummed out, my back arching as he slid inside of me from behind.

"That's it, raise that ass in the air for me to see, baby," he groaned, and the walls of my vagina contracted at the rumbling in his voice.

On instinct, I began throwing it back on Connor, to which he responded by tightening his hands around my hips, and sliding in even deeper. My stomach muscles clenched and I tightened my fingers around the bedsheets, trying hard not to rip them completely from the bed. But the way Connor was moving behind me, and more importantly, *inside* of me, I wasn't going to be able to control myself.

"Oh God, that feels so gooood!" I groaned out, barely able to get the words out of my mouth.

"You like that, baby?"

My mouth opened to respond with a resounding, "*Yes!*" but all that came out was moan after moan. Especially when he adjusted his hips, angling them so that the tip of his cock ring bumped up against my G-spot. That damn bar, adding to an already incredibly pleasurable moment, I erupted again.

All I saw were stars in front of my eyes as the orgasm rocketed through every cell in my body. Behind me I could make out the faint sounds of Connor groaning, his arm flexing around my waist as he also succumbed to an orgasm. The intimacy of the moment was increased when he balled his free hand in my hair, pulling my head back enough to allow his lips to come crashing down on top of mine. Right then, I tried to discern whether I was the giver or receiver of all of this pleasure, but my thoughts were too scrambled.

It wouldn't be until later, as I laid down against Connor's sweaty chest, our bodies fighting to regulate our breathing, that I would realize I was both—I was both the giver of pleasure and the receiver of all the bliss Connor had to give.

Chapter Twelve

Resha

"You're not in your office. Did you go to a coffee shop?" Shauna questioned, only half paying attention to me as she adjusted the setting on her chair. "I know that little girl was in my office when I told her to stay out," she fussed, as she heightened her chair.

"Marley?"

Shauna's gaze returned to the screen as she rolled her hazel eyes. I couldn't help but notice they were a darker hazel than Connor's. "Who else?" Shauna responded. "I know my momma lets her come in here when she's babysitting her and I'm not around. I had three chocolate bars missing from my desk the other week."

I giggled at the fact that Shauna counted all of the chocolate bars she kept in her desk.

"Leave her alone. She's too cute to get mad at," I retorted about her almost four-year-old daughter. Shauna kept a picture of her on her desk—which I saw from time to time—and the little girl had interrupted our call on more than one occasion, barging into Shauna's office while we were on the line. And while my virtual assistant became embarrassed, apologizing for the intrusions, I was delighted seeing her mini-me in her element.

I lowered my gaze as that familiar pang of want raced through my chest. At thirty-seven I was questioning whether or not I would ever get to have the one thing I'd always wanted: a family of my own.

"So which coffee shop are you at? I thought you didn't like the last one you tried to work at."

I startled, being pulled from my self-pity induced stupor. "Oh, I'm not at a coffee shop. I, uh, a friend of mine let me borrow some office space."

"Are you considering renting out an office space?"

I shook my head. "No. My building, they're doing some renovations so it gets kind of loud during the day. I just figured I could use her office for a few weeks while the workers did whatever they were doing during the day." I shrugged to come across casually. "So let's see what's on the agenda for this week." I flipped open my weekly planner, hoping that Shauna would drop the subject.

I wasn't so lucky.

"I like the brick background of the office. Gives it some character. Like those new loft-style condos they're building around me. Those are very in these days."

I nodded and took a sip of the latte I'd made this morning at Connor's. A smile played at my lips at the memory of us riding into his office together.

"What's that smile all about?"

I blinked, looking back to Shauna, who—behind those cat-eye framed glasses—had an eyebrow lifted.

"Nothing, I was smiling at the thought of the loft-style apartments you mentioned. I bet they're nice."

Shauna eyed me as if I were her little girl instead of her colleague. "Nice but expensive. Way overpriced," she finally scoffed.

I let out the breath I'd been holding. "So for this week …" I went on with our meeting, going over the plans for the week, what needed to be taken care of, what could wait, and so on.

"Hey, I noticed a file labeled 'Connor' in the shared folder that you uploaded over the weekend. I opened it and whoa! Is this a new brand you're working with?" Shauna questioned, confused, as we closed out our meeting.

Shit!

I forgot that Shauna had access to that particular folder where I saved all of the pictures I took of Connor that Saturday. Though it was only two days earlier, it felt like that photoshoot was so long ago.

"No, no, it's not a brand I'm working with."

"Oh, because I was going to say … when did you get into working out and protein shakes?" She giggled. "But he is fiiine. Did you find those images online somewhere?"

"Unh, unh. He's a ... it's just a favor for a friend who needed some help with their social media pages."

"Resha?"

I startled at the knocking on the opened door followed by Connor calling my name. Glancing up, I swallowed at the imposing image he made at the door. His long and broad body took up just about most of the width of the doorway, and the way the dark jeans and black T-shirt he wore clung to his frame was enough to have me swallowing. And if that wasn't bad enough, images of the way he'd made my body sing the night before floated through my mind.

"Who's that? Is that him?"

"Shauna, I have to go. Talk to you next week. Bye." I quickly disconnected the call at the same time Connor pushed away from the door frame and headed over to the desk where I sat.

"Hey," I greeted, standing as if I just got caught with my hands in the cookie jar.

"That was Shauna?" he questioned, rounding the desk and peering down at the screen that now displayed the homepage of my blog.

Clearing my throat, I responded, "Yes."

"You didn't want me to meet her?" he teased, a smile tugging at the corners of his lips.

"We were working."

He chuckled. "Anyway, I have to head out for a couple of hours."

"You have a work meeting?"

He paused, and something in his eyes looked uncomfortable. "Something like that. I'll be back around four. My receptionist will be here, so if there's anything you need let her know or call me. I'll have my phone on me. Oh, and I ordered lunch. It should be arriving around one."

"That wasn't necessary, I could've just gotten—"

"You would've lost track of time, and before you know it, would've gone the whole day without eating. All you had this morning was a coffee and one of TKO's protein bars."

Putting my hand on my hip, I cocked my head to the side. "I thought you stood by your products," I teased.

He moved closer, taking my chin in his hand. "I do, and there's a reason they're called *supplements*. They're meant to supplement a well-rounded diet. Not be a meal replacement. Lunch will be here at one." He pressed his lips firmly to mine before releasing my chin and stepping back.

"What're you going to eat for lunch then?"

"I'm picking up something on the way to my meeting. I'll be back by four."

I sighed. "Fine." How was I to argue with a man who wanted to feed me? "I'm going to work on a few posts that I need to finish up, and then I can look through the pictures I took of you on

Saturday and help you with writing out some captions. Hey, I was also thinking you might want to hire a web designer to update your site."

He grunted. "Yeah, Jersey's already sent me over some names of web designers to help with that."

"Good. I can help you pick out one to work with."

He nodded as he stared down into his phone, distracted. "Yeah, that'll be helpful," he finally stated, stuffing his phone into his back pocket and moving closer to lean down and give me a kiss. Never had I experienced a man who was so affectionate. I couldn't say I didn't like it.

"I'll see you later. Remember, anything you need, just ask my assistant."

I shrugged, knowing that he was saying, without words so much, that he didn't want me leaving the building for any reason. I would've told him that I'd go wherever I damned well pleased, but ... well, the look in his eyes told me to can it.

I swallowed my pride as I remembered there was still a stalker out there who'd broken into my home.

"I'm sure I'll be fine. Don't worry about me, I'm a big girl." It was meant to be a joke, but the way Connor's nostrils flared and his eyes narrowed as they slid down my body, there was nothing funny about the way my body warmed.

"I'll be back by four." Connor's voice was thick and rumbling.

My nipples instantly pebbled, and as soon as he departed from the doorway, I fanned myself with a piece of paper from the desk. "Lord, what've you gotten me into?" I purred.

****

Connor

"I really like this one. You need to post this one on the homepage of your website."

Staring down at Resha's grinning face, I grunted. We were both sitting on the floor in my living room, looking over the images she'd printed out from our photoshoot the other week. While we sat there, with my arm wrapped around her shoulders, my hand making small circles over her right arm and Resha leaning into me, she smiled down at the images she'd taken, something came over me. A feeling of complete peace. I'd had this experience before a few times in my life. Once after winning a national championship that I'd been training many years for. The peace of owning my own home and knowing my brother and family never had to worry again because I'd be able to care for whatever they needed.

However, never had I experienced this peace in conjunction with another human being, let alone another woman. It'd only been a week and a half that she'd been staying with me.

"You don't have to go back," I suddenly blurted out, surprising the both of us.

Resha's eyes doubled in size, telling me she knew exactly what I was talking about. I watched as she visibly swallowed. Then her eyes fell, her fingers playing with one of the photographs—it was of me in only a pair of grey sweatpants, mid-jump as I jump roped, staring dead center into the camera. None of my TKO products were in the shot, so the likelihood of the shot ever making onto my social media feeds wasn't very high, but Resha kept looking at it.

I moved my free hand to her chin, raising her face so she could look me in the eye.

"You don't even have an office for me to work in. I can't keep borrowing your empty office space at work. What if you hire another employee?"

Jerking my head in the direction of the long hallway, I stated, "I'll clear out the guest bedroom and you can make that your office."

Her lips pinched and a contemplative expression crossed her face. "Balcony."

I frowned. "What?"

She sighed, and her eyes moved over to the sliding glass doors that led to the balcony of my condo.

"It was my favorite spot in my home. Not my office, or my bedroom, or even the kitchen."

Both of my eyebrows lifted because I would've sworn her favorite room was the kitchen. Every night for the past week and a half that Resha had been staying at my place, she cooked for us, even when I attempted to insist that she didn't have to, or it would be easier to just order something, she was persistent in making a home-cooked meal for the both of us.

"It was where I went to daydream, come up with ideas for my blog or podcast topics. Where I journaled and would drink my lattes in the morning or hot chocolate on cold nights. It was my little sanctuary. I miss it," she finally stated. "Of all of the things this stalker has taken or tried to take away from me, my balcony is what I miss the most."

She looked up at me with apologetic eyes.

I turned and looked out onto the balcony that I rarely used, and then back to Resha, dipping my head to brush my lips across hers.

"You're still staying."

Her smile turned into a giggle. "You can't keep me hostage," she quipped.

Wiggling my eyebrows, I retorted, "Sure, I can. All I need to do is …" I trailed off as I took both of her wrists into one of my hands, pushing them over her head while I pressed her back against the floor, moving over top of her.

"All you need to do is, what?" she challenged.

I parted my lips to respond, but the sound of my elevator door opening caught my attention.

"Connor!" Mark's voice suddenly rang out in apartment as he pushed the door open, entering my place.

"Son of a bitch!"

"Oh, there— Oh shit!" Mark yelped as he rolled over to the foot of the couch, seeing both Resha and I there. His eyes enlarged, but it was Resha who was most surprised.

She squirmed out from underneath me, quickly lowering the T-shirt of mine that she wore back down around her hips, standing and damn near breaking a leg to head up the stairs.

"Eyes on me," I growled at my brother, whose head followed Resha's bare legs up the stairs.

Mark looked back to me a sparkle in his hazel eyes that mirrored my own, chuckling. "If I'd known you had company—"

"You still would've brought your ass over here unannounced."

He paused, pondering that before nodding his head and laughing again. "You're probably right."

"Give me back my damn key," I demanded, rising from the floor of my living room to stand over him.

Mark made a cynical expression. "Yeah right. Like that's gonna happen. Not my fault! I didn't expect you to have anyone over here. This hasn't happened before," he grunted. "I do believe this is the first time we've ever run into a situation like this."

I scowled at the laughter I heard in his voice as he moved behind me, following me into the kitchen.

"What the hell do you want?"

He shrugged as I glared down at him. "Didn't know I needed to make an appointment to see my older brother. It's been weeks since I've heard from you. It's not like we don't live right across the street from one another."

I rolled my eyes. "You saw me at the Underground two weeks ago."

"Yeah, after *I* came early just to catch your attention. By the way, it looks like you took my advice. I've noticed the revamping of your social media over the past few days. Bravo. Who'd you get to take the pictures?"

"I did," Resha's voice responded, causing Mark to look over his shoulder before fully turning himself around to face her.

She stood at the entranceway of the kitchen, in a pair of blue jeans and an off-the-shoulder T-shirt of hers, obviously having changed. Never before had I had an urge to kick my brother out of my place. Even though I'd barely been speaking to him for months now, when he did come over, I never wanted to demand he get out as much as I did in that moment. I wanted Resha all to myself and Mark was getting in the damn way.

"Resha, right?" Mark snapped his fingers as if just recalling her name.

She nodded. "That's right. And you're Mark. Connor's younger brother." She extended her hand, to which Mark took into both of his.

"Connor's much more charming and attractive younger brother, Mark."

Resha giggled, her gaze rising to meet my scowl. Her eyes squinted, wondering what the sour expression on my face was about.

"Don't mind him, he always looks like that when I'm around lately," Mark stated.

"Is that so?" Resha questioned, moving closer to me, placing her hand on my abdomen.

"Unfortunately. Anyway, you're the one who took those photos I've been seeing on his Instagram posts?"

Resha pivoted on her bare heels to face Mark, and I let my eyes drop, admiring the dark brick red color she'd gotten her toes painted just the day before.

"I did take the photos."

"You're a photographer?"

Resha laughed. "Not be any stretch of the imagination, but I've taken some classes on photography, run my own blog for almost a decade, and I do my own posts, so I was able to help Connor out."

Mark whistled. "You more than helped him out. Those photos were practically screaming sex. And now that I see you were the one who was behind the camera I can see why."

My damn head nearly exploded when I watched Mark's eyes rove up and down Resha's frame in the same way mine had minutes before he'd arrived.

"Get the hell out!" I barked, moving to step in front of Resha.

Mark immediately began laughing as I grabbed onto the back of his chair and started pushing him out of the kitchen.

"Connor's usually terrible at taking pictures. He *hates* being in front of the camera! She must be your inspiration, big bro!" He laughed heartily as I pushed him over to the still open elevator door.

"Get out!"

"Fine. I know when I'm not wanted."

"Hey, Mark?" Resha called from the living room, causing us both to look at her.

"Yeah?"

"How about you come over for dinner tomorrow? Around six? I'll cook us something."

I started to tell her that wouldn't be happening but Mark beat me to the punch.

"That sounds great, but I don't mind picking up something for—"

Resha waved a hand dismissively. "No takeout. What is it with you two? I'll cook. Just bring your appetite. Is there anything you don't like or are allergic to?"

Mark shook his head.

Resha's smile grew. "Great. Then we'll see you tomorrow night."

The last image of my brother I had was the cocky grin he tossed my way as he informed us that he would be here with bells on the following evening.

"And don't forget to lock the door behind you!" I called. He was always forgetting to lock the elevator door once he got off on the ground floor.

"The hell did you do that for?"

Frowning, Resha folded her arms across her chest. "He's your brother and you treated him like he was some sort of inconvenience."

I moved closer to her, pulling her into my arms. "First of all, he *is* an inconvenience just showing up out of the blue like that. Especially, when I was about to ..." I dipped my head to the side of her neck, kissing the vein that'd already began beating more rapidly.

"You c-could be n-nicer to him."

"Mmm," I growled, continuing to kiss her sensitized skin and pressing my hips against her stomach, allowing her to feel the bulge growing in my pants. "How about I be nice to you instead? Very, *very* nice."

"That might make up for your behavior." She sighed against my lips just before I captured hers.

There was no more talk of my brother that night.

Chapter Thirteen

Resha

"That was Detective Brookes on the phone," Connor stated as he entered the kitchen.

I slapped his hand as he tried to reach into the pot with one of the slices of bread I set aside to ladle with the beef bourguignon stew I prepared for our dinner with Mark.

"The hell?" he grumbled.

"That's for our dinner. Mark will be here in ten minutes."

"He's late."

"Not his fault he had to stay late at work. We'll eat soon. Here," I moved to the fridge to grab the hummus I made earlier and a bag of the pita chips I picked up from the store earlier in the week. "These will hold you over."

Connor took the proffered snack, looking relieved.

"Did Detective Brookes have any news?" I questioned as I went back to stirring the simmering stew before turning the heat down just to keep it warm while we waited.

"Nothing viable yet but he wants to speak with you down at the station next week."

"Does he think there are any suspects? Last time I spoke with him he said that Jarvis had been ruled out as having anything to do with the break-in."

A shadow passed over Connor's face but it quickly cleared as he responded, "It wasn't him. Jarvis was out of the building for most of the day when your condo was broken into. But Brookes finally got the video footage from your building's security. Wants you to take a look at it to see if you recognize anyone."

I nodded and continued stirring the stew. "Do you think this guy's even still worried about me? I mean, I haven't gotten anymore emails. What if he's gotten it out of his system? You know, like the break-in was what he needed to get over whatever infatuation he had and now he's past it?" The excuse sounded dismal and pathetic to my own ears, but I looked over at Connor, hopeful. That was, until I saw the frown that crowded his face.

"The break-in was this fucker escalating," he informed me as he moved closer, lowering the hummus and pita chips to the counter so he could wrap his hands around my waist.

I sighed as he pulled me against his chest. My eyes closed when the back of my head made contact with his body.

"What're you thinking?"

"That I want this to be over. I hate walking around scared thinking someone's following me or going to leap out of the bushes at any moment." Releasing the spoon I was holding, I turned and buried my face in Connor's chest, needing to feel the comfort only he was able to provide me with. How I'd grown so attached in such a short period of time I'll never know or understand. All I knew was that I drew strength from him.

Lifting my head, I peered up into his face. "Do you ever think about New York?"

A blond eyebrow raised curiously.

"How when we both live here in Williamsport, not even separated by six degrees, with both of our connections to the Townsends, but we met all the way over there?" I shrugged. "I didn't even want to go to that event in the City, and I was so close to canceling that trip but I'd agreed to do some collaborations with other bloggers. I didn't want to disappoint anyone. And then …"

"One night you went to a bar," he finished.

I lifted on my tiptoes and he lowered, our lips meeting somewhere in the middle. Lightning coursed through me, same as it did every time we kissed. Connor's hands moved over my hips to cover my ass, squeezing it through the material of the burgundy skirt I wore with the matching thigh-high boots.

"Dammit!" he growled, pulling back when the doorbell rang.

"At least he rang the buzzer this time." I giggled at Connor's chagrined expression.

"At least," he snorted, his hands falling to his sides as he looked me up and down, his eye pausing on the boots. "You're keeping those on tonight."

I gasped, catching his meaning, and then swatting him with the dish towel I'd placed on the counter as he exited the kitchen because Mark was ringing the buzzer again.

"Hold your damn horses. I'm coming!" he yelled.

Laughing, I shook my head. I'd completely forgotten the conversation that preceded that kiss, which was typical. In the last week, it was only the moments in which I was alone that I remembered I had a stalker, someone who was likely dangerous and had essentially forced me out of my own home. But whenever I was with Connor—which was most of the time, as of late—it just seemed to fit. Like there was no other place for me to be except in his arms, in his home, at his place of business.

Shaking my head again, I reminded myself that this was temporary. Connor was just helping me until whoever this person was was caught and put away. Then I'd be back home and whatever he and I had would likely fizzle out because … well, men seemed to get tired of me easily. Most people in life did.

"Hey, Resha," Mark exclaimed as he entered the kitchen.

Pushing those previous thoughts aside, I gave him a genuine smile, happy to see Mark again. He reminded me of his brother in a lot of ways. Both of their eyes mirrored one another's. Mark's hair wasn't quite as blond as Connor's, nor was it as long. Mark definitely looked more the part of the clean-cut, business exec type, whereas Connor came across as more rugged and gritty. However, their facial features were similar, and in spite of the fact that he was in a wheelchair, Mark's long legs were a testament that he, too, had inherited the family's height gene.

"Hey, Mark, how are you?" I moved closer, throwing my arms around his shoulders for a hug because that also felt natural. He must've felt the same because he didn't hesitate to return the embrace.

"Tired. Today was a long day. The only thing that got me through was knowing I'd have a home-cooked meal at the end of it."

I laughed along with Mark until Connor interrupted with, "Don't get too used to it."

I nudged him, giving him a side-eye. "Be nice. He's just put in a ten-hour day working for what I'm sure is a very demanding boss." My gaze bounced between Connor and Mark.

"Yeah, brother, you heard the lady. Be nice." Mark turned his head to me. "Don't worry about him, he's had a bug up his butt where I'm concerned for months now." He waved a dismissive hand. "It smells delicious in here. I brought a bottle of red wine since I hear it pairs well with the dish you were making. Can I help with anything?"

"That's perfect." I took the bottle from Mark. "And no, you just relax. I've got the dishes already set up at the table. Let's head over because I know your brother's hungry and I assume you are, too, after staying late at work."

I went to grab for the pot but Connor's hand stopped me. Instead, he used the two potholders to lift and carry the pot with the stew behind me as I followed Mark to the dining section of the kitchen. While Connor placed the pot down at the center of the table where I'd already set up the trivet, I put thick slices of toasted garlic bread on each of our plates.

"This looks great," Mark chimed as I ladled the stew onto his dish, followed by Connor's and then my own.

"I hope it tastes as great as it looks." I wrung my hands. "I actually ran out of red wine and was only able to use half of what the recipe calls for."

"Anything made by you will be phenomenal," Connor replied, placing a kiss to my cheek before pulling out my chair for me to sit.

When I did, I paused, noticing the shocked expression on Mark's face across the table. I was about to ask what had him so dumbfounded but his eyes roved over to Connor, who was taking his seat, before he lowered his head, whistling and chuckling to himself.

"Thanks for coming, Mark," I decided to say instead. "Even with your long day."

"Are you kidding? It's rare I get invited over here anymore." His mischievous glint moved over to his brother.

I frowned. "And why is that?"

Mark grunted. "You'll have to ask him."

I looked to Connor, who was taking his first spoonful of the stew. He didn't say anything for a long while, until he swallowed. "This is delicious, a stór."

My heart felt as if it literally skipped a beat at the compliment. It always did when he complimented my cooking, which was every night.

Mark cleared his throat. "He's right, Resha. This is great."

"Thank you. I'm glad they had beef brisket at the grocer instead of the regular stew meat. The brisket adds a better flavor to the stew and the meat is so much more tender."

"Where'd you learn to cook?" Mark questioned.

"My Aunt Donna." I caught Connor's inquiring look out of the corner of my eye. "Destiny was never one for the kitchen, so I think Aunt Donna let out a sigh of relief when I moved in with them and took up an interest in the dishes she made."

"That's cool. Our Ma never taught us much about cooking. Not that either one of us were interested."

Connor snorted. I wasn't certain if he was agreeing with Mark or he was annoyed that Mark was divulging more about their family background than he wanted shared.

"You're awfully quiet." I reached over for Connor's free hand, relieved when he didn't pull it away. He'd become closed off since his brother arrived.

"That probably has something to do with me," Mark confessed.

"Don't fucking speak for me," Connor finally replied.

I squeezed his hand, hating the way he talked to his own brother.

"Someone needs to speak for you since you've decided to go mute," Mark retorted. "Or did you all of a sudden have something to say?"

I got the sense that Mark actually got excitement from this little exchange. I could've been reading it all wrong, but it felt like when a kid that has been ignored by his parents finally gets some sort of reaction from them due to his negative behavior, so he takes it and runs with it.

"I've said everything I needed to say. To you, to Buddy, and anyone else who'll listen. But you assholes don't listen so what's the damn point of continuing to talk?" Connor took a spoonful of his remaining stew.

My head shot from Connor to Mark during the entirety of this exchange.

"Will you just get over it already? It's done. I'm fighting and that's it. And look at me," Mark held his arms out to his side. "I'm *fine*. Nothing's happened to me. Nothing will happen to me."

"You don't fucking know that!" Connor roared, tossing his cloth napkin onto the table. "In case you haven't noticed you're not indestructible. No one is. Taking unnecessary chances is stupid, bonehead, and fucking idiotic!"

"So now I'm an idiot?"

"He didn't say—"

"If the shoe fits, lace that bitch up and wear it!"

I gasped. "Connor! You don't mean that."

"I know what the hell I mean."

"Yeah, he fucking means it. Swears I'm still just his little brother that followed him around and always needed to be protected like when were were kids. But now, because of this ..." Mark slammed his hands against the armrests of his wheelchair, "he treats me even more like an imbecile who can't make his own decisions."

"Start acting like a grown adult capable of making smarter decisions and I'll treat you like one."

Sucking his teeth in disgust, Mark tossed his hands up in the air.

"Hey, how about we all calm down?" I suggested, hating the turn that this conversation had taken.

"I'm out of here."

"No, Mark! Please don't leave," I implored. "At least stay and finish your dinner? You've worked late and I'd hate to see you not eat. I made blueberry pie and bought vanilla ice cream for dessert because Connor said it was your favorite. Finish your dinner and then I can send you home with the dessert if you don't care to eat it here." I felt myself biting my tongue to keep from begging Mark to stay.

The thought of these two brothers being so angry and pissed at one another tore at my insides.

"You went through all of this trouble for me?" Mark questioned.

I gave him a warm smile. "It wasn't a lot of trouble. I love cooking, and cooking for others even more. Stay. Enjoy your meal."

He gave his brother, who continued to eat, a once over before nodding, agreeing to stay.

I pushed out the breath I'd been holding, thankful that he wouldn't be storming out of here. However, when I looked over at the stubborn set of Connor's jaw, I knew the evening wasn't over.

****

Connor

"Dinner was great, Resha, and the pie was amazing. Probably best blueberry pie I've ever had," Mark gushed as we headed out to the living room. "I'm stuffed."

"You're not just saying that are you, Mark? Because I've been told you're something of a connoisseur when it comes to blueberry pie," she giggled, and in spite of the annoyance I still held onto concerning my brother, it evaporated for one full heartbeat in the face of her laughter.

"He's right, baby. Your pie is the best." Wrapping my arm around her waist, I tugged her to me and placed a kiss to her temple. I glanced down to my right when I heard my brother whistling.

"You might be able to soften this guy up after all. I didn't think anything or anyone would."

"Watch your mouth," I grunted.

"You watch—"

"Hey, hey, we made it through dinner and dessert without you two tearing one another apart, why start now?"

"He started it," Mark retorted.

"Are you fucking serious? You sound like a damn nine year old. Hell, I've heard nine-year-old girls sound more mature than you."

"I bet you have. It's probably because you have more in common with them than with anyone else."

"Mark," Resha gasped.

He shook his head. "I'm sorry, Resha. I tried to be civil. My apologies for ruining dinner, but I can't bite my tongue any longer."

"You don't have to do shit. Far be it from me to make you do anything," I grunted.

"Not like that doesn't stop you from trying, does it?" my brother yelled in my direction.

"Oh, so that's what I'm doing? Trying to control you? Instead of protecting you?"

"I don't need your damn protection! I'm not a damn child or a helpless invalid, which you seem unable to wrap your goddamn head around. What the hell is wrong with you?" he bellowed, his face red with anger.

"What's wrong with me? I got my assed handed to me for you! That's what's wrong with me! I stepped into ring after ring, to fight just so you wouldn't have to! And now you're throwing it all back in my fucking face like it didn't mean shit!" I roared, feeling relieved having gotten that off my chest.

Mark, however, looked burdened by my statement His shoulders sank just before he said, "I didn't realize I was such a burden to you."

My gaze narrowed. "Don't be fucking dramatic," I hissed.

"You're right. I need to stop being dramatic. Goodnight, Resha."

"Wait, Mark, don't leave like this," Resha called out, trying to stop him, but he was adamant.

I grabbed Resha by the arm to prevent her from stepping on the elevator behind my kid brother. There was nothing left to be said between the two of us that night. At least, not between Mark and I.

Once the elevator door closed, Resha whirled on me. "What was that about?"

I waved a hand, pivoting from her and heading to the living room to turn on the television to ESPN. Resha had other plans, obviously, because she snatched the remote from my hand, switching the TV off.

"I asked you a question."

"It was about exactly what I said. I busted my ass for that kid and he acts like it didn't mean shit."

"How so?" she questioned, folding her arms over her breasts, remote still in her hands.

I cocked my head to the side, eyeing the thigh-high boots she wore and the tiny portion of exposed thigh that was left uncovered between the bottom of her skirt and the tops of her boots. And although we'd just finished eating, my mouth watered with a different kind of hunger.

"Eyes up top."

My gaze rose to meet hers.

"What was that really about?"

I pushed out a heavy breath. "I'm probably not gonna get my dick wet until I talk, huh?"

"It might not even happen then. Not unless your explanation is *really* good."

I shook my head. "Mark's been fighting in the Underground."

Her perfectly arched eyebrows rose in surprise at first. "So he's a part of the same club you started? That must take talent."

I snorted. "Talent, yeah. He kept it a secret from me for over a year. Him, Buddy, Josh … they all hid it from me."

"Because you didn't want him to join?"

"Obviously."

"Why not? I hope you're not going to say it's because he's in a wheelchair. If that's the case, I know some Disability Rights Advocates who would like to speak with you."

"It's not because of the chair … not all of it."

She unfolded her arms and tossed the remote onto the couch before giving me the *go on* expression.

"We didn't have shit growing up. My ol' man was a former fighter over in Ireland. He moved here a washed-up boxer with little more than the clothes on his back. My mother was a first gen Irish-Catholic who liked to party more than she liked staying home. My parents hooked up one too many times and ended up with me. They married, and a few years later Mark came along. They weren't terrible people but they weren't made for rearing children either. My father taught me the only thing he knew how to do, which was fight. At five years old he put my first pair of gloves on my hands. Turns out, I was pretty good. When I was sixteen, my ma finally had enough of the homemaker life and split. My father had had one too many concussions and started losing his shit. I was left to fend for all of us, and all I knew how to do was fight. So that's what I did. I won more than I lost, but I still got my ass handed to me a few times. But the one thing I had that other fighters didn't was persistence. I never tapped out, never gave up. I had more than myself to think about.

"Anyway, that's how I fed my family. How I kept a roof over our heads. I fought, paid bills, and saved money for Mark's college fund. Put my father in a home when he was fifty-five because he couldn't even feed himself anymore by that time. I fought so Mark wouldn't have to. When he had his accident ..." I trailed off because I refused to think about that horrible time. Clearing my throat, I continued with, "I kept on fighting and began building my own businesses to pay for his medical care so that he'd never have to worry about anything."

Unclenching my fists, I refocused and looked into Resha's watery eyes. I couldn't help the chuckle that burst from my lips when she practically knocked me over as she ran into my arms, firming her lips against mine.

Pulling back, she questioned, "Have you ever told your brother what you just told me?"

I squinted. "It should be obvious. He knows what I did."

She giggled, lowering her head before looking back up at me. "Men really are clueless."

Frowning, I wrapped my arms around her hips and squeezed. A small moan pushed through her lips. "You wanna repeat that shit?"

The smirk that played at her lips told me she did, but instead she said, "I'm saying that maybe your brother has never seen things from your perspective because you never told him. Yeah, he was there but he was a kid when you started fighting. He was what? Sixteen when he had his accident?"

I nodded.

"How much did you understand about the world and the people around you when you were sixteen? And then, to add a tragedy like the one he experienced at such a young age. You took such great care of your brother, he never really had to know struggle outside of his own. Maybe it's time you shared what's really going on inside of your head with him."

I began shaking my head, but Resha cupped my face with her hands. "Just think about it," she implored.

"Yeah, and what about you?"

Her head jerked backwards in surprise. "What about me?"

I lifted an eyebrow, giving her a funny look. "You haven't told Destiny or your aunt about what's been going on with you. Do they even know you're staying here with me?"

She pulled her hands back from my face as if she'd been burned, but I caught her wrists in both of my hands. "I'll take that as a no."

"The timing hasn't been right."

"It hasn't? Since when does the timing have to be right to tell your family that you're being stalked and had a break-in at your home?"

She sighed, her shoulders sagging. "I'll tell them."

"When?"

"When the timing's right."

"Don't you record another podcast episode with Destiny in two days?"

She rolled her eyes. "I'm not telling you my schedule from now on."

I grunted. "Too late. Our schedules are already synced up via the cloud, sweetie."

"Whatever," she mumbled.

"You'll tell her this week."

"Are you asking me or telling me?"

"I'm *telling* you," I responded firmly.

"Fine. I'll talk to Destiny and my aunt as long as *you* speak with your brother."

I frowned, and instead of answering I bent low and hoisted Resha over my shoulder.

"What the hell?" she demanded, smacking my backside as I started for the staircase. "Connor, if you don't put me down right now!"

"I'm going to put you down, baby. And then I'm gonna strip you out of this tempting ass skirt you've been walking around in all evening but keeping on those boots because I want them resting on my shoulders. Finally, I'm gonna spread your legs and eat you out until your eyes roll to the back of your head and you pass out, or until you beg me to stop. Whichever comes first," I finished just as I laid her down on the bed, my hands immediately reaching for the front clasp of her skirt. "How does that sound to you?"

When she didn't respond at first, I lifted my gaze to her face to see her bottom lip trembling and her eyelids heavy with lust. Smirking, I lowered my face in between her thighs to make good on my promise.

Chapter Fourteen

Resha

"Hey!" Destiny called as I entered the studio where we recorded our podcasts each week.

Smiling, I leaned down, hugging my cousin. "Hey yourself. I'm loving that cardigan," I complimented, admiring the leopard print, almost floor-length cardigan sweater my cousin wore.

"Thanks. All I had left clean to wear were some jeans and a couple of bodysuits so I chose to wear the sweater to disguise my back fat and pudge," she stated, pinching the damn near invisible belly rolls at the sides of her body.

I rolled my eyes. "If you say that dumb shit one more time, I'm gonna punch you. No, you know what, better yet, I'm going to call your husband and tell him you're over here badmouthing yourself."

Destiny's eyes doubled in horror. "Resha, stop playing. You know that man I married is a little off his damn rocker."

I giggled. "I know. That's why I said it. Ty don't play about his baby mama."

Destiny laughed, shaking her head.

I teased her but I was serious. Destiny had always been petite growing up. She was barely five-foot-three and was always small and athletic. She looked great, but after having triplets the year before she was self-conscious about the ways in which her body had changed, despite getting back to her pre-pregnancy weight. She did have more hips than she used to, and she sometimes moaned about not being able to get to the gym as often as she liked because life was so busy these days.

"And do you know what? Tyler is already asking for more kids! That damn man."

My heart squeezed in my chest.

Envy, my brain shouted at me. *I wouldn't mind having Connor begging me to have more of his kids.*

Wait, what the hell did I just say?

"What? You didn't say anything."

I blinked and looked at my cousin, realizing I'd asked that question out loud. I shook my head. "Girl, don't pay any attention to me," I giggled, trying to play it off.

"You okay? You seem a little jumpy today. You're not pissed that I had to cancel last week's podcast are you?" She frowned.

I wrinkled my forehead, trying to recall what she was referring to.

"Oh!" I snapped my fingers, suddenly remembering that she did have to cancel the previous week due to their nanny being out with the flu. "Girl bye!" I waved a dismissive hand. "You know I totally understand that you had to take care of your family. Besides, I had something else come up, too."

"What was that?"

"Huh?"

"That came up."

"Oh, uh, nothing just an issue with a brand that wants me to work with them. Apparently, they got in some hot water for their lack of inclusivity or whatever, so they want to push up our campaign." That was a semi-truth. The particular issue had come up with one of the clothing brands I partnered with, and since Destiny had canceled, I was able to take care of it on the day we usually record our podcast, but it could've waited.

"So they want you to go out of town to shoot?"

"No." I shook my head. "The photoshoot will be here in Williamsport with a few other local bloggers."

"That's good. I know you were getting burnt out on traveling so much."

I nodded. "That's the truth."

"I called you a couple of nights ago. Did you get my message?"

I blinked, realizing that I'd totally forgotten to check the voicemail my cousin left me a few days earlier. "I forgot." My nights had been, ahem, occupied as of late.

"Now what if I was calling to tell you something super important?"

Again, I waved Destiny off. "If it was that important you would've called again, sent a text, or whatever."

Destiny sucked her tongue. "I could've been dying somewhere and you wouldn't even know."

"And your ass calls me dramatic? Dying? Really, D?"

She shrugged. "I'm just saying. You've been absent as hell lately. Not returning calls, barely coming over for dinner anymore. Sometimes, I feel like I hardly see you, Resh."

My shoulders slumped as I started to feel guilty because Destiny wasn't totally making things up. I had kind of gone a little MIA, and the fact that so much was happening in my personal life that I wasn't sharing with her, made the pit of guilt in my stomach only grow.

"You're right. Work has really been taking off, and I guess I got a little preoccupied. I'll do better," I affirmed.

Destiny's smile grew. "I know I can do better, too. I've let my homelife kind of get in the way of us spending one-on-one time together. I'll—"

I held up my hand, shaking my head. "Don't ever apologize for being a good wife and mommy." As independent as Destiny was, I always knew she wanted to be married and have a family of her own. We both did. It just sucked that for the last year I'd been left feeling like I was on the outside looking in. But I wouldn't burden her with my bullshit.

"Now, let's get this podcast recorded," I stated clapping my hands and looking around at the microphones and wooden stools we sat at to record. We rented out time at a recording studio in the same building where Destiny rented out space for her main office.

"Let's do that. Hey, I haven't checked the email in like two weeks. Can you scroll through and see if we have a couple of questions from listeners to answer?"

I nodded, pulled my tablet out of my bag, and set it up on the small, wooden table in the corner of the room to look through the joint email we'd set up for our podcast listeners to email with questions. Typically, Destiny checked the email and pulled three to four questions that we'd read and answer at the end of each recording.

"Let me see if I can pick out some juicy questions," I remarked, rubbing my hands together as the email opened.

"I always pick out the juicy questions ..." Destiny's rebuttal faded into the background as the first email I saw caused my stomach to drop.

STOP IGNORING ME, BITCH!

I gulped, biting my bottom lip in fear, my finger trembling as I pressed the email to open it.

Did you like the little present I left for you on your bed? I can't believe you called the fucking cops on me, you bitch! And you've been whoring around with that tall blond guy! I saw you weeks ago leaving the building with him and getting on the back of his motorcycle. That's how you treat me after I've gone out of my way to show you how much I care?!?!?!?!

There was more in the email but I couldn't finish it. My stomach churned with nausea at what I had read.

"You find anything good?"

I startled at Destiny's question and immediately deleted the email, quickly opening another one as she came to stand over my shoulder.

"Y-Yeah ..." I paused to clear my throat. "This one thinks her fiancé is keeping secrets about his total debt and net worth from her. She wants to know what to do about it without looking like a golddigger," I stated, reading the question and trying not to look too suspicious even though my stomach was practically doing cartwheels.

"That's a good one. I definitely have some thoughts to that question. I know you do, too." Destiny bumped me with her hip.

I glanced up, giving her a tight smile. "Sure do. Um, let me pick out another few questions and then we'll get started."

Destiny tilted her head. "Cool. I need to run to the bathroom anyway."

I sighed in relief as she exited the studio room. Quickly, I scanned through the rest of the unopened emails making sure *he* hadn't sent any others. Never before had he sent an email or message to this email address, or any other outside of the account connected to my blog. Opening the trash folder, I scoured it, searching for the email I'd just deleted, and although I hated to have to do it, I sent it to my personal email account. Suddenly, I was relieved that Connor was going to be picking me up from our recording session and going with me to the police station to speak with Detective Brookes.

Once that was completed, I hastily looked through the emails and chose two more listener questions without fully looking them over. Luckily, they turned out to be great questions, one of which was on plus size fashion and the other was on dressing your new body after having a baby. The show went off without a hitch, and since I'd gotten a text from Connor telling me he was running a few minutes late to pick me up, I headed to Destiny's main office with her to talk for a few minutes.

****

Connor

Exiting the elevator, I pulled my cell phone out of the back pocket of my jeans to look up the exact number of Destiny's office. I'd gone up to the floor where Resha told me they recorded, only to be informed by the studio owners that the women had exited a few minutes earlier, having completed their session.

I swore that if Resha even tried to leave this building on her own, there was going to be hell to pay. I'd started to text her as much but refrained when I saw her standing just outside of a glass door talking with her cousin, her back turned to me. From behind, I could admire the form-fitting jeans she paired with a sleeveless white top and a flowy blue, floral shawl or whatever the hell she'd called it this morning. It was the red pumps she'd matched with the outfit that truly caught my eye. I'd taken her to a storage location where she kept a ton of clothing that'd been gifted to her by brands the day before, allowing her to get more clothing since the ones she'd packed from her apartment weren't enough. At least that was what she claimed. And since she'd been using my office space at work, we'd received at least two packages a day from brands sending her new clothes to post on her blog or Instagram.

"Connor?" Destiny's surprised voice called, staring at me over Resha's shoulder.

Resha spun, with wide eyes, to face me.

"Destiny." I nodded.

"What are you doing here?"

I cocked my head to the side, giving Resha a curious expression. "Picking up your cousin," I responded while keeping my eyes locked on Resha's nervous face. Clamping my mouth shut, I gritted my teeth together, recognizing that she hadn't told her cousin anything.

"Really?" Destiny peered back over at her cousin.

At least, I assumed she did because I was still staring at Resha as well.

"Yeah, uh …" she paused, clearing her throat, "we're going to lunch."

"Huh," Destiny huffed, obviously feeling not in the know.

"Right, Connor?"

I gritted my teeth. "Lunch, right." It was true. That had been the plan—to go to lunch, and then head to the police station. It was the second part of that plan that Resha didn't want me to reveal to Destiny. The fear in her eyes was only second to the silent begging I saw there.

"Yeah," I reiterated to Destiny as I draped my arm over Resha's shoulders instinctively. I didn't miss Destiny's eyes moving to my hand, watching our contact. Nor did I care too much either. What I did care about was the way Resha's body, perhaps without her even realizing it, melted into mine.

"Sooo, this is uh …" Destiny trailed off.

"Lunch. It's a lunch. And we have to get going," Resha hurriedly explained.

"Resha—"

"I'll call you later, D. I promise." She didn't give Destiny time to ask another question as she barreled through her explanation and quickly pulled her into a hug. "Give the kiddos a kiss for me. Love you." Resha waved her hand and glanced up at me as she backed away from her cousin.

"Nice seeing you again, Destiny. Give Tyler and the kids my regards."

"Will do," Destiny retorted while still eyeing her cousin who would've been three steps ahead of me if it not for my arm now around her waist, still holding her to my side.

I physically felt the tension exit her body the farther away from her cousin we moved.

Dropping my arm from hers, I punched the button to the ground level where I'd parked my car.

"Am I some sort of fucking secret to you?" I barked as soon as I slammed my driver's seat door closed.

Resha reared back, gasping, eyes bulging. "What?"

"What the hell was that up there?"

"That …" She trailed off and sighed. "I'm not hiding you or what's happening between us if that's what you're thinking."

"That's exactly what the hell I'm thinking. And if you're not hiding us then why the hell did your cousin seem so surprised to see me?"

She averted her eyes, and it took everything in me not to turn her head to face me, to look me in the eye. But she was warring with something.

"You tell me to be honest with Mark, to express my feelings and shit, and then you hide our relationship from your best friend?

The woman you call your sister," I growled, feeling angry for reasons I couldn't fully explain.

"She *is* my sister. Not by blood but in every other sense of the word." Resha turned to face me—the exact emotion I saw in her eyes that first night in the bar was back again.

I had the same urge I'd had that night in New York: to wipe it away from her pupils; to remove whatever the hell it was that was plaguing her.

"But just like you and your brother, I don't share everything with her."

"What does that mean, Resha?"

She shrugged. "I haven't told Destiny all of my secrets, and for the last year and a half ..." She tapered off. "It's been difficult, okay?"

I parted my lips to make her say more. To tell me what the hell she meant by all of this. However, the look in her eyes stopped me. They practically begged for me not to press any further. There was something she didn't want to reveal.

Moving my hand to take her chin in between my thumb and forefinger, I angled her head upwards so she had nowhere to look but into my face.

"You keep secrets from Destiny, your aunt, and God knows whoever else. But not from me," I demanded. "I don't give a shit that they've known you longer, they're your blood. I'm your *man,* and whatever or whoever is putting that look in your eyes needs to be stomped out. I'm the motherfucker to do it."

It might as well have been a blood oath because I meant every syllable with the entirety of my soul. And while I was one hundred percent serious, I couldn't refrain from the laughter that burst from my lips, when Resha damn near leapt across the center console, her lips meeting mine as she threw her arms around my neck.

"I don't know why but I believe you," she sighed against my mouth.

Reaching around, I squeezed her hip with my hand and said, "Because while you may not want to admit it fully right here and now, I'm yours and you're mine."

She stared into my eyes and shook her head slightly, grinning. "If you say so."

"I say so and so do you because last night, you were yelling those very words."

She giggled as she moved back into the passenger seat, putting on her seatbelt. "We're going to be late to meet Detective Brookes."

I grunted, having almost forgotten about the appointment.

"Brookes can wait. You need to eat first. What are you in the mood for?"

"Thai."

"Thai it is. There's a place not too far from the station we're headed to anyway."

"Sounds good."

Chapter Fifteen

Resha

"He what?" I demanded, staring at Detective Brookes in the private room of the police station Connor and I had been shown into after first arriving. It wasn't one of those typical interrogation rooms you see on TV. There was actually a bookshelf in the back corner, and a circular table with four chairs around it, instead of the rectangular-shaped tables. And there was a huge window which allowed you to see down onto the parking lot. Still, the white walls and lack of decor save for the clock on the wall gave a cold feeling to the room.

"That son of a bitch was part of this?" Connor growled, his voice causing me to shudder and he wasn't even directing his anger my way. "I should've killed him that night."

"Then we wouldn't have the information we have now," Brookes retorted.

I frowned, my shoulders slumping in fear. "So wait, Detective Brookes, are you saying I have two stalkers?"

Brookes shook his head. "No, that's not what it looks like. But the man, Oliver Westbrook—"

"The one who attacked me in the alley."

"Yes. Apparently, we've gotten word from a former cellmate of his that he was paid money to rob you. To frighten you and to try to take your purse."

"By who?" Connor and I questioned at the same time.

"We don't know—"

"Fuck, Brookes! You called us down here saying you had news and this is the bullshit you give us?"

I have to commend Detective Brookes. While most would've looked frightened as hell in the presence of Connor's mounting anger, Brookes kept his cool; merely nodding as if in agreement with Connor.

"You don't think I'm pissed also? My hands have been tied trying to get the goddamn video footage from your building's property manager. *These things take time* is all I've been hearing."

"Yeah, well, I've got a few other avenues I can get this information from."

"I'm going to pretend like I didn't hear that."

"You do that," Connor retorted.

"So, wait, how did you find out the guy who attacked me was hired to do it? From a cellmate?"

"Yeah," Detective Brookes answered. "Westbrook is currently locked up at our main facility and he's not saying anything. He was already on parole so this arrest will likely end up in him having to finish out the remaining three years of his five-year sentence." Brookes shook his head, rolling his eyes. "Jackass gets out of prison after two years due to good behavior and ends up going right back in after just a few months of being out. Anyway, while he was in holding here, after he got out of the hospital ..." Brookes paused, pinning Connor with a glare.

Connor glared at him right back, arms folded across his chest as he stood looking down at the detective.

"He must've had a guilty conscience or something."

"Pain has a way of doing that," Connor grunted.

"So it does. Anyway, he'd told one of the other guys in lockup that he was just looking to score some drugs that night and he came across a guy who offered to pay him in drugs to attack you."

I shook my head because it didn't make sense to me. "Why would anyone do that?"

Detective Brookes, for the first time, looked stumped. "Beats the hell out of me. My guess, however, is that he was setting Westbrook up. Westbrook says this guy came up to him on the street, not too far from your building, and had him follow you to that alley. I'm thinking this guy wanted Westbrook to attack you so he could save you and look like a hero, but that's just speculation on my part."

I turned to Connor because there was too much to take in that defied logic.

"What's this guy's name who gave you this information?"

"You know I can't give you that."

Connor scowled, moving closer as he leaned down on his fists on the table. "What the fuck is his name?"

"O'Brien, you know the—"

"If you talk to me about the law, I swear to God I'm gonna beat your ass."

I gasped. "Connor, you can't threaten a cop like that. I'm sorry, Detective," I told Brookes, feeling both mortified and nervous he'd take offense to Connor's words and try to have him arrested.

Again Brookes took it in stride as he waved my apology off and stood. "Look, O'Brien, I get it. You want blood. You want this bastard caught and so do I. But I have to follow the law because that's *my job*. Ms. McDonald, we're doing everything we can to ensure whoever is behind this attack and the break-in will be caught."

"It's not enough," Connor firmly expressed.

I stood, placing my hand on his shoulder, feeling the tension coursing through his body. "I'm sure Detective Brookes is doing everything he can," I stated, hoping beyond hope that was the truth.

Connor tutted, shaking his head firmly. "More can be done." He pushed away from the table, standing upright, taking my hand into his. "We'll see ya soon, Brookes."

Without another word he escorted us both out of the room, slamming the door behind him. I was barely able to keep up with his long strides as we made our way down the hallway to the main lobby of the police station, and out to the lot where he'd parked.

"What was that? Brookes might've had more information to tell us," I asked as we got into the car.

"He doesn't know shit because his hands are fucking tied. But I know someone who doesn't give as much of a shit about circumventing the law."

Lifting an eyebrow, I gave Connor a curious look. "We're not doing anything illegal, are we?"

Connor peered over at me out of the corner of his eye before lifting my hand to his lips. "*You're* not doing anything illegal."

I started to ask what he meant by his statement but I caught myself. I'd rather not know, to be honest. It wasn't until about twenty-five minutes later when we ended up back at Townsend Industries that I started to understand what Connor's remarks meant.

This time, instead of taking the elevator up to Joshua's office, we took the elevator down. My hand tightened around Connor's as he held mine firmly in his grasp. The elevator door opened to what looked like a basement, and standing there to greet us was Brutus. Apparently, Connor had sent him a text message earlier in the day before we even made it to the police station.

"We got the video," was all Brutus said before exchanging a look with Connor and then me.

I lifted my eyebrows. I didn't need to question what video he was referring to. It was the same one Detective Brookes apparently had trouble getting from the property manager of my building.

"Follow me." With a wave of his head, Brutus pivoted on his heels and proceeded down a long hall toward a large set of metal double doors. Pushing a key into the knob, he unlocked the door, revealing a huge, nearly empty basement-looking room. I shuddered as I stepped into the room. I wasn't afraid as I felt Connor's hand move to my waist, but the eerie feeling that came over me was too familiar.

I looked around the concrete room, noticed the wooden chair and rectangular table, and cold feeling of the room. It felt even colder in this room than the room we'd been in at the police station. Without asking, and without anyone having said as much, I knew there weren't very many people who came down to this particular room willingly.

"It's okay," Connor whispered in my ear.

"Sorry about the accommodations ... " Brutus apologized, his eyes scanning the room, "but this is the only location I can take these kinds of meetings during business hours." He nodded at Connor, who responded by dipping his head.

"What've you got?"

Without another word, Brutus opened the tablet he'd brought with him, quickly punched in a code, and pulled up a grainy image. Setting it down on the table so that we all could see it better, he stated, "This is the video footage from the day your condo was broken into."

My eyes traveled from Connor to the tablet. I stepped closer, staring intently at the screen, my heart rate beginning to increase.

"That's me," I whispered. I watched as I exited my condo, bag in hand, and locked the door behind me. I knew I'd locked my apartment up, even though the police asked me numerous times that day if I was sure I had.

"Maybe this was just a crime of opportunity," one of the officers had said, but I knew that wasn't the case.

We continued to watch the video as various angles of my hallway came in and out of the main shot.

"Can't you clean it up?" Connor questioned, obviously aggravated that the video wasn't that clear.

"This is cleaned up. You should've seen it when I first got it."

Connor's response was a grunt.

"Who's that?" I questioned suddenly, pointing to the screen as a figure approached my door.

"This is what I texted Connor this morning that you both need to see."

I frowned and my forehead wrinkled as I concentrated intently on the screen in front of me. I watched what I assumed to be a male figure, wearing a dark hoodie and dark fatigue pants first knock on my door. When he raised his hand again, I saw that he wore a dark pair of gloves, which was likely why the police were never able to get any fingerprints from the break-in.

I held my breath, when, after knocking again and getting no response, the guy looked up and down the hallway, then removed a black case from one of his side pockets, opened it, and pulled out a key to unlock my door.

I gasped. "He has a key to my home!" Frantically, I raised my gaze to meet Connor's stormy hazel eyes. "He could've gotten in even when I was home."

All along I'd assumed he'd used some sort of tool to break-in but it was a regular key.

"H-How could he have a key to my condo?"

"Good question," Brutus replied. "I know he hid his face but is there anything that looks familiar about this guy?"

"Rewind the video back," Connor ordered.

Brutus did so and we watched from the time the guy walked up to my apartment door, going out of his way to not allow the cameras to capture his face.

"He knew where the cameras were placed," Connor noticed.

"And he had a key."

Both men exchanged a look.

But I stared at the screen. "Can you rewind it back again?"

Brutus nodded and did as I asked.

"Pause it."

He stopped the video once the guy got a few feet from my door.

"His walk," I noted.

"Yeah, it's a weird gait," Brutus stated.

I nodded, noticing how the guy walked with a slightly slumped-over stride. At first, I thought it was because he was trying to conceal himself from the camera, but the rounded upper back and the way his feet stuck out to the sides as he walked seemed familiar.

"I've seen that walk before." I squinted and leaned forward, trying to see more as if the video would somehow change and the guy would just turn the heck around, showing his entire face.

"Where?" Connor questioned.

I shook my head, shrugging. "I can't remember. There's something familiar about that walk. I know I've seen it before. Maybe in passing." I stopped, my blood suddenly going cold. "What if this guy's passed me on the street or been following me and I didn't even know it?" I blurted out, feeling terrified.

"Chances are you've encountered him in one way or another. Those meetings were obviously more important to him than they were to you."

I folded my arms over my chest, running my hands up and down my arms, feeling cold even though the room we were in was heated.

"Send this video to my phone," Connor demanded. "What about the DNA?"

Brutus shook his head. "Not back yet. Unfortunately, for that we have to wait on the Williamsport Police Department. Their crime lab has all the samples."

"They're taking too fucking long."

"I'll give my guy at the lab a nudge to see if we can get the sample bumped up the list for testing and analyzing."

Connor nodded but didn't seem satisfied in the slightest.

"I received another email," I blurted out, suddenly remembering the message I'd gotten earlier.

"Through your blog?"

I shook my head. "This one was sent to the email Destiny and I share for the podcast. Neither of us have checked it in a while since the show's been on hiatus."

"Can you open it up?" Brutus questioned.

I pulled out my phone and brought up the email that I'd sent to my personal account, handing it to Connor. His scowl grew fiercer with each word he read.

"This fucker's going to die," he growled, passing the phone to Brutus.

Even Brutus, who much like Detective Brookes didn't seem to get rattled very easily, reacted. A shadow passed over his face and his lips tightened at the message. I hadn't even read the entire email, stopping after the first few sentences because it made me sick to my stomach.

"Hang on, let me make a call to my guy at the lab," Brutus insisted as he passed the phone back to me.

I glanced over my shoulder as he exited through one of the metal doors.

"Is this the only email you've received as of the last few weeks?"

I nodded at Connor's question. "The messages to my blog have stopped. For now, at least. Nothing in my DMs. I haven't received anything outside of the typical messages on Twitter or Facebook. Some are strange but nothing like this." I held up my phone, indicating the latest email.

"We're going to go through them tonight to make sure none of them are from this fucker."

My eyes bulged. "We can't," I insisted.

Connor's brows dipped. "Why the fuck not?"

"Because I receive all types of emails and direct messages from my female followers. Some of them would be horrified if they found out I let anyone else read them. They send me a lot of personal things, seeking advice, sharing stories because they feel lonely."

"Would they be just as horrified to find out the woman they're seeking advice and fashion tips from is being stalked by a psychopath? Would they be as reticent to show those emails if it meant keeping you safe from harm?"

I pushed out a breath, because I knew I wasn't going to win this debate. I'd already been keeping this secret from Destiny which had Connor pissed. I knew he wasn't over that. He wouldn't stand for me keeping messages from him if it meant that they could lead to whoever was behind this.

"I just want this to be over," I sighed, letting my head fall back as I looked up at the ugly cement ceiling.

I felt a shadow fall over me, and Connor's large hands wrapped around my arms, stroking them up and down. Without deciding to, I lifted my head, leaning it against his chest.

"It'll be over soon, a stór."

A different kind of chill ran through me, the same one that always did whenever he used that special pet name with me. I didn't fully know what it meant but I knew it comforted me every time it came from his lips.

"We should have the DNA sample results within the week," Brutus announced as he entered the room again.

Connor glanced over his shoulder as my head lifted.

"The sooner the better."

"I'll see if I can pull some strings down there," a new but familiar voice added.

Lifting up on my tiptoes, I was just barely able to see Joshua enter the room behind Brutus, over Connor's shoulder.

"Resha." He nodded.

"Josh."

"I'm meeting Kay for a late lunch or early dinner, whatever the hell this is. I'll walk you two out."

Connor stepped back, taking my hand in his and we followed behind Joshua toward the elevator that'd brought us down to the basement of this building apparently.

"How's Victoria?" I questioned Josh as we entered the elevator.

His smile was wide. "Perfect in every way. Trying to get Kay to pop out another one within the next year," he chuckled.

"That seems to run in the family. Destiny's complaining Tyler's already talking about more kids." I laughed, shaking my head although a pang tugged at my heartstrings. My gaze immediately moved up to reach Connor's who was already staring down at me. His expression was unreadable, but it was as if unspoken words passed between us.

I dipped my head because I didn't want to believe what I'd just felt. It all felt too good to be true, and ... well, I refused to allow myself to believe in fairytales anymore. Every day, I kept telling myself that whatever was building between Connor and I would fizzle out as soon as whoever was behind this stalking was found, and I had to move back into my place. I'd been living with him for a little over a month now and it still felt like at any moment the rug was going to be pulled out from underneath me.

"Resha? Connor?"

I looked up, startled by the feminine voice that greeted us as the elevator doors parted.

"Hey, Kayla." I waved, feeling slightly awkward to see her standing there.

She must've felt the same because her eyebrows knitted in confusion.

"Kayla," Connor greeted, my hand in his.

I didn't miss how her eyes fell to our clasped hands, surprise registering on her face.

"Kay, I was just walking Connor and Resha out. You were supposed to meet me in the lobby. It's cold out here," Joshua insisted, taking his wife into his arms, looking as if he was going to warm her up, despite the fact that she was already wearing a coat.

"I'm fine. Wanted to get a little walk in after sitting most of the day, so when Brutus called down to the lobby to say you were going to get the car to meet me out front, I decided to walk around. No biggie." She shrugged but Joshua didn't look appeased at all.

"I'll catch you later, Townsend," Connor stated, pulling me away from the couple.

"Bye, Kayla. Good seeing you," I added from afar as Connor all but carried me in the direction of the car.

"Impatient much?" I questioned after Connor held the door open for me to get in before circling the front and getting behind the wheel himself.

"Hell yeah. I didn't need to see Josh get into it with his wife because she didn't listen. Good thing you listen," he mumbled that last part as he began backing out of the parking spot.

"What do you mean *I listen?* Like I follow orders as if you're my damn daddy or something?" I questioned, folding my arms over my chest.

"Here we go," he groaned. "I didn't mean it like that and you know it."

"Well it sounded like that. And I will have you know that I—"

"Look, it's my job to keep you safe just as it's Joshua's job to keep his wife safe. Him thinking Kayla was in one place when she actually was in another is prime time for shit to go awry. I'm just saying, your safety is paramount."

I started to retort but nothing came out when I parted my lips. The fact that Connor had compared his and my relationship to Joshua and Kayla's marriage left me stunned. I swallowed the lump in my throat, trying to shove down the bubbling hope that insisted on rising in my chest.

"I have a surprise for you."

That did it.

Those six words were all I needed to tamp out the burning flame of hope. I swallowed, shaking my head.

"I don't like surprises," I whispered.

Connor didn't say anything as I continued to stare down into my lap, my hands fidgeting with one another. Not until I felt the car stop as we pulled up to a red light, did one of his much larger hands fold around both of mine, causing them to still.

"What just happened?"

"My mom," I pushed out. "That phrase was one of the last things she ever said to me." I blinked and shook my head, attempting to clear my blurred vision.

You're not a twelve-year-old girl anymore. My logical mind worked to convince me of the truth.

"Look at me, Resha."

My head lifted an inch or two, turning to face Connor. I felt his hand tighten around my own.

"There is nothing … absolutely nothing I would do to bring you pain. I'm not your mother or any other motherfucker you've dealt with before. Are we clear?"

I swallowed and nodded once, wanting with every fiber of my being to believe him. To trust that look in his eyes that was saying he was telling me the truth.

I exhaled. "Okay," I stated, as the light changed and he pressed his foot to the gas, to accelerate the car. His hand remained firmly over mine, however. He didn't let his hand move even as we turned into the parking garage of his building, pulling into the spot next to my car.

****

"I don't know why you insisted on cooking tonight," Connor grumbled as I placed the plate of roasted turkey and homemade stuffing, covered in gravy, with sautéed garlicky string beans in front of him at the coffee table in the living room. This was the location where we ate most of our dinners together, each night. And while the bedroom always seemed to get me excited in other ways, sitting on the floor, in front of the couch, with one of Connor's arms wrapped around my waist as we ate and talked, was my favorite time of the day … with our clothes on.

"Cooking relaxes me. And I needed some relaxing," I finally responded while sinking to the floor, next to him. "And don't even act like you want to complain right now, either. Taste this," I rushed, sticking a forkful of turkey and stuffing covered in gravy into his parted lips.

However, when I tried to move my hand back, Connor gripped mine along with the fork as he caught my gaze. Slowly, he pulled the fork from his lips, never blinking nor letting his gaze drop.

I watched as his jaw worked slowly, methodically, once he released the fork free from his lips. A look of pure bliss passed over his face.

"You know I'm never letting you leave, right?"

My brows raised and I giggled but Connor's face held firm. "I'm not joking."

I rolled my eyes, waving him off. "Whatever. Eat. Your food's getting cold."

"There's no danger of anything getting cold around here, baby."

I laughed, taking my first bite of my own meal. It was delicious, I must admit, but I took more pleasure in observing Connor enjoy it as he ate. That was what I really loved about cooking. Being able to provide the people you loved with joy, pleasure, and nourishment on top of it all.

Did I just say love?

I paused, the fork halfway to my lips at the question. I reviewed my own internal dialogue, and sure enough, I had mentioned the word love in conjunction with Connor O'Brien.

You're doing it again, that same voice warned. I was falling too deeply too soon. A habit of mine in past relationships.

Stuffing my mouth full of string beans, I focused on my plate, but trying to forget what I'd just figured out was pointless. Especially with Connor's free hand caressing up and down the side of my body. Peeking over at him, I realized he wasn't even aware of what he was doing. It seemed to come naturally to him, comforting me, holding me, even as he fed himself.

I sighed, longing for something I shouldn't have been.

"What was that?"

I blinked, turning back to his questioning stare. "Nothing."

His lips folded downward and he gave me that look that says *you're full of shit, Resha*.

"How're the green beans?" A meager attempt to change the subject.

"They're gone."

I lowered my gaze and a smirk crossed my lips to see his now-empty plate.

"Do you want more? I made enough for—"

His hand stopped me from getting up. "What I want is to show you something."

He stood, bringing me with him.

"Is this the surprise?"

"Yes. Are you done eating?" he questioned, frowning at the food on my plate.

"I am now."

"If you still need to—"

"Connor," I growled, taking a lesson from him.

He chuckled. "You can finish eating after the surprise. You're going to need your strength for later."

My nipples hardened at the implication and the tone in his voice.

"C'mere," he ordered, pulling me to him as he stepped backwards toward the closed balcony door. He separated the blinds, which he nearly always kept closed, and I gasped at what was behind them.

I watched with anticipation as he unlocked the lock and slid the glass door open, allowing both of us to step out onto the balcony that had once had just a couple of chairs and a small table.

"You re-created my balcony," I gushed, glancing around at the balcony Connor had transformed to look just like the one I had at my condo. Squinting, I moved closer, my eyes taking in the furniture and the low-sitting coffee table. "This looks exactly like the furniture from my apartment."

"It should. It's the same one."

"How did you—"

"Police said you could go back in weeks ago. They'd collected all the forensic evidence they could."

I nodded, knowing this, but I still hadn't been back to my place. Most of it was because I couldn't even think of going back without being gripped by fear. A small piece of the reason was because I didn't want to leave Connor's home, even if he had been okay with me going back to my place. Which he'd made abundantly clear that he wasn't.

"So I had some movers go in and get your balcony furniture and plants while you were working yesterday. They came back this morning while you were recording the podcast to set it up just the way you had it. I'd taken pictures. The fucker that broke into your home hadn't touched anything on your balcony."

I remembered that from that day. I'd been too rattled to recognize the oddness of it. He'd destroyed my living room and my office, cleaned my bedroom but ejaculated on my bed. However, the balcony had remained untouched. None of it made sense but I'd chalked it up to him just not having enough time or not wanting to get caught seeing as how my balcony could be seen from the street below.

Walking around, I admired the set up, running my hand over the loveseat and the wicker table, even noting the lights that'd been strung up around the furniture, illuminating the reading nook I'd created.

I turned to Connor, questioning, "How'd you get them to design it exactly like I had it?"

He gave a one shoulder shrug. "I took photos." He removed his phone from his pocket, pulling up the images of my balcony. He'd taken at least two photos from every angle, ensuring that nothing was missed.

I took one final look around, something warm in my chest settling, and turned to Connor. "Why?"

His face wrinkled.

"Why did you go out of your way to do this?"

He moved to me, pulling me into his arms by my waist. "You said the balcony was your favorite part of your home, right?"

I nodded.

"I couldn't recreate your entire home since that fucker destroyed most of your other belongings."

A smile touched my lips. Connor always referred to the stalker as *that fucker* with so much venom in his voice.

"But I could do this for you. Here. Because I want you to be comfortable. To feel at home as much as possible."

Letting all the air out of my lungs, I leaned against his chest, wrapping my arms around him, and in spite of the cold night air, I'd never felt warmer in my life.

"I need to tell you something and it's probably going to freak you out. You'll probably regret doing this for me and I'll regret saying it but I have to say it because it just doesn't seem like I can hold the words in any longer. And I know it's way too soon, and in light of the way all of my past relationships have gone, I'd be wise *not* to say these words, but—"

Connor leaned back, taking my chin into his hand. "Resha, just fucking tell me you love me so I can say it back already."

Grinning, I retorted, "I love you."

"I love you, too."

I held my breath, pulling out of his arms, and looked around, out into the night air.

"What are you doing?"

"Waiting for the lightning to strike."

"Get your ass over here," he growled, pulling me to him and covering my lips with his own.

An instant moan sounded from my mouth.

I yanked my head back. "Now, I want to give you something," I stated, panting. My hands went to his belt buckle, undoing it along with the button of his jeans. Connor barely had time to figure out what was going on, before I sank to the ground, grabbing one of the couch pillows to place under my knees.

"Resha, what the fu—" His question broke off on a groan when I covered the tip of his cock with my mouth, using my tongue to spread the precum that had already begun to emerge from the tip.

"Shit!" he growled, his hand making its way into my hair.

I'd long since given up the battle of telling him not to pull my damn weave during sex. I simply conceded to the fact that I had to up my appointments with Missy from every six weeks to every four weeks. And since Connor paid for my more frequent appointments, in spite of me insisting that wasn't necessary, my concerns about my hair fell by the wayside as I slid my lips down his cock, and his hand's grip tightened in my hair.

I took him all the way to the back of my throat, before moving almost to the tip again. Fellating Connor was easy. He'd attentively cared for me so easily and effortlessly over the past weeks, that it made me want to take care of him. Bobbing my head on his shaft and hearing the groans escape his lips as his fingers massaged my scalp, spurring me on, I let myself go. Pleasuring him was the only thing that mattered.

When his hips began jerking rapidly, and I felt his balls tighten in my hand, I knew his coming was inevitable. But I didn't release him from my mouth to finish him off with my hand, as I had with past lovers. I wanted to taste him, to feel him inside of my mouth as his come ran down the back of my throat.

"Fuuck!" he moaned and grunted as he shot his load off just where I wanted him to.

I swallowed everything he offered and continued to suck him for even more. It was Connor who eventually pushed himself free of my hold. I felt almost lost at the releasing of his shaft from my mouth but not for long. Soon enough, I was being pulled up from my knees. Connor moved so fast, I didn't have time to inhale my next breath before my legs were wrapped around his waist as he hoisted me up his body, taking us back inside and slamming the balcony door shut.

I saw him close the blinds out of the corner of my eye only a moment before my back was pressed against the wall next to the door, as Connor slid inside of my wet channel. My body tensed up as my hips pressed forward, seeking to access every inch of his. I'd never been so grateful for my decision to remove the stockings I'd worn earlier in the day in all my life. That decision, made to increase my comfort while cooking, allowed for the easy access that my man was taking full advantage of.

"Oh shit!" I yelled as my fingers dug into his upper back, trying to hold myself upright as he pounded into me.

"Fuck, baby, you feel so good!" he growled in my ear, burying his face into my neck, kissing me there.

My entire body shivered and convulsed with all the sensations coursing through it. My eyes rolled to the back of my head at the same time my head pressed against the wall. My mouth went dry from my panting as I gasped, reaching for my next full breath.

Connor moved his hand under my head, lifting it to allow his lips to crash down on mine.

Who needs oxygen? my mind questioned. I'd sustain myself on this feeling alone. My eyes squeezed shut and the muscles of my canal tightened and flexed around Connor's drilling cock. I wanted to yell that I couldn't take anymore, but as usually happened, just when I thought it couldn't get any better and I couldn't handle any more pleasure, my orgasm crashed through my body.

The climax was like a starburst behind my eyes, lighting every cell in my body with its intensity and sharpness. My toes curled and I crossed my feet around Connor's waist, my thighs locking around his body.

"I l-love y-you," I panted, my teeth clattering as I struggled to speak coherently.

"And I, you," he returned, cupping my face with his hands and flexing his hips slightly as he stared into my eyes.

And for a little while I believed I caught a glimpse of forever in his eyes.

Chapter Sixteen

Resha

I'd been in bliss for the past two weeks, ever since I'd told Connor I loved him and he said it back. And he meant it. That was the best part of it. It wasn't just a, *"Yeah, okay, same,"* response that I'd gotten from past lovers. Connor didn't say words he didn't mean. And so, while we still didn't know who my stalker was, as the DNA results hadn't revealed anything about this guy, I felt as if I'd been walking on cloud nine.

There was something to be said for going to bed and waking up next to the man I loved, and being able to say those words so freely. I still went to work with Connor nearly every day. He'd actually cleared out the office next to his, making it officially mine whenever I needed it. On days that I had appointments or meetings at other locations, or needed to run errands, Connor made it a point to take me or make sure I had some sort of an escort. I'd told him hiring extra security wasn't necessary and I would just be careful but he wouldn't hear of it.

Everything felt perfect, but all of a sudden, I started to feel as if everything I was fearing as too good to be true, was just that.

I startled when I heard the buzzer to the door ring. Frowning, I listened Connor's feet padding across the living room floor. Quickly standing from the toilet, I crumpled up the paper I'd been holding and disposed of it in the trash before bunching up some toilet paper and putting it on top of the discarded trash. The other item I had in my hand, I quickly shoved into the pocket of my jeans before rebuttoning them, and heading to the sink to wash my hands.

"I know she's here."

My eyes bulged in the mirror when I heard my cousin's voice. Exiting the bathroom, I headed through the bedroom and down the stairs.

"Were you up there hiding?" Destiny demanded with her hands on her hips, tapping her foot against the hardwood floor.

"Hiding? I was in the bathroom. And what are you doing here?"

"What am I doing here?" Destiny retorted angrily, pressing a hand to her chest as if she couldn't believe the question. "The question is what are *you* doing here? Living here, to be exact," she finished, glaring between myself and Connor, who moved to stand beside me.

I looked up at him only to be received with an *I told you so* expression.

Clearing my throat, I began, "Um, well, yes, I've been staying here with Connor ... wait, how did you know?"

"No thanks to you. But thanks to our hairstylist who loves to gossip, I found out that my cousin, who is supposed to be my best friend, was actually living with a man. When I told her that that wasn't the case at all because I would know it, she informed me how said man dropped her off and picked her up in his car on three separate occasions. Still, I told Missy she had to be mistaken, and while, yes, Resha is currently seeing someone new ..." Destiny eyed Connor, "she's barely even spoken to me about, so she certainly wasn't living with him."

"I—"

Destiny held up her hand. "And then Missy briefed me, in so many words, that I must not be in the know what's happening with my own family, because every time this guy came to pick up my cousin, he made mention of going *home* together." She finally smacked her lips, arms folded as she glared at me, silently demanding an explanation.

I guessed the jig was up.

"Why don't we take this to the living room?" Connor suggested, still giving me that look. I bet his ass was reveling in this.

Sighing, I moved toward the living room, followed by my cousin. I could feel the heat of the glare on my back.

And as if finally remembering her manners, Destiny turned to Connor, saying, "I'm sorry for barging in here like this. It's not you I'm pissed at."

"Oh, I know." He glared at me, cocking his head to the side.

I rolled my eyes. *See if a certain someone gets any head tonight.*

"D, look, I'm sorry for not telling you. This was kind of a sudden thing ..." I paused as I looked into Connor's eyes. "I have a stalker," I blurted out, turning to my cousin.

Destiny's eyes ballooned. "What?!"

Inhaling deeply, I launched into the specifics of what'd been happening over the past few months. My cousin's face grew more and more angered as I spoke. When I finally finished telling Destiny the whole truth, I exhaled deeply, feeling relieved.

"So a random man has been leaving you threatening and harassing messages, following you, and eventually broke into your home, and you didn't tell me?" she screeched.

I winced at my cousin's words, hearing the betrayal in her voice. "I know it sounds bad, but—"

"*But?* How could there be a but, Resha? It doesn't *sound* bad. It *is* bad!" She stomped her foot angrily.

"I know, but just listen," I demanded, holding my hand up when it appeared as if she was about to interrupt me again. "All right, yes, it *is* bad. But I didn't think it was really a big deal at the time. Not before the break-in. I get weird messages often on the blog or in my DMs from random guys. Most of the time, it turns into nothing. They're just lonely dudes who have nothing better to do than to be creepy on the internet. I block them and move on."

"But this wasn't one of those times."

I nodded and shrugged, agreeing with my cousin, before looking over at Connor. "We've been working with the police to figure out who this guy is."

"The police?" Destiny turned to Connor, with a raised eyebrow.

"As well as other avenues," he added, arms still folded over his broad chest.

"So, you've been living with Connor for safety reasons." She nodded as if saying it out loud to herself. "Okay then, you'll come and stay with me and Tyler. We have state of the art security and—"

"That's not happening," Connor interrupted, voice low but firm, instantly cutting my cousin's declaration off.

Destiny blinked, looking between Connor and I.

"Resha's staying right here."

"You don't know how long it's going to take to find this guy, and—"

"Doesn't matter how long it takes." His voice was full of so much finality I found my stomach muscles tightening from being turned on.

"Resha, you—"

"He's right," I stated, staring into his eyes, and swallowing the lump in my throat, preparing for what I had to say next.

"But what if you have to travel, or if Connor needs to travel out of town for work?"

"She'll go with me," Connor answered, staring at me.

"I'll go with him ... unless, of course, I'm too far along to travel," I admitted.

Connor's brows dipped and he cocked his head to the side.

"Too far along for what?" Destiny questioned.

Peeling my eyes from Connor, I turned to Destiny, who as soon as she saw the expression on my face, her eyes fell to the hand that covered my stomach. I hadn't even realized I placed it there until she noticed it. Looking back to Connor, I saw his eyes were pinned to my abdomen as well.

"Are you ..."

Nodding, I answered, "Pregnant? Yes." With the hand that wasn't covering my stomach, I pulled the pregnancy test I'd just been staring at upstairs in the bathroom out of the back pocket of my jeans. I looked at the two pink lines that were present as day before handing the stick over to Connor.

He moved closer, taking my wrist into his hand, holding the stick in front of his face. "I see two pink lines. What the fuck does that mean?" His hold tightened on my wrist, not causing any pain at all, but I could feel the tension in his body as his eyes shifted from me to the test and back to me again.

Grinning, I responded, "It means you're going to be a father."

His entire body stiffened and his eyes bore into mine, a blank expression on his face.

The fear that I'd felt up in the bathroom as I saw those lines for the first time returned.

You did it again. Moved too quickly. Now you've got a child to raise on your own, my own mind began mocking me.

"I know it's way too soon, and heck, we've only been living together for like, barely two months. We haven't even solidified what this relationship is or where we want it to go. I mean ... yeah, sure, we've told each other I love you, and it's true for me, I hope it is for you, but adding a baby into the mix brings a whole new element into—"

"Resha?"

"Yes?"

"Shut the hell up. I'm going to be a daddy!" Connor whooped, just before grabbing me by the face and crushing his lips to mine.

The laughter that bubbled up my belly, through my chest, and out my lips was infectious, effectively breaking our kiss but causing Connor to laugh also as his hands moved down my body, to cover my stomach.

"Holy shit!"

I blinked, remembering that Destiny was still standing there. Moving away from Connor, I went over to my cousin, the second most important person to me in the world.

"You probably have opinions about this. I went from celibate to living with Connor, to pregnant in only a matter of weeks, in your eyes, and—"

"You two are in love?" she questioned.

I looked at Connor and smiled before turning back to Destiny. "Yes."

"And you're going to be a mommy," she gushed, pulling my into her arms, hugging me. "You've always wanted this," she whispered in my ear.

I had to wipe away the tears that threatened to form once she released me from the hug. She was right, I always had wanted this. And it all felt like it was too good to be true. Even as Connor pulled me back into his arm, using his free hand to rest over my belly, it felt as if everything I ever wanted was coming to life, and nothing scared me more.

****

Connor

"Are you sure you want to do this?" Brutus questioned as he pulled into the parking space in front of the abandoned building.

"Never been surer of anything in my fucking life," I affirmed before getting out of the dark Suburban and slamming the door shut behind me.

Moving toward the door, I pulled out the key, unlocking the door and shutting it once Brutus entered, locking us inside. Across the dimmed basement room, I could make out three figures. One was sitting in a chair, still dressed in the orange jumpsuit most criminals wore even when being transported from one jail to another.

Approaching the three men, Joshua's grim face came into view first and he nodded in my direction before his eyes lowered to the man sitting in the chair in front of him, Oliver Westbrook.

The other man to Joshua's right was on Brutus' security team. He'd also acted as the driver for the Williamsport Correctional Facility, that brought Westbrook all the way out here to this abandoned building, so that I could have a one-on-one conversation with him. This wasn't the same building we used for the Underground fights that took place in Williamsport. Much darker fights happened in this building. Ones that most opponents often couldn't get up and walk away from.

How Joshua and Brutus were able to get Westbrook all the way out here, given the legal entanglement due to him still being in prison, were beyond my scope of knowledge. But that didn't concern me either. All I knew was that this son of a bitch had information that I needed and I was going to get it out of him, one way or another.

"Do you remember me?" I questioned, coming to stand over Westbrook, who still had his handcuffs, his wrists bound behind his back.

He looked up, blinking, allowing his eyes to adjust to the light that hung over where we were standing.

When his eyes bulged, fear entering those dark pupils of his, I knew he remembered.

"Good. No need for introductions." Crouching low in front of Westbrook, I began, "You have some information about that night you attacked my woman and you've refused to speak to the police. So, you've been brought here."

He started shaking his head. "I'm not— owww!" His refusal was cut off by a swift jab to his stomach.

Another louder and sharper howl of pain was heard a second later when my right hook connected with his left-side kidney. He crouched over in pain, but just before he could fall out of the chair, I stood, grabbing him by his hair at the top of his head and yanking him to stand as well. His cries of pain fell on deaf ears.

"I don't know who you think you're fucking with here, Westbrook, but I'm not the motherfucking one to try it with. All the laws and constitutional rights that allow you not to talk or incriminate yourself don't apply down here." I paused and looked around the nearly empty basement, turning his head to follow my gaze, so he knew what *down here* meant.

"You can scream as loud as you want and no one will hear you. And those of us that do …" I spun him to face Joshua, the other security guard, and Brutus, before finally turning him back to face me. "We don't give a shit about your pain."

I shoved him back into the chair.

"Now, let's start again. That night you attacked my woman, who the fuck was it that paid you to do it?"

"I don't know." He shook his head. "Owww!" he yelped when my open-palm smack across the face sent him to the floor.

"Try again."

"I-I don't know. Honestly. He came up to me in a dive bar I was hanging out in, looking for my dealer," he confessed.

"Keep talking," I growled, standing over him with my fists clenched.

"I c-couldn't see much of his f-face. He had on dark clothes and a low hat. All h-he said was that he wanted me to follow and rob s-some chick."

"And your stupid ass didn't bother to ask questions?"

"I just needed the money, man! B-But I remembered he said his name started with an S, and he had a funny walk."

"How so?"

"L-Like his feet stuck out to the side and he w-wobbled a bit. I-I thought he was high when he first came up to me because everyone at that bar was high or looking to get high."

"What else did he say?"

"H-He said there was a woman who lived in a building, he gave me the address. He wanted me to follow her when she left the building that night. He said she always went to the same grocery store Saturday nights. He wanted me to follow her down the alley as she walked to a store, and take her bag, maybe smack her around a little bit. Ahhh!" he yelled after I stomped him in the abdomen.

Stepping back, I watched him writhe in pain due to my latest blow and I had to tamp down on the urge to do it again. The image of him hitting Resha, or even just accepting money to do so, pissed me the hell off.

"Piece of shit," I growled, spitting on him. "What the fuck was his name?"

He shook his head and tried to scoot away from me as I barreled down over him again, but the handcuffs on his wrists made it difficult for him to properly maneuver himself around. "I-It started with an S … l-like Santa or something. I just wanted the m-money. Didn't want any more details beyond how much he was gonna pay me."

"And that was supposed to be it? You were just going to rob her, smack her around a little bit, and then what?"

Westbrook shrugged. "I-I don't know. He said he'd be there to console her or something. Look, I didn't ask for details. I just nee—"

"Needed the money. I fucking heard you the first time you said it," I growled and kicked him again for good measure, ignoring the cries of pain as I spun around, turning to Brutus and Joshua.

Joshua's scornful eyes moved from the piece of shit on the ground, up to me. "Santa?"

I shook my head. "The letters and emails she got all were signed off with the letter 'S'." I turned to look at Brutus. "We need to look into her building's property management company and their security staff."

Brutus nodded. "The key."

I grunted in agreement.

"Key?" Joshua questioned.

"The video footage Brutus picked up showed the fucker entering Resha's apartment with a key. Not picking the lock or shouldering his way inside. He had access through a key. I'm thinking it may have been some sort of master key or a copy he made specifically to Resha's home. Someone with that type of access likely worked in the building or lived there."

Joshua nodded. "Makes sense."

"We'll start with current employees of the management company who have access to the building. Checking everyone whose name starts with the letter S."

Brutus pulled out his phone and started typing a message to someone.

I looked to the asshole on the floor, scowling at how pathetic he was. For a fucking high he was willing to attack a woman he didn't know.

"How much did he pay you?" I questioned, moving closer to Westbrook. When he tried to scoot away, I crouched down, grabbing the hair at the top of his head, securing him in place. "How fucking much?"

"A hundred bucks ... b-but I never got the money. He said he was gonna pay me after the job was done, but—"

"You got the shit knocked out of you and sent to jail," Brutus chuckled, as he stood behind me, looking down at us.

"Waste of fucking life," I growled, disgusted, pushing Westbrook away and stepping back.

"P-Please don't k-kill me," he begged when Brutus nodded to his security guy, who then moved closer to us.

"You're going back to the shithole you belong in."

I watched as security picked Westbrook up off the floor, reminding him that he was to keep his mouth shut as he dragged him out of the room and back into the car that would deliver him to the Williamsport Correctional Facility bus. The same bus that just so happened to have had a breakdown on the side of a long, country road while transporting an inmate.

I kept watching as Josh moved beside me to stand. "He won't last long in prison," he stated.

Nodding, I wasn't shy about not caring of the fact that Joshua just confirmed that there was a hit already put out on Westbrook. I wasn't the only one who wanted him gone. Apparently, he'd stolen some valuable items from a dealer he used to work for. *Good riddance.*

"I think that was the first time you hit anything besides a punching bag in at least a decade," Joshua remarked, turning to me.

"Hasn't been that long, but it was worth it," I admitted with my arms folded over my chest, my fingers still itching to punch the shit out of Westbrook. But he wasn't my final target.

"We'll find out who this asshole is," Josh assured, but even the determination I heard in his voice didn't make me feel any better.

"We need to speed this along. The longer he's out there the more emboldened he'll become, and I won't have Resha's life in danger much longer." *Or that of my unborn child.* Knowing that Resha was carrying my child upped the ante on everything. There was no way I was going to let my son or daughter be born into a life where their mother was endangered, for any reason.

"I know that look," Joshua stated, catching my attention.

Blinking, I looked down on him.

"A father, huh?"

I scowled at him, narrowing my eyes. "How the fuck did you know?"

"Intuition."

"Bullshit."

Joshua chuckled before slapping me on the back. "I'm just fucking with you. Destiny was so excited, she couldn't keep the news to herself, so she told all the women. And Kay …" He shrugged. "My wife doesn't *not* tell me anything," he added cockily.

"Yeah, well, your fucking gift better be the biggest one at the shower."

"Oh, I've already planned the gift. Speaking of presents, the property around the corner from me is still for sale."

"Here the fuck you go." The subdivision where Joshua and his brothers lived was just outside of Williamsport and he'd been trying to get me to buy a house there for at least a year.

"I'm just saying, you can't expect to raise a kid in your loft. What? Are you going to put the baby upstairs while you both sleep downstairs or vice versa?" He grunted, looking disgusted at his own question. "And I know you aren't going to move into Resha's condo even once you catch this son of a bitch."

Oh, fuck no, we aren't. Hell, I'd all but had Resha's stuff moved out and had that damn place on the market over the last few days. I'd only stopped speaking with a realtor once Resha asked if we could hold off on the sale for a few months while she sets up her things at my place. Figuring that the stress was probably not so good for the baby, I agreed.

"Exactly," Joshua continued, answering his unasked question. "It just makes logical sense that you two move into our subdivision and let me be the one to sell you your home. Resha would love being so close to her family once the baby's here and so will you."

"Lay off, Townsend. Let me talk to my woman and think about it," I responded out loud but inwardly felt touched at Josh alluding to the fact that he was my family.

He chuckled as we started for the door, indicating he knew my thoughts.

A father. Knowing that I had a family to look forward to and take care of had me considering things I'd never thought of before. Caring for my father and brother had been different. They were my family, and in many ways I'd been responsible for them, but this was just different. Resha, in such a short period of time, had become my world. The baby she was carrying would become *our* world. Every time I looked at her, I saw the hope blossoming in her eyes, with each passing day. She wanted this so badly it almost frightened her.

That was what made me more intent on getting to the bottom of whoever the fuck thought they could impede on her life. I wanted this fucker to know that she was taken and I would spend my last breath ensuring that she was loved, cared for, and protected.

Chapter Seventeen

Resha

I glanced over my shoulder at the burly man who was following me down the long hallway, and rolled my eyes.

"Hey," Destiny greeted as she was the first to exit the conference room of the women's shelter.

"Hey," I greeted, gloomily.

"What's the matter?"

I glanced over my shoulder again at the man in the dark suit, with his hands clasped in front of him as his eyes kept scanning the hallway. "Him," I grunted, nodding my head in his direction.

"That's Abe. He was once our security," Patience announced, as she entered the hallway from the conference room as well. "Hey, Abe." She waved and he nodded back at her, before scanning the hallway again.

I sighed. "Yeah, well, you can take him back. I told Connor I didn't need to be followed around by some big, burly dude all damn day but did he listen to me? No, of course not." I threw my hands in the air, feeling exasperated, especially since I was overly tired due to first trimester pregnancy symptoms.

Destiny and Patience shared a look before bursting out in laughter.

"The hell is so funny?"

"Nothing ... well, that's not true. It's just a little funny to see the other side of things." Destiny shrugged. "Come on," she ordered, pulling me by the arm into the room and shutting the door behind us.

"Hey, Kayla," I greeted, waving at the other woman in the room.

Her smile widened as she raised her head. "Hey, Resha. Glad you were able to make it in. Destiny said you weren't feeling well this morning."

I nodded. "Just a stomachache. Seemed to get better after I had a little something for breakfast," I lied. The ache in my abdomen had been happening off and on since the night before but I didn't want to alarm anyone so I didn't tell Connor about it and I downplayed it to Destiny that morning. Even when the pain increased, I kept hoping that it would just go away. And even while it did subside a little after breakfast, it was still there.

"Oh man, I remember I would be so nauseous if I didn't eat in the morning during my first trimester," Kayla groaned, rolling her eyes as if the memory was too much for her.

"I couldn't keep anything down that first trimester with Kennedy and Kyle. With my second pregnancy, too. My third was a little better but not much."

"Same here. You all remember I was barely able to make it to the SuperBowl because I was so sick. "

"Yeah, Tyler played like crap that first half because he was so worried that you hadn't shown up to the game," Patience added.

I nodded, recalling that time. Patience had been in the bathroom all morning, throwing up her guts, and even after tossing all of her cookies, she was left dry heaving. I shuddered at just remembering it.

"Thankfully, this pregnancy hasn't been that bad. I've had some food aversions, though, and I swear I want to climb Connor every night like a damn tree. I mean, we obviously were going at it like rabbits before which is how I got in this position in the first place, but now? I just want to jump his bones whenever he walks into a room. Any of you experience that?"

"Yes."

"Oh my God, yes!"

"Hell yeah."

They all laughed and agreed.

I laughed along with them, shaking my head. "I had no idea pregnancy did that to women."

"Sometimes," Kayla added. "Sometimes pregnancy can have the opposite effect, or no effect at all on sex drive."

"Yeah, well, I have a theory," Destiny chimed in.

"Oh Lord, here we go with you and your theories," I teased.

Giggling, Destiny said, "Hear me out. I think being married or with virile men like the ones we're married to, or in your case, living with, is the reason our sex drives were catapulted like they are during pregnancy. Something with the hormones and evolution and whatnot." She shrugged.

I gave her a side-eye. "Whatever, cousin. All I know is I'm tired as hell any other time of the day, but if Connor walks into the room, *any* room, my libido stands up and says *hello!*"

We all laughed, high-fiving as we agreed.

"Enough about my sex drive, let's get on with creating some outfits for these ladies. I hear Lena has a job interview for a paralegal position?" I asked, glancing around the room at the three women.

Patience nodded. "Yes. She completed her paralegal course study a couple of years ago, which she did in secret, mind you. Unfortunately, she wasn't able to start searching for a job until she broke away from her ex." Patience shook her head, sucking her teeth. "He was a piece of work. Anyway, we were able to help her get her foot in the door with some local agencies and headhunters, and now she actually has two job interviews. She needs some help in her confidence, so we've been doing mock interviews with her over the last couple of days and now she needs your fashion sense to bring it all together."

I clapped my hands, rubbing them together, feeling excited to be able to help in this way. I met Lena a few times before when I'd come to the shelter. She was in her mid-twenties and had a backstory like many of the women who came to the shelter for help.

"What time will she be here?"

"Eleven-thirty. Her interview's the day after tomorrow."

I nodded. "Good. We should be able to find her an outfit, and I can give her some makeup and styling tips also."

I spent the next thirty minutes picking out a couple of outfits for Lena to choose from, as well as giving some tips to a few other women who were staying at the shelter, and in the midst of looking to reinvent their style. Destiny, Patience, Kayla, and I laughed and talked as well, all of the women almost giddy with excitement for Connor and I. Kayla mentioned, more than once, how it would be nice if Connor and I moved into the subdivision where they lived. Glancing over at Destiny, I got the feeling that she'd put Kayla up to telling me about an available property just around the corner from all of them.

"I'll think about it," I finally stated once the last woman from the shelter left for the day. "Hey, I need to go to the restroom," I told the women before we began closing up the shelter's office for the day.

As soon as I stepped outside of the conference room, my hand went to my stomach while the other one held onto the doorknob to prevent me from doubling over in pain.

"Are you okay, ma'am?"

Startled, I looked up, remembering that Abe, the security Connor hired, had been out here the whole time.

"I-I'm fine. I just need to use the bathroom," I told him before straightening myself and turning on my heels to head to the restroom in the opposite direction. Once there, I burst into one of the stalls, hoping and silently praying that I was imagining things. That what I was experiencing were normal symptoms, and being a first time expectant mom who was worrying too much.

However, as I sat down on the toilet and saw the red stains on my panties, I realized that I wasn't making it all up. And that I wasn't just worrying for nothing at all.

****

"I'm sorry, but you're having a miscarriage."

A literal stab to the heart would've hurt so much less than those seven words, stated by my gynecologist as I sat on the examination table, after having just had an ultrasound.

"H-H-How can th-that b-be?" I stammered out through quivering lips. I was just there the week before getting an ultrasound. This same doctor had determined I was between six and a half to seven and a half weeks pregnant. Everything had looked good. Yet, there I was sitting in an exam room, being told by the same doctor that my baby was no longer.

"These things happen, sometimes," she answered in an irritatingly affirming voice. It fell on deaf ears. Everything she said after that seemed to hit me in the chest and bounce right off. I had to ask the same question two and three times because my brain just wasn't absorbing what she was saying.

"Resha, normally, at your stage in pregnancy, I tell my patients to let the miscarriage run its course."

"Run its course?"

"To let it happen naturally. The body will do what it needs to do. But given your history of fibroids, I think it might be better for you to get a D&C."

Grabbing my stomach, I turned away from the doctor. I knew what a D&C was. I had a friend, a fellow blogger, who had a miscarriage a few years ago, and needed to get one.

"I recommend you do one as early as today. I'm going to admit you for inpatient care as well. Just so we can monitor you for twenty-four hours after the procedure. To be on the safe side."

My head was spinning but I agreed. "Let's get it over with," I told her, my voice barely audible.

Doctor Rodriguez gave me some final words before heading out of the room, presumably to make the arrangements for the procedure. Her office was right next door to Williamsport Hospital, so I assumed that was where the surgery would take place.

"Resha?"

My heart sank at hearing Destiny's voice as she entered the room. Once I saw the blood in the bathroom back at the shelter, I couldn't hide the truth any longer, and I broke down and told Destiny what happened. She held my hand as I made the emergency appointment with Dr. Rodriguez's office, as well as had come with me, driven by Abe the security guy.

When I lifted my head, the tears I held back overflowed. Destiny rushed into the room, taking me in her arms as I nearly collapsed into the shock and grief of the moment.

"Connor is on his way. I called him to tell him where we were."

"No, no, no." I began shaking and crying. "H-He can't know. I don't want him here."

"Resha, he has to know. He's the baby's father."

"There is no more baby," I cried, covering my face with my hands.

"Oh Resh …" Destiny's words broke off on a sob as she pulled me into her arms. "It's going to be okay," she murmured repeatedly as she stroked my hair and back, consolingly.

I heard the words but couldn't believe it. Nothing would be okay after this. Not me. Not Connor and I. And certainly not the baby I was carrying. Everything I had hoped for changed in one instant and there was nothing I could do about it.

Chapter Eighteen

Connor

Maybe I should've been here, I kept repeating to myself over and over again. Instead of being out trying to be a fucking vigilante, I should've been with Resha. I suspected the night before she hadn't been feeling well, but she hadn't made a big deal out of it and so neither had I. Although I mentally kicked myself in the ass for going out to that meeting earlier, I told myself that had been for the protection of my family. But she needed me there, with her.

As I rushed through the doors of the hospital, searching for the floor Destiny had told me to meet her on, it took all of my strength not to punch a hole through the fucking wall.

"Destiny!" I yelled, seeing her down the hall when I pushed through the door from the stairwell. I'd had too much pent-up energy to wait for a fucking elevator.

"How is she? Where is she?" I questioned, searching over her head, looking farther down the hall for Resha.

"She's in that room, waiting for the nurses to come in and prep her for the procedure."

I squinted. "What procedure? What's going on?" Destiny hadn't told me much over the phone. She'd just said that Resha had been in pain and they'd gone to her doctor's office and that I should meet them there. While on my way, Abe, the security I'd hired, texted me to tell me to head to the fourth floor of the hospital instead. No more information had been given, even when I texted Destiny to ask about Resha and the baby. Resha's phone had gone to voicemail the three different times I tried calling her.

"I think Resha should be the one to tell you what's happening. She's in there." Destiny's head tilted in the direction of the door to my right.

I moved to the door, lightly knocking, before turning the knob and entering. "Resha, baby," I called as I entered the room, seeing her laying on her back in a light blue hospital gown.

She didn't stir at all. She just kept staring at the ceiling, eyes blinking every so often and her chest rising and falling, indicating that she was breathing. Outside of that, she was so still I would've thought she was asleep.

"Resha," I said again, taking her left hand into both of mine. It felt so cold, I began rubbing it to warm her up as I took a seat in the chair next to her bed.

"What are you doing here?" she finally asked, just above a whisper.

My head sprung backwards, shocked by the question. *What am I doing here? Where the hell else am I supposed to be?*

"I'm here because you're here. You and the baby," I affirmed, reaching to place my hand over her stomach.

Resha's entire body jumped as she pushed my hand away from her stomach.

"There is no more baby, Connor." With that statement, she looked directly at me.

I could see the redness of her eyes. She'd been crying, but now no tears fell from her eyes. As if she was all cried out for the time being.

I don't know which hurt worse—hearing the words she'd just shared, or knowing that she'd been crying and I wasn't there to comfort her. Both of those thoughts, however, killed something inside of me.

"There is no more baby," she repeated.

It stung just as much to hear the second time around. But nothing hurt more than her next statement.

"And there's no more us," she blurted out.

"What?" I questioned when she pulled her hand from mine.

"You heard me."

"You're not making any sense."

"I'm making total sense. We've been walking around, living in some sort of fantasy world for months now. The baby pulled us even deeper into that fantasy, allowing us to fall further into the lie that there really was something between the two of us. And now, the baby's gone and so is the fantasy. We were just two lonely ass people who met one night at a bar in New York, and just so happened to live in the same city." She shook her head resolutely before continuing.

"Thank you for helping me the night of the attack and with the break-in and everything but I think it's time we end things. Let's not delude ourselves any further into thinking this is something it was never meant to be. After this procedure is over and I'm released from the hospital, I'll be staying with Destiny and Tyler for a little while, and then I'll either get a new place of my own or stay in a hotel. Either way, you don't have to feel obligated to keep saving me." She turned back to stare at the ceiling, her hands clasped, covering her chest.

I stood, to allow myself to fully see her face. It was expressionless. She wouldn't look me in the eye—just kept concentrating on the ugly popcorn ceiling of the hospital room.

"You could at least look at me after you lie to my fucking face," I growled.

Her lips pinched and she narrowed her gaze, her eyes rolling over to me. "I'm not lying."

"Bullshit, Resha."

"Don't curse at me. I'm telling you the truth! And we both know it. You're no longer obligated to take care of me. I'm letting you off the hook. I'm not carrying your child anymore, so you have no more ties to me. You're free! Go do whatever the hell it was you were doing before we met. Go on! Get out!" she yelled.

I grew angrier, my hands gripping the railing of the bed to keep from shaking her by the shoulders. I recognized the fragile state she was in even if she didn't.

"Get out I said! Get out!" she yelled continuously as I moved away from the bed. It was only when my hand touched the doorknob that she ceased yelling. "I don't want you here when I wake up," she stated firmly before turning to stare up at the ceiling again.

I wasn't going to make her see reason. Not in the state of mind she was in. And even if I thought I could, a second later, the doorknob that was still in my hand, twisted and I was forced to step back as two nurses entered the room.

"Oh, hello," the first one said, obviously surprised by my standing there. "Ms. McDonald," they started, "we're here to prep you for the D&C ..."

I didn't say anything as the nurses began to explain to Resha what the process for prepping her would entail. I pushed through the door and moved passed Destiny, who looked stunned but didn't say anything. Needing fresh air, I made a beeline for the stairwell, keeping focused on the exit all the way at the bottom, four flights below, until I pushed through the doors. My lungs burned as I deeply breathed in the cold, winter air.

My baby was gone.

Our baby was gone.

****

Resha

See? I told you. That part of my mind that always seemed to know the right thing to say to make me loathe myself even more was active again. The previous twenty-four hours had kicked my ass, and just when I felt as if I couldn't get any lower, my mind reminded me that I was here alone, again.

Well, not exactly alone; I remembered Destiny had arrived a little earlier and was now at the nurse's station checking to see when the doctor would be in to discharge me. I ached at the reminder of going home with her while I recuperated. Just the idea of living in her home and seeing her and Tyler interacting with their three babies while I'd just lost my own nearly killed me.

Add to that the heartbreak of realizing what Connor and I had wasn't real, and all I wanted to do was sit in a corner and cry myself to sleep until I never woke up again. But I couldn't do that. At least, not right now anyway.

Sitting up in the bed, I made sure I had all of my belongings that Destiny had brought to the hospital for me packed up in a duffle bag. We were just waiting for the doctor to come in and give me the okay to leave. I didn't know whether I wanted the doctor to hurry up or to continue delaying my departure from the hospital. I'd thought getting the actual D&C would be the hardest part of all of this. But I'd been asleep for that. Hadn't felt the procedure that allowed the doctor to stick a scraping tool into my uterus and remove all of the cells that once were a fetus out of my womb. No, that hadn't been the hardest part.

The most difficult part of this so far was waking up and not having Connor there to hold my hand. The worst part of losing this baby would be to walk out of the hospital doors to my new reality. Or, what was my old reality. A life without Connor O'Brien and the child we'd conceived together.

I swallowed and wiped a tear from my eye, refusing to let myself go into a full-on meltdown again. I could save that for another time.

"Hey, I just checked at the nurse's station," Destiny told me as she knocked and entered the room. She pushed the shoulder-length curls, which I'd gotten redone the week before, back behind my ear. "The doctor should be here soon to sign off on your release."

I nodded, hating the way her voice was filled with so much tenderness and pain on my behalf. I was starting to understand why, when she'd experienced the loss of her own baby, all those years ago, she'd sent me away after a few days of staying with her, saying she needed time alone. I got it now.

"Here he is," Destiny said as the door of my hospital room pushed open, assuming it was the doctor. But it wasn't.

"What are you doing here?" Destiny hissed when Connor's large frame filled the doorway.

I stopped breathing altogether as his glare moved from my cousin to me.

"That seems to be a popular question around here." He moved inside of the room, like he owned it, stepping around Destiny as he made his way over to the bed where I sat.

"She doesn't want you here," Destiny protested.

I dipped my head in shame. I told Destiny that Connor had just left without saying much and that I didn't want to see him. I hadn't told her that I kicked him out after yelling at him and breaking up with him.

Somehow Connor knew I hadn't shared the whole story with Destiny because he looked at me and said, "Still keeping secrets, huh?"

He didn't wait for me to respond as he turned back to Destiny. "What she wants has been overruled. Thank you for being with her yesterday and today but I'm taking over from here on out."

I gasped at the same time my cousin did.

"I don't want you here," I insisted, speaking up for the first time since he entered the room.

"And I just finished telling your cousin, in so many words, that what you want doesn't matter."

My eyes bulged. "What the hell do you mean what I want doesn't matter?"

"Exactly what I said, a stór."

I was forced to move my head back slightly when Connor bent low enough to get his face even with mine. I'd never seen such a look of determination and fierceness in a man's eyes.

"You seem to be under the misguided impression that I give a shit what you want right now. And that your yelling and kicking me out of your hospital room has any bearing on what the fuck I'm doing or how I'm going to treat you. Let's get one thing straight, it doesn't. Especially in the state you're in."

Placing my hands on my hip, angered, I questioned, "What the hell does that mean? The state I'm in."

"Emotional," he stated flat out, rising to his full height, crossing his arms over his chest. "The research I've done over the past twelve hours says it's to be expected. In addition to the loss we've experienced, your hormones are also all out of whack which creates periods of intense emotion and whatnot. So, if you think I'm not going to be around to see you through this, or that I'm going to let you spend however many weeks at your cousin's …" he paused to glance over his shoulder at a silent Destiny, "you've got this all fucked up."

Not bothering to wait for my response, he gave me one final look before reaching around me, grabbing for the bag of my belongings that Destiny had brought for me earlier that morning. After securing the bag over his shoulder, he lifted my forest green, wool coat from the bed and held it open for me to step into.

"It's cold outside. Let's go," he insisted when I obviously hesitated.

My eyes went to Destiny, who continued to stare at the two of us, as if in somewhat of a daze. Connor's growling sound, the same one he made when growing impatient, pulled my gaze back to him. The noise only ceased when I stepped forward, spinning around to place my arms in the sleeves of my coat, allowing him to put it on me.

"I can button the damn thing myself," I asserted only after he attempted to start buttoning it for me.

"Then do it and let's go."

Pursing my lips, I glared at him but didn't say anything.

"We have to wait for the doc—" I began a few seconds later, having forgotten that I hadn't even gotten the doctor's approval to leave the hospital just yet, when there was a knock on the door.

"Dr. Mills," Connor greeted with a nod of his head, catching me by surprise.

How does he know this doctor?

The doctor nodded at Connor. "Ms. McDonald, how are you feeling?"

I cleared my throat, not knowing how to answer that question.

"Physically?" he clarified.

"Okay."

He nodded, seeming to understand that, while I felt okay physically, aside from some cramping—which was normal—I wasn't *actually* okay. But he couldn't do anything about that.

"Well, your lab work from this morning came back and all your numbers look good. So, I'm okay with discharging you. You remember the instructions given to you by your doctor, right?"

I nodded, but of course, Dr. Mills had to go over everything my own gynecologist had told me the day before, yet again. When I saw a look exchanged between Connor and Dr. Mills, I got the impression that the doctor had been somewhat coerced into the amount of care and detail he was giving me. However, I didn't think too much about it. My head was heavy with the emotions and I just wanted to get in bed and lay down, and not get back up for the foreseeable future.

"I'll call you later, Resh," Destiny finally said as Connor held the door open for both she and I to pass through. "It'll be okay. Let him take care of you," she whispered in my ear while pulling me into a hug.

I didn't respond. I couldn't respond. The truth was, my heart felt like it expanded at the thought of being taken care of by Connor. Yet, my head remembered everything I'd endured over the previous twenty-four hours. That knowledge sank down into my heart and it contracted again under the weight of my grief. It didn't feel like everything would be okay.

However, even as those morose thoughts ricocheted around in my head, causing it to spin, the moment Connor slipped his large hand around mine, walking us out of that hospital, I felt something pushing against the heaviness of the grief. I wouldn't dare call it hope—I'd been hopeful just forty-eight hours prior, and look how that'd turned out—but I felt comfort in knowing that after experiencing such a hard loss I wasn't walking out into the world alone.

Chapter Nineteen

Resha

"I'm going out for a few hours. I left the chili on the stove and the cornbread in the oven to keep it warm."

I nodded slightly, not verbally responding, as I turned the pages of the book I was barely reading. Though I wasn't looking at him, I felt when Connor moved from the balcony doorway, closer to the couch I was sitting on. A breath later, I felt my shoulders being covered by yet another fleece throw blanket, as if I wasn't already covered in two of them.

"It's cold out here, a stór. Maybe you should come inside and read."

"I'm fine," I stated curtly, turning yet another page I hadn't read.

Connor stood over me, staring down, but I kept my eyes on the words I didn't truly see.

It'd been like this for three weeks, since I'd gotten back from the hospital—Connor ordering food, day after day, keeping it warm on the stove or in the oven, covering me with excess blankets as I sat outside on the balcony. Very few words were being exchanged between the two of us, even when he accompanied me to Dr. Rodriguez's office for a follow-up visit to see how I was doing. He'd asked me how the visit went since he sat out in the lobby, and I'd told him *fine*, my usual answer to that question these days, but that was all I gave.

"You need to eat, Resha."

I almost flinched at the growing impatience I heard in his voice. *Good.*

Maybe he'll get so impatient with me that eventually he'll give up, recognize that what I said in the hospital was true and that we really have nothing in common, and he'll let me go on my way without a fuss. Most men in my life seemed to have operated that way. Even my own father who'd been with my mom up until I was one year old, and then decided that we weren't enough for him, and he split.

But Connor wasn't my father. He wasn't the type to quit so easily. I remembered that as he leaned down, placing a kiss to my temple, letting his lips linger there for just a moment. It was a brief exchange of intimacy, but enough to warm me up more than the three blankets I wore on the outside balcony on this cold, wintery day. Regardless, the coldness that still lingered in my heart, was fiercer than the outside temperatures. In spite of Connor's devotion, the iciness lingered.

And when he walked away to wherever it was he went on Tuesday nights, although I wanted to call to him to ask where he was going, I refrained.

Probably to go see another woman.

One who could give him children if he wanted them.

That was when the tears started again. Thank God, he left just before they started because they always felt like a faucet I couldn't turn off. I'd expected the crying bouts to let up by then but they still came and I couldn't stop them. Not when I was alone. It was as if my body knew it was safe to let them flow, at least for a little while.

"Pull it together," I grunted at myself, feeling foolish for yet another meltdown. I'd barely been ten weeks pregnant, how was I still so emotional over losing something I never really had?

Shoving the book aside, I picked up my tablet and attempted to go onto Instagram, but I couldn't bring myself to do it. When I clicked on the web browser, the page I'd been reading previously opened up.

What Caused Your Miscarriage?

That was the title of the article. I'd read it over and over, and at least ten others just like it over the past three weeks. But this time, instead of reading the article, I scrolled down to the comments sections. That was always where debates and arguments occurred. Women shared their experiences of miscarriage, how they changed their diets or started working out more, and viola! They got pregnant easier, or were able to hold the pregnancy for a full forty weeks. I read the comments of these articles incessantly, searching for what I'd done wrong.

Was it the cup of decaf coffee I'd switched to in the morning? Some comments said that even decaf had small amounts of caffeine in it which could affect the baby. A woman commented that all the chemicals and BPA in the plastic bottles and cleaners she used caused her infertility, and when she switched to organic and natural, she got pregnant.

I read to the point of obsession, so much so that I didn't hear or see the man sneaking up on me, until he reached out, touching my leg.

"Oh!" I jumped out of my damn seat, grabbing my chest with my free hand, my heart palpitating.

"Sorry, Resha. Didn't mean to scare you," Mark stated, a concerned expression covering his face. However, his hazel eyes reminded me so much of his brother's that it was difficult to feel anything aside from relief at seeing them.

"No, no worries, Mark," I responded, pushing out a heavy breath, trying to regulate my breathing.

"I called your name as I entered the apartment but you were so enthralled in what you were reading, I guess you didn't hear me." His eyebrows shot up as he glanced at the tablet still in my lap. "What *are* you reading?"

Closing out of the web browser, I shut down the tablet and set it on the coffee table in front of me. "Nothing. H-How are you?" I questioned, clearing my throat and readjusting the blankets over my body. Mark had been stopping by more frequently over the past few weeks, in particular when Connor wasn't home. I started to suspect Connor put his brother up to it, to have someone watching over me while he wasn't here.

"I'm good. Busy day at work but no big deal."

I snorted derisively, but then felt guilty as I looked at Mark. "Sorry."

He shook his head. "Nothing for you to be sorry about."

I sighed. "Is Connor putting you up to this? Visiting me while he's out doing God knows what and with whomever?"

Mark's brows knitted in a way that signaled his confusion. "No one puts me up to anything."

"You sound like him."

He shrugged. "He practically raised me."

I almost let out a smile. Almost. And then I remembered the baby that Connor wouldn't get to raise because of my own body's failure to sustain a pregnancy.

"You don't have to keep coming. I don't need to be coddled, and I'm sure you have things to do."

"Have you eaten?"

I frowned. He obviously wasn't about to take my bait.

"I'll take that as a no. I think I smelled some chili coming from the kitchen. I'll go make us some bowls."

I silently watched as he rolled backwards until he had enough space to turn and head through the balcony doorway, and presumably over to the kitchen. I heard sounds of him moving around in the kitchen. I thought of going in to help him, but it felt like such a task to bother with getting up from my seat. Luckily, Connor's kitchen had been outfitted to be handicap accessible. He told me as much when I asked about the spacing in his kitchen when I first moved in.

For when Mark comes over. He ain't shit as a cook but if he ever gets the inkling, the kitchen's set up for him already.

It warmed my heart to think he'd considered his brother's needs even when picking out his own home. That was one of the first inclinations I got that Connor would make a great father.

"This looks great," Mark interrupted my ruminations as he pushed his way over the balcony doorway with a tray of two bowls on saucers with cornbread on the side for each of us.

I just stared at the food for a moment, but then Mark said, "You know I tell the Big Guy if you don't eat."

I glared at him before leaning in and taking the bowl and spoon. "Traitor," I murmured before putting a spoonful of the chili into my mouth. For a full two seconds, I savored the richness of the chili powder, onion, peppers, liquid smoke, and a touch of sweetness from the tomatoes, in the chili. Admittedly, if I'd been in a different space and mood, I'd classify the food as delicious—I might even be looking up where Connor had purchased it from to find out the recipe to recreate it myself, but not that day.

"It's great, isn't it?" Mark questioned.

Glancing over, I saw that he was nearly halfway done with his own bowl.

"It's okay."

He chuckled. "Jealous it just might be better than yours?"

I gave him a half smile. "I can do better."

"You'll have to prove that one to me, sis. I haven't had your chili yet."

I blinked at the nickname he'd bestowed me with.

"Don't give me that look," he stated slyly as he broke off a piece of his cornbread and popped it into his mouth.

"You called me *sis*."

He gave a one shoulder shrug as he chewed. "That's what you are, pretty much anyway."

"Am I?"

"Any wife of my brother's will be my sister."

I squirmed in my seat, looking down into the bowl in my lap.

"I'm not his wife."

Mark snorted. "You live together. He's closer to you than anyone else I've seen him with. Hell, he calls me to come look after you when he's not around. My big brother doesn't call on me to do *anything* for him. He's used to it being the other way around. So, you mean a hell of a lot more to him than you realize because he does things for you that he's never done for anyone else."

My heart ached at Mark's words. They should've made me feel better. He was saying them to lift my spirits, I guessed. Unfortunately, their impact was the opposite of what he'd intended. They made me feel worse. Connor was giving so much and I couldn't give him anything in return.

"Don't do that to yourself," Mark insisted, moving closer to me and placing a hand on my knee.

"Do what?" I questioned, sitting up straight and wiping a wayward tear from the corner of my eye.

"Beating yourself up over what happened."

I began shaking my head. I didn't want to talk about *what happened.*

"I know, I know," he began, apologetically. "You don't want to talk about it and I'm not about to try to make you. The last thing I need is for you to get upset, start crying, and Connor come home to see you upset … he might try to kick my ass, or worse toss me over this balcony." He jutted his head toward the balcony's railing, smirking.

That pulled another small smile from my lips. I wasn't ready to laugh just yet. Didn't know if I ever would be but Mark had a way of lightening my mood.

Clearing my throat, I said, "Thanks for coming," before taking another spoonful of my chili.

"Thanks for eating. Connor would be pissed at me if he knew I was here and couldn't get you to eat something."

I rolled my eyes as I placed my half empty bowl and half a piece of cornbread onto the coffee table. "Well, you can report to him that you saw me eat."

"Good. Now that that's out of the way, wanna play cards or something? What? What was that look?"

I blinked and shook my head, not even realizing I'd worn my emotions in my expression. "Nothing."

"It was something."

I sighed. "It was just your asking to play cards reminded me of the night I was attacked in that alleyway. Connor stayed with me all night at my apartment. One of the things he did to keep me awake was ask me for a deck of playing cards. He teased me about my pink cards."

Mark snorted. "Sounds like my brother. Who the hell has pink playing cards anyway?"

"I got them for breast cancer awareness month," I defended.

Mark rolled his eyes. "Whatever. But that does explain why it's all cute and frilly out here on his once, all-black, barely any furniture balcony," he stated, looking around. "He did this for you."

I glanced around as well. "He decorated it exactly how I had my balcony at my own place."

"See?"

My gaze connected with Mark's.

"He wouldn't do this for just anyone."

I didn't say anything but it hurt too much to know that.

****

I laid in bed, scrolling through photos I'd taken of myself weeks ago, trying to decide which one I was going to post on my Instagram that day. I was getting messages from concerned readers, inquiring as to why I hadn't been posting much in recent weeks. Clearly, I wasn't ready to tell the entirety of the internet why I'd taken a semi-break from posting. Plus, there was the whole concern about brands and sponsors who required I post their content a certain amount of times in order to hold up my end of our contract.

Sighing, I sat up, having chosen a picture, and began typing out a caption to go along with it.

"Goddamnit!" Connor growled from downstairs just moments before a loud crashing sound frightened the hell out of me.

"What the—" I questioned, jumping up from the bed, and started running down the stairs. My heart raced as I feared the worst.

"Shit!" I found Connor mumbling to himself as he looked at the spilled contents on the kitchen floor.

"What's going on?" I demanded.

He spun around, facing me, his eyes going wide for a moment before narrowing in ... shame? Embarrassment, maybe?

"You weren't supposed to hear that."

"Sweetie, I think the whole damn building heard that," I countered. "What are you doing?" My eyes went to what appeared to be some sort of soup concoction on the floor with the black soup pot in the middle of it all.

"Screw them," he growled.

"Connor?"

"I was trying to make that beef stew or soup you made weeks ago, all right?" he grumbled, tossing his arms up in despair. The look of despair in his expression pulled at the muscle inside of my chest.

Taking a step closer, I stopped and finally took a good look at him. At *all* of him.

"Oh my God!" I blurted out before doubling over in laughter. The laughter came out of nowhere, and every time I thought it died down, all I needed was another look at Connor standing there in my *Queen of the Kitchen* apron, which was adorned with colorful cupcakes and pink frills, to start cracking up all over again.

I don't know how long it took for me to sober up, but doing so consisted of me wiping away tears.

"I can't believe you're wearing my apron." I giggled some more, still unable to totally stop.

"I haven't heard that laugh in weeks."

That did it.

The sincerity in his deep voice tugged at something else inside of me, and the laughter was replaced by some other force when our eyes connected. It was at that moment, I also realized that Connor wasn't wearing a shirt underneath the apron. Letting my gaze move lower, I saw he was wearing my favorite pair of grey sweatpants. And for the first time in nearly a month, my body felt like a light switch turned on.

"Started to believe I'd never hear it again."

I dipped my head before peering back up at him. He was standing directly over me. "I was starting to believe that I'd never laugh again," I confessed, rising up on my tiptoes, allowing my lips to meet his. Apparently, the fear I'd been having about never being able to be physically intimate or vulnerable again was unfounded.

But Connor pushed away from me, turning to the floor. "I need to clean this up."

Sadness now filling my chest cavity, I merely nodded. "I'll make us something."

He snorted. "No way. You're supposed to be resting. Taking it easy. I'll just order us—"

"No." I shook my head adamantly. "I've rested enough and I can't eat another take out meal. I'd almost rather eat whatever it was you spilled on the floor, than have another delivery order up here."

Stepping around Connor and the mess on the floor, I went to the refrigerator, pulling it open to see what there was to cook. For a man who hated cooking, Connor sure kept a well-stocked fridge. I pulled out some Brussel sprouts and chicken thighs to bake, and took out a few sweet potatoes from the basket on the counter to prepare. All the while, I watched Connor clean up the mess on the floor, stick the soup pot in the dishwasher, and then remove the apron.

That familiar tingling sensation began throughout my body as I observed him in the middle of the kitchen, shirtless, in only a pair of sweatpants. He moved closer, staring me down as well. Tilting my head upwards, I closed my eyes, readying myself for the inevitable. However, all I felt was his arms move over my head and then the material of the apron around the back of my neck, as he placed it on me, tying it at the back. Blinking my eyes open, I stared up in confusion.

"I'm going to take a shower." He stepped back, giving me one last lingering look before turning and heading up the same stairs I'd just come down.

Shaking the negative thoughts that started moving through my head, I went back to preparing our dinner, all the while trying to convince myself the inevitable wasn't happening. Still, as I prepped and seasoned the chicken to go in the oven, I couldn't shake the thought that what was between Connor and I really was over.

Chapter Twenty

Connor

"I'm heading out for a few—"

"Are you cheating on me?" Resha demanded as she stared at me from the balcony couch where she'd been working for the past hour.

My first response to that idiotic question was total and utter confusion. My second was to lift her from that damn couch and shake some damn sense into her. Luckily, I decided to go with my third reaction, which was to ask, "A stór, what in the hell are you talking about?"

I was just barely able to contain the anger in my tone.

She remained silent for so long, I started to believe she wouldn't answer me, and that shit just wouldn't fly.

"Don't get shy on my now, baby. You had enough words in you to ask that dumbass question, now backup why you would even think such a—"

"Because you're always going out every Tuesday evening at the same time. And it's not for a work thing or meeting. I know your schedule."

I lifted an eyebrow, cocking my head to the side.

Pushing out a heavy breath, she tossed the blankets that'd been covering her body to the side, standing.

"Yeah, I did it. I called your assistant and asked her if your Tuesday meetings were on your schedule and she said no. In fact, she said she had strict instructions to always keep your Tuesdays clear." She moved closer, coming to stop directly in front of me, arms folded, appearing defensive. "Look, Connor, if that's what this is, if you're seeing someone else, just tell me. I know what we've experienced the last month or so could be detrimental to any relationship, and I obviously haven't been the most intimate person lately because—"

"Have your coat and shoes on in the next five minutes."

She blinked, looking astonished.

I moved aside, glaring at her, waiting for her to follow my abrupt instructions. "You can either do it yourself or I'll do it for you."

With a crease in her brow, Resha moved passed me, heading upstairs. Two minutes later, she came down the stairs in a pair of tennis shoes that were, naturally, designer, and a pink and purple color that matched appropriately with her off-the-shoulder striped sweater and dark denim jeans. Even sitting around the house, she had a natural style about her that many women wished for. I carefully watched as she put on the long, burgundy coat that hung from the coat rack by the door.

"Ready?"

She nodded, obviously still confused but willing to allow me to take the lead. Taking her hand into mine, I led us onto the elevator, and down to the garage level of my building, where my car was parked. Typically, I'd take my motorcycle for this trip—it allowed me to think and clear out my mind, both on the way to where I was headed, and while driving back home—but since Resha was with me, I opted for my SUV. Not for one moment had I forgotten that the fucker who was stalking her was still out there, on the loose. So far, checking the records of the security staff and the property management company of her building had revealed nothing.

"Where are we going?" she finally inquired after about five minutes of driving in total silence.

"To answer your question," was all I responded with. Glancing over, I saw her tuck her bottom lip into her mouth. She wanted to ask more but was afraid to. I didn't say anything, partially because I was still pissed that she could even think that I'd want to see someone else. And secondly, because I was mentally kicking my own ass for not being up front from the beginning. I was about to reveal a secret with her that only one other person in my life knew.

Fifteen minutes later we pulled up to the parking lot of a huge brick building. Surrounding the building was a spacious yard, that in the summer was filled with green grass and colorful flowers. During the winter, however, as it was, patches of snow were visible, only showing few spots of dried, dead grass. The scene was still nice for people who liked that sort of thing. I made out two people on the walking trail around the building, one pushing the other in their wheelchair.

"What is this place?" Resha questioned as she squinted, peering up at the bronze plate across the top of the front entrance that read 'Williamsburg Nursing Home and Rehabilitation Center'. Resha turned to me. "What's this?"

"Where I go Tuesday evenings." Taking her hand in mine, I led her across the parking lot and down the sidewalk that led through the front entrance. As soon as I entered the door, the receptionist smiled at me.

"Mr. O'Brien, nice to see you again," the older woman intoned before her warm, brown eyes moved to Resha who was standing beside me.

"Mrs. O'Hare, this is my lady, Resha McDonald," I introduced, wincing a little when I said her last name.

"Ms. McDonald, a pleasure to meet you."

"You as well," Resha responded before turning to me, still confused, obviously.

"Is he awake?"

"Sure is. He's in his room at the moment, wasn't feeling too well earlier."

I frowned. "Is he coming down with something? Need to be taken to the hos—"

"No, no." She waved me off. "He just didn't sleep well last night." She shrugged. "You know how it goes sometimes. He was a little grumpier than usual this morning from lack of sleep. He rested this afternoon after I reminded him that it was Tuesday and you were coming to see him."

Guilt filled my chest as I nodded and turned to pass through the main doors, after signing in along with Resha. I still held her hand in mine, and she was silent as we made our way down the long hallway, her free hand moving over to cup my wrist, signaling her questioning and how uncomfortable she was with not knowing what was happening.

We turned right, and passed a number of doors before stopping at room 132. I knocked lightly and pushed the door open. The first person I noticed was a nurse's aide, who I was familiar with.

"Mr. O'Brien." He nodded and stepped aside.

"Samuel," I called.

The man sitting in a wheelchair at the window shook his head a little, mumbling.

I nodded at the aide and he turned Samuel's wheelchair.

"Samuel, it's me, Connor." A small smile crested on the man's face. I turned to Resha. "Resha, this is Samuel. Not Sam, Samuel."

"No! Don't call me Sam," Samuel slurred but was adamant as he slapped the side of his wheelchair.

"N-Nice to meet you, Samuel," Resha spoke before turning to me and then back to the dark-haired man in the wheelchair. At first glance, anyone could see that he was younger than me, so the last place one would expect him to be was a nursing home.

"R-R-R-"

"Resha," I stated, helping Samuel out. Letting Resha's hand go, I moved to Samuel, kneeling next to him. "Samuel, this is Resha. She's come with me today to meet you. Is that okay?"

For a split second, Samuel's eyes focused as he looked Resha up and down. He didn't say anything, but he braced his hands on the side of the chair, placing his feet on the floor instead of the footholds. When I realized what he was trying to do, I depressed the lever that held down the wheelchair's brakes, to allow Samuel to push off of it to stand.

"H-H-Hi, R-R-Resha," Samuel managed to get out as he stood up from the chair.

Resha moved closer, taking the hand he extended to her. "Hi, Samuel. It's nice to meet you."

"C-C-Connor my friend," he told her. "H-H-He your friend, too?"

Resha's coffee-colored eyes moved to me before returning to Samuel. "I suppose so."

My chest tightened in anger.

"You're p-p-pretty, I-I-I think."

"Easy, Samuel," I stated, rising from the floor. "That's my woman you're trying to seduce." Taking his hand, I freed Resha's from his hold. No, I wasn't jealous, per se, but I didn't like any man but me touching her.

"Samuel's right. We're friends," I turned to Resha, hoping that somehow this made sense. I couldn't say the whole story right then but I would later. I just needed her to see where and how I spent my time on Tuesday evenings when I was away from her. The only reason I'd leave her, even for a few hours out of the week. It was to follow through on a commitment I'd made many years ago and I was nothing if I wasn't a man of my word. Even when it hurt to leave the woman I loved while she was in such pain.

But Resha must've understood how important this was to me. She must not have needed the words right away because she went along with Samuel and I as he showed us the old baseball trading cars he'd had since he was a kid. This was something he did every time I visited, no matter how many times I'd seen it. Then he turned on the television in his room, turning to the fighting match he had the aide record and waited to watch specifically during my visit. It was a few hours before Resha and I left, having stayed to enjoy meatloaf, mashed potatoes, and string bean dinner they always served on Tuesday nights.

"That's where you go on Tuesdays," Resha stated as I got behind the wheel of my car in the parking lot of the nursing home.

Sticking the key into the ignition, I turned to her to explain. "Samuel is a fighter. Was …" I corrected. "About ten years ago he was an up-and-comer in my division. For a year and a half, his trainer and manager had been asking me to put him on my list of fights. I was only doing about two to three fights a year. I'd made enough money and earned enough clout that I could spend most of the year training and still get paid millions for doing a single fight. Plus, I had my businesses going by then. I didn't need fighting to pay the bills any longer. I was already considering retirement but fighting was all I knew so I kept at it.

"One year, I finally decided to take the fight. It'd be worth a lot, and what the hell?" I shrugged. "What I didn't know was that Samuel was already suffering from a severe concussion, from a fight he'd had earlier that year. Instead of taking more time off like his doctors advised, his manager kept pushing him to fight. On the outside, he looked fine, but he wasn't. He lasted all of three rounds in the fence with me. I knocked him out. A knockout wasn't unusual, and I expected him to wake up with some smelling salt. He didn't. I stood there in the middle of that cage and watched as medical staff rushed to his aid. Later that night, I went straight to the hospital to find out that Samuel was in a coma. Doctors gave him about a fifty percent chance of waking up. Over the next few weeks, brain scans revealed that even if he did wake up, he'd never be the same. I felt like total shit."

Pausing, I stared Resha in the eye. "Samuel's entire team abandoned him in that hospital. He was no longer of use to them, and couldn't make them any money so they left him there to die. He came from a rough background, his family had been living off of him and when he couldn't provide for them, they left him, too. Eventually, the small amount of money that he had saved ran out and he was to be shipped to a state facility. I couldn't live with that shit on my conscience. The money I earned from the fight went to pay his medical bills. After a month in a coma, he woke up. I paid to move him to this nursing home so he would be taken care of and receive the rehabilitation he needs.

"I come every Tuesday to visit him because no one else does. I was him once. Had my circumstances been just a little bit different, it could be me in that damn room and not Samuel. I got lucky. I had Buddy who never forced me to take on a fight I wasn't ready for. Who made sure I got paid double what I was worth, and who introduced me to businessmen who showed me where the real money was, so I didn't have to always put my body on the line. I retired after that last fight with Samuel."

"How come you run the Underground?"

I nodded. It was a reasonable question in light of what I'd just revealed. "We all need an outlet of some kind. Most of the guys in the Underground don't want to fight for a living, they just need a place to let their demons out. But one of our only rules is that we don't allow headshots."

"That was your rule."

I nodded. "I've seen what repeated blows to the head can do to a person." I looked back, through my rear window toward the nursing home.

Resha's hand covered mine. "I thought you didn't want me anymore."

Her admission pulled my gaze from the building to hers. Cupping her face with both of my hands, I questioned, "How the fuck could you even consider that?"

"You always just said you were going *out,* and ..." She trailed off until I shook her face slightly. "You've barely touched me in weeks." She pushed out a breath as if the admission nearly killed her.

"Baby, you were healing."

"I know, but ..." She pulled back.

"But what?"

"But it's been weeks. Physically, I've gotten the all clear from my doctor. But lately, every time I get close to you and think you're going to kiss me, you make an excuse. Like the other day in the kitchen, you had to go and shower. If you're not attracted to me anymore, just say so—" The last half of that sentence was pushed back down where it came from when I pressed my lips to hers, effectively cutting her off.

Moving her hand to my crotch so she could feel the growing monster in my jeans, I pulled back. "Does that feel like I'm not attracted to you anymore?"

Looking dazed and a bit confused, she shook her head.

"Baby, I had to make that shower a cold one and jerk off while I was in there ... twice."

"Why?"

"To keep myself from mauling you. Seriously, every goddamn night you lay in bed next to me I have to remind myself not to give into my animal instincts to rip every inch of clothing from your body and make you scream my name like I've been yearning to hear for weeks now. I didn't want to push you too fast. I know you're still hurting from losing our baby. We both are, by the way."

"Oh." Her eyes dropped from mine. "I thought you didn't want me since I couldn't have a baby, and you went and found someone else."

"Resha ..." I pushed out a breath, giving myself time to get my thoughts—which were jumbled with anger that she could even fathom such a thing—together. "A stór, I would cut off my right fucking arm and beat myself with it before I did anything like that to you."

She frowned. "Thanks for that imagery."

I chuckled before pulling her to me again for a kiss. "What I'm saying is, there is no getting rid of me. You're stuck with me. Do you know how much it killed me to introduce you as Resha McDonald at the front desk?"

Her forehead creased. "That's my name."

"Resha O'Brien sounds better."

Her eyes ballooned.

"Baby, if trying for another baby is what you want, I will put a hundred babies in your womb."

"And what if ..."

"Then we'll adopt or steal a kid or borrow one from someone. I don't give a shit. We'll have the family that we both crave. In our own time and our own way."

Turning to my left hand that still cupped her face, she kissed the inside of my palm. "How can you be so sure?"

"Because I don't believe in coincidences."

More confusion on that pretty face of hers.

"It was no coincidence that we met in that bar in New York, or that yours was the first face I saw when I walked in, or that the loneliness that I saw in your eyes pulled me to you because it mirrored my own. You were right about what you said in the hospital. That night, we were two lonely ass people, looking to not be so alone. But it became so much more than just that. It's not a coincidence that we both lived in the same city and found one another months after our first encounter. And I know for damn sure it's not a coincidence that we fell in love. That was destined for us."

I paused, moving my thumb to wipe away the tears that streamed down her cheeks. She didn't need to form any words. Her tears told me enough. And when she moaned into my mouth as I pulled her in for a kiss, I knew that neither one of us could hold out any longer.

****

Resha

"Don't be soft with me tonight," I pleaded, staring up into Connor's eyes, my back pressed against the wall of the elevator as he hovered over me.

His lips pressed together, and for a second he looked hesitant.

Circling his neck with one arm and bringing his head down to meet my lips, I kissed him with everything I had inside of me, before pulling back. "I don't need you to be soft or gentle with me tonight, Connor. I want you. All of you," I said just above a whisper.

I wasn't in the mood to be treated with kid gloves. I wanted to be handled in only the way Connor could. I wanted to be desired, cherished, and loved all while being thoroughly sexed. I needed the feeling of being pushed to the edge, all the while feeling incredibly safe, that only came from being in his arms. It'd been weeks since I'd felt that. Weeks since I allowed myself to feel anything other than grief. Now, I wanted more. The grief was still there. It would be for a long time, but right then I wanted my man more than anything else.

Connor's lips crashed down on mine, pulling a moan of gratitude from me. His kiss was all-consuming, just the way I needed it. Somewhere in the far off distance I heard the elevator beep as it came to a stop. My heart sank a little when Connor pulled back, to allow himself to reach for the button that would open the elevator door directly into his apartment.

"I won't take you for the first time in a month, in our elevator."

My heart sank and rose at the same time. Something I never knew was possible. It sank because I thought I might burst into flames and die if I didn't have him inside of me at that moment, but rose at hearing him call this place, this elevator, *ours* without hesitation.

"Just make it quick," I demanded.

"Oh hell no, baby. I plan on taking my time wit— What the hell?" he raged suddenly, causing me to look from him to the middle of the living room.

A wide-eyed Mark sat there, eating a plate of the leftover baked chicken and vegetables I'd prepared a few nights before.

"Welcome home. Glad to see you got outside for a little while, Resha," he stated calmly. "This chicken is delicious, by the way. Lemon pepper? Can I get the recipe?" he questioned, before cutting another piece from the plate in his lap and devouring it.

"Get the hell out," Connor demanded.

Mark gave Connor an impish look. "How wonderful to see you, too, brother. Is that how you welcome me these days?"

"Get out."

"Babe, don't be rude," I interjected.

"Yeah, *babe*. Especially since you failed to call me and tell me that my stopping by tonight wouldn't be necessary." Mark put his knife and fork down on his mostly empty plate and rolled himself to the kitchen.

I followed, and Connor followed me.

"As you can see, you're not needed tonight. Get out."

"You're so mean," I said over my shoulder.

"No, what I am is horny as a motherfucker and ready to throw my brother out on his ass," he stated low in my ear, the rumbling in his voice reaching down, in between my thighs.

"I heard that."

Mark's comment pulled my attention back to his now frowning face. Suddenly, his face morphed into a grin and he shrugged.

"But I see that I'm not needed and my belly is full, so I'll take that as my cue to leave." He rolled past us, out of the kitchen.

"Good to see you looking better, Resha. By the way, that burgundy color really works for you."

"Thanks, Mar—"

"Bye, and don't forget to lock the fucking door on your way out."

Mark chuckled.

Spinning, I placed my hand on my hip, giving Connor a glare.

"What? He always leaves that fucking elevator unlocked. Did the same shit as a kid, leaving the door unlocked." He shook his head as if he were a father, thinking of his unruly child. It was such a turn on.

"I'm glad you two are getting along better."

Connor grunted but didn't say anything.

"Mark told me you called him and told him your issues with his fighting. Your *real* concerns."

"Yeah well, whatever."

"You're so cute." I found it funny that Connor didn't hesitate when it came to openly expressing his feelings with me but it was a different story with his brother.

"Still. You could've been nicer."

His eyes narrowed, and a spark entered them. One that had my nipples budding beneath the fabric of my bra.

"You don't want me to be nice tonight, remember?" And before I could respond, he took one step in my direction, bent low, and circled my thighs with both of his arms, hoisting my over his shoulder.

"Connor!" I yelped, feeling a twinge of fear for the briefest of moments. It was a natural reaction, but then the warmth filling my body reminded me who had me. I knew he wouldn't let me fall, even as he carried me up the stairs. Still, I smacked his backside just to be able to feel the muscles of his ass beneath the jeans he wore.

"Oof!" I blurted out when he dropped me onto the bed, causing me to bounce a couple of times. He wasn't going to be gentle that night, and I started to wonder what the hell I'd been thinking telling him that in the elevator.

His gaze was focused and intentional as he roughly unbuttoned my belt and jeans, yanking them down my thighs, calves, and eventually off my body.

Rip!

I gasped at the sound of my lace panties tearing underneath the strength of his determination.

"Connor, you ripped my damn panties!"

"Your fault," he grunted as he moved to cover my body, taking my mouth with his.

I groaned against his lips as my core began to ache with need. My entire body started to feel weak, and I sent up a silent thank you that I was already lying down because I didn't have the strength to stand on my own two feet.

His large hands felt underneath the sweater I wore, moving it up my body and over my head. He was so deft at removing my bra, I felt like I blinked and it was off. I watched as he tossed it over his shoulder, dipping his head as he pushed both of my breasts together and covered my nipples with his mouth. I practically felt a waterfall gushing between my thighs as my back arched into the feeling of his hot mouth. I let my hands intertwine in his hair, disposing of the band he used to hold his long locks back.

"Ooh! Baby, that feels so good," I moaned.

But before I could get too comfortable in that position, Connor flipped our bodies over and slid down on the bed a ways, while holding me in place by the waist. He was so damn athletic and dexterous that he would have me in positions I never dreamt of moving in before.

I found myself with my knees pressed against the bed as my pussy lips hovered over his face. He was especially fond of this position. I'd found myself self-conscious in the beginning but this was quickly becoming a favorite of my own. Especially when Connor pulled my waist down to his face, and pressed my lips apart with his tongue, circling my clitoris.

Tossing my head backwards, I held onto the headboard for dear life as I let out a wail of a scream. My entire body sighed in relief at being in this position and receiving this kind of pleasure again. It'd been a month since Connor and I had made love and he was letting his mouth make up for lost time.

My sudden and thunderous climax was his reward, and he sopped up the physical evidence of my orgasm with the fervor of someone who's been waiting all year for their Thanksgiving dinner.

"Jesus!" I breathed out, struggling for air.

"Jesus can't save you tonight, baby," he growled, pressing my back against the bed while simultaneously lifting my left leg over his shoulder.

I was so dazed, I couldn't even recall when he'd removed his clothing, but I sure as hell felt all of him when he began pressing himself inside of me.

"So fucking tight," he groaned, again his tone electrifying every nerve ending in my body. He wrapped one arm around my leg, trapping it to his body, allowing himself free entry into my canal however he wanted.

"Tell me you're mine," he demanded, pushing inside of me all the way to the hilt.

"I'm yours," I conceded, repeatedly with each thrust of his hips. There was no way I could ever be anyone else's.

Lifting my hands to circle his neck, I pulled his head down to meet mine, kissing him with all the promises I was too tongue-tied to actually say in that moment. This small position change allowed him to push even farther inside of me and I let out a small scream. Connor responded by biting my lower lip and sucking it into his mouth. At the same time, the tip of his cock, along with the ring he still wore, hit my G-spot at just the right angle and all I saw were stars exploding.

My entire body shuddered with the release of my second orgasm for that night. Connor kissed me through it, his hips continuing to surge forward over and over again, as the walls of my vagina milked him for his release. His body obeyed, granting him his first orgasm of the evening.

But that wasn't to be his last. We went at it like rabbits until the wee hours of the morning, relieved and elated to have this sort of intimacy back between the both of us.

Chapter Twenty-One

Connor

"Who threw you away?" I questioned as Resha's head rested against my chest and I let my fingers glide up and down her sweaty arm. Part of me felt guilty for putting her body through so much exertion, after being intimate for the first time in a month, but I couldn't help my damn self. I'd been jerking off in the shower, alone, for the better part of a month, just to not be an asshole and push her too far too fast.

But as we laid there, in the dark, our bodies completely sated—for the time being, at least—I asked the one question I'd been wanting to know the answer to for weeks.

"Was it your mother?" I pressed when she didn't answer at first.

Slowly, her head lifted, her face turning to meet mine. "How'd you know I was thrown away?"

I shook my head, pressing my free hand behind my head. "Because you've always got one foot out the door. Using any and every excuse to push me away before you get pushed away. Making up excuses in that cute little head of yours as to why this can't or won't work out. And don't give me that shit about past relationships. I know you've had some boneheads before but those fuckers ain't me and there's a reason you try so damn hard to not see that. Was it your mother?"

I went back to the question I'd asked previously because I knew the truth was there. Resha had admitted some things about her mother but not much. She didn't talk about her life before she went to live with her aunt, uncle, and Destiny.

"Yeah," she finally admitted just a hair above a whisper. "But she didn't just throw me away. She *gave* me away."

"To your aunt and uncle."

She shook her head. "They didn't come until later." She paused, turning away from me before facing me again. Sitting up in the bed, she reached over me to click on the nightstand lamp. "If I'm going to say this, I want to be able to see you when I do."

I sat up also, leaning my back against the headboard, and waited for her next words.

"I've never told anyone this. Not Destiny, not Aunt Donna, or my uncle before he passed away."

"We're spilling all of our dirty laundry today, baby."

She nodded and tucked her knees underneath the oversized AC/DC T-shirt of mine she wore. Ordinarily, I'd be pissed about someone stretching out my shirt like that but Resha wasn't anyone. I could get a new T-shirt, and to be honest, I would let her stretch that one out as well.

"My mother was a drug addict. You already know that. My father left not long after I was born, and was in and out of jail until he was shot and killed when I was seven. Both my parents were hardly around. Anyway, one day, I remember my mother frantically searching our small, dirty hotel room for something. The hotel was where we lived at the time. She got us kicked out of so many apartments. I asked her what she was looking for and she said her check. She got paid from the government and would use the money to get drugs. I was twelve and knew the cycle by then. I'd intercepted the check and paid our bill at the hotel with it and bought some food so we'd have a place to live and food to eat.

"Of course, she was pissed. She stormed out of the hotel room after yelling and berating me. I was numb to it all by then, however. I was proud of myself for prioritizing the important things with that money. But an hour later, my momma came barging back in the room, almost frantic, telling me to get my jacket and come on. 'I've got a surprise for you,' she said. I asked what it was and where we were going but she wouldn't answer. Just told me to hurry up as we walked down the back alley by the hotel, across the street, and down another block to what appeared to be an abandoned building.

"It wasn't abandoned. There were people there. They all had the same look in their eyes that I'd seen in my momma's. They all were high or looking to get high. It smelled awful, and I noticed some people passed out in the corner of one room, two men beating up a woman who begged for them to stop in another, and even scared looking kids in there who were younger than me. But my momma ignored it all as she tugged me by the arm down a long hall.

"'I need you to do a favor for me, baby, okay?'

"It was the nicest voice she'd used with me in a long time and I started to get a dreadful feeling in the pit of my stomach. Especially after a tall man entered the room behind her, shutting the three of us in.

"'You actually brought her. I didn't fucking think you was gonna bring her.'

"'I did. Just like you asked, Tone. Here she is. You got the stuff?'

"Tone took a long drag of the cigarette he was smoking before his dark, cold eyes moved over to my mother in disgust. 'Yeah, I got it.' He slammed a baggie in my mother's outstretched hand and said, 'Now get the fuck outta here.'"

"I saw her turning to the door and I panicked. She was going to leave me alone with this evil looking man.

"'Momma!' I called to her, and for a moment she paused, turning back to me.

"She moved to me, kneeling down. 'It'll be real quick, I promise, Resha. He just wanna talk to you a little bit.' She stood up and quickly moved to the door, slamming it behind her.

"I yelled for her to come back but she didn't. My screams became louder when the man approached me, his hands reaching for me. It was then I realized my mother had sold me to this man to get high. She sold my virginity to her drug dealer because I'd spent her government check on rent and food instead of drugs."

Resha paused, wiping tears from her eyes, and I thanked God because I couldn't hear anymore. The rage that filled my body was too overwhelming. I'd have to go find this fucking Tone guy and beat him to within an inch of his life, let him get all healed up, and then repeat the process, over and over for years to come. And that would assuage only an iota of the rage inside of me.

"I got lucky, somehow," Resha finally continued. "I don't know how but I managed to kick him in his crotch through his pants. Hard enough that he doubled over, releasing me. I squirmed away from him, crawled to the door, and opened it, running down that hall and out of the building. I didn't even bother to stop and look for my mother. I ran all the way back to the hotel. I locked myself inside, putting a chair underneath the lock so even she couldn't get in with her key. The next day I got the keycards changed so my mother could no longer get in. Not that she tried. She never came back to the hotel after that day. A part of me thinks it was because even she was so ashamed of what she'd done that she couldn't bear to look at me. I stayed in that hotel room for a month, by myself. It was only when the school I'd been attending contacted my aunt and uncle, who I'd put down as the emergency contacts, that anyone came looking for me.

"When Child Protective Services gave me over to my aunt and uncle, and they asked what happened or where my momma was, I made up a story saying she'd left one day and just never came back. That I was too scared to leave the hotel because maybe someone took her. Eventually, they believed it. They hadn't realized her drug habit, as they referred to it as, had gotten so bad. I didn't even want to think about that day in that horrible building so I didn't tell them the whole truth."

I sat there, still too full of rage to respond though it had toned down some. That was the moment I started to hate yet another person I'd never met. The first was Resha's stalker. The second was her mother. Hell, my own mother wasn't exactly Joan fucking Cleaver but she'd never given me or my brother away for a fucking score. She at least had the decency to leave us in the care of our father when she got tired of being a mother. My father wasn't perfect, either, but he loved us the best way he knew how. Seeing how shit that happened more than twenty years earlier still affected my woman and our relationship pissed me off all over again.

Pushing away from the headboard, I cupped her face in mine. "You know she was fucked, right? She threw you away because she was all kinds of fucked up in the head, and it had absolutely nothing to do with you. Who you are or what you deserved. Tell me you know that!" I demanded, nearly choked by my anger.

She smiled through the tears, actually giggling before she nodded her head. "You have a way with words."

I shook her face in my hands again. "Tell me you know the truth."

"I do ... logically. I've been to therapy in the past over it. Well, technically, I went over my past relationship troubles and found out a lot of it stemmed from my childhood. But logic doesn't always supplant emotion."

I nodded, understanding. The most logical people in the world often did the most illogical things due to irrational emotions.

"When your logic fails you, come to me. Don't shut me out or push me away by trying to get rid of me. You're stuck with me, in case you didn't understand that as of yet."

Resha's eyebrows rose as she cocked her head to the side, her mouth parting. A small smile crested on my lips as she took in the deeper meaning behind what I'd just said.

"Did you just propose to me?"

"Yes," I answered without equivocation. "I don't have a ring yet, but—"

"Yes!"

And for once, it was her lips that crushed against my own, sending me back to the mattress. A deep chuckle pushed past my lips as Resha continued kissing every inch of my face.

"Good. Now, let's get started on making a family," I growled, my hands moving to the T-shirt, removing it from her body.

I was pretty certain by the number of times I released inside of my future bride that our child was conceived that night.

****

Resha

"Well, well, well, look who decided to finally show up," Destiny chimed as she pulled open the door for Connor and I.

Glancing over my shoulder, I rolled my eyes before turning back to my cousin. "Hello to you, too," I stated, reaching in and hugging Destiny.

"Hey, Ty, come look what the cat dragged in. I hope you still recognize her, it's been so long since either one of us have seen her."

My stomach dropped as I entered my cousin's home. "Being a little dramatic, aren't you?" I questioned as I removed my coat.

"She's not."

Spinning around, I was confronted with Destiny's husband, Tyler, who had the same look of disappointment on his face as his wife.

"We've rarely seen you in months."

I sighed, greeting him with, "Hi, Tyler," as he pulled me in for an embrace.

"Let up on my woman, the both of you," Connor interrupted, placing his arm around my hip. "She's been a little preoccupied." He dipped his head, pressing a kiss to my temple, sending my pulse racing due to both the physical touch of his lips and his defense of me.

Tyler raised an eyebrow while Destiny crossed her arms over her chest. "Oh don't think I don't know who's been taking all of my cousin's time lately," she blurted, tapping her foot against the hardwood floor of the foyer.

"Anyway, we're glad to be here. Is Aunt Donna here?" I questioned, looking around, wondering why my aunt hadn't come out to greet us yet.

"She was here but we took her and the kids over to Ty's parents' house to spend the evening with them."

I nodded. "I bet she loved that." I smiled, feeling a little guilty for not having seen my aunt in weeks, although I called her a couple times a week.

"Come in. Dinner's still warming up but I made my first charcuterie board."

"You? In the kitchen?" I giggled at the glare Destiny gave me over her shoulder as we moved down the hall toward their dining area.

"I could hardly believe it myself," Tyler added.

"You're domesticating my cousin."

"What the hell is a charcuterie board?" Connor inquired.

I couldn't help the laugh that fell from my lips. "Babe, it's like an appetizer board full of meats, cheeses, crackers, olives, fruits, or vegetables. There are all different types but the ones with cheese and crackers are my favorites," I admitted.

Connor nodded and shrugged as if he didn't find something like that all that impressive. I reached up on my tiptoes to press a kiss to his lips on instinct. It was one of the many things I loved about him. He was strong and protective, and even with a number of successful businesses and a championship fighting career behind him, he remained rooted and down-to-earth. He was still a kid from the rough side of town who had to fight his way up, even though he rubbed shoulders with people like the Townsends.

"This looks amazing, Destiny. You did a great job." I turned back to the table where the board had been set out, at the same time my stomach began growling. "Great timing, too. I'm starving."

I sat when Connor pulled out a chair for me. Smiling at him as he sat next to me, I turned and didn't miss the look that Destiny and Tyler exchanged before taking their own seats.

"It's so quiet here without the kids," I commented, realizing just how calm the house felt without the three kiddos around. My heart strings tugged a little at missing them. Immediately after the miscarriage, I couldn't bear the thought of seeing the children every day. I barely knew how I was going to make it staying with Destiny while I healed, when I tried to push Connor away. Thankfully, I didn't have to deal with that since he stepped in and took me back home to his place to recover. But now, I realized how much I missed them.

"Yeah ..." Destiny paused looking to Tyler before turning back to me. "We wanted a night with just adults for once." She gave me a tight smile which lead me to believe she wasn't being completely honest. However, she obviously didn't want to say it out loud in front of everyone so I let it go.

Instead, I focused on the food in front of us, taking a few crackers and a few different cheeses with some grapes from the charcuterie board. We ate and talked about upcoming plans and whatnot. Tyler was expected to resume his career in the NFL in the coming summer after having taken a leave of absence to be home with Destiny and the kids their first year as a family of five. It was a controversial decision, one he actually got a lot of heat for in the public eye, but sitting across from the table from him, I saw he took it all in stride. He knew where his priorities were. That thought had me turning and looking to Connor, who I had no doubt would make the same kind of decision for us, when we became a family.

If we become a family.

I still had a ton of fear regarding whether or not I could actually get—and keep—a pregnancy. I'd read so many stories of women who had multiple miscarriages, or whose husbands left them because they couldn't get pregnant, or who had come to accept that motherhood would never happen for them. I didn't want that to be me. And yes, Connor was right, we certainly could adopt or get a surrogate, I just didn't want to feel as if I were robbed of the experience of going through pregnancy with the man who would be my husband. Even though I knew that experience wouldn't keep a marriage together.

I was learning to let go of all of those fears but it wasn't easy. Just the week before, Connor had caught me reading yet another article on miscarriages. He'd yanked my tablet out of my hands.

"Is this why you wanted to work out with me so badly?" he'd demanded.

Sheepishly, I admitted it was. Most of the articles discussed doing your part to ensure a healthy pregnancy and that included eating better and working out, which I loathed. But I'd asked Connor to show me a few workouts I could do to get in better shape. He started taking me to the gym with him each morning. Little did I know his "gym" was actually the place where the Underground fights were hosted. He made up his own workouts, which were so much more hardcore than anything I wanted to do, initially. But I thought the more I sweated the better shape I'd be in, and thus, the better the chance of getting and staying pregnant.

"Working out is not a punishment for your body," he'd insisted. I'd cried at those words because I'd slowly began to want to punish my body for betraying me by miscarrying. I wanted to cause it pain the same way it'd pained me, and somehow my future husband could see that. Now, I was limited to working out three times a week, not more than thirty minutes each time, until I built up enough stamina—mental and physical—to workout for the purposes of health and overall well-being. I was getting there.

"Oh my god! Look at that ring!" Destiny's words called my attention back to the table, as she openly gawked at the princess-cut sapphire stone, surrounded by two aquamarine stones, all set in a rose gold band, that I sported on my left ring finger.

I glanced over at a proud looking Connor.

"Something else you care to tell us?" Destiny asked.

Swallowing, I nodded as I peered down at the ring that I loved so much. Not just because it was gorgeous but also because it wasn't the typical engagement diamond ring, and Connor had carefully incorporated both of our birthstones in the ring. He didn't necessarily believe in or even know much about zodiac signs and whatnot, but he knew I did.

"We're engaged," Connor and I both responded at the same time, sharing a smile.

"When did this happen?"

"Three weeks ago," I answered without thinking.

"Three weeks?"

I pivoted to face Destiny at hearing the shriek in her voice. She looked appalled, and moreover, hurt. My heart sank.

"My cousin and I need to talk privately," she stated, standing from the chair and glaring at me to follow her.

"We can—"

"No, you both stay here, please," Destiny cut off Tyler who'd started to stand.

I stood, and followed Destiny down the hall to one of the spare bedrooms they had on the first floor, noting that Destiny shut the door behind us.

"What the hell is going on?" she demanded.

"What? Connor and I got engaged. I didn't tell you because—"

"It's not just that, Resha, and you know it. You didn't tell me about the engagement, but you also didn't tell me about the fact that you were living with him for months. And yeah," she held up her hands to cut off my interjection, "I know ... that was initially because your home was broken into and you were or *are* being stalked. Which, again, you never told me about. And this had been going on for months before you even met Connor."

I flinched.

"What? What was that look?"

"I actually met Connor almost a year ago when I was in New York ... we, uh, we kind of were a one-night stand kind of thing." Clearing my throat, I turned away from my cousin. Not because I believed she'd judge me but because it was just one more thing that I hadn't revealed to her over the past year.

"See what I mean?" She tossed up her hands, looking hurt and bemused. "It's like you've kept me out of your life for months. Outside of the podcast and your trips to the women's shelter to work with us, I hardly see or hear from you. What's going on, Resha?"

My shoulders slumped as I pushed out a heavy breath, moving to the large sleigh bed to sit on the side of it. I didn't want to admit what I was about to say but I didn't want lies between my cousin and I any longer—she was my best friend and closest family member.

"I was jealous," I admitted.

When I didn't hear anything, I lifted my gaze, meeting Destiny's bewildered look. "You're going to have to explain."

Rolling my eyes at myself, I began with, "I know. When you and Ty started dating and it moved so quickly, I was apprehensive. I didn't want you to get hurt like you had in your last marriage."

She nodded, moving next to me to sit on the bed. "You told me all of that."

"Yes, but I also watched how happy he made you and how protective he was over you. The man was ready to lose his whole career to defend you. So, I started to recognize what you saw and I was happy that you found love again. But it also made me yearn for more as well. Then you two were married. Just like that. No engagement, no save-the-date or wedding invitations. You just came back from vacation with a new last name. A new name I had to find out via the grapevine, instead of hearing it from the source."

"Resh, I told you—"

This time I held up my hand. "I know what you said, D. Still, it hurt to not be a part of that, and I knew how childish and juvenile it sounded to be jealous and happy for you at the same time, while also feeling left out of this new life you were starting. So, I kind of shut down. Blocked it out and told myself that it was fine, we all change, life changes us and we have to adjust. I'd be there for you whenever you needed. Then the triplets came and I was overjoyed you finally got the family you always wanted, but again, it made me assess where I was in my own life. My business and career were going very well, I had friends but no one to come home to at night. That loneliness I'd felt ever since I was a child being left alone at night by a mother who cared for drugs more than me began to well up, and it became almost painful to visit you so often …"

Pausing, I turned to my cousin, feeling like shit for admitting all of this out loud. I hated the way I'd been feeling toward Destiny and her life as of late, but it wasn't until recently that I realized the ways in which I'd acted out on my jealousy. By shutting her out of the pivotal parts of my life.

"I'm sorry, D. I know it was messed up, but I didn't even realize that's what I was doing at the time. I just …"

"I get it," she finally said. "After I lost the baby and went through my divorce I shut the world out. Even you for a little while."

I shook my head. "But this was different—"

"Not really. I was in pain, and instead of letting you or others help me, I shut you out. You were in pain also. Hurting and lonely and so you shut me out."

I let her assessment sink in. "I guess it was somewhat similar in that regard."

"Anyway, heffa, if you do that shit again, expect for me to curse you out and tell Mama about it!" she announced, standing from the bed to move in front of me with her hands on her hips. "Don't laugh. I'm not playing, either!"

I covered my mouth to smother the giggles. "I know you're serious. I'm sorry. It won't happen again. At least, I'll try not to let it happen."

"Good." She pulled me up and into a hug.

"Now that we're confessing stuff, I should tell you the reason we sent Mama and the kids over to Ty's parents' house was because I was afraid that being around them would be too painful for you."

"I figured that's what that look was about."

Destiny's eyebrows raised before she flinched, sheepishly. "It was that obvious, huh?"

"Only a little, and I love you for caring."

Pulling back from the hug I'd just given her, she inquired, "But how *are* you doing? With the miscarriage and all?"

It'd been a while since my cousin and I had spoken. Our podcast had been on hiatus ever since I'd gotten out of the hospital because I just didn't have the emotional energy to do it. Thankfully, she understood.

"Most days are good. I still get sad about it, of course, and cry when I need to. Connor has been my rock." I gaze upward, remembering the many nights he held me as I cried or I talked to him about my fears of never having our own family. When I initially met him, I never would've thought he would be so patient, kind, and caring enough to just listen to me as I babbled on about fears, or talk me off the ledge when I believed we wouldn't work out for one reason or another. He was calm and reasoning when he needed to be. But other moments, he barreled right through my feelings, letting me know that I was on some BS and he wasn't having it. Most of those times, he was right, also.

"Good. You two look really happy together. And I can't wait to start planning your wedding." Destiny's face brightened as she smiled.

Frowning, I stuck my hand on my hip and questioned, "How do you know I'm not going to run off an elope on a yacht or something?"

I swear my cousin grew by about six inches in height when she sassed, "Because as much as your ass has kept from me over the last year, you know I would beat your ass for eloping!"

Laughing, I shook my head. "You're right. Anyway, I don't want anything big, to be honest, and—"

"Have it here."

"What?"

"At the house. We have plenty of room for all of your and Connor's family and close friends."

I paused, mulling it over. Destiny and Tyler's property was very spacious. Close to two acres, I believed, which should be large enough for the type of intimate wedding Connor and I had been discussing.

"I'll talk to my fiancé about it."

Destiny's face opened up in a wide grin as she pulled me into a hug, and in that moment, I knew where we'd be having our wedding. After distancing myself from my cousin and best friend for so many months, it only felt right to let her do this for Connor and I.

"One last thing. What's the news on this stalker? Should I be concerned?"

The weight of that question settled around me just as I started to feel lighter. My shoulders rose and fell, revealing my bewilderment at that situation.

"To be honest, I don't really know. I haven't gotten any emails, messages, or anything in weeks. Connor and I have been back to my place to clean it and to get a few more of my belongings. He won't allow me to go there alone." I rolled my eyes.

"As he shouldn't."

"I knew you'd take his side." Truth was, I didn't want to go to my place alone, either. For obvious reasons, I didn't feel safe there, and Connor's loft felt more and more like home. To be honest, wherever he was felt like home.

"I'm taking your side. I want you safe."

"Thanks, D. But the truth is I think possibly he's moved on. Perhaps this guy, whoever he was, found something or someone special to fill his time and he's lost interest in me."

"So maybe he's stalking someone else. That's your hope?"

"Of course not, D. I'm just saying, he could've found a real girlfriend to occupy his time, or a hobby or something, and he's done with obsessing over me."

I said those words with all the hope I had in my body. I really wanted them to be true. I didn't want to have to think about someone following me whenever I went out alone, or have to look over my shoulder every time I stepped out my door, but the pit in my stomach that rose up as Destiny gave me a *stop being delusional* look, was all I needed to know that I was living in a fantasy.

Chapter Twenty-Two

Connor

"Is this really even still necessary?" Resha whined as she tossed another puny ass punch in the direction of the mitt I held up with my right hand.

Lowering both hands, that wore punching mitts, I gave her a hard glare. We were standing in the middle of the same ring where my Underground fighters fought. She'd somehow convinced me to do another photoshoot for my TKO products for social media purposes and my website, which I obliged, but only under the notion that she switched her workouts up to self-defense lessons that I would teach her.

"If it weren't necessary, I wouldn't have you doing it."

She awkwardly folded her arms due to the boxing gloves she was wearing. Admittedly, she looked cute as hell in the purple workout leggings and grey, sleeveless top she wore. The clothes perfectly outlined the hips, ass, legs, breasts, and everything else I loved so much.

"But how do I know this guy is even still out there? Oh! Maybe he got hit by a bus and, you know, is out of commission or died and we're doing all of this self-defense nonsense for no reason."

"There's always a need for self-defense All women should know how to protect themselves."

"I know. I've taken self-defense in the past."

"How long ago?"

Her eyes dropped to the floor.

"I knew it."

"It was like six or seven years ago, I think," she mumbled.

"And you haven't practiced anything since, have you?"

She defensively put her hands on her hips. "I don't like to sweat."

"You like sweating for me," I reminded her.

An annoyed smile crept onto her face. "That's different. And I'm just starting to workout now. Can we take it slowly?"

"Babe, we're only here three days a week. I need to teach you what I can in the limited time I have you down here. What if you're ever presented with a situation where you have to defend yourself?"

"How would that even happen?" She held out her arms. "Either you're always with me or the security you've hired. I'm never alone. He scared the hell out of one of the cameraman at the photoshoot yesterday, by the way."

"Who? Gary? Good, that's what he's there for." Gary was one scary looking motherfucker. I knew it, and it was the reason I specifically requested Brutus send him to the photoshoot Resha had to do the day before for a company she worked with. Abe had moved on to another assignment. Her work assignments had been picking up since she was feeling better, but that meant I couldn't be with her at all times. Hence, the need for additional security.

"Yeah, well, unless you know something I don't know—"

"He's still out there, Resh."

Her mouth snapped shut.

"How do you know?" she finally questioned.

Removing the punching mitts from my hands, I tossed them to the side and moved closer to her, taking one of her hands into mine to begin removing her boxing gloves.

"Brutus and I, along with Detective Brookes, have been looking into the security personnel of your building. At first, we didn't find anything. Everyone hired by the property management company looked above board. But their records were incomplete. That's why it's been taking so long to track this fucker down. Turns out, they hired a company off the books, to not have to pay premium prices for security. They've been lying to their residents when they say all the security staff is trained and has gone through a background check."

"That's what I was told when I first moved in." She slid her right hand out of the glove I loosened and I tossed it to the side. Nodding, I moved to remove the second glove. "It's what they told everyone, except it's a lie. A lot of the security staff worked under the table so there are no records. We've had to ask a lot of questions, knock on doors, and even knock a couple of heads to find out the real names of former security staff in the building. I believe it's someone who used to work there."

She looked at me with a wrinkle in between her eyebrows. "But you said you know he's still out there. How?"

"He's still messaging you. I didn't want you to find out, especially after the miscarriage, so I had Brutus hack into all of your email and social media accounts and scan them for messages from him. I delete them before you ever get a chance to see them and then block the email addresses."

"How …" She paused. "So he's still emailing me? Sending messages?"

I nodded slowly.

"And you just delete them without telling me?"

"Don't get pissed. You weren't checking your email or other accounts often, so it wasn't difficult to hide messages from you, but it was enough for me to know that that fucker is still around. Still obsessing over you."

She sighed, dipping her head and moving in close to me, resting her forehead against my chest. "I just want this to be over. I want him out of our lives so we can move on."

Lowering my lips, to place a kiss to the top of her head, I assured, "He will be gone, a stór. I promise you with everything that I am. That fucker will be found and taken care of."

The tingling in my fingers signaled how much I meant the words I spoke. I used to get that same feeling before every fight. It was my body's way of telling me it was *game on,* and anyone who dared stand in my way when I got this feeling would have to either lay down or get put down. Most of the time, it didn't matter which one they chose, but in this case, with this fucker, I was all set to put him down like the dog he was.

****

Resha

"All right, cousin, what's on the agenda for today?" I questioned as I placed my bag down on the desk in the studio where we recorded our podcast. We were back, finally, after nearly a two-month hiatus.

"I was thinking since we've gotten so many questions while we were away, we should do a listener Q and A episode. We talked about it before, remember? We just never got around to it. What do you think?"

I nodded. "Sounds good to me. Let's do it."

"Great. I've already gone through our emails and gotten a list of twenty questions. That should fill up the hour. You look cute by the way," she commented.

"Thank you. I had that shoot with the plus size fashion brand I told you about. They're expanding their workout line and saw some of the pictures I've been posting lately in my workout gear."

Destiny lowered the cup of coffee she'd been sipping on. "Oh, here, this is for you. A white chocolate mocha latte with whipped cream." She handed me the second drink she had.

"Oh my goodness! Thanks, this is just what I needed." I moaned as I closed my eyes at the first sip of the warm beverage.

"So they liked the workout pics, huh?"

I gave her a side-eye. "Don't start." Destiny had been trying to get me to workout with her off and on for years.

"What? I'm just saying you look—"

"All right, enough, enough. Yes, I have been working out more and I'm actually liking it. Having Connor be my own personal trainer doesn't hurt. Have you seen that man in a pair of grey sweatpants? Sheesh!" I fanned myself with my hand as Destiny giggled.

"No, but I've seen Tyler in grey sweats and yeah ... I get it."

We both laughed as we prepared the studio and the microphones to record the podcast. The questions that Destiny had picked out were pretty good. More than one listener had questions about my love life, noting that I seemed happier and even glowing in my latest Instagram and blog posts.

"I don't discuss much about my personal life for reasons, and you faithful listeners know that. But I will say that I'm happy," I responded to the question while also happily playing with the engagement ring on my finger.

"Well, that's that on that," Destiny summarized before moving on to the next question.

The show went a little longer than we'd anticipated, turning out to be about an hour and a half. But at the end, Destiny and I were happy with the way it turned out, and we scheduled it to go live the next day.

"Okay, I'm going to head home and start cooking dinner before Connor gets in," I told Destiny as we hugged one another good-bye.

"All right, Resha. I need to head to my office and get in an hour of work before leaving."

"Don't work too late."

"Pssh, and have Mr. Townsend show up here, looking crazy because I wasn't home on time? No thank you."

I laughed at the thought because I could imagine Tyler doing just that. Then I spun around and came face-to-face with Gary, the scary looking security guard Connor had put on request for me. Laughing, I recognized I had my own protective man to worry about.

I nodded at Gary as I passed, and he followed me into the elevator and down to the parking garage where my car was parked. He'd followed behind my car for most of the day after I put my foot down and insisted that I didn't need to be driven everywhere. Connor finally relented, giving me the modicum amount of space I needed to breathe.

About fifteen minutes later, I found myself pulling into the parking garage of the home I now shared with Connor. Gary followed me up to the elevator and rode up with me, presumably to do his normal sweep of the loft before heading down to the entryway of the elevator until Connor arrived home. It was our nightly routine.

Patiently, I waited on the elevator while Gary stepped off, looking from left to right.

"Hey, Resha, I— What the hell?" Mark barked.

"Put your goddamned hands up!"

"No, Gary!" I went running off the elevator to stand in front of Mark who Gary had his gun aimed at. "This is Mark, Connor's brother!" I assured, my eyes falling to the barrel of the gun, my heart pounding in my chest.

Gary's dark eyes slowly moved from mine to look over my shoulder, and he lowered the gun. "Mark O'Brien. You work at Townsend Industries."

"Yeah, man, what the hell was that?" Mark questioned as he rolled from around me.

"Connor said he had a brother. Wasn't expecting you to be in here," Gary explained.

"I'm starting to think I need to call before I come over," Mark grumbled.

"That would be helpful," I added, giving him a side-eye.

He returned it with a sheepish look, obviously remembering the last time he'd dropped by unannounced.

"I'm just going to check out the rest of the place and head down to my regular post," Gary stated.

I pushed out a heavy sigh. "That was unnerving." I leaned down to give Mark a hug, which he returned.

"Tell me about it. That guy looked like he was ready to blow me the hell away."

"He was. According to Connor, all of these guys are ex-military. Anyway, what's up?" I asked.

"Not much, had some free time and wanted to check-in with the siblings."

I giggled every time he referred to me as his sibling, just like with Connor.

"You two decided on a date yet?"

"Hmhm." I nodded. "The first day of spring, March 19th."

"Nice. Where at?"

"Destiny and Ty's. Connor agreed to the location."

"Sounds perfect. I'll have my tux ready to go."

I grinned, knowing that Connor planned to ask Mark to be his best man but I didn't want to ruin that surprise for him so I kept my mouth shut.

"You want some lemonade? I made it fresh-squeezed last night."

"Anything you make, I'm eating or drinking. Lead the way."

Mark followed me in the kitchen, and we sat and talked for a while over some Hershey kiss cookies I made earlier in the week. Mark loved them, and I told him to take the leftovers home. I planned on making chocolate lava cakes for dessert that night, which Mark made me agree to save him at least one. Since the recipe I had made six, I figured that wasn't much of an issue.

"My sweet tooth's been acting up lately," I confessed.

Mark shrugged as I walked him toward the elevator door. "You've been working out. You've earned it, right?"

I laughed. "I don't think that's how it works."

"Does for me." He popped another cookie into his mouth.

"You keep that up and those aren't even going to make it to your place."

"I need the extra energy. I've got a fight tonight at the Underground." He winked at me.

I shook my head before bending down and giving him a hug. "Just be safe."

"What's the fun in that? See ya later, sis."

I watched as he rolled onto the elevator.

"And don't forget to … lock the door," I mumbled the last bit since the door had closed before I could fully get my statement out. Connor was always complaining about how Mark forgot to lock the door and anyone could just walk in.

I wasn't too worried about it since I knew Gary was still downstairs, keeping watch. He wouldn't let anyone up that didn't belong here.

With that, I headed for the kitchen to prepare a garlic and herb linguine dish with shrimp scampi and broccoli. I wanted something kind of light for dinner since I would be making a decadent dessert. About halfway through cooking the main dish my phone rang.

"Hello? Gary?"

"Hey, Ms. McDonald, I'm sorry to bother you but, uh …"

I started to get nervous. Never in my wildest dreams had I envisioned a man as big and scary looking as Gary sounding this … anxious. Afraid.

"Gary, what's the matter?"

"It's my daughter."

I blinked, my head jerking backwards, not expecting that sentence to come out of his mouth.

"You have a daughter?"

"Yeah. I'm a single father. Anyway, she's only seven and her school just called me saying her ride never showed to pick her up for the after-school program she attends on days I work late. She's all alone down there and—"

"Go. Go get your daughter!" I insisted.

"Are you sure you'll be all right?"

Looking at the clock on the wall I nodded even though he couldn't see me. "Connor will be home in another thirty minutes. The door is secured and locked. I'll be fine. Go get your child."

"Thanks so much. I'll make this up to you and Mr. O'Brien. I promise." He sounded like he was already walking or running in the direction of his car.

"Don't worry about it, Gary. Take care of your family."

I hung up knowing a little more about the man who protected me. Apparently, everyone had their weaknesses. Gary's was obviously his daughter. I smiled to myself as I continued cooking, wondering if Connor would sound like that about our daughter in the future. I could envision him being just as protective over our own little girl as Gary. Or teaching our son how to box. I couldn't wait for those moments. And when fear tried to creep in, reminding me that I couldn't know for sure that those times would ever come to life, I remembered

Connor's steadfast assurance that we—us, he and I, and our family—were no coincidence.

Those thoughts had me singing along to the workout playlist I'd decided to make to help get me through some of the more challenging workouts that Connor had been putting me through lately. I thought about sharing it with my followers on Instagram as I stood at the kitchen counter, stirring the contents for the lava cakes in the mixing bowl, when I heard the elevator door open. Looking up, a smile crossed my lips as I noted the time.

Placing the bowl down, I wiped my hands off with a towel and straightened the apron I wore before heading out of the kitchen to welcome my man home.

Unfortunately, the man who greeted me as the doors of the elevator opened wasn't my man at all. No, this man with dark brown hair, beady brown eyes, standing at about five-foot-eight with a slight bend and an awkward gait was not Connor.

The sneer on his face told me he wasn't there to do any good. The gun in his right hand confirmed this.

"I've been waiting a long time for this, Resha."

The way he said my name made my skin crawl, and suddenly I remembered where I knew this guy from. I'd come face-to-face with my stalker many times before.

Chapter Twenty-Three

Connor

I watched the fucker look over his shoulder repeatedly before he tried the lock of the elevator that led directly to my loft. Rage seeped inside of me when it opened, unobstructed by a lock or the fucking security guard that I hired to keep Resha safe. Getting out of my car in the empty parking space I parked it in, I knew Resha was up there by herself while that fucker made his way to her.

Adrenaline began coursing through every vein in my body, and I headed to the secret entrance into my apartment that no one else knew about. The main elevator was too loud and would alert him that I was coming up. That could put Resha in even more danger. I needed to get the drop on him before he had time to think, or hurt her.

Punching in the code to the secret entrance, I barged through the elevator doors as they opened, pressing the up button to my floor. This particular elevator let me out down the hall from my loft, where I then used a key to open a door that led directly into the spare bedroom that resided on the main floor of my loft. It was the bedroom where I'd set up a desk and office space for Resha's new computer, even though she still came to work in my office most days when she didn't have shoots.

Moving quietly, I could hear the fucker yelling at Resha, saying how much he loved her and demanding to know how she could betray him by shacking up with another man. I toed out of the heavy boots I wore as to not make any noise against the hardwood floor. Moving slowly down the hall, I could see Resha standing there with her hands suspended in the air, looking frightened as hell. The fucker was now pointing his gun directly at her. I couldn't take watching that scene any longer.

In two quick steps, I made it to the middle of the living room, wrapping my arm around the fucker's neck from behind.

"Wh—" was all he was able to get out before my bicep and forearm began crushing his windpipe. This had been a favorite move of mine in many fights where anything was legal. Usually, however, I used the move just to put my opponent to sleep for a little while. This time, that wouldn't be the case. This fucker was going to sleep permanently.

Dropping the gun, he thrashed and used his fingers, trying to claw his way out of my grip. It wasn't working. I felt nothing as I replayed the fearful expression on Resha's face just before I put him in this death grip over and over in my mind. The satisfaction was better than any belt I'd won in the ring. I literally felt the life draining out of his body. He was dying, and with the last few slaps he gave to my arms, I could tell he knew it.

Once I was certain that he was dead, I let up, tossing his body to the floor. I stood there staring for moments just to make sure I didn't catch a twitch of activity.

Out of the corner of my eye, I spotted movement. Looking up, I caught Resha's stunned face moving from the lifeless body on the floor to me.

"You never gave me a chance to use my defense moves."

I grunted and stepped over the body, tugging her into my arms, smashing my lips to hers, all the fear I'd felt pouring out of me.

Pulling back, I stared into her eyes, my hands running all over her body, assessing. "Are you okay? Did he hurt you?"

She shook her head. "Yes. And no, he didn't hurt me, but that's the second time I've had a gun pointed at me today."

My eyes bulged and she quickly explained the situation that happened with Gary and Mark and how she interceded.

"Okay, well you and I are going to have a fucking discussion about running in front of guns," I demanded.

"But it was Mark and he—"

"I don't give a shit. Mark knows how to protect himself. I taught him well. He would've been fine. Trust me. And speaking of Gary, where the hell—"

"He has a daughter …"

I gave Resha an *and?* expression, to which she explained how he had to leave early.

"He's lucky if he doesn't get my foot up his ass."

"Don't do that. He sounded really concerned for her."

"Yeah, whatever." I pulled out my phone to call Brutus and let him know that his special clean-up crew was needed.

After hanging up, I looked at the pile of shit on my floor.

"I know him," Resha stated, moving next to me. "He worked as a security guard in my building about a two years ago. Mainly at the reception desk. I first spoke to him when Destiny and I used the building's gym to work out. He creeped me out even then. I went down to the gym a few times by myself but it seemed like he was always there. So, I stopped going. A few months later, I didn't see him anymore. I asked at the front desk and they said he'd been relocated. I later heard through building gossip he'd been fired for sleeping on the job or something like that."

"Explains how he knew where you parked, your apartment number, and was able to get a key to your place. You remember his name?"

"Santos. Santos Lovato. He yelled it at me just before I saw you behind the stairwell. But when he worked in my building everyone called him Ricky."

"Sounds like Santa. That was one of the leads we got," I explained when Resha gave me a quizzical look.

A few people we talked to had mentioned a Ricky, but they didn't know his first name.

I led her into the kitchen to sit and remain while Brutus' crew showed up to remove the body as well as any evidence that Santos Lovato had ever been there. They would head over to his place as well to delete any evidence of his obsession with Resha just in case someone tried to trace his disappearance in the future. But according to records, he didn't have much family, no friends, and had infrequent employment. Chances are no one would miss him much.

Epilogue

Resha

Nine months later

I sat in my hospital bed, staring down at my little miracle, tears filling my eyes, unable to wipe the smile from my face even if I tried. Looking into the sleeping bundle in my arms, I silently wished for him to open his eyes just so I could catch another glimpse of those hazel eyes that mirrored his father's.

"He's so handsome," Destiny gushed as she stood beside my bed.

I lifted my gaze to my cousin. "I thought my wedding day was the happiest day of my life, but … well, it may have just gotten moved to number two on the list."

Destiny reached over, lightly running a hand over little Colin's head. "I don't think your husband would mind you saying that."

I smirked and looked down at our son again, thinking over all that transpired over the last year. And as it turned out, I got pregnant again soon after the miscarriage. I waited until our wedding day to reveal the news to Connor, as part of my wedding gift to him. He'd picked me up and spun me around on the dancefloor that Destiny and Tyler had set up in their spacious backyard especially for our nuptials.

It wasn't until my new husband put me down that he turned me to face, outward, looking over the bushes, beyond Destiny's yard, out to see some of the neighborhood houses in the distance.

"That one …" He pointed over my shoulder. "That's the one I have Joshua holding for us."

I turned, my mouth ajar. "Holding?"

He nodded. "I won't let him put it on the market. I haven't made the purchase yet. Need to see if you like it. If it'll fit your needs for office space and closets and all that shit, but it's ours if you like it."

I giggled at his constant interjections of curse words even when being romantic. And as it turned out, I loved the house. It was perfect for my home office needs, the yard was big enough for a backyard pool and playground set, and for hosting parties and events. We were all moved in by the time I was six months pregnant. And on the days I woke up afraid that this was all just a dream, or something was going to destroy our happy ending, Connor steadfastly reassured me we were in this together and there was nothing we couldn't take on as a team.

"You ready to take this little guy home?" Destiny questioned.

"Never been more ready for anything in my life."

Connor had gone down with a member of the hospital staff to assure them that we had a carseat and it was strapped in properly.

"My husband's taking an awfully long time," I told her, my head raising.

"Yeahhh … about that …"

"He's freaking out, isn't he?" I giggled, shaking my head. He'd been so strong throughout all of this. I knew the time would come when the weight of what we were about to take on, truly hit him.

"I wouldn't call it freaking out so much as—"

"Mrs. O'Brien," a nurse interrupted Destiny as she entered the door, rolling a wheelchair ahead of her.

I had my cousin hold Colin while the nurse helped me from the bed to the chair. Taking my son back into my arms, I felt ready to head out, as the nurse began pushing me.

"Hey, sis, looks like we're twins," Mark joked as I exited the room.

"You must be the jokester in the family," the nurse chimed in behind me.

"Jokes aren't the only thing I'm good at," he added, smoothly, and not for the first time I noticed how similar Mark looked to his brother. The O'Briens were definitely a handsome family. Connor had shown me pictures of their father. They both took after him. And even at just forty-eight hours old the baby in my arms already looked the spitting image of the man who helped conceive him.

"What the hell do you mean you don't know the safety rating of the damn car seat? This is my family we're talking about here!"

The anger caught my attention and pulled my gaze toward the bellowing man down the hall.

"Of course I fucking checked the rating before purchasing but that was months ago. You don't know if there have been any recalls since then, do you?" Connor demanded of the staff standing behind the nurses' station.

I looked up at my cousin. "Not freaking out, huh?"

"I was trying to be nice."

"Hey!" I called as the nurse rolled me closer to my husband. "Are you trying to wake your son up?"

Connor looked down at me and then the baby, a timid expression on his face, which I found extremely sexy. "Did I?"

I shook my head and he sighed in relief.

"But how about we take Colin home before he wakes and needs to be fed again, huh?"

Connor nodded, placing a soothing kiss to my forehead, before giving another light kiss to our son's forehead. My heart broke open again for like the hundredth time in the two days this little guy had been here on the planet.

"Ready to go home, Colin?" I whispered while Connor moved behind me, pushing the wheelchair as Destiny and Mark flanked my sides.

I loved his name. Connor and I had gone back and forth. Once we found out it was a boy, I wanted him to be a junior but Connor nixed that idea. He wanted his son to have his own identity which I didn't understand at first. We bickered over it until one day I was looking through names and said, *"What about Colin?"*

It was close enough to his name that they would almost have that in common, but it was his own name, his own identity. Connor liked that idea and we stuck with it. And as we entered the elevator and I stared down at my son, I knew the name was fitting.

"Next stop, home."

Connor leaned over me from behind, placing another kiss to the top of my head. I took his hand into one of my own while keeping Colin resting in my lap and other arm. Destiny placed her hand on my shoulder and I looked up at her through tears. My Aunt Donna was waiting for me at our home, deciding she'd stay with Connor and I for a few weeks to help care for her *new grandson* as she referred to Colin as. This was the family I'd always longed for.

Who knew one lonely night in New York would've turned into all of this?

The End

Looking for updates on future releases? I can be found around the web at the following locations:
Newsletter: Tiffany Patterson Writes Newsletter
FaceBook private group: Tiffany's Passions Between the Pages
Website: TiffanyPattersonWrites.com
FaceBook Page: Author Tiffany Patterson
Email: TiffanyPattersonWrites@gmail.com

More books by Tiffany Patterson
The Black Burles Series
Black Pearl
Black Dahlia
Black Butterfly
Forever Series
7 Degrees of Alpha (Collection)
Forever
Safe Space Series
Safe Space (Book 1)
Safe Space (Book 2)
Rescue Four Series
Eric's Inferno
Carter's Flame
Emanuel's Heat
Non-Series Titles
This is Where I Sleep
My Storm
Miles & Mistletoe (Holiday Novella)
Just Say the Word
Jacob's Song
The Townsend Brothers Series
Aaron's Patience
Meant to Be
For Keeps
Until My Last Breath

Tiffany Patterson Website Exclusives
Locked Doors
Bella

Printed in Great Britain
by Amazon